Najila

A Novel

C. J. Illinik

Kregel
Publications

Najila: A Novel

© 2007 by C. J. Illinik

Published by Kregel Publications, a division of Kregel, Inc., P.O. Box 2607, Grand Rapids, MI 49501.

Library of Congress Cataloging-in-Publication Data
Illinik, C. J. (Carol J.)
Najila : a novel / by C. J. Illinik.
    p. cm.
    1. Princesses—Iran—Fiction. 2. Iran—History—640–1500—Fiction. I. Title.
PS3609.L57N33 2007
813'.6-dc22   2007018863

ISBN 978-0-8254-2907-1

Printed in the United States of America

07 08 09 10 11 / 5 4 3 2 1

Acknowledgments

Grateful thanks:
To my husband, Bob, for making our meals while I wrote the first drafts, and for inspiring me to go to Turkey in the first place.

To Mrs. Linda Blair, Dr. Neal A. Boliou, Mrs. Pat Collins, Mrs. Lorene Richardson, Mrs. Peg Sorter, and Mrs. LaVerne Sawyer, outside readers who judiciously critiqued various drafts.

To those who read *The Tablets of Ararat* and urged me to write another novel. To those who wanted to know more about Najila, this is especially for you.

To Reverends Paul H. Boliou and Levi Johnson for theological information.

To Dr. Wayland Stephensen, MD, who graciously consulted with me on frontal lobe trauma.

To Professor William G. Millington, who many years ago rebuilt my self-esteem when it had sagged to zilch.

To Professor E. Polzin, whose U.S. history class at Long Beach City College, also many years ago, kindled my then nonexistent interest in humanity's past.

To the helpful and conscientious Kregel Publications staff.

And especially to my managing editor and friend, Stephen Barclift, whose encouragement and belief in me kept the writing going, and to Becky Fish who worked wonders with her brilliant final edit.

Late Eleventh & Early Twelfth Century Konstantinoupolis

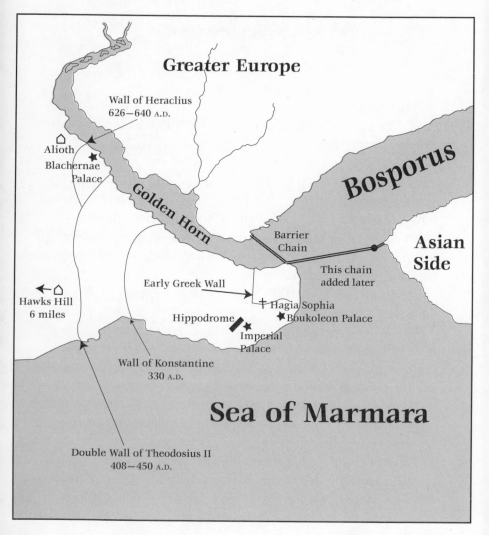

Greater Europe

Wall of Heraclius
626–640 A.D.

Alioth
Blachernae
Palace

Golden Horn

Bosporus

Barrier
Chain

Asian
Side

This chain
added later

← Hawks Hill
6 miles

Early Greek Wall

✝ Hagia Sophia
★ Boukoleon Palace

Hippodrome

Imperial
Palace

Wall of Konstantine
330 A.D.

Sea of Marmara

Double Wall of Theodosius II
408–450 A.D.

Book One

Doukas–Komnenous Family Tree

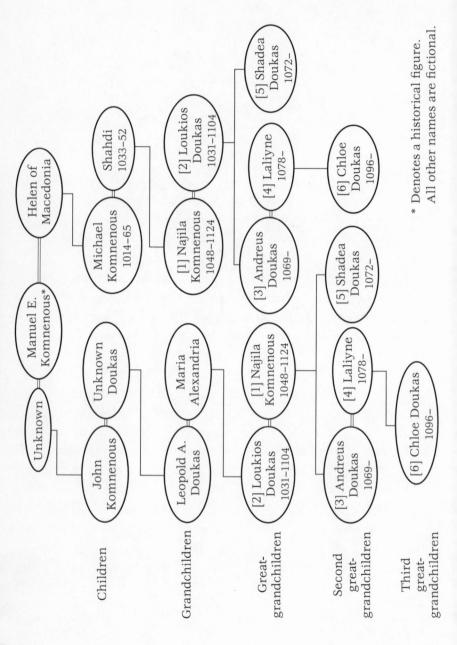

* Denotes a historical figure. All other names are fictional.

Prologue

Groaning, the fifteen-year-old girl arched her back. The baby lay great under her ribs, compressing her lungs. Panting, she opened her mouth wide. With every breath, she struggled to eke sufficient relief from the humid air to sustain both herself and the precious life she bore.

Already more than a week overdue, young Shahdi awkwardly reclined on padded mats the servants had spread on the broad, elevated ledge surrounding the Byzantine embassy's lovely rectangular pool. Only occasionally did the hint of a breeze whisper a cooling mist from the turquoise pool's bubbling fountain. It was never enough.

The summer of 1048 in Baghdad had proved to be exceptionally uncomfortable, with endless, debilitating heat. Despite the courtyard's refreshing pool, lush vegetation, and glazed ceramic tiles, the atmosphere always became unbearable by noon when the sun reached its peak. The temperature would be lower within the thick embassy walls.

Shahdi laboriously shifted her cumbersome bulk to a sitting position and tentatively stretched. Oh, how her lower back ached. It had bothered her all morning.

Supported by Zahra, her lady-in-waiting, and followed by her twin Nubian fanners, Tala and Taraneh, Shahdi rose and started to waddle from the courtyard. Instant, excruciating pain lanced her abdomen. Doubling over, she clutched her immense belly. A second contraction made her cry out. Even in her discomfort, Shahdi managed a weak, relieved laugh. At last, her baby was on its way.

Cupping his ear, Michael Doukas Komnenous, the Byzantine envoy to Persia, politely leaned forward to better hear the musical strains that reverberated in the cavernous throne room. He knew that the caliph admired the popular poet Nã ser-e Khosrow, whose philosophical qasidas were quoted throughout the Arab world. Though he spoke both languages well, Michael found it difficult to translate the ornate Farsi and Arabic mix.

The poet droned on, his voice echoing in the columned hall. Michael, ever the diplomat, listened with feigned intensity; ideological poetry was not his forte. Participating in a stimulating political discussion or haggling strategy during a military enclave was more to his liking.

A light tap on his shoulder interrupted Michael's reverie. He turned to see one of Shahdi's Nubian fanners, Taraneh.

Agitated at the imposing sight of the caliph, Taraneh clasped and unclasped her hands. She gave him a slight curtsy before speaking softly so only Michael could hear. "It is Lady Shahdi's time. She calls for her husband."

Michael sprang to his feet, spilling a bowl of nuts and dates from his lap. With a great crash, the ceramic bowl shattered on the tiled floor, scattering its contents everywhere. The poet stopped his recitation in mid sentence. The caliph frowned, and his florid face reddened even more.

Except for Otrygg Harald, his Viking bodyguard and close friend, Michael was taller than everyone else in the room. His height alone commanded respect. "Apologies, Excellency," Michael said, bowing to the caliph. "I am told that Lady Shahdi's . . . er . . . that our child is about to be born. I regret that I must leave."

The caliph could not fathom the excessive attention Michael granted his woman. Nor would he accept the Christian teaching that a husband should take but one wife; the caliph had three, as permitted by the Qur'an. Highly annoyed by the interruption, the caliph dismissed Michael with a flick of his fingers.

✝

Shahdi carefully loosened the wrappings that embraced the treasured bundle she cuddled at her breast. Joy and love overwhelmed her ecstatic heart. Then a thought sobered her, and she hid her face from Michael.

"I know that you wished your firstborn to be a son. I hope a daughter does not disappoint you, my husband."

Michael peered down at the plump pink cherub upon whom Shahdi adoringly gazed. Inexplicably humbled in the presence of such a miracle, he didn't know quite what to do. He smiled diffidently at his young wife.

"How can I be displeased with something that is a part of you, Shahdi?" He bent to brush his lips lightly across her forehead. "Our daughter is a gift. Not only is she God's gift, but she is also a gift from my darling Shahdi. She is a gift to both of us from God."

Michael knelt on the floor by the bed and took Shahdi's small chin in his large hand, gently turning her face toward his. "Your mother and father hoped for a boy, but it is of no significance to me whether I have a son now or later. Having a son is not as important to me as it is to your Islamic relatives." Michael gave her a mischievous grin. "Besides, we have many years to produce one."

Remembering her ordeal carrying and delivering this large child, who had stressed her delicate frame to its utmost, Shahdi promised herself, *I will not soon go through that again.*

She gave the infant's tiny button nose a feather-light tap. "Her eyes are tightly closed, so you cannot see their color," she said, decidedly relieved that she had not failed Michael after all. "They are enormous and golden brown like a fine topaz. Do you think Najila is an appropriate name for our daughter?"

"'Brilliant Eyes.' Yes, it is perfect, as you suggest, beloved." Michael's gaze lingered on the infant's petite features. "Najila is truly the name for one so beautiful."

Chapter 1

Four Years Later

Little Najila had not been allowed to enter the bedchamber for three days, but she had constantly hovered nearby. Normally an energetic and boisterous four-year-old, she was subdued by the somber mood of everyone she encountered in the embassy halls. Now, she hesitated outside the partially opened bedchamber door.

Geometric designs of alternating light and shadow, cast by the elaborately carved windows, papered the walls of the room. Najila's mother lay pale and motionless, except for the shallow rise and fall of her breast. Taraneh and Tala, ever faithful and devoted, cooled her feverish body by sweeping broad feathered fans. Tears rolled down their bronzed cheeks.

Najila had heard the story of how the two women, when they were twelve, had been given to Shahdi when she herself was but a two-year-old toddler. Maturing alongside her, they were treated as family, becoming companions rather than slaves.

Najila's father sat next to the bed. His red-rimmed eyes had purplish blue pouches under them. Najila tiptoed to him. He did not chase her off as he had previously done, and she climbed onto his lap.

"How is my mother?" she whispered.

"Things are not well with her, Najila. The caliph's physicians have not helped by bleeding her." He put his free arm around

Najila and quietly said, "They only worsened her condition. I am afraid we must soon prepare for her marvelous journey."

Najila squirmed in expectation. Innocently gazing up at her father, she asked, "Where are we going? Are we taking a boat trip on the river? Perhaps we can visit the caliph's menagerie." Both prospects delighted her, especially the latter. She laughed, clapping her hands. The special palace garden complex was her favorite place in the whole world—particularly the area that formed the caliph's fine personal zoo filled with odd-looking animals from all over the earth.

Michael drew a prolonged breath. "Your mother shall travel to heaven, where God and his angels will watch over her. It is impossible for us to go with her right now, but when you and I have lived our lives, we will also go to heaven."

"Is my mother dying?"

"It is so," Michael mumbled. Najila's baffled expression pained him. Living in a mansion within the palace compound, she had been protected from the outer world. And though Shahdi had never completely regained her strength after giving birth to her, Najila was extremely healthy. Death was a stranger.

"Is the baby going to heaven also, Baba?" Najila probed.

Her question pierced Michael's heart to the very core. He and Shahdi had so looked forward to having another child. Now his dream—their dream—was about to end. For Najila's sake, he mustered a response. "The baby must stay with its mother."

Najila frowned. "I want to go, too, Baba."

Michael pulled Najila to his chest and hugged her tightly. "The baby has lived too short a time within your mother to survive without her. But you can. It is God's design."

"Is it like the birds? They fly away and then return the next year. Will my mother return next year?"

"Going to heaven is not the same as the seasonal departure of fowl, Najila. People remain in heaven for eternity." Seeing fear clouding Najila's face, Michael assured her, "Heaven is marvelous, to be sure. A day is coming when we will be in heaven, also. Then, we shall see our beloved Shahdi again." *But would Shahdi be there?* Michael wondered. He wasn't sure.

"When?" Najila demanded.

Michael sighed. "Many years may pass before we follow her, but your mother's memory will forever be with us, inside us, deep within our hearts."

Michael saw that Najila still did not comprehend death's finality, but he could think of nothing else to say that might console her when his own heart was beyond solace.

Najila wrenched free of Michael's arms and screamed. "I want to go with my mother!" Sobbing, she fled the room and ran through the deserted corridor that led to the children's quarters.

Michael froze, mute, his empty arms spread wide as his daughter's rapid footsteps echoed eerily on the polished marble floor.

Safe in her chamber, Najila threw herself onto the bed.

Najila clutched Michael's hand as they walked in the spacious private gardens surrounding the caliph's palace. Michael, lean but powerfully built, towered over her. Copper highlights glowed in his shoulder-length auburn hair; Najila's raven locks reflected sparks of the sky's blue.

On this day, neither one appreciated the giant shade trees imported from lands all over the world after the Abbasid Caliph Al-Mansur founded Baghdad three hundred years before. Nor did they take notice of the exotic flowers and blooming trees that perfumed the air. It had been eight days since Shahdi left them, and father and daughter had drawn even closer in their shared grief. Najila had at last accepted the inevitable, though barely.

Michael stopped near a gushing fountain, one of dozens in the park. As he squatted down to face Najila at her level, a silver and amber cross suspended on a silver chain fell free of his tunic and swung to and fro. Najila always fingered the weighty object when she sat on her father's lap for storytelling. She liked to stroke and smell the satiny, fragrant amber, which was bezel set into the silver. Especially enchanting to her was the ancient dragonfly forever entombed within the yellowy resin, its wings outspread across the arms of the cross.

"How did the dragonfly get in there?" She gazed expectantly at her father.

"Once, the amber was soft and sticky, so that the dragonfly became stuck in it. Then the resin hardened." Michael had often wondered just how long ago that had happened.

"Where did it come from?"

Michael began to create a new story for her. "The Vikings came to Konstantinoupolis in a long warship that had brightly painted shields along both sides of its hull.

"Usually the Vikings came to attack the settlements or sell slaves. This time, though, they sought trade, not battle. They came from way up by the North Baltic Sea. They followed the Dnepr River south to Kiev, the new capital of the Russian State. The river was in spring flood, full of debris and hidden sandbars. Sometimes they could row when the water was deep enough, but other times they were compelled to carry the heavy ship from one spot to another.

"When they reached the Black Sea, the Vikings, who lifted and dipped the oars with practiced cadence, did not miss a stroke. Their steady rhythm created a bow wave that spread in an ever widening V, with the boat's high prow making a hissing sound as it plowed through the water."

Michael leaned over and hissed in Najila's ear, making her duck her head and laugh.

"When the wind picked up, a sail was raised. Only then could those very tired men rest. Each man sat on a carved, wooden chest which, along with his personal belongings, held trade goods: skins, walrus ivory, and the most treasured of all merchandise, amber."

Michael bent from the waist and squinted at Najila, his voice dropping to a conspiratorial whisper. "A husky, red-haired man named Eyvind-the-Seeker owned the finest specimen, an immense translucent chunk with the dragonfly, but none of the other men knew he had it. Eyvind told me that he had discovered it half-buried in the sand on a Baltic beach."

"This very one!" Najila declared, patting the nugget on the cross.

"Yes. The same. I had to bargain long and hard for it," Michael told her. He recalled how the grizzled old Viking seemed reluctant to part with the spectacular piece. In the end, Michael knew he had paid too dear a price, but he had never regretted it.

The cross arced slowly back and forth. Najila stared at it absentmindedly, half hypnotized by the motion. As the sun shone through the swinging amber, a golden light darted across her father's brocaded silk robe. She reached out to snatch it, but Michael stopped her. Taking her little hand into his great one, he said, "This light is like your mother's spirit. It is there, but you cannot catch it."

When Najila didn't answer, he said, "Someday, the dragonfly cross will be yours." *However, not until you know its real meaning,* he thought. Standing up, he added, "Though your grandmother endlessly argues against my religion, you have to learn about Jesus Christ, who was crucified on a cross such as this."

"What is crucified?" Najila asked.

"It is a gruesome way to kill someone. It happened over a thousand years ago in an old city called Jerusalem, which yet exists toward the setting sun and south from Baghdad."

Najila grew silent, sorting those facts in her mind. "Is Jesus in heaven with my mother?"

Even in his sorrow, Michael felt pride in her inquisitive mind. "Yes, Jesus is in heaven. Your mother . . ." He paused, terribly saddened, shuddering with renewed grief. Shahdi had never accepted Christianity. According to the Scriptures, she was not in heaven. What could he say to comfort Najila without lying?

But Najila didn't wait for him to answer. "Was Jesus a nice man?"

Michael breathed a sigh of relief; he could honestly answer that one. "Jesus was not only a nice man, but he was far better than any man. He was the Son of God, perfect, without sin."

"Then why did they kill him?"

"Jealous priests, the Romans, and other foolish people had him murdered." Michael paused. He knew that what he had told her wasn't totally accurate, but it was the best he could do at the moment. "Do you see?"

Najila solemnly bobbed her head. "I think I do. Grandmother Shafiqa told me Jesus was a prophet like Muhammad."

Shafiqa has had too much influence on Najila, Michael thought. He would have to spend more time with his daughter if he expected her to become familiar with the four Gospels and the Old Testament prophecies concerning Jesus Christ.

"Jesus was more than a good man, more than just a prophet, Najila. Remember, Jesus is the living Son of God, and it is written he will one day return to rule the earth."

But Najila was not convinced; how could someone who was killed still be alive? Deciding that it all was beyond her understanding, she asked no further questions.

Chapter 2

Michael and his chief courtier, the eunuch Julian, rode down a palm-lined street paralleling one of Baghdad's many canals that diverted the water of the Tigris River. The canals had been constructed centuries before, mainly to nourish the city's lush gardens. Known as the Marble City because of its marbled palaces, bridges, walls, and mosques, Baghdad hummed with enormous energy.

The two men shouted to be heard above the snorting and braying of animals and the noisy tirades of merchants touting their wares. The loud voices of determined shoppers haggling for a better deal added to the din.

Close behind the two riders, Najila lounged in her gilded, scarlet and saffron palanquin. Four ebony-skinned Nubians, wearing matching red and yellow kilts, supported the conveyance.

The party was returning to the Byzantine ambassador's mansion situated within the royal complex. Sixteen-year-old Najila was never permitted to venture unaccompanied beyond the compound walls. Bored to distraction, she had begged for an outing, and Michael had finally agreed, taking the opportunity to test the mettle of his three-year-old filly, Sabiya, in a crowd.

Fascinated by the surrounding commotion, Najila peered through the translucent silk curtains at the jostling throng. As the riders and palanquin proceeded, the mob parted to either side like a turbulent sea split by a fast-sailing ship's prow.

Michael's hot-blooded, half-broken Arabian mount exercised every possible excuse to shy. Foam streaked the animal's sleek, dapple-gray coat, and sweat darkened her saddle blanket. Michael's strong hand and expert horsemanship were all that kept the filly in line.

Julian, astride an ancient, mild-mannered bay, shuddered. "She will cause your death yet, my friend. Why do you choose a beast so difficult to manage? It would sorely try my patience."

Michael merely laughed. Doubling the reins around his fist, he automatically shifted his hips to counterbalance the filly's sudden diagonal lurch. "Come, Julian, what would everyone think if they saw me straddling your elderly dog?" He laughed again. "Sabiya represents Byzantium's unconquerable spirit and glory. Besides, I savor the challenge."

Julian snorted. "Ha! I pray Sabiya does not represent a fall from glory." He lashed out with his quirt at a beggar who grabbed at the bag slung across the pommel. The thief cursed and backed away, lofting his arm with a fist-in-elbow gesture of contempt.

Noting the eunuch's offended frown, Michael guffawed. "See, Julian? They accost you, yet they fear to approach Sabiya the Terrible. Someday, I shall teach her to sink her teeth into the hides of such riffraff."

"And have the law after you for damaging a citizen?" Julian chided. "Even our esteemed caliph could not help you then."

"You are right as always, my wise friend. Anyway, a poor beggar is not worthy of queenly Sabiya's ire." Michael chuckled. Enjoying the banter, he continued to torment Julian. "I hear the Norman war horses rear on command during battle. Sabiya will learn to do the same one day. Such a feat would surely complement and aid my fine swordsmanship."

Taking the bait, Julian grimaced. "And I'll pray to our holy God that Sabiya doesn't break your neck meantime. Besides, I believe those same war horses are stallions, not skittish fillies."

A tinker clanged on a pot, and Sabiya gave a giant leap forward. Still firmly seated in his saddle, Michael easily controlled his jittery mount. Frustrated, Sabiya pranced in place at a thirty-five-degree angle to the street and shook her head, jingling her silver bit and bridle ornaments.

It had been a good day for all except Julian, who fretted over Michael and Najila as a mother doted over her brood. "We are home at last," he sighed with relief as they rode into the courtyard. "I was afraid I might be forced to scrape you from the street and carry you home prostrate in Najila's divan."

"You worry too much, old soul," Michael replied, handing Sabiya's reins to a groom. He was giving the portly Julian a hand off the equally rotund bay when a courtier rushed up to them.

"My lord, a messenger arrived while you were gone. He brings grave tidings," the man panted. "The Hungarians have seized Belgrade."

"This is serious news," Michael exclaimed as he and Julian crossed the courtyard's broad expanse toward the manse entrance. "The Byzantine empire shrinks year by year. It is the fault of Emperor Konstantine X Doukas. When he decreased the military's power, he antagonized the army and wrenched out its heart."

Julian nodded. "To give the clergy and scholars increased say in diplomatic affairs may have been a good idea to begin with, but he cannot successfully fight a war without the military's full support."

"Did you ever meet him?" Julian asked. He removed his tall pointed cap, revealing a bald pate rimmed by a halo of white hair.

"No. I have not met His Majesty, Emperor Konstantine X Doukas," Michael disdainfully answered.

Julian snorted. "Well, that spendthrift has nearly bankrupted the empire."

"Truly an inadequate ruler," Michael agreed. I being in her favor, she appointed me an envoy. When she died I was allowed to remain the ambassador to Baghdad, because I am descended from both the Komnenous and Doukas noble houses. Furthermore, I understand the Seljuks and Arabs as well as any Westerner can."

"That you surely do, Michael."

Michael stretched and something in his back clicked. "I am getting old!" he groaned.

"Old at fifty?" Julian scoffed. "Who would know it? You hide your age well."

"I am ready to retire, Julian, though I suppose Konstantinoupolis has somewhat forgotten me, isolated as I am here in Baghdad. But the world is changing as we speak. Is not Solomon, Hungary's new king, more a threat to Byzantium than the Seljuks? He appears just as clever as the Seljuk commander Tugrul, who was able to take Baghdad without a fight. Ten years have passed, and I still tremble with apprehension when I recall that day," Michael said, throwing his arm across Julian's shoulders.

"Ever since the Seljuk victory, I have expected orders to return to Konstantinoupolis. What think ye, Julian? Shall we write a letter to Konstantine X? Ask for my release? I weary of Arab and Seljuk machinations. And it is time for Najila to see her father's homeland."

"Ah, to live my last days in lovely Konstantinoupolis." Julian sighed. "Tell me when to write the missive, and it is done. So be it."

Chapter 3

Late one evening five weeks later, before Michael and Julian got around to sending the letter of Michael's resignation, the caliph summoned Michael to the palace. It was not out of the ordinary for the Muslim leader to insist on Michael's presence at an important meeting or impromptu celebration, but Michael knew of nothing scheduled for that night.

Heading toward the palace, he and Julian walked leisurely through the caliph's gardens. The fragrance of night-blooming jasmine permeated the air. Brilliant crystalline stars and a thin crescent moon shining through lacy, date-palm fronds striped the yellow-sand path. Noting that the palace was not brightly lit, as was usual for a feast or special entertainment, Michael grew uneasy.

A lion-like roar shattered the silence. Both men flinched, though the sound was merely produced by a peacock roosting in a nearby tree. Making light of his jumpy nerves, Michael commented, "There is an edge to the atmosphere tonight. Perhaps a sandstorm gathers on the horizon."

"Humph!" muttered Julian, embarrassed at his own timidity.

Once inside the palace, the two men followed a turbaned guard to the mogul's private quarters. As Michael and Julian started to enter the royal apartment, the caliph commanded, "Step back, eunuch! I speak only with the Byzantine envoy, Michael Komnenous."

Michael gave Julian a brief nod, and the eunuch quietly moved aside, letting Michael enter the room alone.

The caliph sat cross-legged on a raised and pillowed platform. He noisily sucked a draught of cooled and filtered smoke through the tube attached to a bubbling, bejeweled narghile at his feet. Exhaling a dense cloud that slowly encircled his head, the pompous ruler examined Michael through slit lids.

"I have received a document ordering your return to Konstantinoupolis." A sneer distorted the caliph's mouth. "It seems Byzantium has much trouble these days."

Despite the caliph's menacing tone, a frisson tickled Michael at the thought of going home. "What manner of trouble?" he asked courteously, carefully suppressing a grin.

"I have just learned that Arp Arslan and his Seljuks advanced east and have taken Armenia. The Brave Lion continues to bite and digest bits of Byzantium one by one," the caliph jeered, his attitude even more imperious than usual.

Arp Arslan had become ruler of the Seljuk Turks in 1063. Fanatic in his quest to overcome all infidels, the fierce warlord had led his Islamic army progressively west. Armenia was crucial to Konstantinoupolis's economy. Its loss hurt. The big question was what land Arslan would seek next.

Though Michael's expression remained stoic for the caliph's benefit, the announcement that Konstantinoupolis had at last beckoned thrilled him. The difficult decision to leave was no longer his to make.

Moments later, as he and Julian left the palace, an exuberant Michael declared, "We will depart Baghdad as soon as possible."

Chapter 4

Though Michael was eager to start for home immediately, there would be no long-distance travel in midwinter. Around Baghdad, the weather remained relatively mild, but deep snow blocked the higher mountain passes to the north.

When he had been a newly appointed envoy to Baghdad—and a much younger man—Michael had just himself to worry about. What route he traveled did not matter. Now, however, he would have the responsibility of a beautiful (if unpredictable) daughter, her lady-in-waiting, and a cranky mother-in-law. Because of them, he would have to choose the most opportune time and the easiest and safest route home. They would wait until early spring before leaving for Konstantinoupolis.

Michael and Julian sat upon a cushioned bench within the ambassador's private atrium where they could talk without being overheard. Lingering winter weather chilled the dry air of February. Both men wore heavy, embroidered robes over their indoor garments and tucked their hands into their sleeves for warmth.

"I would rather not take Shahdi's mother with us," Michael confided to Julian. "But besides me, Shafiqa is Najila's only close relation. She has cared for Najila since Shahdi died."

"Shafiqa is rather up in years. Can she survive such a long journey?"

"Hah!" Michael snorted. "Shafiqa is as tough as an old brood hen. She will survive, if only to torment me."

"Shafiqa is still trying to convert you?"

"She does not cease." Michael's brows turned thunderous. "Personally, I do not mind her lectures; I can resist her haranguing. Have I not always been a true follower of Jesus Christ? But," he went on, "my mother-in-law confuses Najila, until the girl does not know what to believe. But my daughter shall also become a follower of our blessed Lord; I'll have it no other way."

Never reluctant to voice an opinion, Julian pursed his lips and blurted, "Do not take Shafiqa to Konstantinoupolis. Her influence is too great. Is it not enough that Zahra, Najila's lady-in-waiting, tends Najila as she tended Shahdi? Is Shafiqa's presence needed?"

Spreading his arms in a hopeless gesture, Michael cried, "I do not have a choice. I am helpless. Najila insists that her grandmother accompany us. My daughter honors Shafiqa as if she were her mother."

Julian dared say no more. He merely nodded in sympathy. Verily, Shafiqa was unbearable at times.

Michael abruptly changed the subject. "Have you learned what caravans will soon leave Baghdad for Konstantinoupolis? I am anxious to be gone."

Julian slid a folded parchment from a pocket deep within his robe. Unfolding it, he peered at the fine script. "Two are scheduled to depart at the end of the month: one heads directly to Trabezund via Tabriz, and the other goes to Antioch." The eunuch ran his index finger down the list. "A third caravan departs Baghdad for Antioch early next month. From Antioch we can travel by land or sea the rest of the way. I hear that daily at least one ship heads to a Byzantine port. Another sails straight to Konstantinoupolis once a week. I truly think going from Antioch to Konstantinoupolis by sea is best."

Horrified, Michael groaned. "Our holy God in heaven! Let me see that list. I could not tolerate another voyage across the Mediterranean during the spring storms."

Remembering their former seagoing ordeal, Julian felt for Michael, but his personal choice was to go entirely by water. Knowing it was faster and that he himself never became seasick, Julian continued his effort to change Michael's mind. "There is the shorter sail to Tarsus. One is never sure, however, to catch a northbound caravan out of Tarsus. Those that head north are few and haphazardly scheduled. Also, at this time of year, there is the threat of avalanches in the Tarsus mountain passes. I have to believe that traveling by sea all the way is best."

"Julian, you know how ill I become when aboard a ship. And to endure Shafiqa's unending quacking while suffering with a bout of that abominable affliction would be beyond any man's patience. It is surely beyond mine."

"Lady Zahra and I will keep Shafiqa occupied," Julian promised, dreading the prospect.

But Julian's vow eased Michael's churning stomach not in the slightest. "We will take the overland caravan to Tabriz," he declared. "The sooner, the better."

When told she was leaving Baghdad, Najila's querulous wails rang throughout the embassy. All her life, she had heard rumors that the Byzantine capital was unbearably humid in the summer, freezing cold in the winter, and bathed in fog the rest of the year. Every bone in her body protested.

"My home is not Konstantinoupolis; home is here in Baghdad, where my mother is buried," she screamed at her father. "And it means leaving Baghdad's beautiful parks, sparkling lakes, and lovely animals. Never!"

Her suite became a disaster area. She flung a gown here, a veil there. Heaped clothes covered every surface, including the thick Persian carpets. She had carelessly scattered jeweled diadems, necklaces, rings, and bracelets across the top of her dressing table. A sunbeam straying across the brilliant stones reflected a thousand shards of color onto the high ceiling.

Elbows akimbo, Zahra stood frowning in the arched entry to Najila's bedchamber. "My lady makes our packing unnecessarily difficult," she scolded the disheveled girl.

"Good! It will delay our leaving Baghdad." Najila's curly dark hair stuck out from her head at every angle, resembling dried grapevine tendrils. Her cheeks were streaked with tears, and her eyes red and swollen. Still in the midst of her childish tantrum, Najila plucked a delicate purple tunic off her bed, ripped it asunder, and tossed the remnants to the floor.

Just then, Michael appeared in the open doorway. Thrusting Zahra aside, he stormed into the room. "What is going on in here? My daughter's living space is the pen of a camel." He waved a sheer piece of purple gauze in the air. "You have so many clothes to spare that you destroy them?"

He threw down the flimsy fabric and marched to the dressing table. "These things should have been packed by now." Jabbing a finger at an exquisite emerald necklace, Michael bellowed, "You have had weeks to do this, Najila. We go at first light tomorrow. If these baubles are not ready, we leave without them."

Najila paled. She had never seen her father in such a rage. "Yes, my father," she said, meek at last.

Finally! He disciplines the spoiled child, Zahra thought, smiling behind her hand. No one could blame her for the mess. Michael's timely appearance on the scene relieved her of the onerous job of managing the willful, unhappy Najila. Appeased, Zahra moved to a heap of clothing piled on the floor and bent to pick up an elaborately embroidered vest.

"Stop at once, Zahra! This chaos is for Najila to put in order. It is her clutter; she must restore it," Michael roared.

"As you wish, my lord," Zahra bowed low, if only to hide her amusement. Darting a sideways glance at the cowed Najila, she promised Michael, "Lord, your daughter will be prepared by morning." Straightening her aching back, she added, "Is that not correct, my lady?"

Nodding vigorously, Najila began to rapidly gather her possessions.

"By day's end. No later," Michael shouted as he stomped out.

Chapter 5

A caravan was no safer from marauding land-based bandits than a ship was from the pirates that haunted the inner seas. For the protection of Michael's caravan, Julian had managed to round up three-dozen mercenaries as escorts. After inspecting them—a diverse mixture of several nationalities, religions, and races—Michael appointed Otrygg Harald, his huge, red-haired, Viking bodyguard, as their leader.

Michael and Otrygg had been friends as boys when Michael's family lived near the Konstantinoupolis palace and Otrygg's father had been a member of the emperor's elite, axe-toting Varangian Guard. At maturity, Otrygg had inherited a place in the guard, too. Nevertheless, Michael had little trouble luring Otrygg away from Konstantinoupolis by promising him adventure and wealth in far-off Persia. Of all men, he trusted Otrygg most. Michael knew the Viking would sacrifice his life for him and anyone else in Michael's immediate family.

Long before dawn, with Julian and Otrygg's help, Michael assembled his household servants along with Otrygg's men. Over a ton of baggage was loaded on loudly protesting pack camels. As dawn broke, they headed in a long line toward the city's fringe, where outgoing caravans mustered. Fortunately, a light drizzle had settled the insufferable dust usually associated with moving men and beasts; the air was clean and crisp.

Carrying his gigantic, double-bladed axe, Otrygg approached Michael. "Everything is nearly ready," he said, speaking in

Latin, Old Byzantium's primary tongue. "I must warn you, Michael, your rich caravan needs more reliable defenders than this rabble Julian has hired. I do not like leaving the lady Najila so vulnerable."

"They will have to do. There is no time to find others," Michael replied, also in Latin.

Otrygg Harald spat. "I fear the men Julian has chosen are true to none but themselves. I sense they resent me. There may be trouble because of it."

Michael thumped Otrygg's immense biceps, twice the circumference of his own well-muscled arms. "As always, my old friend, I can count on you to meet the challenge. Our way is through desolate and hostile territory. There is bound to be difficulty ere we are home. Meanwhile, cultivate your men's loyalty."

Otrygg Harald drew a formidable scimitar from his sash. Placing it smartly against his cheek, he saluted Michael. "I will try, but it will not be easy."

Following the ancient trade road through the rugged Zagros Mountains, the caravan took weeks to reach Tabriz. The area had belonged to the Abbasid Caliphate before the Seljuk Turks conquered it. As long as the predominantly Muslim caravan remained in Seljuk-occupied territory, it was relatively safe from attack.

The weather became their principal adversary. At higher elevations, it was especially unpredictable. The light vehicles had not been built to shield their occupants wholly from cold or wet. Najila never knew if freezing rain would drench her or if snow would overburden the litter. A heavy snowfall caused the carriers to periodically stop and lower the three palanquins so the roofs could be cleared. Thus, the entire caravan, already slowed to a crawl, was progressively delayed.

As a result, they often failed to arrive at a caravanserai, a traveler's hostelry, by dusk. When that happened, the Syrian caravan master ordered a halt at a suitable place. Najila could barely wait for the setup of her felt tent and a nice plate of hot food. She spent those nights huddled between thick pads of wolf pelts, for which the solicitous Otrygg had bartered grain and other goods earlier along their route.

No question about it, she was undeniably miserable. Despite the many layers of fur enfolding her, she shivered uncontrollably. Her chattering teeth prevented a sound slumber, but dozing as she reclined in the palanquin, she recovered some lost sleep during the day.

If the weather allowed, Najila hiked alongside the palanquin in an effort to get warm and loosen up. More often, she walked to relieve the endless tedium of travel. At first, her feet developed huge blisters, and her whole body ached. As she toughened, the exercise trimmed and enhanced her plump, seventeen-year-old figure.

The caravan steadily ascended the sloping plain until they came to Tabriz at forty-five hundred feet, with colder temperatures yet. Five mercenaries immediately deserted, and Otrygg recruited better-qualified replacements, among them a stranded fellow Viking, the only survivor of a longboat wrecked the previous fall on the Caspian Sea while on a trading mission.

Forced to idle three days in Tabriz, Najila had a chance to explore the city, Zahra accompanying her in the well-guarded palanquin. They found Tabriz to be dirty and cluttered. It lacked the striking architecture, canals, and aqueducts that made Baghdad so attractive. Though more than two decades had passed since the devastating earthquake of 1041, partially collapsed buildings and debris still littered the back streets.

Thinking the women might need a reprieve from living in tents, Otrygg arranged for them to stay at an inn that looked to be free of parasites and vermin. After her third sleepless night in a row—due to biting fleas—Najila was grateful to be on the road again.

The caravan next headed north and west toward the Doğubayazit caravanserai. Additional camels and cargo arrived from the Far East, expanding the train, until at times it would stretch to almost a mile long.

Chapter 6

A few days' journey out of Doğubayazit, a motley band of a dozen or so booty-seeking ruffians spotted the caravan's gilded palanquins. Otrygg's sharp eyes saw the distant silhouettes of the raiders on top of a ridge, and he instantly commanded the caravan to close ranks. Lances at the ready, pointed outward, his men encircled the milling camels and drivers. Otrygg saw to it that Michael's company kept well within the perimeter for maximum security.

Expecting an easy triumph, the bandits charged. Instead of a quick victory, they encountered a wave of arrows launched by Otrygg's infantry, followed by a wall of mounted men wielding lances. Though skilled horsemen, the raiders were no match for Otrygg Harald's efficient fighting force on their much taller camels. After a brief skirmish, the would-be robbers were exterminated. Otrygg's troops captured seven hardy steppe ponies as a bonus.

Shouting triumphantly, Otrygg's nearly unscathed brigade cantered up and down the unmolested, cheering caravan as it regrouped. But when Najila noted that many a mercenary's lance bore a bloody, severed head, she buried her face in her furs.

✠

Late that same afternoon, when the caravan halted for the night and camp was finally organized, Michael and Otrygg came to Najila's tent.

"Najila, come see the prize Otrygg Harald won for you," Michael called.

Zahra opened the flap. "Your daughter sent me to tell you she is feeling ill, my lord." When Zahra saw what Otrygg held, she clapped her hands in delight. "For Najila?" she whispered.

"It is so," Michael answered.

Otrygg grinned, and his ruddy skin flushed an even deeper red.

Zahra called into the tent to Najila, "My lady, you must see the gift your father and Otrygg have brought you."

Curiosity getting the best of her, Najila rose from her bed and peeked out. She gasped. "Is he truly mine?"

"That *she* is," Michael said, drawing a shaggy black steppe pony closer to the tent entrance.

Najila stroked the battle-weary animal's velvety nose. The mare waited patiently, her lids half closed. Najila scowled. "But I cannot ride."

"Otrygg Harald and I will teach you while we travel. You will no longer complain that you are bored."

Najila threw her arms around her father's neck. "I have always wanted to learn to ride like a man."

Michael rolled his eyes upward. Byzantine women were rarely seen astride a horse. Persian women? Never! Would he not create an unmanageable monster by teaching his willful daughter to ride? He remembered all too clearly the fountain episode of ten years ago. . . .

Zahra put down her spindle and ball of carded wool. Getting to her feet, her sharp eyes missed nothing as she glanced over the

courtyard to see if her wards were behaving. All was well. As usual, midsummer in Baghdad was torrid. Playing quietly with a medley of clay animal figures, Najila and two other seven-year-old girls sat near the partially shaded pool. One of Najila's playmates was the daughter of a servant, the other of a noble, but all children under the embassy's roof were treated equally. Michael had ordered it so when he had first come to Baghdad.

As soon as Zahra hustled indoors and out of sight, Najila shot a sly look at her companions and leaped into the turquoise pool. Giggling, the other two quickly followed.

Created for an envoy's private meditation, for his serene viewing, the lovely fountain and its shallow basin with glazed tiles immediately became an aqueous, rough-and-tumble playground. The girls splashed each other until water saturated their light cotton tunics and sizzled on the sun-heated, foot-blistering tiles. Their intricately coiffed hair soon hung in limp, twisted tendrils.

Laughing and coughing, Najila clambered from the pool. Standing on the rim, she stripped off her dripping tunic and stood naked and unencumbered like a lithe, bronzed statue. A sense of intoxicating freedom enveloped her as she stretched out her arms, spun around, and belly-flopped into the pool. She knew just how to flatten her dive so that she didn't scrape her head on the bottom.

Like sheep led to slaughter, Najila's playmates copied her, but only one child made a successful dive. The second girl came up crying and holding her forehead. Blood streamed down her face, chest, and belly, tingeing the water pink, while Najila and the third girl stood by helplessly.

It was this scene that Zahra beheld when she returned. At her side stood one of the newly arrived guests, a lad about Najila's age. Appalled, Zahra roughly shoved the boy back into the building, then raced toward the pool screaming, "Najila! Get out of the water!" Gathering up the wet tunics, she cried, "All of you dress and go inside! Right now!"

Ignoring Zahra's stern command to don her tunic, the injured girl, unclothed and weeping, ran through another door into the embassy to find her mother. *Najila's remaining companion obediently drew on the tunic Zahra thrust toward her, but Najila pretended not to hear Zahra. Instead, she dove underwater.*

As sleek and lissome as a river otter, Najila swam around the rectangular pool's central fountain. Gasping for air, she surfaced at the opposite side of the pool, which lay shadowed by the embassy balcony. The strange boy had come back into the courtyard, and Zahra was busy hustling him away from the shocking sight.

Resting on her haunches, the water level just below her eyes, Najila grinned.

When Zahra returned, she was accompanied by two female servants. Despite the three women's pleading, Najila, giddy with exhilaration, refused to come to them. Finally, they managed to catch her and wrap her in a towel, but not before the adults were as wet as the wriggling, slippery little body they clutched.

When Michael returned to the embassy after an all-day conference with the caliph, Zahra told him what had happened. "Najila caused a child to be hurt," she complained. "Najila might have been injured, too."

"Fortunately, she was not," he grunted. "And the day was extraordinarily hot. Would that I were young enough to do the same."

"My lord, it is difficult to control her," Zahra persisted. "She needs a stronger hand than mine."

Michael shook his head and studied his seventeen-year-old daughter as she fondled the black mare. *Najila has grown up a lot since then,* he thought. *But she can still be quite a handful.*

Chapter 7

Najila soon discovered that her heavily brocaded Persian women's apparel was not at all suitable for riding a horse. Michael silently chuckled at his daughter's attempts to mount her pony while clothed in a long robe and a duo of ankle-brushing skirts.

But sympathizing with her plight, he managed to discreetly obtain a pair of loose trousers and a figure-hiding tunic like those worn by Byzantine nobles. An Arabian head scarf, called a *kaffiyeh*, and a warm cloak completed her new outfit. Swearing the man to secrecy, Michael employed the caravan leather worker to make Najila a set of supple, goatskin boots.

Michael and Najila often rode together, she on the calm steppe pony that she named Jahara because of the jewel-like white spot situated just below the mare's shaggy forelock. Michael always rode his spirited Sabiya. He insisted that Najila wrap the scarf around the lower half of her face whenever they rode within sight of the caravan. No one, however, paid attention to her disguise; everyone else covered their faces, too, especially when the torrid sun baked the ground and huge dust clouds, stirred up by hundreds of hooves and feet, choked them.

The three women who Otrygg and his men guarded were the caravan's only females. Yet in her riding outfit, Najila always managed to slip in and out of her palanquin or tent without being recognized by anyone other than the members of her immediate entourage. The camel drivers believed Najila to be a slender young boy who galloped back and forth on his black mare. If anyone did suspect that a highborn woman rode at Michael's side, no one mentioned it. They dared not trifle with the lordly former ambassador and his formidable Viking companion, whose eyes ever followed the whereabouts of Michael's daughter.

But Najila's conservative grandmother made clear her opposition. "Najila's garb is indecent," Shafiqa spat at Michael. "What kind of father are you to let her dress so . . . so . . . so like a man?"

Having long had enough of his mother-in-law's interference, Michael subdued with no little effort the impulse to rattle Shafiqa's stubborn bones. Instead, his teeth showing in anger, he hissed, "That which my daughter wears is my concern and mine alone. She is comfortable, and the clothes make her ride much safer." With that, he marched off, shaking his head. Only temporarily silenced, Shafiqa stomped her foot and balled her fists.

The black mare's short-coupled gait was extremely rough at the trot. At first, Najila suffered stressed muscles and intensely painful saddle sores. Michael pretended not to notice when she stood in her stirrups, constantly shifted her position in the saddle, and refused to sit at meals without calling for an extra pillow to be placed beneath her. Nevertheless, Najila endured her apprenticeship, and she eventually overcame her inadequacies. By the time they reached Doğubayazit, she had become a fairly decent equestrienne.

The caravan rested for several days at Doğubayazit. Michael and Najila were guests at the villa of a wealthy noble, a Doukas cousin of Michael's. Their quarters were an incredible luxury after weeks on the road. Above all else, Najila relished a leisurely perfumed bath twice a day.

Father and daughter spent many hours together, something they had rarely had time for in Baghdad. One morning, they sat in the villa garden, watching tamed Egyptian geese competing for food scraps. Michael idly twirled the silver and amber cross hanging from his neck. Thinking of Shahdi, his expression saddened as he told Najila, "This will be yours when I die. Your mother would not wear a Christian cross, though she cherished it because I gave it to her."

Najila shuddered. The thought of her father dying was anathema. "You will live a long life, my father."

Michael lifted the chain over his head. He put the cross to his nostrils and inhaled the resin's scent. "Whenever I smell amber, I think of your mother." He sighed and gently kissed it. The resin was warm and velvety, as Shahdi's lips had been.

Suddenly, a ray of sunshine shimmered through the amber, illuminating the preserved insect within. For a fraction of a second, its four wings appeared to quiver, the dragonfly reborn and poised for flight.

"Are you sure that I have not related the story of how the cross came to be?" he asked.

Najila shook her head. "Hmm. Perhaps. When I was very small. If so, I have forgotten it."

Recalling the day when he stood alongside the sleek Viking war craft, brightly painted shields lining its gunwales, Michael seemed to peer inward. "Previous to my appointment to Persia, I bought the amber in Konstantinoupolis from an old Viking. The Viking ships usually brought slaves down from the north. This one bore amber and other inanimate objects. I had to bargain an entire morning for the beauty you see here."

Najila reached out and caressed the amber, then delicately sniffed her fingertips where they had touched it. Her mind searched the past. "It is the first perfume I knew," she whispered.

Michael looped the chain back around his neck. Speaking more to himself than to Najila, he murmured, "Later, after

I arrived in Baghdad, met your mother, and we married, I designed the setting and had a Persian silversmith complete it. It was my wedding gift to her."

Najila leaned over and hugged him, her eyes filling with tears.

"The entire population bristles with tension," Otrygg remarked to Michael as the two men led the column into Iğdir, a mountain town near the endlessly changing boundary between Byzantine and Seljuk territories. Fortuitously overlooked by Seljuk forces, Iğdir lay within Seljuk-controlled Armenia, and the inhabitants were naturally edgy. One never knew when Seljuk raiders might appear on the horizon.

The uncomfortable atmosphere made Michael eager to be in Byzantium proper, where he would feel more secure. "I will be glad to leave this place," he growled to Otrygg and Julian. But the caravan didn't leave as soon as he would have preferred, because of the additional travelers who came day and night to join it.

Najila, on the other hand, especially enjoyed the exciting chaos that occurred during a preparation for departure. Strange cultures and languages intrigued her. Incognito, she rode Jahara among the shouting men and complaining beasts of burden. On the morning her caravan was to leave, she was up before dawn to observe a group of cursing men reloading stacks of priceless Persian carpets on protesting camels.

To one side, barely visible in the dim light, a short, fat monk struggled to adjust an awkward-looking load on a bony pack donkey. Dust discolored the monk's faded black habit, and Najila noticed that he had a pronounced limp. She watched as the monk's waist-length beard caught in the knot he had used to fasten the cargo ropes.

Najila expected an irritated outburst at the very least, then marveled as the monk patiently freed his beard and tucked it into his belt, all while the donkey repeatedly tried to bite him. Then the monk calmly retied the knot and double-checked his bindings. Seeing how solicitously he attended to his baggage, Najila wondered what an obviously impoverished monk carried that warranted so much concern.

Shafiqa had proven difficult from the beginning as Michael had feared. She continued to harangue him over Najila's horseback forays, declaring that no man would marry a girl who acted so brazenly. Michael merely shrugged and tried to avoid his mother-in-law, though not always with success.

Tempers grew testy, particularly Michael's. On the day Shafiqa went too far, the heat had become intolerable, forcing the caravan to stop in midafternoon. Michael had settled down in the shade under a canopy temporarily erected in the treeless landscape.

Najila galloped up and slid Jahara to a halt. Dismounting, she collapsed on the rug beside her father, saying, "Ah, it is cooler here, is it not?"

Michael anticipated a few peaceful moments alone with his daughter, but to his annoyance, Shafiqa shuffled up to them. Seeing her granddaughter clothed in riding attire, she scolded, "Allah hides his face when my granddaughter goes out in a man's clothing, riding astride as a man."

Weary beyond telling, rank with perspiration and trail grime, Michael could no longer bear Shafiqa's insufferable grousing. "Najila is my daughter; she does as she does with my blessing," he snarled. "And another thing, though I respect your faith, you shall not teach it to Najila. We go to a Christian city, Najila is the daughter of a Christian, and she will become a Christian. I have decided." Michael didn't look at Najila, who listened to the altercation with her mouth hanging open. Never before had she seen her father outwardly oppose her grandmother.

Shafiqa started to stammer something, but Michael waved her away. "Be gone, old woman. I will hear no more." He lay back, dropped his head onto his saddle, and closed his eyes.

When she realized that Michael would simply ignore her, Shafiqa shuffled off, mumbling that he was forever "damned." From then on, she openly shunned him. Secretly, she continued to instruct Najila from the Qur'an.

Chapter 8

"What glorious freedom!" Najila shouted at Jahara's backward-pointed ears. She cantered on alone within sight of the caravan but out of anyone's hearing.

The caravan had wound along endless valleys, across broad arid plains, and through range after range of rugged mountains—months of them since they had left Baghdad. Najila's body was as slim as the male youth she imitated. It only enhanced the exotic Persian features she had inherited from Shahdi: her mother's long-lashed topaz brown eyes slightly upturned at the outer corners; the olive complexion; her full mouth. Michael's Greek and Roman ancestors had bequeathed her prominent cheekbones and an aquiline nose.

As time passed, a few caravan members began to suspect that the boy who rode the little black mare was no boy at all—and only one young woman accompanied them, she of the fancy palanquin within the aristocratic cortege.

Sometimes Najila, who felt secure in her disguise, rode along with Gregori, the shy Armenian monk. He thoroughly enjoyed her company, though he assumed she was an intelligent lad. When Najila told Gregori her name was Ali, he never dreamed she was the enigmatic passenger in the gilded palanquin. He told Najila that he was a muralist, that he had been sequestered at St. Jacob's Monastery on Mount Ararat, and that he was now traveling to Cappadocia. What he did not tell her was that he carried precious artifacts, including several items recovered from Noah's ark, to a safer monastery located in a hidden Cappadocian valley. He would reveal that to no one.

Speaking Latin or Greek, and even a bit of Armenian, they discussed religion, most often Islam versus Christianity. Najila's contralto voice did not betray her femininity. One day, she declared, "I know about the crucifixion of Jesus Christ. I have also heard that he supposedly died for me . . . or that he died for my sins. I cannot remember which."

"Both are true, Ali," Gregori said, pleased at his young companion's interest.

Puzzled, Najila asked, "How can it be that he died for me? This Jesus lived long ago; I live today; I did not know him."

Gregori straightened in his saddle. Before her eyes, the rather dowdy and rotund monk seemed to grow in stature, become more confident. His speech resounded with renewed authority as he answered her question according to Cappadocian theology.

"Jesus Christ is part of the Trinity as stated in our Nicean Creed: God the Father; God the Son, and God the Holy Spirit. All these entities are divine. Though they are three, they are also one; they have existed since time's beginning. Do you understand?"

"No!" cried Najila, confused. "How are three persons one? It is impossible."

"Are you familiar with the Greek word *homoios*, Ali?"

"Yes."

"You know then that it means of *the same substance.* God the Father, God the Son, and God the Holy Spirit have always been and forever will be. Though we speak of them as separate identities, they are *homoios*; they are the same.

"I still do not understand."

"Ah!" Gregori gently responded. "You have a father, correct?"

Thinking the monk referred to Michael, afraid he had seen through her disguise, Najila held her breath.

Gregori waited for her answer.

"Hmm. Yes, of course," she murmured tentatively. "But what has that to do with my sins?"

Gregori impatiently shook his head. "Let me answer one question before the other." He lifted two fingers. "Your father is at the same time his father's son. Is that not also true?"

She nodded.

"And when you are a father, your father will be a grand-father." He lifted a third finger. "Do you see?"

Najila thought she was beginning to.

"Hence, your father can be a father, a son, and a grandfather. If a mere, earthbound man can be all these at once—as well as an uncle, a cousin, and a grandson—is it not possible that our omnipotent God might have more than a single identity?"

"I suppose so."

"Here is another example. A man can feel the fire burn his hand, think about the pain of it, and snatch his hand away, all at once. Each function is distinct, yet together, they are one with or a part of the man. All are of the same substance. *Homoios!*"

"I try to understand, but it is written in the Qur'an there is only one God. The Qur'an does not say there are three Gods, only Allah. It teaches us that Jesus Christ and his mother, Mary, were great prophets."

Sighing, Gregori declared, "If one tries to explain the Trinity, he may lose his mind, but if one denies it, then he loses his soul."[1] Slowing his donkey, he pulled a thick parchment scroll from his habit. "Do you read Greek?" he asked.

"Of course," Najila answered. "Arabic and Latin, too."

Amazed, Gregori stared at Najila. "Where did you learn so many languages?"

Realizing she had nearly given her secret away, Najila fumbled for an answer. "Uh . . . tutors taught me."

Gregori wondered to whom the strange boy belonged and who had hired tutors for him. But he didn't want to pry. Instead, he handed Najila the scroll. "This contains the four holy Gospels: Matthew, Mark, Luke, and John. It tells the story of Jesus and how your sins can be forgiven. I rendered the illuminations myself," he mumbled, modestly dropping his eyes.

From then on, at every opportunity, despite the palanquin's jouncing and lurching, Najila managed to read the beautiful document's ornate Greek script. She perceived that she was not the perfect human she believed she had been all her seventeen years.

She began to remember things from her childhood, things that tugged at her heart: her suave, dignified father on his knees, humbly praying at his personal altar; his regular visits to the embassy chapel to confess his sins to an Orthodox monk who traveled from a distant monastery especially for that purpose; her father vainly beseeching her mother to join him in his belief.

Najila soon realized that her Muslim grandmother had more faith in Allah than she herself did, despite her grandmother's persistent teachings. Faith! That was the whole idea. Now she knew. She had never truly had faith.

Najila's wonder increased as she read the scroll. When she had a problem with it, she had only to question Gregori, who then patiently instructed her in the matter. She became quite fond of the round little monk. As for Gregori, he had lost his heart to the mysterious veiled girl in the palanquin, and he remained unaware that she and the clever youth Ali were one and the same.

By the time they reached Erzurum, Najila was ready to settle down, settle somewhere, anywhere, as long as she could luxuriate in a nonmoving environment. She longed for better food, a softer bed, and daily baths, with attendants ministering to her every whim. Her inability to keep immaculately clean bothered her the most.

"I did not want to leave Baghdad. Now, I cannot wait to reach Konstantinoupolis," she admitted to her father.

"I am sure that you will like Konstantinoupolis; it is a fair and fascinating city," he told her. "Wonderful statues and fine churches and monasteries line the streets. There is the famous Hippodrome—"

"Hippodrome?" Najila interrupted. "What is that?"

"It is a monumental structure, the largest in the city. I sometimes think it is the most important building in all Konstantinoupolis, even more important than the coliseum or the emperor's palaces."

"It has something to do with horses?" Najila asked.

"Yes, it is famed for its chariot races, but other competitions and events are held in it, also."

"Do you mean chariot races are run inside a building? I cannot imagine such a place."

Michael laughed. "The Hippodrome is a huge, roofless oval with seats at one end and along both sides. A low wall divides it down the middle. On the wall are statues of illustrious people. Twelve chariots—they erupt out of twelve gates that open at the same instant—race around the wall. Magnificent, bronze horses stand atop the gate tower. It is too much to describe. It has to be seen."

He sighed, recalling the riotous colors, the boisterous crowd, and the rich medley of smells. "I have not seen it for twenty years."

Just then, the Syrian caravan master rushed up to them on his tall camel. "Soon we come to a narrow canyon," he yelled. "It is especially dangerous because of the many landslides that occur in it. We must hurry through." Surreptitiously glancing at Najila, the Syrian's expression showed no indication that he recognized her. "It is best," he pronounced, "that the ladies ride

in their sedans. Horses are often unmanageable through here."
He loped up the line to warn the others.

"Do as he says," Najila's father said.

"I do not—"

"Enough!" He glared at her. "Our caravan master is an experienced guide. It is obvious that he knows who you are. If he
believes you would be safer in a divan than on a horse, then
he is to be obeyed. Go!"

Bristling at the implication that she was a weak female, Najila
galloped Jahara to the palanquin and turned the mare over to
a servant. Still raging at the indignity, she stopped her bearers
and threw herself into the vehicle.

"A woman cannot handle a nervous horse? My father and
that dog of a Syrian know nothing," she huffed.

Chapter 9

Progressing in a single file, the caravan carefully negotiated a narrow trail along the north wall of the deep gorge. Below, a powerful river gouged the chasm's floor. Boulder-strewn cliffs loomed above, steep and treeless, their unforgiving walls magnifying the sun's torrid rays. Man and beast labored on with their heads down, their plodding steps raising swirling, choking clouds.

Michael rode toward the front of the procession, watchful for any impending trouble, but his retinue lagged far back in the fragmented line, in a part of the caravan that was still traversing the wide valley leading up to the entrance of the canyon. To Najila, the journey seemed endless. She lay in her palanquin, her pores oozing perspiration that dried almost instantly. Her Nubian bearers suffered even more. Their breath rasped, and their sweat-streaked, ebony skin was covered with dust, becoming the same sienna hue as the surrounding soil. The four bearers changed every hour to rest and slake their thirst, lowering the palanquin and relinquishing the long handles to fresher men.

Another servant led the three-month-old colt that Michael's mare Sabiya had delivered during the journey. At the beginning of its weaning, the colt constantly whinnied for its dam. Najila often had the baby brought to her side, where she tried in vain to console it.

Najila's chief concern, however, was for her grandmother. The trip was proving too much for Shafiqa, who had sunk into an unusual lethargy. Najila and her father also worried about Zahra, who had lost weight and lacked her normal vibrant energy. Each elderly woman, riding in her own palanquin, endured frequent bouts of diarrhea and dehydration.

A sort of muffled thundering aroused Najila out of her apathy. She parted the curtains to gaze upward. The cloudless sky gleamed luminous and blue, but when she peered forward, she saw what appeared to be billows of dust roiling in the distance. Too weary to give more than a brief thought to what had caused the phenomenon, Najila dropped the curtains and collapsed back on her pillows. She listlessly swatted a pesky fly that had taken advantage of the brief opening. The insects were intolerable.

Desperate shouts rose above the clatter of rapid hoofbeats. Her curiosity piqued, Najila stuck out her head again, squinting against the blinding sun. Sensing that something bad had happened, she shivered despite the searing heat.

A low rise in the terrain obscured the trail beyond the point where it left the narrowing valley to enter the canyon. All at once, a cluster of running camels, and then donkeys, emerged from behind the hill and charged toward the palanquins. Drivers followed as panicked as their animals. The madly dashing horde divided and hurtled to both sides of Najila's bewildered, cowering party, just in time to avoid overrunning them.

As Najila tried to gather her wits, her friend the monk and his two donkeys sped into sight. The pack on Gregori's baggage donkey had loosened and swung wildly beneath its belly as it galloped nose-to-tail behind the saddle donkey. The terrified beast contorted its body, repeatedly bucking and kicking at the frightening burden that banged its ribs.

Fortunately, Gregori's well-tied knots held fast. He frantically hauled on his saddle donkey's reins, at last controlling his frenzied mount and bringing the two animals to a panting halt.

Gregori and his animals had narrowly escaped being crushed, but within the gorge, an enormous slide had carried several donkeys and their drivers to the canyon bottom. If the caravan units had been traveling closer together, many more could have perished. Those who had been traveling before and after the slide had come to a confused halt, the men and animals milling in scattered, disorganized groups.

Najila didn't hear the full story of the catastrophe for nearly three hours. Michael had been riding Sabiya right in front of Gregori when the landslide hit, but he had not been seen since. The monk eventually informed Najila that her father was missing. "I am going to assist the searchers," he told her. "He will surely be found."

Awaiting news, Najila paced and chewed her nails. Zahra and Shafiqa occasionally joined her vigil, though their weakened conditions soon drove the older women into the shade of their palanquins.

It was dusk before Otrygg and his men approached the Doukas retinue. They bore a crude litter, on which lay a motionless form, the face covered with a kerchief. Verging on hysteria, Najila ran to meet them. When the Viking ordered the men to set their burden at Najila's feet, she recognized her father's blood-soaked tunic. Horrified, she threw herself across Michael's body and wept. She tore at the kerchief that hid his face, but clotted blood glued the silk to his lifeless flesh.

The big Viking gently untangled the cloth from the girl's fingers and lifted her off Michael's stiffening corpse. "Mistress, you must not look upon your father yet. Go to your divan until I make him fit for viewing."

Najila screamed once—a shrill, anguished howl—and sank to the ground. Zahra rushed up and fell to her knees, embracing the prostrate girl. Noting Otrygg's distraught expression, Zahra raised a questioning eyebrow. Otrygg slowly shook his head, and she realized that Michael was beyond help.

"He was alive when we discovered him at the bottom of the canyon," Otrygg explained, his eyes red and watering. "He never regained consciousness, though, and died before we could get him to the top."

Najila was mute and unresisting as Zahra guided her away from the awful scene.

Chapter 10

They buried Michael in a shallow grave among the rocks. His entire entourage attended, as did the Syrian caravan master and a few drivers. It was especially for Najila that Gregori performed his first funerary mass.

Najila cried until no tears were left. She no longer pretended to be a boy, cantering Jahara up and down the line. The steppe pony was forgotten. Her beloved father was gone, never to return to his beautiful Konstantinoupolis, never to show her the wonderful things he had so eloquently described. She was living a horrible, impossible nightmare. Denial and bitterness hardened her heart.

One afternoon, soon after Michael's funeral, Gregori came to speak to Najila, who had retreated behind the curtains of her sedan. Just as he was about to announce his presence, he saw the black steppe pony grazing next to her palanquin where Zahra had tethered it. Suddenly he stopped, shocked. How could he not have known? It all made sense now. The slender boy Ali and the mysterious, lovely Najila were one and the same. Remembering their intimate conversations, he felt like a fool.

Steadying his faltering nerve, he softly called, "My lady, I have come to bring you our blessed Lord's comfort."

The monk's kindly offer only enraged Najila. "Now, I am an orphan, as you are," she cried, flinging aside the curtains, her glare defiant. "You have often said God loves me, and God is merciful. Would a loving, merciful God take my father from me? Take my mother along with her unborn baby when I was still a child? Did a merciful God allow a crazed bear to maul your parents, murder them, when you, too, were but a child?"

Najila's scorn devastated the little monk. He did not know how to answer her grief-wrought questions. He merely stared at her, then turned away, shattered.

Even Shafiqa was unable to pacify her granddaughter. When she made an effort to lecture Najila on Allah's ambiguous benevolence, the girl hissed, "Let me be. Allah does not exist, nor does my father's Christian God."

They were delayed four days while the men cleared the trail of the slide's detritus. When that task was accomplished, what was left of the caravan continued onward toward Konstantinoupolis.

Due to passing time and Gregori's patient ministering, Najila's bitter attitude softened enough so that she once asked him to hear her confession. She made him believe that her mind and emotions were finally healing. Nevertheless, when the caravan reached Sebaste and the road to Konstantinoupolis was in sight, Najila's awareness of her terrible loss returned, as did the despair and bitterness.

In Sebaste, Gregori bade Najila and the other two women a reluctant good-bye, but Najila declined to acknowledge him. When he sadly left to feed his animals, Najila beckoned to Otrygg. Handing him a silk-wrapped packet, she snapped, "This is my father's cross; give it to the monk. Perhaps it will protect him. It did not protect my father." She withdrew into her divan, yanking the curtains shut.

Stunned, Otrygg remained where he was by Najila's divan. Was it not only a few days before the slide when Michael had

made him promise to see that Najila inherited all his possessions, including the valuable, cherished cross? Made him promise to watch over his daughter if something should happen to
him? The Viking mourned his longtime friend deeply. That
Najila could part with an object so precious to her father baffled
him. Pondering life's vagaries, Otrygg went to seek Gregori,
hoping to persuade the priest to refuse the cross.

Gregori sat on a boulder, his eyes staring at nothing. He
flinched when he saw Otrygg approach.

Otrygg held out the wrapped cross. "The lady Najila asked
me to give this to you. However, I do not believe that—"

The monk's forlorn expression stopped the Viking's protest
in mid sentence. Changing his mind about asking the monk
to reject the cross, Otrygg thrust the package at him. Gregori
took it with both hands. Letting its wrapping fall open, Gregori shifted the cross to one flattened palm. Tears made muddy
tracks on his dusty cheeks. Four cabochon emeralds winking
in the bright sunlight reminded him of Najila's eyes. Three
inset rubies glowed like her moist lips. "Why did she do this?"
he moaned.

Seeing Gregori's anguish and overwhelmed by his own grief,
Otrygg was unable to say or do more. He could only shrug his
great shoulders, turn, and stride away.

Gregori stood, his head bowed over the pendent. The heavy
chain looped around his wrists, binding him to Najila's image
as bridle and bit bind a horse to its master.

Chapter 11

Though the last leg to Konstantinoupolis was uneventful, Najila seemed to waste away. Growing wan and thin, she stayed aloof even from those who had attended her from infancy. Shunning Zahra and Shafiqa, who repeatedly tried to comfort her, she shadowed Otrygg Harald. Rarely employing her palanquin, and then only to nap briefly, Najila resumed riding Jahara, openly dressed in a man's garb, unveiled and sitting astride. Shafiqa and Zahra were horrified.

Even Otrygg was appalled at her contempt for everyone and everything. Much to his frustration, Najila often took off at a reckless canter down some remote ravine, or repeatedly crisscrossed any foaming stream that the caravan happened to be following. The surefooted, tough little steppe pony kept her safe.

Besides her father, Otrygg was the only man with whom Najila had ever had a close relationship. At forty-eight, he was a mere three years younger than her father had been when he died, and he was thirty-one years older than Najila. In Najila's eyes, the handsome Viking was her father's embodiment. She admired him, felt indebted to him, and almost worshipped him as a father figure.

As for Otrygg, his feelings for Najila went far deeper than he dared admit. He could hide his innermost thoughts of her from Najila, but he couldn't hide them from himself.

On a rare day when Najila rode silently by Otrygg's side at the head of the troop, he reflected on her continuing depression. Hoping to gladden her spirit, he decided it was expedient that he reveal what awaited her at their destination.

"The Komnenous family owns a vast estate outside Konstantinoupolis called Hawks Hill," he told her. "It now belongs to you."

Najila pondered this extraordinary information. Raising a skeptical eyebrow, she twisted in the saddle to face him. "I own property? My father never told me. He just said we were going to Konstantinoupolis." It still made her throat ache to mention her father. She swallowed hard to prevent the tears that easily gushed forth these days.

"Your father inherited Hawks Hill shortly before leaving for Baghdad. At his . . . er . . . death, it became yours."

Despite an effort not to show it, she was intrigued by Otrygg's news. She asked the Viking, "Have you seen Hawks Hill?"

"I know it well. It was my home, as it was my father's and your father's."

"You lived at Hawks Hill?"

"Yes, until I was of an age to join the Varangians."

Najila frowned. "I do not understand. I thought the Varangians lived at the palace."

"True. My father was a member of the emperor's elite Varangian Guard, and he dwelled on the palace grounds while serving the emperor. After my mother died, when I was only a small lad, my father sent me to Hawks Hill. Your grandparents took me in, treating me as a son and your father's brother. When my father retired, your grandfather hired him as captain of the Hawks Hill guards. I naturally became a Varangian when I was old enough, but I resigned from the guard when Michael persuaded me to accompany him to Persia."

Najila then asked, "What happened to Hawks Hill when my father was assigned to Baghdad? Are my grandparents living there yet? It is strange, but I cannot remember my father ever talking about them."

"No, they died long before you were born. When Michael left, he assigned the care of Hawks Hill to Leopold Alexander Doukas, his cousin. You are to claim the title for yourself upon your arrival."

Najila couldn't help but relish the exciting prospect of ruling such a noble-sounding estate. She gave Otrygg a tight-lipped smile, but the icy chill due to her recent loss remained unchanged.

Chapter 12

When they at last neared the famous city in October 1065, Otrygg Harald's sensitive nose detected a familiar odor long before he saw the walls of Konstantinoupolis. He closed his eyes and breathed deeply of the salty, fecund air. His biceps twitched as if they strained at a longboat's graceful, narrow-bladed oars. Ancient runes of his Viking ancestors sang in his genes. His heart raced. He had been too far and too many years away from the sea.

Each time they ascended a rise, Najila could more clearly see the Golden Horn's busy harbor and Konstantinoupolis's undulating western skyline on its opposite bank. Anticipation of soon being enveloped by the fabled city's great walls had her insides deliciously quivering.

The fall harvest was at its peak. Equally burdened beneath ponderous loads of produce destined for the city's consumption, people and animals now crowded the road. The huge, clamoring throng intimidated Najila, and she fled to her divan, having given Jahara to a groom. A cart jostled the palanquin, and Najila glimpsed piles of green melons, larger than any she had ever seen, with ugly, warty skins. At the impact, one melon rolled off the cart to the ground and shattered. To Najila's amazement, despite its moldy-looking husk, the fruit's orange-hued interior appeared as fresh and juicy as the melons she had eaten in Baghdad.

A column of donkeys, each carrying a giant heap of straw, overtook the slower caravan. All Najila could see of the little animals were their long-eared heads and spindly legs. They resembled the hay stacks she had beheld on nearby farms—only these small stacks moved.

Najila waited impatiently while customs officials strutted among the members of her retinue. Important with their power, efficient, and stone-faced, they pried into every item of baggage, including her most personal possessions. Vendors plying their wares between the men and animals shouted that water, tea, and food were available.

Minutes stretched into hours. Finally, after paying the customary bribes and receiving the necessary permits, Najila's party was allowed to go on. Led by Otrygg, the caravan headed toward the harbor.

Expecting to be immediately bedazzled by a plethora of royal palaces and splendid churches, Najila was disappointed when they entered the Asian portion of the city. It seemed a bit scruffy: the streets unswept and the churches, houses, and shops neglected.

"Not until we cross the Bosporus Strait and enter Konstantinoupolis proper will you see the city's best part," Otrygg explained when she expressed her trepidation.

Unfortunately, in order for Otrygg to make arrangements for their crossing, they were forced to stay overnight in a run-down inn that was deplorably filthy. Otrygg had chosen it because it was reputedly safe and served fairly decent food. Though the three women spread furs on their prickly straw pallets, they slept little, spending the night scratching bites and pinching fleas and lice between their fingernails.

Meanwhile, Otrygg spent his evening and two hours the next morning in various taverns, seeking vessels capable of transporting them across the strait.

By midafternoon, Najila's party, along with their animals and belongings, were aboard four Viking-inspired *knorrs*,

square-sailed cargo ships that could also be rowed. The wind
had picked up, and the crossing was not smooth. White caps,
peaking and flowing over the heavily laden boat's prow,
foamed out through the scuppers. At every tack, the grimy,
patched sails popped, and the rigging squealed and groaned.

Najila had never seen such a churning expanse of water. She
experienced fear, yet at the same instance, her senses were tit-
illated by the strait's unique beauty. She discovered that, unlike
her late father, she was not prone to *mal de mer*.

The Golden Horn, an arm of the Bosporus bounded by verdant hills and terminating at the Black Sea on the north end and
the Sea of Marmara on the southernmost end, supported one
of the world's most prolific fisheries. As the *knorrs* approached
the Golden Horn's western side, the local fleet was leaving for
a night of fishing. Taut, multicolored sails hovered above the
water like butterflies fluttering in a stiff breeze above a puddle.
Nearly every small boat had a protecting eye painted on its
bow, and each carried a lantern on its stern. When at night the
wind died and the lanterns were lit, the light attracted fish into
the nets.

Waiting in her palanquin, which rested on a dock as their
goods were unloaded, Najila appraised her new surroundings.
This was more like what she had expected. Nothing, abso-
lutely nothing, matched the grandeur of the magnificent Hagia
Sophia, which stood atop a hill and dominated the landscape.
Najila had first seen the enormous church from the Asian side.
Even at that distance, Hagia Sophia's spherical dome—the larg-
est in the world—towered over the structures around it.

Once their goods were unloaded, they traveled slowly west,
lengthwise along the bustling peninsula. Najila sometimes felt
like a beetle trapped on a teeming anthill. Moving through the
congested streets of Konstantinoupolis at such a leisurely pace,
however, gave her the opportunity to examine closely everything they passed.

Larger-than-life antique statues lined the wide thoroughfare. Her entourage skirted four-story buildings, gold-leafed monuments of every size and description, and marble obelisks that touched the very heavens. Such visual stimulation after months of travel through so much sparsely populated wilderness overwhelmed her.

It seemed that every block bore multiple churches. Otrygg, riding guard beside her palanquin, described them for her. "Most of these churches contain reliquaries inside: an arm, a finger, or some other anatomical feature that supposedly belonged to the saint to whom the church is dedicated."

To Najila, who had been taught by Shafiqa that to create even an image of a human was wrong, the idea was evil. No matter how she tried, she could not relate the worship of body pieces to her father's Christian beliefs.

They spent the night in a far cleaner inn and, after a bugless, solid night's sleep, got an early morning start. Once they had passed through Konstantinoupolis's three western walls, exiting the city through the St. Romanus Gate, Najila could no longer stand to ride in the confining palanquin. "I have to get out of here," she pleaded to Otrygg. "Please bring Jahara to me." The big Viking immediately complied.

The cortege followed an old Roman road west of the city. Sabiya's blue-gray colt pranced on a lead held tightly in Najila's right hand. Though the motherless colt had been sired by a royal stallion, the shaggy steppe mare bared her teeth and flattened her ears whenever the colt tried to nurse, forcing Najila to concentrate on keeping the frustrated colt's line from tangling in Jahara's legs.

Suddenly, Otrygg stopped their progress and trotted up to Najila. "We approach Komnenous holdings. It is not befitting a lady of your station to be seen dressed as you are. It is especially improper for her to ride . . . ah . . . ride astride. My lady would be wise to return to her palanquin."

Najila made a disgusted face at Otrygg. Nevertheless, she dismounted and handed Jahara's reins and the colt's lead to him. "If my cousin has not seen a woman on a horse, he soon will," she snapped as she climbed into the palanquin. But before commanding the bearers to lift the vehicle and to continue onward, she reached for the skirt she kept handy under a pillow. Undergoing a series of contortions in the palanquin's limited space, she managed to gather the voluminous yardage around her legs, thus hiding the offensive male attire—at least from the waist down.

The closer they came to Hawks Hill, the greater Najila's apprehension. Her stomach churned, and she was slightly nauseated. Here she was bound for an inheritance that was overseen by an obscure relative. Beyond that, she knew nothing about the mysterious property.

Dusk was about to fall as they entered the grounds of the vast Komnenous estate. Her curiosity intensifying by the minute, Najila tied back the divan's curtains and stared out. Many of the cultivated fields had already fallen under the scythe. Others, luxuriant with unharvested grain, gleamed in the golden light of the brilliant sunset. Horses and cattle—faint black silhouettes against the darkening sky—grazed peacefully in the farthest fields.

Over the centuries, most of the virgin forest had been cut to build and repair Konstantinoupolis and its ships, but on Komnenous land, some woods remained in parks. These had become isolated islands where wild game still ranged, mainly boar and deer that were nurtured and hunted by the nobles and their friends. All at once, she realized it all belonged to her, Najila Doukas Komnenous.

Chapter 13

The estate's residents had received early word of the travelers' impending arrival. The nobility and house servants queued under the massive portico to watch the newcomers approach along the fir-lined entrance road.

As her party neared the manse, Najila leaned out of the palanquin as far as she dared and tried to see the assembly waiting to greet her. Which of them was her father's grandnephew, her remote cousin, the man who would have to turn his home over to her? She dreaded their inevitable encounter.

Dominating everything below it, the great Komnenous manor house stood atop the area's highest hill. The structure's main section rose to four stories, and the wings to either side were three stories tall. Two huge Corinthian columns, their caps carved in the most elaborate Greek style, miniaturized the humans waiting between them. Behind the Corinthian columns, a pair of simpler Doric columns framed the building's arched doorway. The Komnenous crest adorned the keystone of the arch.

A dome topped the end of each wing, and a bigger one—a small copy of the dome on Hagia Sophia—rose just behind the portico. Red tiles, in the Roman style, roofed the entire manor, including the domes. Pink-tinted stucco coated the walls.

The manor rivaled the Baghdad caliph's palace in grandeur, but its handsome design combined Greek, Roman, and Byzantine architecture rather than Persian.

Upon their arrival, while Zahra helped Najila from her palanquin, Shafiqa, garbed in black and heavily veiled, examined the place with a buzzard's eye. The old woman's swiveling head was the only thing that revealed her intense interest in the activity going on around her. Beneath her veil, Shafiqa wore a satisfied smile. From her initial glimpse of Najila's rich and expansive inheritance, Shafiqa had determined that she herself, by right of seniority, would take charge—once everyone settled in, that is. Her granddaughter would never be able to manage it all at her young age.

Najila started for the portico's bottom stair, but Shafiqa's bony fingers clawed at her arm. "Hold your head high like a princess should," she hissed. "These people must realize that you are in command now."

Najila automatically straightened her shoulders and lifted her chin. Of course, she *was* a princess. Did her mother not have royal Persian blood?

Otrygg moved forward and tucked Najila's arm into the crook of his. The Viking's large size suddenly made Najila feel like a little child. She instantly reacted, wrenching her arm away from Otrygg's restricting hold, then stepped in front of him so as to become first to climb the wide marble staircase.

As she ascended the broad staircase, Najila kept her eyes downcast to avoid tripping on her skirts. Reaching the top, she raised her eyes to the man who faced her.

"Welcome to Hawks Hill," her father said.

Chapter 14

When Otrygg saw Najila sway, he quickly stepped to her side and took her arm. His strong hand bracing her elbow, he whispered, "Are you ill, my lady?"

"Baba," Najila said through tremulous lips; then she shook her head. "For a moment I thought he was my father," she explained in rapid Persian to Otrygg. She doubted that anyone amid the reception committee could understand that language.

Briefly mistaking her cousin Leopold Alexander Doukas for her dead father was an understandable error. Manuel Eroticus Komnenous and his wife had sired a son named John. After his wife developed a long and fatal ailment, Manuel had a midlife liaison with a famous Macedonian courtesan, whom he had brought home in the guise of a companion to his wife. When his wife eventually died, the fickle Manuel discarded his mistress for a younger woman, though by then, the courtesan had given birth to Michael, Najila's father.

Manuel's first son, John, like his father, dallied with a Greek courtesan. The result of that liaison was Leopold Alexander.

Michael had been two years older than Leopold, but as small children and on into their early teens, they were often mistaken for one another. The twin-like resemblance hadn't lasted, however. At maturity, Leopold stood an inch and a half shorter and outweighed Michael by sixty pounds. Michael had been clean shaven until he left Baghdad. Leopold had grown a full beard, which his personal barber meticulously curled every day. Such abundant facial hair was not fashionable, but recently it had become Leopold Alexander's attempt to hide the puffs and sags wrought by his wanton lifestyle.

Recognizing Najila's plight, Otrygg nodded to her and interceded. "Forgive me for speaking out of turn, my lord. Lady Najila is astonished because you remind her of her late father, Michael Komnenous."

"So I have been told." The man's smile did not extend to his eyes, and his tone was unmistakably hostile. His expression was more a sneer as he boldly examined the tall Viking. "Who is he who speaks for this child?"

Waving a hand in Najila's direction, ignoring Otrygg entirely, he spoke to the man at his side. "Am I to assume that this infant is my cousin?"

Struggling to keep his volatile temper in check and his face bland, Otrygg studied the pompous individual who confronted them. He had never met Leopold Alexander. He intensely disliked what he saw. "I am Michael's true friend and his daughter's protector," Otrygg declared. Next he asked, his voice a low, warning growl, "Am I to presume that I am addressing Michael's cousin?" Whether from intimidation or because he simply refused to, Leopold Alexander did not favor Otrygg with an answer.

While all this occurred, Najila had had a chance to scrutinize her cousin, whose beard and flowing flamboyant robes had at first disguised his wobbly double chin and large protruding belly. His jet black hair featured a startling white streak that began above his right eye.

Leopold Alexander Doukas might be called handsome, she mused, *except that he seems somewhat effeminate and far too fat.*

Even according to Byzantine standards, Leopold Alexander was overly embellished. Precious gems encrusted his elaborately embroidered robes. Jewels glittered on his shoes. Every finger sported a flashy ring, and he wore pretentious emerald and ruby earrings in both ear lobes.

He is a gaudy, overfed rooster, thought Najila. *How could I ever have mistaken him for my father?*

Her cousin offered Najila his hand, which she reluctantly accepted. Though the temperature was quite warm, Leopold's palm and fingers were unexpectedly cold and clammy. Najila almost jerked her hand back, but with remarkable self-control, she refrained. Instead, she graciously returned his insincere smile, declaring, "Yes, I am Michael's daughter, Najila. You are my cousin Leopold Alexander Doukas, of course."

"I am he," Leopold verified.

Najila blushed as his eyes undressed her. Still holding her hand, he suddenly pulled her to him. Because she resisted, he whispered, "For the customary kiss, my dear. Those who watch expect it of us."

Unlike Leopold's slobbery, lingering kisses on both her cheeks, Najila's kiss was a single quick peck on one cheek, followed by instant retreat. His displeasure evidenced by his sour countenance, Leopold turned toward the manor's high arched entrance, motioning Najila to go before him.

As she entered the unlit entranceway, Najila hesitated, wishing Otrygg would catch up. The Viking had stayed close and now walked immediately behind Leopold. Najila threw him an appreciative glance and swept into her new home.

The interior of Hawks Hill was more luxurious than Najila could have dreamed. A wide, dimly lit hall, beginning just inside the dark apse, led to a magnificent rotunda, whose pink marble walls contained four Roman arched doorways. Niches between the openings held life-size marble and bronze statues. Najila's Islamic upbringing caused her to avert her gaze from the predominantly nude figures.

The rotunda was covered by the dome she had noticed in back of the portico from outside, and each of the three floors above ground level had a projecting balcony. Ornately carved, glistening, off-white marble railings rimmed the balconies. To Najila, it looked like tiers of delicate lace encircled the exquisite room.

Instead of the thick, sound-muffling carpets to which she was accustomed, an intricate marble and glass mosaic decorated the floor, causing footsteps to ring and voices to echo. The detailed mosaic illustrated the solar system as Byzantine astronomers pictured it—Sol and the other planets circling the earth. Gold-enameled glass chips depicted a stylized sun that gleamed realistically in the late afternoon light that streamed through narrow, vertical windows set in the room's curved wall.

"Hawks Hill is the most beautiful place I've ever seen; I cannot believe my father left it all to me," Najila breathed to Otrygg.

"You and your party must be weary after your long journey," Leopold Alexander purred. "Come, I'll show you to your chambers."

Chapter 15

On entering her bedchamber, Najila immediately spotted a great canopied bed that dominated the room. She squealed with delight and threw herself backward on it, sinking almost out of sight in furs and thick comforters. Uttering a huge sigh, she remained supine, fingers locked behind her head, and gazed raptly around the room. Zahra and Shafiqa continued to direct the servants who lugged in trunks and bundles.

"Sleeping here, I may die of pleasure," Najila breathed.

Though too somber for her taste, her three-room suite contained furnishings as lavish as the rest of what she had seen so far of Hawks Hill. She vowed, however, to replace the drab and toneless, patterned-silk wall covering and the heavy, lined drapes that shrouded the ceiling-to-floor windows. Brighter colors and airier fabrics would be more suitable.

With the drapes tightly drawn, the candles in a pair of triumvirate iron sconces provided the only illumination for the room. "Zahra, please uncover the windows," Najila said. But she had forgotten that the hour was late and the sun had fallen below the horizon. Even with the draperies open, the meager twilight coming through the windows added very little light to the room.

Though it had been a lengthy and tiring day, and Zahra felt a bit queasy, she dutifully began to remove and shake out clothes from one of Najila's traveling chests. Spreading a splendid red satin gown on the huge bed alongside Najila, she began to smooth its wrinkles. Gold and silver peafowl, their embroidered tails fanned in full display, embellished the wide skirt. Lacy Persian designs ran vertically across the bodice and down the sleeves.

"Lord Leopold Alexander told the Viking that we are to eat at the tenth hour," Zahra advised Najila; Zahra never called Otrygg by his given name. She gave the crimson gown one last pat. "You must look your best for your formal presentation to the lord's household, followed by a banquet in your honor."

"Whose household?" Najila snapped at the unsuspecting Zahra. "Must I remind you? Hawks Hill is mine now."

"Oh, my mistake, grand lady," Zahra groaned. "Well then, you must make a good impression on *your* household." She held up Najila's favorite gown of pale blue silk, which was strewn with intertwined paisley designs rendered in tiny seed pearls. "This gown is not wrinkled as much. It might be a better choice."

Najila shook her head, mildly contrite. "I love the blue, but I seem to have more confidence when I wear red; I feel good in it. Anyway, no one will expect me to be perfect tonight after months of travel. If anyone dare criticize, it will be the last thing they say in this house; I will demand that they depart on the morrow."

Zahra rolled her eyes.

Shafiqa had been desperately searching the connecting apartments where she and Zahra would stay. She finally found a chamber pot, which she employed immediately. *Oh, to have a young bladder again like my granddaughter,* she mused as she shuffled, greatly relieved, back to Najila's room.

From the instant Shafiqa had first seen the great mansion, she had been plotting how to say what was on her mind. She eyed her granddaughter slyly. "Najila, as a princess of Persia, it is below you to discipline the servants personally. Leave that duty to me." Ordering people about, especially servants and slaves, suited Shafiqa's contentious nature, but deep down, she feared that Najila would not grant her the total power she relished.

"You may do so, my grandmother, but come to me before you do anything," Najila enjoined, "The final decision will be mine. Always!"

Shafiqa gritted her teeth, but held her tongue.

Najila's introductory meal at Hawks Hill was a strained and embarrassing disaster. In a deliberate faux pas, her cousin Leopold positioned Najila and Shafiqa together near the end of a long table, while Zahra stood behind them, ready to render her services if necessary. Leopold sat at the center of the table, the traditional seat of honor.

Though unfamiliar with local customs, Najila and Shafiqa still recognized the seating as a profound insult. As the legal and sole inheritor of Hawks Hill, Najila should have been in the host's chair.

"I will never forgive him for this," Najila mumbled to her grandmother. "Not as long as I live."

Shafiqa, her face flushed with anger, rose and left the table without excusing herself.

Najila believed that her cousin Leopold was testing her, and she did not mean to fail. She would not be chased off. Suddenly hungry, she used her dagger to stab a succulent squab from the serving platter. As she chewed a juicy morsel on her dagger point, she noticed that next to her plate lay a strange object made of finely wrought silver. One end obviously served as a handle, but what of its opposite end? If she had to, she would be hard put to describe it. Flattened, it had side-by-side, pointed branches. She decided to ignore it and dug into her food with her dagger as had been proper in Baghdad.

Chewing on a thigh of venison that she gripped in both hands, Najila peered over the dripping meat and surreptitiously examined the others at the table as they ate. They were making use of the odd-looking utensil. Out of the corner of her eye, she watched the man next to her. He jabbed at a potato with the object's branched end until the potato broke into pieces; then he used the implement to carry a large piece to his mouth.

When the man turned to talk to the woman to his right, Najila picked up her own device and awkwardly tried to imitate the other diners. After a few bungled attempts, she discovered that the utensil made it easier to manipulate bites than did a dagger.

Of course, Shafiqa did not witness Najila's newfound skill. Silently chuckling, Najila planned how she would enjoy teaching her grandmother its application at the morning meal.

The region's strong, resinous wines flowed freely. Soon the boisterous voices of the feast's participants overwhelmed the poor musicians struggling to make themselves heard above the din. Despite the cacophony, Najila could hardly keep awake as the interminable evening progressed. She started as the loud chatter, the rattling of dishes, the music, all ceased at once. Every eye focused on a trembling old man, who stood before Leopold.

"A new star having a tail has appeared," cried Leopold Alexander's astrologer.[1] "It is a harbinger of a dire event."

Pandemonium spread throughout the hall. Cutlery clattered to the floor; tables overturned. Screaming, shoving, and pushing, everyone rushed outside. The alcohol-numbed men and women stood quivering beneath the clear October sky, staring with dread at the sinister omen.

Feeling they were but strangers, and a bit bewildered by the turmoil, Najila and Zahra waited until the panic had somewhat subsided, then followed the throng out into the crisp, night air.

Najila had no fear of the unusual streak of light. "I saw a drawing of it," she commented. "My father used to bring books on astronomy to me from the caliph's library."

Not as well educated and far more superstitious than her young companion, Zahra shivered. "Let us go inside, my lady. Be that what it may, there is an evil look about it."

Chapter 16

In the days following the comet's appearance, Leopold Alexander disappeared from sight. Rumor, carried by Zahra to Najila's quarters, had it that he was consulting his astrologers.

Najila had little interest in what her cousin did or didn't do; she was relieved to be free of his imperious presence. Besides, she needed time to recover from the long, arduous journey from Baghdad, and she felt a bit reluctant to immediately tie herself down to the unfamiliar responsibility of running a large household.

Eager to learn the extent of her inheritance, she used the opportunity to explore Hawks Hill and its lands. She learned that the main building contained a grand reception hall, two dining halls, each with its own kitchen, and twenty-eight sleeping rooms. Five bedrooms of the twenty-eight were part of self-contained suites. A dozen rooms on the top floor were occupied by house servants.

Otrygg made a point of accompanying Najila as she rode across the estate's rolling terrain, becoming acquainted with the families that farmed there. Everywhere they went, they heard talk of the comet, but Najila was too filled with the landscape's splendor to dwell on a shooting star. The reds and golds of fall enchanted her. She noticed that the brilliant colors shone especially bright at dusk, after a rain shower had polished the vegetation. She had seen nothing like it in Baghdad.

One day, while they stopped to watch a herd of soft-eyed does, a rutting stag barked in the distance, the strange sound echoing across the hills. It attracted the attention of the does, and their ears swiveled in unison toward the buck's call. Still grazing, they began to gradually move toward it.

"I have never seen such beauty," Najila commented to Otrygg.

"Nor have I," he murmured, glancing over at Najila's radiant face.

On that same day, caught by a sudden downpour, the two riders took refuge in a thick grove of tall conifers. Sheltered by the pines, whose needles shed rain like a duck's feathers, they remained relatively dry. When they emerged from the grove, a double rainbow greeted them, two perfect arches that bridged the dark gray sky to the northeast.

Coming home, they happened to approach Hawks Hill from a different angle, more from the rear than they had before. Najila saw that the dome that topped the manse's western wing had changed: it was sliced like a citrus fruit with a missing wedge. Amazed, she reined Jahara to a halt. Even as the two riders watched, the aperture shrunk, and its doors clanged shut. Najila then realized that the dome's roof was made of metal and not tiled like the rest of the manor roof.

"It is an observatory, like the caliph's, Otrygg."

"So it seems. I do think this is larger, though."

"I must see what is inside," Najila exclaimed, her excitement growing by the second.

"Take care, my lady. It may be dangerous," Otrygg said, peering up at the high, forbidding tower.

"There is no threat within an observatory," Najila scoffed. "I only want to see if it is the same as the caliph's."

Otrygg shook his head in despair. "Your curiosity will cause me trouble yet. Sometimes, I find it is difficult to keep my promise to your father—to keep you safe."

"My father is dead. I care for myself." Najila retorted, toss-ing her head. Kicking Jahara to a canter, she sped toward the stables.

Otrygg, loping after her on his slower gelding, did not catch Najila until they both reached the stable yard. His expres-sion was stern as he dismounted, but he said no more to his young companion. He grimly took Jahara's reins and led the horses off.

On entering the manse, Najila could hardly wait to investi-gate the mysterious tower. Instead of changing out of her riding clothes and into more ladylike attire, she immediately started for the wing that held the observatory. She thought it would be easy to find, that all she had to do was to follow the corridor that spanned the entire front of the building.

In doing so, she somehow became confused. Coming to the corridor's easternmost end, she discovered a north–south hall perpendicular to the one she had just traversed, the two form-ing a T where they joined. She paused at the intersection, try-ing to decide which way to turn. Before she could make up her mind, a servant girl exited through a door to Najila's right.

Najila ducked out of view, giggling to herself. What was she doing, acting like a guilty child in her own home? She straight-ened and marched boldly down the hall just as the servant entered another room and closed the door behind her.

Avoiding the room into which the servant had gone, Najila tried the rest of the doors. Some disclosed empty rooms; others led to furnished sleeping chambers. The door at the hall's far end was the only locked one.

That search yielding no sign of the place she sought, she about-faced and checked the other end of the hall. Opening every side door, she found the rooms were identical to those in the last section. She entered a room that dazzled her with sunlight. She stopped, puzzled. The sun was not coming through the windows as it ought to at this hour of the afternoon.

Suddenly, she realized she was in the wrong wing. Irritated at her stupidity, she returned to the main corridor and walked to the west instead of to the east, going straight to the end door in the western tower. It was not locked.

When she inched open the heavy door, she discovered an upward-spiraling stone staircase. The sun had descended to the horizon and did not light the dim passageway as Najila would have preferred. The narrow, shallow stairs were barely illuminated by unglazed slits set in the outer wall, put there for bowmen to use in case of a raid. Wrought-iron sconces were mounted every few feet on the walls, but the torches they contained were unlit.

Najila cautiously ascended the murky, twisting stairwell. At the uppermost step, she was stopped by a stout, planked door. Gripping the handle, she was ready to push open the door when she heard what sounded like a heated discussion occurring on the other side. She recognized her cousin's snarl but not the second man's voice.

"I will not let a mere girl take away what is mine, what has been mine for nearly a quarter century. See that she disappears without a trace. I want it done before the Nativity celebrations."

Najila froze. Chills scurried up her spine. She did not wait to hear more. Thoroughly frightened and newly awakened to the fact that Otrygg's warning did have merit, she stumbled back down the winding passageway. Returning to her quarters, she told nobody what she had overheard, not even Zahra. She knew without a doubt, however, that she had to dispose of her cousin Leopold before he harmed her. She would discuss the problem with Otrygg on the morrow.

Chapter 17

It was the hour after the evening meal, and Zahra and Shafiqa had disappeared into their own quarters. Growing sick with fear, Najila had eaten very little. She had changed her mind about waiting until morning to tell Otrygg; she would let him know immediately what she had heard in the tower. She finally found him in the big central kitchen, stoking his brawny frame with food.

Seating herself next to him on the rough-hewn bench, she blurted, "Something awful happened this afternoon." Her entire body shuddered. "You were right to be afraid for me, and I am truly sorry I spoke harshly to you." She then told him what she had accidentally overheard.

Otrygg's already ruddy face reddened more. He slammed a huge, clenched fist onto the table, rattling the dishes and spilling his wine. Raging, he leaped off the bench and paced the room. "Evil gorges your cousin's heart. I was convinced of it at my first glimpse of him. I never have believed we could trust him."

At first, Najila had felt only fear, but now she felt anger—anger tempered with relief, because she knew without a doubt that Otrygg would protect her. Still, danger surrounded her at Hawks Hill. If her father were alive, he would have sent her cousin Leopold packing. A sob caught in her throat at his memory, and she covered her face with her hands. "Perhaps it is meant that I should leave here," she moaned.

"Surely not!" Otrygg instantly moved to comfort Najila but stopped short of touching her, his upraised hand poised above her shoulder. He turned away so she could not read his expression. Standing by a window, his back to her, he said, "Your father left Hawks Hill to you, and to you alone. As for Leopold Alexander Komnenous . . ." Swinging around, his eyes glaring, Otrygg vowed, "I will slay and quarter the man."

At Najila's horrified grimace, the corners of Otrygg's mouth lifted, and he feigned a yawn to hide his smile, adding, "Or would you have me spirit him so far away you would never have to again see him? My lady, you have only to tell me what action you wish me to take, and it is done." He hissed his short sword from its scabbard and thoughtfully rubbed his thumb along the well-honed blade.

Najila wearily massaged her forehead. "Whatever we do, we cannot delay. My life is at stake, as are the lives of you and the others. I do not know how we can be safely rid of him, but we have to do something soon. Rumors are that he has powerful connections at the palace."

She placed a small hand on Otrygg's massive forearm, and her fingertips sensed the tension in his muscles. Without Otrygg, she would be lost. "The star with a tail was an omen of terrible things to come. I am almost sure of it. Otrygg, you have to help me; there is no other person who can."

Najila recoiled as a cloaked specter strode rapidly toward her. Even on the valley's dark floor, bordered by soaring mountains that blocked the moon's light, she knew the phantom was a man. She stared at what looked like an enormous bird perched on his shoulder.

She thought she recognized him, but she wanted to be certain. Her heart raced as she attempted to close the distance between them, to meet him face-to-face, but her legs would not obey. She could not move. Wanting to cry out, she found she had no voice. Immobilized, her eyes straining to see him better, she could do nothing but wait as he approached.

At last, he stood before her. She tried to see his features, but they were shadowed and indistinct. The moon eerily leaped into the sky over the surrounding peaks, and a metallic object gleamed in the man's hand. He held the dragonfly cross, her father's cross, the same one that she had given to the monk Gregori. Her heart nearly burst.

The apparition offered the cross to her, and she eagerly reached for it. As she did so, the bird—a great hawk—sprang off the man's shoulder. Its talons snatched the silver chain, and the bird soared upward, the pendant dangling wildly as the creature flew. The man roared. His hood fell to his shoulders, and she saw the jet black mane with its white blaze. He was not her father at all. It was her cousin Leopold.

A sudden rumbling and crashing sounded from above. She looked up. The entire mountainside came grinding down upon her in a slow-motion slide.

Najila awakened in a state of shock, trembling and gasping. A silent scream choked her. It took her a minute to realize she was actually in bed—in her own bed, in her own room at Hawks Hill.

Echoing from the courtyard below, the clatter of hooves and wheels created a tremendous din. *That noise must have spurred my bad dream*, she thought. Flinging off the covers, she ran to the window and separated the heavy drapes.

Peering out, she saw that bedlam had taken over the courtyard. Men gripping torches scrambled to attend a large, three-horse chariot and three carts towed by bullocks. Adding to the turmoil, a dozen or more horses, each led by its own groom, milled at one end of the area. The distended nostrils and wet coats of the animals steamed in the freezing air, as did the breath of the handlers.

The chariot contained two men. As Najila watched, one man stepped down from it, jogged up the stairs, and disappeared out of her sight beneath the portico.

The second man, who had remained in the vehicle, handed the chariot's long reins to a servant and jumped to the ground. He shouted for the others to unload the cart's baggage, after which they began to hurriedly lug it into the manse. When the carts had been emptied, the man reentered the chariot and signaled for the carts and grooms to follow him out of the courtyard.

What was that about? Najila wondered. Still drenched in perspiration from her nightmare, she began to shiver in the brisk breeze that flowed through the window. She released the drapes, dashed back into her warm bed, and lay there thinking. No member of the household had mentioned an expected guest, and was it not too dangerous to travel after dusk? Whoever had come to Hawks Hill in the middle of the night and surrounded by such a large company, had to have been someone important and daring.

The next morning, when Najila left her chambers and entered the main part of the manse, the servants seemed to perform their duties with unusual cheer and spirit. Entering the dining hall, she asked a maidservant, "Who arrived at Hawks Hill during the night?" The serving girl merely ducked her head and scuttled off.

Just then, dressed for travel, Leopold entered the room and stalked to a large, polished bronze panel. Otrygg had not had a chance to get rid of Leopold, who didn't appear to be the slightest menace at the moment. Rearranging his elaborate, fur-collared cloak, he inspected his reflection. Turning this way and that, he smoothed his mustache and fussed at his beard. Not otherwise acknowledging Najila, he boasted, "The emperor has summoned me to the palace, where he is to receive the Bulgarian ambassador."

Najila bit her thumbnail in order to avoid laughing aloud at her cousin's vain contortions before the mirror. "I saw an illustrious man arrive by chariot late last night. Is he a noble?" she stammered, smothering a giggle.

Leopold Alexander snorted. "Eh? A noble? Yes, of course." He again spun before the mirror. "It was my noble son, home from a horse-buying trip to Spain. He has been gone many months." Without so much as a glance in Najila's direction, he stalked from the room.

Najila considered this new piece of information. Leopold Alexander had never spoken of a son. Neither had her father. Nor had Otrygg, for that matter.

In the days following, while Leopold was away at the emperor's court, Najila asked everyone about the son, but no one would even admit that he was on the premises. Though she watched for him, he never reappeared. It was yet another riddle for her to ponder. *What is going on around here?*

Chapter 18

Though Otrygg had been away for nearly twenty years, the palace complex and its maze of corridors and wings were still familiar, as was the fabled underground labyrinth. While a Varangian, he had learned every inch of the multiple royal compounds. Now, because he might need their support, he had come to seek out old acquaintances.

Canvassing the palace and surrounding area for members of the Varangian Guard, Otrygg was soon disappointed. He knew no one, except for two footmen who had been mere boys, brand-new recruits, when he had left Konstantinoupolis to go with Michael to Baghdad. They did not remember him. It saddened Otrygg profoundly to learn that former comrades in arms had either retired—most to the northern provinces—or had been killed in the border wars. Others had merged into the local population.

Giving up his search for a helpful Varangian, he next looked for Julian, the eunuch who had served as Michael's personal counselor. He hadn't seen much of the older man since they had arrived in Konstantinoupolis from Baghdad. On his return, Julian had immediately reentered the court and become immersed in politics, which befitted his natural bent. Otrygg suspected that Julian had the emperor's respect and confidence.

Julian's father, a member of the minor nobility with lofty aspirations for his eldest son, had seen to it that Julian was

castrated while still a baby. Castration of their sons, particularly of the eldest, was commonly practiced by the realm's
lords. Julian's noble ancestry and castration almost ensured
him an eventual position among the emperor's close advisors.
Though his father was long dead and would never realize it,
Julian had more than fulfilled the man's goal. He had achieved
an important post, ranking just under His Honor, the high
chamberlain.

After making several inquiries of people he met in the palace
halls, Otrygg found Julian as he was leaving a meeting in the
emperor's council chambers. Otrygg hardly recognized the old
eunuch, who had gained considerable weight due to participation in numerous, extravagant royal feasts during the months
spent as a court official. Julian's chins had tripled, and his
mildly plump body had become obese and flabby.

On seeing Otrygg, Julian's face lit with pleasure. He enfolded
the giant Viking in a welcoming embrace, the top of his bald
pate bumping the underside of Otrygg's chin. "Otrygg Harald,
old friend, where have you been? I expected a visit from you
long ago."

"This is the first time I have been free to come to the royal
palace, and I have sorely missed you, Julian." The tall Viking
drew back and studied the eunuch. "It appears court activities
agree with you." He chuckled. Then his expression sobered. He
drew Julian out of the corridor and into an anteroom.

Otrygg examined the room for unwanted ears before lowering his voice to a near whisper. "Lady Najila is in danger. You
can help."

Julian threw up his hands, fingers a flutter. "How awful! You
know I will do anything, *anything*, to help Michael's beloved
daughter." Concerned about Najila while enjoying the hint of
conspiracy, he looked around and whispered, "But what is the
nature of the danger?"

"It is thus." Otrygg went on to explain that Leopold Alexander was plotting some sort of unpleasantness—perhaps going

so far as to kill Najila. "She overheard him planning something with another, unidentified man. That's all we know about it. Najila lives day and night fearing for her life."

Julian stood with his chin cupped in his hand. Then he smiled. "I have a suggestion. Just the other morning, I received word that an aide to our Byzantine representative in Moravia was assassinated. I may be able to arrange for the treacherous Leopold Alexander Doukas to take his place." Julian shook with silent mirth at his inspiration, his quivering stomach rippling his robes. "I'm sure that Emperor Konstantine X Doukas will approve the appointment. Leopold has been a thorn in the emperor's side with his endless wheedling for this or that favor."

"You are a clever soul, Julian. Though Moravia is not distant enough to suit me, I have heard the Moravians are still warring with their neighbors, the Czechs and Magyars. People are being assassinated right and left. That and their border difficulties should thoroughly occupy Leopold Alexander. He should find little opportunity to invent trouble for Michael's daughter."

"Do not underestimate him," Julian warned, shaking his head. He winked at Otrygg, his eye nearly vanishing in the folds of his rosy cheek. "But an accident could occur; Leopold may fail to arrive at his new post."

"I am aware of his duplicity, but I have done all I can short of murder to keep him away from Najila. His fate is now in your capable hands, Julian."

"And in Konstantine's, do not forget. The emperor must be consulted."

Assured by Julian's words, Otrygg relaxed. "Meanwhile, can you find an excuse to summon Najila to Konstantinoupolis? To the palace itself? As heiress to the Komnenous estate, she needs to learn court procedures and protocol. Here, you can watch over her, and I will alert the Varangians to be on guard as well."

"The court presents its own intrigue and danger. I truly believe Najila is far safer at home with you there to personally protect her."

"I suppose you are correct. She would be in peril wherever she happened to be." Otrygg tapped Julian on the shoulder. "So be it. Najila will remain at Hawks Hill with me. I leave the details regarding Leopold Alexander Doukas up to you, my good friend."

Otrygg turned to go but not before cautioning the eunuch. "No one can know that you and I have spoken. Agreed?"

"Agreed."

Chapter 19

Upon his return to Hawks Hill, Otrygg related to Najila the plan to petition the emperor to assign Leopold to a remote border country. Otrygg did not mention the possibility that Leopold might never reach Moravia, nor did he want her to know the details of the plot. "He cannot leave soon enough to suit me," he declared. "I will not be at peace until your cousin is safely at a distance where he is unable to harm you."

"I should appeal to the emperor myself," Najila answered. "You should not put yourself in such an obsequious position just for me. You have been absent too long from the center of power. Other than Julian, who at court remembers you after so many years? Konstantine X Doukas was not on the throne when you left, and he has since replaced the others with his own people, those loyal to him."

Otrygg shrugged. "I really did nothing; I only told Julian what you overheard outside the observatory door, and he came up with the solution. It is he who will seek a private hearing with Konstantine. Even so, knowing of Konstantine's reputation for letting his subordinates do his dirty work, Julian may have to make the ultimate decision. Besides, if you had approached his majesty on such a personal quest, it might have hurt your credibility."

Najila shook her head. "What credibility? I probably have less of it than you. Nobody knows me." She paused, mulling over what she had just said. "Whatever happens, I should go to the palace. Show my face around the city. She frowned. "I would rather wait, however, until my cousin is gone. When do you think we will be rid of him?"

"As I have said, not soon enough. But plans are already underway."

"You always have been there for me, Otrygg Harald, ever since I was a small child. You would not believe how your presence has especially comforted me these recent weeks." She hugged him affectionately.

Oh how he wanted to return her embrace. Restraining the impulse with tremendous difficulty, he gently pushed her away and gave her a sad smile instead. "And I will always be here for you, Lady Najila. I intend to stay close . . . to . . . eh . . . guard you." He turned his head so she couldn't see the sudden liquid in his eyes. His back to her, he said, "I must go. Send for me if you need me."

With that, he hurried off, escaping her allure, silently cursing the difference in their years. She deserved a better suitor, one more youthful than an aging giant well past his prime, his sword no longer keen.

✝

Julian acted swiftly. By the end of the following week, Leopold Alexander Doukas had been assigned to Moravia and had departed. Julian sped to Hawks Hill to break the news.

"Leopold Alexander Doukas not only is formally banished, but also, according to Michael's bequest, the emperor forced him to relinquish control of Hawks Hill to Michael's sole heir, Najila," Julian chortled to Otrygg. "Leopold hardly had time to pack his gaudy clothes. He was profoundly shocked at how his life so quickly changed."

Both men roared with mirth.

No one in the household, including the servants, seemed to miss their former master. Najila experienced a new freedom, although to begin with, the responsibility of managing a huge estate intimidated her. She found herself running hither and yon throughout the day. Every night, she literally fell into bed and was asleep before Zahra finished covering her.

Najila's very first official action was to dismiss her cousin's astrologers. As soon as word came of their patron's reassignment, they had come simpering to her quarters, spouting depressing divinations. She was not sorry to be liberated from their slinking around, their vague threats, and their ominous portents.

Next, Najila asked Zahra to gather the servants, including the stablemen and groundsmen, in the main hall. It was time she became acquainted with everyone, and they with her. She was at her writing table, studying the long list of Hawks Hill's staff in preparation for the meeting, when Shafiqa rushed into the room, florid with anger.

Shafiqa glared down at Najila. "It is improper!" she wailed. "You have given Zahra, a servant herself, authority over the staff, when I, as the eldest member of your family, should instruct the slaves."

Najila bristled. "There are no slaves at Hawks Hill, Grandmother. My father would not have allowed it, nor will I. The servants stay of their own will."

"We had slaves in Baghdad. My family has had them forever. They are necessary."

Najila clicked her tongue. "We are no longer in Baghdad, and I want a staff that truly wishes to serve me. Those who have no heart for such service can depart Hawks Hill."

Shafiqa refused to cease her tirade. "The emperor has slaves!"

"The emperor is the emperor, and I am what I am, and I am someone who will not permit you or anyone else to dictate how I behave within my own home. Let it be, Grandmother. It is my decision to make. I will not have it otherwise. Favor us both, and say no more."

Shafiqa's lips tightened to a thin line. Where in Allah's name did her granddaughter's stubborn nature come from? *Surely not from me,* she thought. Muttering to herself, she stalked from the room.

Though Najila hated to offend her grandmother, she knew it made no practical sense to have more than one person try to rule the household. She cast a sympathetic look in the direction of Shafiqa's departure and then rose to go to the great hall.

The chattering slowly came to a stop as she entered the huge room. Every pair of eyes peered at her. Feet shuffled in a nervous hiss on the terrazzo floor. The crowd was larger than Najila believed the estate could support. Obviously, her list had not been complete. Scanning her audience, Najila noted that, besides the manse's immediate staff, the outside men had brought their wives and children. She wondered if they had brought their families out of fear, curiosity, or respect. Whatever the case, she hoped that her next words would put them at ease.

"Lady Zahra is more experienced and will manage Hawks Hill while I learn what is needed to improve things," she explained to the rapt throng. "You overseers will report to her. Hawks Hill will continue to function with designated foremen, simplifying communication between the workers and the main house.

"Meanwhile," she assured them, "I will remain available to hear your grievances, no matter who you are." Wild cheering erupted.

Najila's organizational method was actually not much different from what had previously been practiced at Hawks Hill, although her small changes resulted in a far more relaxed environment than the pall of depression that had surrounded Leopold Alexander. She had learned much from observing how her father ran his Baghdad embassy, and she was determined to encourage happy faces and whistling as the norm while people performed their jobs.

During her short talk, Najila had noticed a broad-shouldered, narrow-waisted man standing among the stablemen, his arms loosely folded across his chest, his legs spread wide. Taller than average, though not quite as tall as Otrygg, his arrogant pose and mocking smile dismayed her. What had she done to deserve such disdain?

He insisted on catching her eye, and she kept focusing on him. Something about him resembled the man she had seen arriving by chariot that late night, two months past, but that mysterious entity, richly adorned and supposedly Leopold Alexander's son, could not possibly be this grimy stable hand. Her face grew hot as he nodded at her, his lips curling again in an impudent grin.

When Najila's presentation ended, she went to greet each individual personally, clasping hands and asking questions about work and families. She had finished with the last family when she realized she had not encountered the man who had so boldly stared at her. In vain, she sought him, but he had apparently merged into the crowd and disappeared.

She left the hall unaccountably irritated that she had not met him. All that night, the illusive stranger's arrogant grin invaded her dreams.

Chapter 20

Spring arrived at last. Najila felt the young season's energy in her blood. On rising, she had fastened her bedchamber's thick draperies wide open. Through the mullioned glass, the dawning sun cast sheets of pink-tinted light across the oriental carpets and onto the opposite wall. Thrusting open the heavy sash, she let in a brisk breeze.

"I am going to ride today!" Najila declared as she sat on the edge of the bed and pulled on a kidskin boot.

Shivering in the chilly room, Shafiqa tugged her black shawl about her shoulders. "I rather you did not. And close that window before I freeze to death."

Instead, Najila went to get her cloak from the coat rack. "I must ride; I have neglected Sabiya's colt and Jahara long enough. Now that spring is here, I have to attend to them. Jahara will be as frisky as a kitten, and the colt needs training. Besides, I have yet to name him." Before this morning, even seeing the colt in which her father had expressed so much pride had hurt too much.

"Najila! You cannot go out dressed so," Shafiqa cried, dismayed. "You are the lady of a great house. What will everyone think?" She clucked her tongue. "You are a disgrace to Allah."

Najila merely shrugged. "My disguise is sufficient." She examined her reflection in the vanity mirror. "When I dress like this, no one other than you, Otrygg, and Zahra knows who I am—unless you tell people, that is." Najila shot her grandmother a warning glare and reached for the Mongolian quirt that hung on the wall near her bed. She absentmindedly slapped the quirt against her thigh. She didn't mean it as a threat, though Shafiqa fearfully backed away.

Najila threw her a sly grin. "If I went out wearing nothing, Allah would not care."

Shafiqa gasped in horror and clapped a hand to her mouth. "Blasphemy!" she hissed between her fingers. "Why do you torment me by uttering such a thing?"

Suddenly, Najila regretted her unkind attitude. After all, her ailing grandmother, her mother's mother, was the only member of her immediate family who was still alive. Tossing the quirt on the bed, she gathered the frail little form into her arms.

"I truly am sorry I cause you distress, but it is necessary that I escape my onerous duties for a while. Working the horses and riding are the only activities that offer me genuine peace. It has been months since I have been astride a horse. Think how cumbersome my skirts are. If I want to mount, they tangle my legs. It is impossible to get up on a small pony without help, and Otrygg is often too occupied to accompany me. And to dismount? Well, it is absolutely obscene."

Visualizing the ridiculous sight of her last fiasco in a full-length skirt, Najila had to giggle. The bulky material had been pinched between Jahara's ribs and the stirrup leather as she awkwardly climbed off, making her fall backward into the stunned Otrygg's arms. Fortunately, he had caught her and held her tightly—far too tightly, she remembered as an afterthought.

Shafiqa softened. "I forget how it is with you, so like your mother. And like me in many ways. Though I am unhappy about it, your father would be pleased to have you ride again."

"I will be home for the midday meal," Najila promised.

Shafiqa's worried frown deepened. "Otrygg is going with you, of course?"

"I do not know."

Najila had no intention of letting Otrygg or anyone else join her. She wished to be alone. Ignoring Shafiqa's last feeble protest, she slipped out through her chamber doorway and casually sauntered through the manse's least-traveled maze of corridors. It was early, and she encountered only one maidservant, who was too preoccupied scrubbing the floor to look up at the wearer of the dainty boots who hurried past.

Aware that she would require help in handling two excitable horses, Najila concluded she would have to befriend one of the grooms. Hidden in a nearby grove, she unobtrusively analyzed the stable hands as they performed their chores. Almost an hour later, she casually strolled into the main yard.

It surprised her only mildly that none of the men, who were intensely involved in their work, paid her notice. Choosing the youngest among them, a new man who had just gone to sit by himself on a barrow, she approached him. "Are you too busy to share a few words with me?" she asked.

The boy, for that he still was, was elated to see standing before him a slender lad near his own age. "I am about to eat my meal. Will you not join me?" He moved aside, giving her room to sit.

"I have eaten, but I am glad to talk with you," Najila said, settling down on the barrow alongside him.

"Have some bread. I have enough." When the boy generously offered her a piece of his meager slab of barley bread, Najila knew she would risk his friendship; she accepted the coarse bread. Munching a bite, she asked, "I have not seen you around here. What is your name?"

"I am called Elias. What do they call you?"

Najila hesitated, pretending to have too big a mouthful to immediately answer. It gave her time to consider how she could let him in on her secret, to reveal who she actually was.

Finally, she decided to do it. "I am not as I appear," she quietly murmured. With Elias looking completely puzzled, she added, "I really am Lady Najila."

Elias drew back, his expression one of scornful doubt. "If you are Lady Najila, then I am the empress Zoe."

"In very truth, I am she. Come with me into the stable and I will prove it to you."

Reluctantly, Elias followed, not knowing what to expect. As soon as they entered the stable breezeway, Jahara heard Najila's voice, and she began to whinny loudly. When Najila entered her stall, the mare rested her head on the girl's shoulder, all the while softly nickering. Najila removed her cap and shook out her long hair.

Elias dropped to his knees. "My lady!"

"Get up, Elias. Someone might see you and discover who I am. You must keep this quiet. We can talk about it here in Jahara's stall."

A few days later, Najila groomed Sabiya's yearling while she covertly observed Elias. The lad, she had learned, was the son of an estate serf. He trotted and galloped Jahara in a nearby field until sweat drenched the mare's coat and she no longer shied at every leaf tumbling in the wind or flinched at a bird winging by her ears. It became clear to Najila that Elias had a way with horses.

Because the morning was so perfect and because Sabiya's name is Arabic for "morning," Najila chose to name the colt Behras, which is Persian for "beautiful as day."

Mounting Jahara, who was barely subdued after her workout, Najila waved good-bye to Elias and rode off. She held the mare at a leisurely walk, pointing her head toward a remote area on the estate to which she had not yet ventured. By the time the sun had reached halfway to its apex, Jahara's sweat-soaked coat had dried, and Najila urged her to a gentle trot, then to a collected canter, heading her into wooded terrain.

Lack of use had weakened Najila's leg muscles, though she had not lost her natural balance. Closing her eyes with pleasure, she relished the fragrant air rushing past her face. She never saw the low-hanging tree limb that knocked her from the saddle.

Chapter 21

"Foolish child!" the watching man growled. *What was the youngster doing, riding so recklessly and trespassing on Hawks Hill land, anyway?* To avoid being seen, he crouched behind a thicket and waited as the slender boy on the small black horse sped toward him through the trees.

As horse and rider came closer, he recognized the animal. It was Lady Najila's steppe mare. And there was something awkward, not quite right about the way the lad rode astride the horse's back; he appeared a bit too stiff, swaying slightly out of synch with the rhythm of Jahara's hoofbeats.

The watcher's stare grew more intense, then widened. "The young rider's eyes are shut!" Before the astonished man could cry a warning, the horse dashed beneath a low-hanging branch. The limb smacked the horseman square on the forehead with the impact of a powerful warrior's mace, knocking the rider into a reverse somersault across the horse's rump and tail. The boy hit the ground with a muffled *thud* and lay unmoving.

Jahara cantered off as the man ran to the motionless figure. Seeing at once that the boy was unconscious, possibly seriously hurt, he squatted beside him. Blood had begun to soak the oriental burnoose that wrapped the lad's head and lower face.

The man rose to his feet and looked helplessly around. No one else was in the vicinity and a light rain had started to fall. He needed to get the injured boy to shelter. One of the estate's many little chapels was nearby. He would take him there and then go for aid. Lifting the lad's weight with ease, the tall man headed for a tiny structure beyond the next rise.

Najila's first sensation when she regained consciousness was of terrible pain in her forehead. Opening her eyes, she slowly became aware of her surroundings. Where was she? Gasping, she tried to sit up, but her right arm refused to obey. A wave of excruciating pain streaked down her arm from her shoulder to her thumb.

"I think your arm is fractured, and it looks like your shoulder is dislocated." The man's voice, deep and calm, soothed her. "Can you stay by yourself while I seek help?"

Najila turned toward the voice. Her vision was blurred by the blow to her head and by blood streaming into her eyes. She could not quite make out his features. She dimly saw that he had broad shoulders outlined by colored light. Colored light? Stained glass? How could she be in a church when she had been riding in the open countryside?

Gradually, the kaleidoscope of brilliant light faded, and she once again lost consciousness.

Seeing that the lad's face had become as pale as a death mask, the man anxiously bent and pressed his ear to the boy's chest. He reared back, unnerved, stumbling into a column as he retreated from the limp body sprawled on the chapel's hard terrazzo floor. A moment passed as he gathered his wits; then he again approached the prostrate form. Reaching down, he drew the blood-soaked burnoose aside, exposing the boy's face. An oath exploded from between the man's clenched teeth. "It cannot be!"

Lady Najila! Wonder of wonders. He smiled wryly. Her disguise had been a success, he had to admit. Bringing aid to her would force an end to his own anonymity, but he hesitated only a beat before running from the chapel to find help.

While the man had carried Najila from the site of her accident to the chapel, Jahara had circled and returned to the scene of the mishap. The mare now foraged close by. The man's own steed had apparently wandered away and was nowhere in sight. Unwilling to further delay his urgent quest for help, he yanked free a clump of new grass. Walking slowly toward Jahara, he offered the mare the tidbit in his outstretched palm. Jahara raised her head and perked her ears. Nostrils fluttering in a silent whinny, she trotted up to him.

As soon as she neared, he grabbed the reins, leaped aboard the mare, and mercilessly whipped her to a full gallop in the direction of the manor.

Najila awakened in her own bed, the room darkened, the drapes tightly drawn. Shafiqa and Zahra hovered at her bedside.

"What happened to me?" Najila tried to say. The words came forth as a rasping honk, sounding more like a throttled goose. When she attempted to change into a more comfortable position, she discovered the effort to be impossible, the agony overwhelming. She glanced down and saw that her arm and shoulder were bound and strapped to her torso. Her headache was unbelievable.

Everything was so vague: Jahara's joyous canter flowing beneath her; the blessedly sweet spring air; a paralyzing blow followed by oblivion. She remembered a strange man leaning over her, silhouetted against colored light. "Lie there," he had said and had gently prevented her from rising.

Her throat was awfully dry. "Water!" she managed to whisper. Zahra carefully supported her head and placed a goblet to her cracked lips. Despite a surge of nausea, Najila sipped most of the water. Things were becoming clearer, as was her voice. "Why am I here?"

"You were knocked from Jahara when she went under a low tree branch. A stableman found you," Zahra told her.

Shafiqa stepped forward. "He is not a stableman. He . . . he is . . ."

Flashing Shafiqa an admonishing grimace, Zahra interrupted her. "We can tell Najila about it later." She threw Shafiqa another pointed glare, which caused the old lady to snap her mouth shut and angrily narrow her eyes.

Biding her time, Shafiqa reluctantly let Zahra minister to Najila. Later, she promised herself, she would personally let her granddaughter in on the real news.

Chapter 22

Depressed and bored, her right arm immobilized, Najila sat by a window in her bedchamber and stared pensively at the far-off hills, which were a softly shaded lavender-blue in the dusk. A sound of iron shoes clattering and clanging in the courtyard below shattered her black mood. When she leaned forward to see what was going on, a sharp pang jolted her arm and shoulder.

Groaning, Najila leaned back and shut her eyes until the pain subsided. Slightly dizzy, she rose gingerly from her chair to peer over the sill. The commotion outside had accelerated. An elegantly clothed horseman fought to control a high-spirited bay stallion on the uneven paving stones. Accustomed to smaller Arabian horses and steppe ponies, she had never before seen such a long-legged, graceful steed. Its thick wavy mane fell to its breast, and its tail dragged on the ground.

The stallion arched its powerful neck as it tried to take hold of the bit in its teeth, only to be constricted by taut reins in the rider's firm grip. Najila marveled at the perfect balance between man and horse, moving as a single, harmonious unit. She so longed to get a closer look at the gorgeous animal and, yes, to study its skilled passenger.

The stallion suddenly reared. Najila gasped as the dying sun lit the tall rider's face. She recognized the man whose smile had mocked her during her welcoming speech in the great hall.

"Ho, there! Take my horse," he cried, and two yardmen rushed to grasp the animal's bridle. The rider dismounted, handing the reins to one of the men. Najila withdrew from sight as the man started up the portico staircase—but not before his gaze had locked with hers.

"Zahra! Where are you? I need your help." Standing with difficulty, Najila unsuccessfully struggled to gather together the front edges of the cape Zahra had placed across her shoulders. Her injuries—the break and dislocation and the multiple scrapes and bruises—caused her to grunt from pain. Nevertheless, she was able to hobble slowly to the closed door. She was about to reach for the bronze handle when the massive door was flung open, narrowly missing her injured arm as she awkwardly twisted to avoid being struck.

Zahra entered, surprised to see Najila out of her chair. She held up an arresting palm to someone behind her, saying to Najila, "My lady, the person who rescued you and brought you home has come to pay his respects."

His respects? Najila clasped the cape closer over her breast. Surely, Zahra did not intend that a strange man should come into her bedchamber. "I do not wish to see anyone, especially him," Najila hissed to Zahra.

Zahra stepped out and said something to the man, then returned, shutting the door. "I have told him he has to wait until you are presentable," she said. Guiding the protesting Najila to a chair, she gently helped her to sit. "He has been here before, but you were not fit to see him. This is the proper time. I asked him to come so you can express your appreciation."

"No, I—"

"Be quiet while I tidy you." Zahra smiled, arranging the cape around Najila and fastening the silk tie ribbons at her neck. After giving a fluff and a pat to Najila's hair, Zahra appraised her. She nodded. "Now, nothing but your feet and head show. And they are quite lovely." She strode to Najila's bed and closed the canopy drapes to conceal the rumpled bedclothes.

Somewhat mollified, Najila sniffed. "Well, perhaps . . ."

Before Najila had finished speaking, Zahra opened the door, curtsied, and said, "My lady is ready to give you an audience, my lord."

The tall stranger entered the room. He wore a nobleman's garments, and his manners were that of a genteel, educated person. "Good afternoon, Lady Najila. I pray your pain has lessened." He stood in a relaxed posture, his eyes seemingly searching for a delicate hand to kiss. None was offered from under the blue velvet cape.

Hearing his voice, Najila dimly remembered the same deep baritone comforting her at the scene of her accident. She faintly recalled kind phrases that had soothed her as she lay half in, half out of consciousness. When she realized that the two mysterious men—her rescuer and the shadowy form that had arrived in the night—were one, emotion warred with curiosity, swirling in her mind like leaves caught up in a stream's eddy.

Seeing Zahra's arched brow, Najila recalled her manners. "I am advised that I must thank you for rescuing me. I do thank you." *There,* she thought. *It is done.*

She tried to avert her eyes, but it was difficult to avoid his steady gaze. Ill at ease with his presence in her boudoir, she wished he would leave. Still, her inquisitive nature prevented her from immediately dismissing him. Besides, Zahra was also present, wasn't she? And Zahra had ushered him in.

Impulsively, Najila decided to take the opportunity to discover more about him. "What do they call you?" she asked, coyly tilting her head.

He threw her a crooked grin, while performing a dramatic genuflection. "In the year 1031, my father christened me Loukios Alexander. Friends and lovers call me Loukas or Lucius."

Ignoring the reference to lovers, she did some quick figuring. *So, he is older than I am by seventeen years.* "Be assured, Loukios Alexander, I am grateful for your aid," she purred, then hesitated. What else was there to say? Embarrassed, she turned away and stared out the window, murmuring, "I grow weary. Please leave."

Instead of exiting at her abrupt dismissal, Loukios moved to where she had to face him. "I have more to say. You are young and naive, but as the lady of the manor and a noblewoman with the responsibility of Hawks Hill's complex upkeep, you should never ride alone. Nor should you be seen wearing the clothing of a man."

Najila felt anger bubbling up, and she began a caustic retort, but Zahra, who had not left the room, hastily interrupted. "My lady, this is the son of your cousin Leopold Alexander Doukas."

Najila's mind reeled. The man was her cousin? Then she noticed his resemblance to Leopold . . . and to her father. How had she missed it? Why had she not made the connection? Because she had believed that the son had departed Hawks Hill with the father. Had he been here all along? If so, where was he staying? She had a million questions.

Shorter than Otrygg, but taller than Leopold and her father, Loukios had the broad shoulders and narrow hips of a horseman. His skin was darkly tanned; he had the weathered complexion of one who spent many hours outdoors. She noted that his lips were beautifully shaped like a cherub's double-curved bow. Long, thick lashes shielded large golden-brown irises that had the barest tint of green. His smile revealed brilliant white teeth, and his nose was aquiline.

Despite her instinctive antagonism toward anyone associated with Leopold Alexander, she couldn't help entertain the notion that, even fully clothed, Loukios reminded her of the nude marble Apollo that resided in a niche in the manse's entrance rotunda. She blushed and ducked her head so he couldn't see her discomfort.

"I shall come again, my lady. After you heal, if you will have me."

A brief, submissive nod was all Najila could manage. When he left, the room suddenly seemed empty and cold.

Chapter 23

Healed from her injuries and pain free except for an occasional twinge in her upper arm or shoulder joint, Najila had come to Shafiqa's quarters to check on her grandmother's condition. Shafiqa had begun their residence at Hawks Hill with gusto, asserting her authority whenever she could get away with it. Lately, though, Najila rarely saw her grandmother, and just that morning, Zahra had confided to Najila that Shafiqa was not well.

It was noon, and Najila found Shafiqa still in bed, uncovered and apparently dozing. From where she stood, trying not to be overt about it, Najila cast anxious glances at her grandmother. Without the black scarf she wore to cover her gray hair and drape her thin corded neck whenever she left her private quarters, Shafiqa looked much older than her actual age.

Seeing Shafiqa's lids flutter, Najila went over to her and quietly took her hand. "Are you unwell? I am concerned for you, Grandmother."

Shafiqa's eyes opened slightly, and she sighed. "I don't like it here. The damp air is bad for me. I want to go home to Baghdad."

How many times had Najila heard those complaints repeated?

Shafiqa tossed on her pillows. "I am too hot, Najila. Get someone to fan me!"

Patience, I must have patience. Najila lifted a fan from the side table and began to waft the feathers to and fro over the frail form on the bed. "Grandmother, you are too ill to make the trip to Baghdad. Besides, it is the wrong season to begin such a trek," she added, hoping to postpone yet another argument. Even if Shafiqa remained at Hawks Hill, Najila believed her grandmother would not last the coming winter. She seemed to have faded in recent days and stayed close to her own rooms, no longer walking the considerable distance down the stairs to dine with Najila and Zahra. Instead, she demanded that her food be brought to her.

"You and Zahra can take me home." Tears coursed down Shafiqa's sunken cheeks.

Najila wanted to be charitable, but Shafiqa's wish could never be fulfilled. "I am sorry you are homesick, Grandmother, but I will never go back to Persia. My home is here at Hawks Hill." She stopped fanning and took Shafiqa's tiny, blue-veined hand in hers. "I need Zahra here, too. Without her, I could not manage."

"Then have the Viking escort me," Shafiqa insisted.

That might be just the solution, Najila silently agreed. *I could arrange for her to go next year in the spring when the weather warms—if she makes it through the winter.* She gently squeezed Shafiqa's hand. "Otrygg might like to make the journey, I think. Perhaps he could take you. I can only ask him." There was no harm in giving Shafiqa hope.

A determined smile broadened Shafiqa's pinched mouth. Temporarily pacified, she dropped Najila's hand and sat up. Her voice instantly stronger, she said, "Thank you, Najila, dear one. It is something to live for."

Najila left the room, shaking her head. Would she never anticipate her grandmother's ploys?

✢

Najila rapidly became too involved with the affairs of Hawks Hill to give more than an occasional thought to Loukios Alexander Doukas. She did, however, take time to go to the stables almost every morning, leaving less urgent household issues in Zahra's capable hands.

Riding her sturdy little steppe mare, Najila spent an hour or two exploring the estate's farthest corners. Instead of going alone, she took Elias along. The boy knew the extensive lands by heart, all the tracks, every hidden glade, each natural spring. She enjoyed his company immensely, and they became good friends, like brother and sister rather than mistress and servant. Having seen Elias puttering about the stable, doing no specific job, she asked him one day, "What duty do you normally perform?"

"I serve my master, but my master is in Spain," Elias replied. "He has been gone these many weeks."

The boy's remark confounded Najila. "What master, Elias? Am I not the sole mistress of Hawks Hill? Do you not serve *me?*"

At her words, Elias looked absolutely wretched. "For sure, you are my mistress, Lady Najila," he stammered, blushing. "I meant only that I serve Lord Loukios Alexander . . . when he is here."

The boy's answer bored into Najila's mind like a tick into her skin. She was speechless, but just for a moment. She leaned over and grabbed the rein of Elias's horse, jerking both their animals to a stop. "Loukios Alexander Doukas?" she nearly screamed, ire twisting her beautiful features. She had not seen Loukios since he had come to pay his respects soon after the accident when she was still weak and hurting. Fully recovered now and able to defend herself against his clever tongue, she was eager to spar with him at his level. It vexed her that he had not kept his promise to visit her again.

"Elias, do not tease me. Loukios Alexander is no longer at Hawks Hill. I have seen him only once since his father left for Moravia." *Actually twice,* she silently amended her statement.

"It is not so, my lady. Lord Loukios spends much time here."

"Why?"

Visibly trembling, Elias stuttered out, "He . . . he . . . manages the horses."

Najila raised an eyebrow, and Elias attempted to explain. "He oversees the breeding of mares and the training of young animals."

Then why have I not seen Loukios Alexander Doukas in the stable yard? she wondered. He had been away, Elias had said, but how did it happen that no one had mentioned him, whether he was absent or present? For some reason, Zahra had concealed the truth from her: Leopold's son had surreptitiously remained at Hawks Hill. He had not been exiled with his father, as Najila had naturally assumed.

"Zahra owes me an explanation," she declared aloud. Spurring Jahara into a swift canter, followed by a very worried Elias, she pointed the mare toward the stables.

Wanting to learn more, Najila loitered in the stable while Elias unsaddled the horses. "Why does Loukios Alexander go to Spain?" she prodded.

Elias shrugged. "He often travels great distances to buy horses. Sometimes he goes on a noble's errand."

"A noble's errand? Humph! Whatever would that be?"

"It is not for me to know, my lady." The boy averted his eyes.

"Does he dwell at Hawks Hill?"

"No, he has a house near Konstantinoupolis. Sometimes he takes me there."

Sensing his misery, Najila felt sorry for Elias; her difficulty with Loukios Alexander Doukas was not his fault. "You have done no wrong. It is a problem I must deal with, not you. When will Loukios Alexander again be here?"

"He is expected to return from Spain on Tuesday of next week, my lady." Elias drew off Jahara's saddle and hoisted it onto a rack. "Tuesdays through Fridays are when he comes to Hawks Hill, always before noonday."

Will not Loukios Alexander be surprised to find me waiting to greet him? Najila thought, smiling as she envisioned their encounter.

The days passed too slowly. Finally, it was Tuesday, and Loukios was due to arrive. Skipping her morning meal, Najila hurried to the stables. She had barely slept the previous night, so charged was she with her mission to get to the bottom of the "Loukios Problem." She would not allow anyone to mock her position or her authority, especially not the son of Leopold. But although she made it to the stable compound quite early, Loukios Alexander was already there.

His back to her, Leopold's son, was on his knees, examining the left hind hoof of the great bay stallion on which she had seen him mounted that dark night weeks ago. She stopped to watch him work.

Loukios must have seen her enter the yard. He rose slightly, bracing the horse's hoof firmly against one muscular thigh. Poised there, his jaws wrestling a hay stem, he critically examined her from head to toe.

"Apparently your injuries healed well while I was in Iberia, Lady Najila. You are more beautiful than ever, despite . . . despite the man's coarse garments that you wear."

Marching up to him, she snapped, "What I wear is my business, not yours." She put her fists on her hips. "And by the way, what are you doing here, Cousin? Why are you not in Moravia with your father?"

"Long before you came, it was arranged for me to be here, and here I shall come when I please . . . sir." He bowed his head, trying to hide a silent chuckle, but she saw his shoulders shaking.

Sir? Had he called her sir? And had he laughed at her riding clothes? When would it end? Her face burning, she turned and fled into the barn.

Standing in Jahara's sweet-smelling stall, she stroked the mare's neck. *The man is impossible. He acts as if he owns the place.*

Though Loukios Alexander patronized her, thus far, he had done nothing to threaten her position. Nevertheless, she did not trust him. He was, after all, Leopold Alexander's son. In any case, it was best that she rid herself of Loukios Alexander Doukas, just as Otrygg had rid her of the man's father. She stalked off to seek the Viking's counsel.

Chapter 24

Though Leopold Alexander had been summarily dispatched, Loukios Alexander, the son, remained at Hawks Hill. When Najila implored Otrygg to do something about Loukios, too, Otrygg seemed strangely unwilling to comply, saying, "I don't presently have time. A matter in Konstantinoupolis requires my attention." That very day, he abruptly left the premises without informing her when he would return. She could do naught to detain him, as Otrygg was neither slave nor servant to be ordered about.

Najila next sought Zahra's help.

"I am too busy managing everything else. Besides, it is beyond the scope of my duties," Zahra told her, clicking her tongue. "You, the lady of the manor, are the person obligated to tell someone when to leave."

Not only was Najila hurt, she was positively baffled that these two faithful retainers, who were normally obedient to her slightest whim, had refused to oblige her. So she set out to perform the deed alone.

She thought she knew where to find Loukios. If he were at Hawks Hill, he would probably be down at the stables. She decided to confront him there instead of sending for him. But before facing Loukios, she had her hair perfectly coiffed and donned her most feminine outfit. Studying her reflection in the tall bronze mirror, the same mirror where Leopold had primped, she decided that she appeared proper enough.

Leaning closer to the mirror, she tried making different faces until she found a haughty one that she believed made her look dignified and authoritative.

Najila found Loukios in the stable yard's center, instructing the grooms how to lunge a young filly. She hid behind a building, intending to approach him when he was free and alone. Cautiously peeping around the corner, she scrutinized the area. Freshly whitewashed, stone-walled barns surrounded the rectangle on three sides. Cleared of manure and recently raked, the grounds were as neat as the manor's rooms. The many deciduous trees, mostly poplars that had been radically pruned for firewood during the winter, were fully leafed and provided pleasant shade.

It slowly dawned on Najila that, whenever she went to the stables, the yard was immaculate, the tack repaired and polished, and Behras's and Jahara's stalls always well padded with clean, golden straw. So far, she had never had reason to instruct or correct the stablemen.

It suddenly occurred to her that she was hearing the sounds of several unfamiliar horses. She was accustomed to the gentle nickering of the steppe mare, the playful frisking of Sabiya's colt, and the stamping and shuffling of the matched pair of sturdy draft animals stabled nearby, but it sounded now as if there were five or six additional horses in the stable compound. Keeping to the shadows to avoid being seen, she explored the nearest barn, despite her inappropriate attire. Whose horses were being stabled in the formerly empty stalls and runs? And who was overseeing the operation? Certainly not Zahra or Otrygg.

It did not take much thought to arrive at the answer. Elias had already given it to her. Loukios had brought in other horses, and Loukios was responsible for the fine condition of the entire site. The realization made her unaccountably uneasy. Perplexed, she entered Jahara's stall and slumped on the fragrant bedding. So recently determined to oust Loukios, she now had become uncertain of the best course of action. The more she questioned herself, the more she wondered whether it would be wise to demand that Loukios Alexander vacate her property.

Najila's musing was interrupted by the sudden appearance of Loukios in the doorway of Jahara's stall. Apparently he had come to exercise the mare. Astounded to see Najila there, he asked stupidly, "What are you doing, sitting among the horses dressed in such finery?"

Najila awkwardly scrambled to her feet, self-consciously smoothing the pleats of her pale green satin gown. She instantly regretted the daring neckline and tried to gather about her the loose-sleeved overgarment sewn of velvet and strewn with seed pearls.

Bedazzled, Loukios paused in mute admiration, his eye drawn to a string of pearls that wove its way through Najila's raven hair, and to a pair of pearl strands that dangled alongside her cheeks. The dim light and dusty haze created an ethereal aura that enhanced her exquisite beauty.

"I . . . I . . . I came to see Jahara," Najila stammered at last, breaking the silence. "The last time I rode her, her right fore-leg seemed . . . rather lame." When Loukios said nothing, she regathered her composure and snapped, "I do not wish to talk here." As she turned to leave, one of her delicate slippers caught in the deep, tangled straw. She tripped and began to fall, stumbling against Loukios. He automatically caught her in his arms and steadied her.

For an enthralling, breathless moment they stood motionless, their bodies intimately pressed together. Staring upward, Najila saw Loukios's hazel eyes widen. Almost as quickly, he dropped his arms. With the release of his support, she nearly toppled. This time, though, he didn't catch her, and she had to grab onto the door frame. He waited, still silent, while she recovered her slipper and slipped her foot into it.

When she exited the barn and reentered the courtyard, Loukios followed. The older stablemen, who knew her by sight,

had returned to their chores, but two new men immediately
ceased their work to ogle her. Unused to seeing a beautiful and
elegantly dressed woman in such an environment, they hooted
their appreciation.

Loukios shouted angrily, "Get back to work! There is much to
be done." The men instantly obeyed.

Hugely embarrassed and desperate to leave, Najila murmured, "I must speak with you. Can we go elsewhere? Where
we have privacy?"

"I know a quiet spot. Come with me," Loukios demanded,
roughly gripping her arm, causing her to shrink from his hold.

Profoundly uncomfortable in her cumbersome velvet and
satin skirts, Najila allowed Loukios to drag her at a rapid pace
to a hidden, walled enclosure off the main yard. Not only had
she never been there, she had not known it existed.

Despite her anger and vexation, she couldn't help but delight
in the enclosure's small garden. Flowers blooming in a dozen
beds perfumed the air, and a four-tiered fountain created a
light mist, reminding her of Baghdad's lush gardens and water
features.

Loukios led her to a marble bench near the fountain but far
enough away to prevent splashing water from staining her
dress. "Why did you come here in a costume resembling that
of an empress, in a gown that barely covers your shoulders?
Your other garb is more suitable to the stables," he growled
furiously.

Najila bridled. "You once mocked my riding clothes. Now you
criticize me when I dress like a woman. I see that there is no
pleasing you." Standing up, she glared down at him. "I came
here to tell you that you have no right to take charge of my
stables or my servants."

When Loukios said nothing in his defense, Najila raged on.
"Are all those horses yours? If so," she snapped, "who gave you
permission to bring them to Hawks Hill? I want you and your
animals off my land at once."

"Wait a minute," Loukios at last protested. "I thought I was helping you learn how to run Hawks Hill by yourself."

She realized he was amused. "Help me? I do not need you or your aid," she huffed. "You patronize me, and like your father, you aspire to steal what is mine."

His easy humor disintegrated. "You are wrong, my lady. I house my horses here because my own facility outside of Konstantinoupolis is inadequate, because Hawks Hill has more room, and because the grooms are well trained—by me."

"You have not explained why you did not tell me about all this," Najila spat out. "And why did everyone keep your presence at Hawks Hill a secret?"

Frowning, he shrugged. "I know nothing of secrets, and I am sorry you think I deceived you. I did not mean to." He held forth his hand, palm up and fingers spread in an appealing gesture. "My wish is for things to be status quo . . . with your approval, of course, my lady."

She had to confess he really had done no wrong. With her eyes cast down and her silk-clad toe drawing little circles on the dirt path, Najila answered quietly, "I suppose you could stay. I have to admit, you are marvelous with the horses, and unoccupied barns are a waste." She threw him a derisive smile. "I shall charge you rent, however."

Grinning, Loukios stood and took her hand. "I do furnish my animals their feed and bedding, so the fee should be inconsequential." Before she had a chance to argue the point, he suggested, "Visit Alioth, my home near Konstantinoupolis. Perhaps then you will understand my predicament."

Unimaginably thrilled by his touch, she hesitated only a second before answering him. "That would please me." She sighed. "I had but a short glimpse of the city when we traveled through it, coming from Baghdad. Is it possible that I might see more of it if I come to visit you?"

"You have not yet seen the palace?"

"Otrygg and Julian talk of taking me, but so far, it has been just talk."

Grinning, Loukios Alexander bowed low. "Then I am just the one to introduce you to Konstantinoupolis, Lady Najila Komnenous."

Chapter 25

A visit to Alioth didn't happen right away. To manage the immediate household and the estate's extensive agriculture was all Najila and Zahra could accomplish. Their work seemed endless. Driven to do a thorough job in her father's memory and physically stressed by daily covering the great manor and the estate's vast acreage, Najila was totally exhausted every night.

Ultimately, she became grateful that Loukios had taken charge of the stable area, freeing her of that responsibility. Three weeks later, when he again pressed her to visit his estate, she was ready for a break and eagerly accepted his offer.

The weather was perfect for the trip. Najila, Loukios, and their entourage left Hawks Hill just after sunrise. During the night, a light rain shower had moistened the dust that usually arose in clouds from the unpaved road that stretched from Hawks Hill to the old Roman road, which was paved with stones.

Loukios and a properly gowned Najila rode ahead of the baggage cart that carried Zahra and Najila's two maids. Four armed men on horseback guarded the party. The distance to Loukios's estate was not long, and Alioth was not far from the great city's double wall beyond the Blachernae Palace. Nevertheless, they had to pass through sparsely inhabited land where bandits preyed on travelers, rich and poor alike.

During the short, tedious journey, necessarily slowed by the lumbering cart, Loukios revealed to Najila his plan to upgrade his horse-breeding operation. "I want to meld Arabian, Iberian, and Mongolian bloods," he told her.

Tilting her head and frowning, Najila asked, "What is an Iberian? I am familiar with Arabian horses. And why put a little steppe horse into the mix? What is the advantage?"

"Because I specialize in chariot horses, I constantly experiment with bloodlines; I am trying to breed a larger, more powerful animal," he explained. "The pureblood Arabian has plenty of fire, but its bones are delicate, and it lacks stature. The Iberian or Spanish horses are taller with heavier frames. I saw them race in Iberia. In fact, I purchased my bay stallion there. He is a former chariot steed, but his right foreleg was injured in a crash. It can no longer take the strain of racing."

When Najila's expression saddened, Loukios patted her arm, saying, "He is actually better off now. Once, he was a famous champion, many times earning the laurel and palm. Trained and accustomed to my touch, he has become an exceptional riding horse and a considerate breeder."

Loukios rode for a while in silence, thinking. "The Arabian and Iberian types alone should give me what I want," he continued, "except that I seek a particular color pattern, which naturally is of the least importance."

"What kind of pattern?" Najila asked, intrigued.

"It all began three years ago when I was hunting northeast of the Black Sea forests. I saw a strangely marked steppe pony, white with dark spots over its entire coat, something like a leopard."

"I saw a leopard at the caliph's zoo in Baghdad," Najila said. "It was a beautiful cat. I cannot imagine a horse with spots like a leopard, though."

"The horse I saw did not have exactly the same pattern of spots, nor were the spots as uniform. It was at such a distance— and part of a large herd—that I cannot be sure of what I saw. I know that I desire to own one."

His description stimulated Najila's memory. "I saw a similar animal near Tabriz."

Loukios's excitement increased. "Do you mean you actually saw such a horse?"

"It was mostly white with only a few spots."

"My eyes did not deceive me then; the pattern does exist."

Najila shook her head doubtfully. "They are probably rare. We have each seen but a single one. If you do find another, will its owner part with it, sell it to you?"

Shrugging his broad shoulders, Loukios smiled and muttered in so low a voice she barely heard his words, "If the Lord wills it, it will be so. I can only try to achieve my dream."

"Your plan is sound; it interests me. I would join you in your endeavor," Najila declared, attracted to Loukios's ambitious idea.

Loukios instantly responded, "I have to travel far, go to other lands, be away for long periods of time. The conditions are not always desirable. It is certain to be a challenge. You could not go with me."

Ignoring this last comment, Najila exclaimed, "I love challenges. They keep life from becoming a bore. And Cousin Loukios Alexander, I am in a position to aid you."

Had she not clearly heard him? To have a woman on his hands wherever he went? Never! Though he wanted to shout at her, Loukios managed to control his temper. In a normal tone without a hint of rancor, he quietly said, "I must go alone."

Najila smiled coyly. "Oh, I do not mean that I should accompany you. I dare not be gone from Hawks Hill for more than a few days at a time. My duties are too many. But if you let me, I will help fund and equip your quest."

Loukios sighed with relief. "That is very kind of you. If my program is to start next year, I should leave soon, before the summer heat."

"On my return to Hawks Hill from Alioth?" Najila asked.

"Yes! I will see you safely back to Hawks Hill, then immediately prepare for my departure. That is my intent."

"Let me know what you require and when you need it," she said, nodding.

Upon her arrival at Alioth, Najila was surprised to discover that Loukios did not own a property comparable to hers. Instead, his estate consisted of a dozen or so agers, or fields; a modest, two-story, squarish dwelling; and several unremarkable outbuildings. It wasn't its lack of grandeur but the location that impressed her. Situated on a knoll, the main building afforded a panoramic view of Konstantinoupolis and the northern end of the Golden Horn.

The entrance porch to the house was a miniature of Konstantinoupolis's four-sided Chalkoun Tetrapylon. Like the original, the smaller version had four stout, square columns supporting a steep, blue-tiled, pyramidal roof. At its peak, a bronze weather vane modeled in the shape of a winged goddess rotated with every puff of wind.[1]

Loukios showed Najila to her second-floor quarters. While Zahra folded and stored garments in the abundant and spacious cupboards of the sleeping room, Najila and Loukios stood on the wide balcony. Gazing southeast toward Konstantinoupolis and the Bosporus, Najila could see the city's three greatest walls: the farthest built by the Greeks close to the peninsula's tip, the nearest erected by Heraclius in the seventh century, and the middle wall built in the fourth century by Konstantine himself. As no foreign power presently threatened the city, the massive linked chain that in time of danger was strung shore-to-shore across the opening to the Konstantinoupolis harbor had been dropped. Ships of every size and from many nations gently rocked with the tide, protected within the harbor's encompassing hills.

"How glorious!" Najila exclaimed. She inhaled deeply, relishing the unfamiliar, salt-laden air. "It is difficult for me to believe you would ever want to live elsewhere. If I were in your place, I could not bear to be apart from this scene for long."

"I love everything about my home, but I am afraid I have grown too accustomed to it. Watching your awe renews my appreciation."

"I would never grow tired of something so lovely."

Stirred, Loukios moved closer to Najila and dared to put an arm around her waist. Pleasantly surprised that she didn't rebuff the sudden advance, he bent and rested his cheek on her soft, raven hair. "And I would never grow tired of someone so lovely as you, Najila," he whispered.

Chapter 26

Both floors at Alioth had wide, eastward-facing balconies that overlooked the same view. Loukios, Najila, and Zahra, their ever-present chaperone, breakfasted on the first-floor terrace, which was roofed by the second-floor balcony. A flourishing garden strewn with statuary and fountains surrounded the house, but on this morning, dense fog concealed everything beyond a hundred meters.

The trio wore heavy cloaks against the fog's clammy, sea-scented chill. Given the option by her host, Najila had chosen to breakfast outdoors, not because she particularly enjoyed the damp atmosphere, but because she felt less uncomfortable there than in the more intimate, interior dining area.

Though Zahra groused that she was chilled to the bone, she was determined to suffer through it and remain with Najila while Loukios was around.

Servants on whispering feet came and went, deftly setting delicacies on the table and removing empty dishes. Loukios gestured toward the swirling mist. "You cannot see due to the fog that there is not sufficient room here for a profitable horse operation."

"I guess I will have to take your word for it." Najila laughed. "At least for now."

He adored her laughter.

"I know that we are cousins," Najila stated. "Zahra was the first to tell me that you were Leopold's son. Is that not so,

Zahra?" Najila asked with a sardonic lift to the corner of her mouth, brows innocently arched. The previous night, she had made up her mind. She would not tell Loukios that Zahra and Shafiqa had known about him long before she did and that the information had been kept from her.

"But I am curious. How exactly are we related?" she asked him as she tore a piece of bread from the fragrant, freshly baked loaf.

Unperturbed, Loukios sat back in his chair, his fingertips forming a steeple as he watched Najila sop her bread with a spicy mutton gravy.

"Manuel Komnenous is my great-grandfather. His son John sired my father late in life. Rumor has it that John had overindulged his wine, and . . . er . . . forced himself on my grandmother, the widow of a Doukas. My father was raised by his mother, my grandmother. I never knew her." He grimaced. "Such alliances permeate the Komnenous and Doukas families—my father did the same as his father did."

"You mean . . . ?"

"Yes. Unfortunately, I am the illegitimate son of an illegitimate son. My birth was kept very quiet, though the resulting scandal affected both families. But by now, the talk has abated, and few remember what happened. Maria Alexandria, my mother—she was born in Thrace—died soon after I was born, and I was raised by nuns in a Greek convent. As a child, I hardly knew my father, and as far as I know, your father, Michael, and I never did meet."

Najila suddenly paled, and Loukios, thinking his tale too crude for her, quickly apologized. "I am sorry if I offended you. Did your father not tell you of these things?"

Najila reached across the table and touched his hand to reassure him. "You have not offended me. To the contrary, it is only because my heart still aches when I hear my father's name," she said, biting her lip. "He never spoke of his relatives here. I was unaware of your side of the family until just this past year." She uttered a deep sigh. "Our leaving Baghdad, and the day my father perished in that horrible landslide, seem so far in the past, yet at the same time they are as fresh as yesterday."

Mulling what Loukios had said, Najila clicked her tongue. "So my grandfather is your great-grandfather? I am surprised. I thought we were more distantly related."

"The women involved were different, so we are merely half cousins, maybe even less. Also, a liaison between John Komnenous and my grandmother has never been proven, and my father denies it ever occurred. Though he actually is a Komnenous, he calls himself Doukas. By doing so, he believes he can smooth a path for his colossal ambition. His appointment to Moravia has undoubtedly started him on the road to an eventual position within the palace, which is his real goal."

Najila flinched and looked away. Loukios knew nothing of her and Otrygg's conspiracy to have his father assigned to a remote and dangerous country. She fervently hoped Loukios would never discover the part she had played in it.

"And your mother?" Loukios asked. "She was not a Byzantine?"

"My mother, Shahdi, was a Persian princess. She died in childbirth when I was four. I barely remember her." Her mood saddened, and tears welled in her eyes. "They said the baby was a boy. My little brother. He died, too, the same day."

"How agonizing for you," Loukios commiserated, his expression sympathetic.

At that moment, a manservant came to Loukios and whispered something. Loukios stood. "Our transportation is ready to take us to the city. Have you had enough to eat?" At Najila's nod, he took her elbow and helped her to her feet. "Perhaps our visit to the palace today will give you cheer."

"I am sure it will. I need only a short time to get ready. By what means do we travel? By cart?"

"I have a palanquin waiting to carry you. It passes easily through the city's narrow streets. A cart is too broad, and the animals required to pull it add to the difficulty."

"We ride in the palanquin together?"

"No." He grinned. "You and Zahra will ride in the palanquins. I will be on horseback."

"I would prefer to ride a horse, as well."

Loukios frowned. "That would be most improper," he scolded. "Surely, you want to impress the court favorably. You are extremely elegant dressed as a noblewoman, but you would create quite a scene wearing the mannish apparel in which I have often seen you."

His mocking failed to aggravate her. "I was teasing," she laughed. "Forgive me. You are right, of course. Though I look forward to being presented to the emperor, I am afraid my knowledge of court etiquette is not as exemplary as it should be."

He bowed. "Your teasing matches my own. It is like jousting with words. As for your manners, I shall be there to advise you. You will perform well; I have no doubt." His voice softened. "The emperor will think you as exotic and lovely as do I," he added. "Besides, your father's old friend, the eunuch Julian, is awaiting us." At Najila's happy smile, he took her hand in both of his and pressed her palm against his chest. On an impulse, he said, "Please call me Loukas."

She felt his heart's strong, rapid beat. Without pulling her hand from his, she answered, "With you and Julian near to guide me, I will be certain to make a fine impression. I do not wish to stand alone before His Royal Majesty, Konstantine X Doukas." She cocked her head. "And in what way are we related to *him*, Loukas?"

"I may tell you on the way," he promised, his spirit soaring. She had spoken his name in its familiar tense. She had called him Loukas!

Chapter 27

From Alioth to the palace grounds, which stood at the tip of the peninsula, was a distance of more than six kilometers. During her first traverse of the city, Najila had been somewhat ill, due to the long, hard trip from Baghdad. She had been grieving her father's death, as well. This time, however, she was alert and seeing everything through fresh, eager eyes.

The inhabitants of Konstantinoupolis numbered about a million. The largest city in Europe, it was a conglomeration of rich and poor, the meanest lean-to sharing a wall with some rich man's lofty mansion. Few residents were of pure Greek or Roman ancestry. They were a diverse mix of peoples with roots throughout the Byzantine empire, the only criteria for citizenship being to use the Greek language and to join the Orthodox Church.

As Najila's party progressed, her excitement grew. "What is that?" she repeatedly asked Loukios as some spectacular landmark or other came into view.

Loukios rode alongside Najila's litter, pointing to this world-famous church or that ancient memorial, while contributing a knowledgeable account of its origin. To be heard over the street clamor, he had to shout. "Najila, we travel west to east on the Mesê, Konstantinoupolis's main thoroughfare. On holidays and during special celebrations, processions come this way. They usually end at the Hippodrome, which is a copy of Rome's Circus Maximus."

"My father told me all about the Hippodrome," Najila shouted back to Loukios. "He said it seats one hundred thousand people. I am anxious to see it for myself."

"To be sure," Loukios promised. "If we stay here in the city for a few days, I can show it—and more—to you."

"That would please me," she yelled.

They were nearing the Hagia Sophia, and Najila almost tumbled from her palanquin when she leaned out, craning her neck to see the very top of the imposing dome. Her bearers staggered as the weight they bore abruptly shifted to one side, but Najila was so absorbed in what she was seeing that she barely noticed their stumbling attempt to regain their balance. "When may I see inside St. Sophia?" she shouted to Loukios, her head swiveling as she gaped at the magnificent structure they were passing.

Alarmed at Najila's precarious position, Loukios tensed to catch her if she fell. Before addressing her last question, he warned her, "Take care. I do not want to scrape you off the street's surface." To his relief, and to the relief of her bearers, Najila withdrew into the divan, but she bundled and tied back the curtains to create as broad an opening as possible.

Rolling his eyes upward and giving thanks to whatever angel was assigned to protect reckless women, Loukios straightened in his saddle. "We can attend a mass this week. It is too bad that you were not here for the Easter celebration. It is a most moving experience. Still, we can attend next year, if you wish."

Imagining the pomp and color, Najila answered wistfully, "I would like to." But then she remembered the Muslim instruction she had been given by her grandmother since childhood, and she also remembered how hostile Shafiqa was toward anything having to do with Christianity. Why, then, did she now succumb to Loukios's charisma and the great Christian church's awesome attraction? She would have to let Loukios know she had changed her mind. Tell him that she did not want to attend a Christian service after all, especially one that celebrated the death and resurrection of the prophet Jesus.

An overwhelming mixture of exotic scents distracted her from further contemplation. Scanning the shops that lined both sides of the Mesê, she saw that they all held perfumers. She wanted to comment about it to Loukios, but he had trotted ahead and out of earshot.

Suddenly, the bearers halted and gently lowered Najila's and Zahra's divans to the cobblestone paving. Najila frantically searched the milling horde for Loukios's stallion, but horse and rider had disappeared. She was feeling just a hint of panic when Loukios reappeared and immediately dismounted.

Clutching the horse's reins in his left hand, Loukios offered his right hand to Najila. Grasping it gently, she stepped out of the palanquin. A uniformed groom took the reins from Loukios, and Loukios led Najila toward the palace entrance. Silenced by the amazing scene that lay before her, she stopped and stared.

They had entered a huge, walled enclosure, the royal compound that lay in the shadow of the Hippodrome's enormous stands, which extended to the right and left. In front of her stood the palace itself, one of more than four thousand palaces in the city. To Najila, its facade and turrets resembled a much larger version of Hawks Hill, except that everywhere she looked, she saw signs of extraordinary wealth. Gilding covered the bronze doors, and the Doukas crest above the entrance had been crafted in vividly enameled precious metals that were encrusted with jewels. Brightly colored glazed tiles adorned most of the rooftops.

The throng of people included representatives of various nationalities, classes, and ages. Konstantinoupolis's nobility, dressed in fine clothes made from the costliest silks and brocades and embroidered with precious and semiprecious gems, roamed the area. Both sexes wore exquisite jewelry of gold and silver laden with emeralds, rubies, sapphires, and pearls.

Though she was used to Baghdad's riches, what she saw here far exceeded anything she had seen in Persia.

Remarkably speechless, Najila allowed Loukios to lead her by the hand like a little child while he described what they saw. "This is the Boukoleon Palace, where the emperor lives. The entry to it is called the Brazen Entrance. The Boukoleon is the main part of a complex that has halls of state, throne rooms, and libraries within its walls. Those I have named are only some of it. It also contains gardens, baths, and more than one stadium. And beneath the buildings that are visible above ground is another labyrinthine maze."

Seeing Najila's awestruck countenance, Loukios smiled and asked, "Are you aware that Konstantinoupolis holds two-thirds of the world's goods?"

This was news to Najila, and she raised one eyebrow to show her skepticism.

"Does it surprise you?" Loukios asked, smiling. "We are not merely wealthy. We have used our wealth to build orphanages, houses for the poor, hospitals, and a two-hundred-year-old university, the Pandidaktirion. Many institutions of learning are in Konstantinoupolis, as well as others throughout Byzantium."

If Loukios was trying to impress her, he had succeeded. Recalling an incident while they had traveled the Mesê—when a man had run out to sweep up the stallion's droppings almost before the animal had finished—Najila commented, "Konstantinoupolis is uncommonly clean."

"So it is. The streets are swept every day, and our sewage disposal system equals Rome's efficiently designed system. The Aqueduct of Valens, which we passed under on the way, carries refreshing water from east of here to a reservoir. Other aqueducts do the same, their waters channeled into several reservoirs, some of them underground. That is why we have all the free water we need. You probably noticed servants and slaves obtaining it from the abundant fountains installed across the city," he said, as they entered through the Brazen Entrance.

Peering at the ceiling overhead, Najila saw that it was covered with mosaics. Beneath her feet, the floor was laid with fine marble in an undulating design of red, emerald, and white. The walls were lined with the same marble.

Such grandeur! She could barely absorb it all.

"Tomorrow we shall see the fabled floating throne," Loukios promised. "There is none like it on the entire earth."

Najila had heard of the mystical throne while living in far-off Persia. She shivered in anticipation.

Chapter 28

Najila's accommodations within a palace wing were unbelievably luxurious, even more luxurious than her quarters in the Baghdad embassy had been. That night, she and Loukios were invited to a feast given in Najila's honor by the noble men and ladies who were Loukios's closest friends. The meal included thirteen courses, among them wild boar and venison from the Black Sea coastal forests, three kinds of Bosporus seafood, and several varieties of fruits and nuts shipped from Egypt's delta and from southern Persia. In addition, there were more appetizers and side dishes than any one person could possibly sample.

Many choice wines were offered, which Najila rejected due to her Muslim upbringing. Neither would she eat the boar, which was, after all, only pig meat. She used a fork as if she had never dined without one, and on this particular evening, it was in constant use. The feast and entertainment lasted well into the next morning.

Najila slept uncharacteristically late the following day, her gluttony having resulted in a night of tossing and turning. It was nearly noon when Zahra's voice woke her. "Lord Doukas asks after you. He wonders why you were absent at the morning meal."

Najila made a gagging sound and pulled the silk sheet up over her head. "Do not speak to me about food."

"That is no answer," Zahra laughed. "Come, you must awaken." When Najila refused to move, Zahra spoke in a sterner tone. "Lord Doukas wishes to take you to see the emperor's throne room today. Shall I tell him you are too ill to accompany him?"

Throwing off the bed covers, having achieved a swift and miraculous recovery, Najila sat bolt upright. "Tell him to wait . . . please, Zahra?"

No, no! Loukios wouldn't dare to leave without her. Najila jumped from the bed. "What am I to wear?" she cried. She anxiously dragged things from cupboards and drawers, flinging clothing here and there.

Zahra was more controlled. "Quickly!" she said, taking Najila by her shoulders to stop the frenzied search. "First, you should have a bath, though it must be brief." Zahra went to the door, opened it, and shouted for hot water to be brought.

Snatching a grape from a cluster in a nearby fruit bowl, Najila popped it into her mouth, mumbling, "A little fruit should sustain me." Chewing the grape, she studied her sleep-ravaged reflection in her hand mirror. "My hair! It is as shaggy and tangled as a wild goat's winter coat. Can you fix it?"

"You know that I can." Cheerfully humming, Zahra worked on Najila. The bath, dressing, and the application of cosmetics took only an hour and a half. In Najila's case, it was a record.

Loukios's wait had been worth every minute. Freshly bathed and combed and smelling like sweet herbs, Najila finally came to him, clad in a deep maroon gown sewn from the finest velvet. Over the maroon velvet, Zahra had placed a cream-hued, floor-length silk cape, edged with summer stoat fur and fastened at the shoulder with a diamond brooch. Even after several hundred years, this style cape, or *clamys*, was still popular among affluent Byzantine women.

Najila's dark, shining hair was simply coiffed in a braid around her head. The braid was wound with a strand of pearls held in place by diamond and pearl combs. Long, filigreed gold earrings set with tiny seed pearls dangled from her ears.

Najila's face beamed with excitement. Seeing the exquisite form approaching him, Loukios suddenly realized how much he desired her. "You look very nice." Though he tried to conceal his turbulent emotions, his voice trembled as he complimented her.

"Today, the Bulgarian representative is being presented to the emperor in the Great Throne Room. We can still see the beginning of the ceremony if we hurry." Loukios grabbed her arm, and giggling like children, they dashed through the myriad corridors and halls and down a graveled walk. Amazingly, they encountered few other people. Those they did meet stared after them, appalled by the well-dressed couple's lack of dignity.

"It is good you know your way," Najila panted, hitching her skirt higher to keep up with him.

"Indeed, a stranger might easily become lost," Loukios said, not in the least breathless. "But I learned how to navigate the palace compound long ago." He stopped at the entrance to a large room in the Magnaura Palace. "Ah, here we are!" He quickly adjusted his own appearance and checked hers. "Your hair has loosened. Let me correct it."

As his fingers delicately tucked in a straying tendril, a delicious thrill coursed through Najila's body. But before she understood what had happened or could react to his touch, Loukios had taken her elbow and was leading her into the majestic hall.

The room was crowded with standing citizens. Najila's initial impression was of opulence and extravagant ornamentation. Every eye focused on the magnificent golden throne that stood six steps higher than the main floor. On the throne sat the sixty-year-old emperor, adorned in glittering, bejeweled robes.

Though his very presence commanded veneration from those attending him, his slumping posture and graying flesh proved that the rumors were accurate: Konstantine X Doukas was a sick man.

Awestruck, Najila could not take her eyes off the throne itself. Observing how it enthralled her, Loukios whispered, "It is known as Solomon's throne. You have yet to see what it can do."

At that instant, the magic began. Najila gasped as the throne slowly rose into the air. At the same time, jeweled enamel birds, perched on the branches of man-made gilded trees placed at each side of the throne's staircase, flapped their wings, moved their heads, and warbled. Life-size, gilded lions stood guard on each side. The beasts lashed their tails, in synchrony with their roaring, and their mouths opened and closed, displaying ferocious teeth and flicking tongues.[1]

The throne continued to rise until everyone had to tilt back their heads to keep their eyes on the emperor as required. At first hushed in reverent awe, the court now shouted and clapped in appreciation of the fantastic spectacle. Despite their position at the back of the hall, Najila cringed, clasping Loukios's arm tightly as the monumental throne ascended toward the ceiling. Loukios gently loosened Najila's iron grip. Firmly holding her hand at his side, he smiled down at her and whispered, "Is this not extraordinary?"

Najila could only nod.

The Bulgarian representative moved to a position closer to where the throne had been at rest. He stiffly genuflected. In order to see the man who occupied the throne, the fat Bulgarian had to arch his back and neck painfully. His face flushing with humiliation, he spoke in halting Latin instead of Greek, though from where they stood, neither Loukios nor Najila could make out his exact words.

"He is angry," Najila said.

"The Bulgarians have always hoped to conquer Konstanti-noupolis," Loukios explained. "One Bulgar ruler, Simeon—he called himself Tsar of all Bulgarians and Byzantines—tried to take the Byzantine throne in the ninth century . . . and naturally failed."

Ignorant about much of Byzantine history, Najila asked, "Is not Bulgaria a part of Byzantium?"

"Yes, it is. Since we have ruled them, however, there have been constant uprisings, and men have claimed to be Tsar of Bulgaria as recently as twenty-seven years ago. They are a stubborn people."

"I have not made the acquaintance of a Bulgarian," Najila remarked quietly. "Perhaps they would rather be free," she added, remembering how the Persians chaffed under Arab rule. But Loukios had lost interest in relating historical facts and was growing restless. Trying to make sense of barely audible diplomatic maneuvering bored him. "Let us go," he whispered, tugging at her hand. "I want you to see the royal gardens."

The imperial gardens, lying between the buildings and the sea wall at the bottom of the hill, were partitioned by shady walks and trickling water. Loukios and Najila paused by an arresting fountain that featured a large, golden pineapple above a silver basin. "On special occasions, wine flows out of the pineapple," Loukios told her, "and pistachios and almonds bobbing in the wine fill the basin."

She flinched and drew closer to him as an Egyptian ibis flew past, its swordlike bill thrust forward and its wings extended in a silent glide.

"Do not fear the bird. It is only challenging a peacock that came near its mate," Loukios said, using the opportunity to protectively encircle Najila's waist with his arm.

Walking on, they reached the top of a gigantic marble stairway that led down to the emperor's own harbor, the Boukoleon. Royal barges and yachts floated tranquilly at wharves adorned with painted, life-size sculptures. From their high location on

this beautifully clear day, Najila and Loukios could plainly see
the Golden Horn in its entirety. To the south lay the Sea of Marmara, its vibrant, azure hue spanning the southern horizon.

Retracing their steps up the hill toward the Boukoleon Palace, on their way to the courtyard where they had first entered,
Loukios indicated yet another impressive building. "This contains the royal birth chamber. It is built of purple stone. That is
why imperial children are said to have been *porphyrogenitus*, or
'born in the purple.'"

Before they exited the royal complex, Loukios had shown her
a polo ground, the royal riding school, and two pools for swim-
ming. By then, Najila had become a bit light-headed from so
much exercise, and she regretted her restrictive clothing and
inadequate footwear.

"Let us return to my quarters, Loukas," she begged. "My feet
are swelling like overripe melons, and I can hardly breathe in
these clothes."

Chagrined that, in his enthusiasm, he had overdone the tour,
Loukios apologized. "I never should have shown you everything
in one day. I am truly sorry, Najila." He stooped and swung her
into his arms. "I will carry you. It is but a short distance."

"No, I—" Najila started to protest, but the painful, throbbing
blisters on her feet outweighed her sense of impropriety, and
she immediately changed her mind. "I do not want anyone to
see us like this," she whispered in his ear.

"There is no one about; everyone is attending the reception
or is busy at his designated duty," Loukios insisted. "We are
alone, except for that fellow over there."

Najila glanced over his shoulder, then snuggled her face
against the smooth skin of his neck. It was true: the only person she could see was a gardener trimming a distant hedge. "I
suppose it is acceptable then," she murmured, content to stay
right where she was.

Chapter 29

L ater that same year, 1067, Konstantine X Doukas died. His demise was attributed to everything from poisoning to strangulation, either of which had its precedent in Byzantium's royal record. Rumors flew, expanding with every carrier. Poor Konstantine's eight-year reign had been fraught with tension due to the escalating threat to Byzantium's eastern borders by the Seljuk Turks. It was compounded by the empire's loss of Belgrade to the Hungarians, who were led by their ambitious new king, Solomon. In the same year, the Seljuks had taken Armenia. Though the Byzantines still held the coastal towns and their ports, the Turkish Ghazi were gradually gaining control of the greater part of Anatolia. Byzantium retained but a shadow of its former splendor.

Loukios had returned just that week from a fruitless, three-month quest in the northern steppes, searching for the elusive spotted horse. Dejected because of his failure, and worried about the empire's tenuous condition, he sought diversion in Najila's company on an early morning ride.

"What will Eudokia Macrembolitissa do now?" Najila asked, idly twisting Jahara's mane as they rode at a leisurely walk. "Eudokia is in good health and is still quite active. Do you think she plans to rule alone?"

"It is hard to say." Loukios sighed. "We will have to wait, see what she does. My guess is that she will soon find another

husband. Unless no one knew of it, she never played an important part in politics. I cannot believe she is about to begin."

"Do you think Konstantine was murdered? There is talk
of it."

Loukios enjoyed Najila's fine mind that always challenged
his own. "Oh, I think he likely died a natural death. I am sure
that Julian will have more inside information." He twisted in
the saddle to look back at her. "But let us not continue to discuss
such mournful tidings. I have heard enough of them recently."

Loukios reined the stallion onto a narrow, rarely traveled
path, Najila following closely. "I want to show you where you
had your accident," he shouted over his shoulder. "Go to the
place where I first saw you." He had meant to take Najila back
to the forest chapel long before now, but he had not had the
opportunity.

Najila had explored most of the estate. Nevertheless, she had
not found the small church. Trying to recall details of the incident, she said, "I remember little of it . . . your face looking
down at me, lights of many colors."

Loukios laughed—a deep hearty sound that she adored.

"You were in another realm that day. You were so pale, and I
was so worried."

Najila did not miss the intense expression in Loukios's eyes
as he helped her dismount at the chapel's door. There was a
subtle difference in his attitude today. Though she was unsure
of its meaning, it unexpectedly thrilled her. To conceal her confusion, she bent to examine the chapel's moss-covered founda-
tion stones. "Who built this church? It looks very old."

"That I cannot tell you," Loukios answered. He tethered the
two horses to nearby trees and unbolted the door. "Apparently,
it was built long before Hawks Hill manor. Local gossip has it
that there once was another, smaller, house where the manse
stands today. Perhaps the person who owned it also built this."

"I was unaware that there had been a dwelling before Hawks
Hill. Does no one know to whom it belonged?"

"No. Only that it was long ago, before the Doukas and Komnenous families gained prominence." He threw open the chapel door and stood aside so Najila could enter ahead of him.

"It is extraordinarily beautiful in here!" she breathed, clasping a hand to her breast. She had not been hallucinating that day when she was in and out of consciousness. Stained-glass windows set high up just beneath the exquisite chapel's vaulted ceiling emitted brilliant colored light. Wherever there was wood, it was richly carved and polished. The artfully crafted floor, inset with a geometric design, gleamed with inlaid marble, glass, and gold mosaic. Twirling to see it all, Najila asked, "Who cares for this?"

"I do," Loukios answered, amazing her even more.

"I love color, especially when it is stained glass."

"Did you know that the Romans first used it in their windows?"

"Byzantium owes a lot to the Romans, does it not?"

"Do not forget the Greeks," said Loukios, chuckling.

"Yes, of course. The Greeks, too. I cannot forget my allegiance to my heritage, can I? But then, I am Roman and Greek on my father's side, pure Persian on my mother's. Do you not see them all in my face?" She smiled shyly, beguiling him further.

They had become as close as a man and woman could be with a minimum of physical contact. Indeed, he relished Najila's companionship, but he wanted more of her. He leaned nearer, his breath warming her neck. "Roman? Hmm. Perhaps the nose," he whispered.

He reached out and gently held her chin, tilting her head so he could better examine her features. "Greek and Persian? Definitely! The brow and nose are Greek. Those eyes have to be Persian. It is an excellent combination." He grinned wickedly, causing Najila to break out in nervous giggles.

Suddenly, Loukios became serious, and his pupils widened. He leaned forward and lightly brushed her lips with his, not a true kiss, but a sweet, tender seeking.

Startled, Najila jumped back, her face flushed. Instantly regretting his action, Loukios quickly began to describe the chapel's carvings. During the rest of their outing, the atmosphere between them was formal and proper.

That night, Najila lay in her bed, dreamy eyed and sleepless. She knew that something special had been added to her and Loukios's relationship that day. She wasn't sure what it was, but it was a something that felt most pleasant.

Lying on his back in his own bed that same night, arms under his head, Loukios came to an astonishing conclusion. "I love and want to marry my cousin Najila Doukas Komnenous, mistress of Hawks Hill!" he bellowed at the ceiling.

Chapter 30

Byzantium did not have long to wonder what the twice-married dowager Empress Eudokia would do, now that Konstantine X was dead. In less than five fortnights, she had a new husband, one of her generals, whom she dubbed Romanus IV Diogenes and installed on the throne at her side. The new emperor, however, was not popular with certain factions of the local nobility.

Loukios invited Najila to the Hippodrome for the crowning of Romanus as emperor of Byzantium. They started for Konstantinoupolis at dawn. Zahra accompanied Najila as far as Alioth, but she refused to go to the coronation, wanting neither to suffer the dusty roads nor endure the big-city confusion. Instead of riding horseback, Loukios sat next to Najila in a luxurious, lightweight, two-wheeled cart. Walking behind the cart, as chaperones, were two of Loukios's personal house servants.

Ever ready to celebrate, citizens and noncitizens alike had traveled from Byzantium's most distant provinces and now jammed the streets of Konstantinoupolis. Slowly guiding the sorrel mule through a maze of side streets that were barely wide enough for the cart to pass, Loukios brought his small group to a position where they could see clearly and hear the events occurring in and around the enormous Hagia Sophia.

Sitting on the high cart's comfortable padded seat would afford Loukios and Najila a panoramic view of the procession that followed the formal coronation rites. Their chaperones stood in front of the cart, one at each side of the mule.

In the main ritual held within the huge church, the patriarch would bless and place the crown on Romanus IV Diogenes. In her imagination, Najila pictured the man seated on the throne while dignitaries representing the world over made obeisance to him. She knew the ceremony had been completed when she heard harmonious chanting issuing from the church:

Holy, Holy, Holy. Glory to God in the highest and peace on earth. Many years to thee, O great king and autocrator!

Waiting for the procession to begin, Najila was fascinated by the wealth of exotic and colorful sights. The varied robes worn by passersby piqued her curiosity. When Loukios explained that it was customary for the city's doctors to be attired in blue, she remembered that the African physician who had once attended her during a bout of fever had worn blue robes.

"Artists, musicians, and poets dress in bright scarlet, and philosophers wear dull, 'contemplative' gray." Loukios laughed at his own joke.

"Why do the ascetics enclose their hair in those nets?" Najila asked.

"Perhaps it is because they like to be creative—or different," Loukios answered, smiling. "I have never put the question to an ascetic."

Before she could ask him anything else, an awesome outcry erupting from hundreds of throats inside the Hagia Sophia throbbed in the air. She heard its sonorous echo bouncing back from every section of the city.

"Glory to God who has made thee emperor," chanted the great choir.

"Glory to God who has made thee emperor," answered the people.

"To the glory and exaltation of the Romans."

"To the glory and exaltation of the Romans," responded the people.

"Many, many, many."

"Many years on many years."

"Many years to thee, the servant of God," proclaimed the choir.

"Many years to thee," chanted the people.

It seemed forever before the front of the procession came into view, heading in their direction down the wide Mesê. The procession was led by the patriarch's entourage of priests, who carried a great silver cross, inlaid with gold and encrusted with dazzling jewels that gleamed in the sun.

Tears flooded Najila's eyes, and she had to turn away. The poignant memory of her father's precious cross, with its glittering gems and warm, amber hues shredded her heart. She had long regretted relinquishing the dragonfly cross, so cherished by her father, to the monk Gregori. "Oh, how foolish I was," she mourned aloud.

Startled, Loukios asked, "What did you do that was so foolish?"

In vain, Najila tried to compose herself, but the tears continued to flow. "During the journey from Baghdad, in my grief over my father's horrible death, I made a hasty decision to rid myself of something I should not have."

Loukios took her hand in his. "Would it help to tell me what happened? Can you bear to tell me?"

"I think I can now, Loukas." She hiccupped. Ignoring their surroundings, she told him. "It was thus. My father had a beautiful cross of amber and silver that he had presented to my mother as a bridal gift. It meant so much to him after she died. He always wore it, and I played with it as a child." She bowed her head, her shoulders trembling. "And I gave it away! How could I have done such a terrible deed?"

"Do you know where the cross is?" Loukios asked. He was concerned that she might become hysterical.

"I gave it to a monk who was on his way to a monastery somewhere in Cappadocia."

"There must be a way to get it back. I will find it for you."

Loukios's confident optimism cheered Najila. Employing a sleeve to dab at her eyes, she said softly, "That may be possible. Let me think about it." Glancing around, she saw that no one was paying attention to her; every eye was intent on the procession. "I am sorry if I have made a spectacle of myself, Loukas," she apologized, squeezing his hand.

"It is nothing," he murmured, again taking note that she had used the familiar form of his name.

As the last of the procession paraded before them Loukios reluctantly released Najila's hand and gathered up the reins. "Ho! It is time we went to the Hippodrome for the public ceremony." He clucked to the mule. As they began to move, he happily whistled in time to the snappy beat that a passing trio of minstrels banged out on tambourines. Could life be any better than it was at that moment?

Chapter 31

Loukios led Najila into a private box among several set aside for nobles at the edge of the arena. He gave his two trusted servants a purse containing several gold byzants, instructing them to buy the finest wine and delicacies from the vendors who were hawking their wares at the event.[1]

As there was little to drink that was safe or that appealed to her, Najila had begun to sip a bit of wine when away from home. Loukios had shown her the passage in the New Testament where the apostle Paul had written, "Stop drinking only water, and use a little wine because of your stomach and your frequent illnesses."[2] He had also quoted an admonishing passage: "Do not get drunk on wine, which leads to debauchery."[3]

"So you see," he had explained when Najila remarked that the verses seemed contradictory, "we are to drink wine in moderation. The apostle Paul was wise. He knew that wine would help our stomachs, especially during the hot summer months when our drinking water often smells unpleasant and turns slightly green." That had convinced her.

Before the public crowning and the spectacle that followed, Najila had an opportunity to observe the Hippodrome in its entirety. Loukios told her that it had originally been constructed for chariot racing, but it was now used for many other forms of entertainment as well, including imitation hunts and "whodunit" plays. The structure was about 400 meters long and 148 meters wide. Down the center of the oval track lay the spina, or spine, which was adorned with larger-than-life statues and other works of art, some quite ancient. Most notable was a tall obelisk that had been taken from Egypt's Karnak temple and placed in the Hippodrome in the year 390. Stone barriers marked the pivoting points at the ends of the spina.

Neither the new emperor nor his court officials had yet entered the purple-draped imperial box, the kathisma, which stood at the northeast end of the Hippodrome and abutted the Augustaeum Square. As called for by tradition, Empress Eudokia would sit in her own box outside a church that overlooked the Hippodrome.

Najila immensely enjoyed watching people, particularly the emotions that danced across their faces. With interest, she studied the individual women and men garbed in the latest fashions, noting that there were representatives from many countries and provinces.

Loukios, talking with great animation to a couple in the adjacent box, did not hear Najila's sudden intake of breath. She pounded his arm to get his attention, and he turned to see why she had hit him.

"He's gone!" she cried, again scanning the crowd for the dreaded face she was certain she had seen. "I saw him, but he has gone."

Her nemesis, Leopold Alexander Doukas, who was supposed to be in far-off Moravia, had disappeared into the milling multitude.

"Is something wrong?" Loukios asked innocently. He had not heard her words above the noise. "Are you feeling ill?"

Najila glared at him. The pulsating roar in her head more than offset the clamor in the Hippodrome. Never had she been so angry at someone. Her fists clenched, she hissed between gritted teeth, "I just saw your father, Leopold Alexander. I thought you and Otrygg told me that he was in Moravia."

Loukios stared at her, dumbfounded. "He is in Moravia. You could not possibly have seen him. If he were back, I would certainly be aware of that fact."

Najila barely kept from hitting him. "You lie! It definitely was Leopold Alexander."

"It could not be. You mistook another for him," Loukios insisted.

Najila could not be persuaded otherwise. "I know who I saw." Convinced that Loukios had deceived her, she refused to look at him. "Take me home. I wish to return immediately to Hawks Hill."

Loukios shrugged and answered in an equally hostile tone, "I will do as you request, Lady Najila, but not until after the ceremony."

Najila moved to the far end of the box and studiously ignored Loukios. He had betrayed her. And so, apparently, had Otrygg.

The arrival of the emperor, who was carried into the Hippodrome on a great shield, and his opulent public coronation, were a slow-motion blur for Najila. Miserably disappointed in Loukios, and half sick with apprehension about the return of Leopold Alexander, she repeatedly scanned the nearby boxes, hoping—and yet fearing—that she might again catch a glimpse of her rival. All she wanted was to return to Hawks Hill, to protect what was rightfully hers.

Chapter 32

Otrygg was stunned by Najila's allegation that he had collaborated with Loukios and had deceived her regarding Leopold Alexander's whereabouts. Though the Viking towered over her as they stood in the great dining hall at Hawks Hill, Najila berated him like a fierce wren defending its nest.

"Why? Why did you not tell me that he was back? I trusted you, Otrygg." Her shrill accusations echoed through the huge room, while the stern-countenanced portraits of her ancestors stared down at Otrygg in judgment, causing him to feel unreasonably contemptible and small.

Spreading his arms wide and looking heavenward for help, Otrygg bellowed, "Our holy God knows that I have proven my devotion to you many times. Is that not true?" He felt like shaking Najila until she regained her senses. She had unjustifiably vented her wrath and frustration on her father's longtime best friend. Moreover she had insulted her loyal champion.

As if suddenly becoming aware of the foolishness of her accusations, Najila abruptly extended her hand. "Of course you are not at fault. I should never have suspected such a thing of you. It is because I am so afraid of Leopold Alexander. I do fear he will succeed in his threat to kill me."

Thrilled by her touch but tortured by his intense emotions, Otrygg's first reaction was to draw away. He hesitated a moment, then enfolded her petite hand in his.

"I realize you are upset. However, you do not have to worry. I will go to the palace tomorrow to determine whether Leopold Alexander is back in Konstantinoupolis. Julian will know what is going on. He is privy to everything concerning our royal court, as well as that of the foreign courts. I will not return until I discover the truth."

Three days later, Otrygg returned to Hawks Hill and immediately sought out Najila. After searching the manse and surrounding grounds, he found her near the stables in the secluded garden. At the sound of his approach, she turned her face from him, but not before Otrygg saw her tears. He hated to reveal to her what he had discovered in the city, but she must be told.

He sighed and got straight to the point. "You were right, Najila. You did indeed see your cousin, Leopold Alexander Doukas. He is in Konstantinoupolis, living luxuriously on the palace grounds in a nobleman's house."

Najila wheeled around. She stifled a sob before blurting out, "I wish never again to see Loukios Alexander. He must remove his beasts from my stables, and hereafter he is not to show his face to me."

Though Otrygg subconsciously considered Loukios a rival for Najila's affection and was admittedly jealous of him, honor demanded that he defend the younger man. "Hear me out, Najila," he said. "You should not condemn Loukios for something he did not do. On my way here, I stopped by Alioth to confront him. When I asked him why he did not tell us his father was in the city, he said he knew nothing of it. He claims that he was as shocked as you were when you told him you saw Leopold Alexander at the coronation. Until I came and confirmed the news, he thought you had seen someone who simply resembled his father."

"I do not believe him. Loukios has deceived you too, Otrygg."

Though it stung him to continue to plead with her on Louki-os's behalf, Otrygg persisted. "Loukios says he will look into the matter and keep us apprised. He wants to see you as soon as possible."

"Well, I do not wish to see him. Not until he proves he is innocent."

Otrygg scowled. If he were in Loukios's position, nothing would keep him from Najila's side. Finally, he said, "It will be difficult to keep Loukios away."

Najila shrugged, as if giving in. "Then what do we do, Otrygg?"

"About Loukios?"

"No. About my cousin Leopold. He is a danger to me, as well as to Hawks Hill. The more distance there is between us, the more comfortable I shall be."

"I believe his disappearance can be arranged."

"That is what you said before."

Otrygg cringed. What she said was true. "This time, however, I will do my best to have him permanently removed to a remote corner of the empire."

But Otrygg's efforts to dispose of Najila's cousin were defeated from the start. When Julian tried to convince the new emperor to send Leopold to a far-flung province, some high-ranking associates, powerful nobles behind the throne, had enough influence to thwart the plan.

Otrygg personally brought Najila the bad news. "We tried, but Leopold's power has grown too strong. "I truly do not know what our next step should be, short of . . . short of assassination."

Najila shook her head. "Then we would be acting just like him. I cannot let you do it."

"Julian and I will think of something," Otrygg promised.

Over the following days, he and Julian searched for another solution, but they could not produce a new plan.

Najila's normally jubilant, optimistic spirit sank into despair.

Chapter 33

The specter of Leopold Alexander Doukas and the memory of his threats to harm her haunted Najila day and night. Fearing for her life, she ceased to ride the estate alone and went to the stables only when accompanied by Otrygg or Elias, the stable hand. Even in their presence, she no longer enjoyed the feelings of freedom and independence to which she had been accustomed. She didn't sleep well, her appetite diminished, and she lost weight.

"Something has to be done," Otrygg told Julian during a visit to the palace. "Najila is wasting away before our eyes."

"I have tried my best," the eunuch replied, "but I do not have the influence with Romanus IV that I had with Konstantine. Leopold Alexander has many friends close to the emperor. Romanus is a man who listens to those who wield their wealth and influence. Still, I am beginning to believe that Eudokia is the real power behind the throne. Why she married Romanus is incomprehensible. He is more interested in carousing with the men he used to command than in governing Byzantium."

"I have to agree, Julian," Otrygg replied. "But if Romanus is difficult to reach directly, can we not entice one of his former comrades-in-arms to persuade him to send Leopold to an unsettled frontier? If it were up to me, I would personally deliver him to the Hungarians. Better yet, he should be sent to the Seljuks."

Julian laughed, nodding. "Except once the Hungarians or the Seljuks acquainted themselves with Leopold and his duplicity, they would surely send him back to us, just as the Moravians did, to rid themselves of him."

"Or mount his head on a stake," Otrygg muttered. "In any case, he would be an utter fool to trifle with either the Hungarians or the Seljuks."

"Nevertheless, Otrygg, your idea just might have merit—and it would certainly solve our problem with that toothless old lion. Give me a few days. I will seek out someone whom we can trust to whisper your suggestion into the emperor's ear."

"That old lion may not be as toothless as we would prefer, but it is a chance worth taking. I am concerned about Najila's health, and even more so for her sanity." Otrygg began to pace the room. "Keep me apprised of your progress."

Tapping a finger on his chin, Julian mused, "Something else occurs to me. Could it be that Leopold Alexander is planning an attempt at the throne? Do you suppose he has returned because he and his cohorts are orchestrating a coup d'état?"

Otrygg halted in mid stride. "Now that would not surprise me. Still, the thought of it chills my blood. If a coup d'état has even the remotest possibility of success, it must be stopped."

"Sever the lion's tail, eh?"

"It is the head I would rather see severed," Otrygg declared.

"Is everything ready?" Najila asked Zahra. The sun had already risen above the eastern hills. They were preparing to go to the Zeuxippus baths where high-society women gathered to bathe, receive massages, display the newest fashions and jewels, and trade choice tidbits of the most recent gossip.

"Yes. I left orders that the cart and guards are to be here within the hour. They will soon arrive."

"You sent word to the palace, informing the empress that we will be staying there tonight?"

"A week ago, but Eudokia has not responded. I wish you were staying here within the relative safety of Hawks Hill," Zahra pleaded. "It is too dangerous in the city. You should at least wait for the empress to reply."

Najila nodded slowly. "I know it could be a risk, but from what I have heard, it is easier to learn what is happening around the throne while at the Zeuxippus baths than anywhere else outside the court. And there is the chance that I, or you, might hear additional disclosures at the palace and—"

"As I always wear the *hijab* in public, few people know my face," Zahra interrupted, referring to her customary veil. "And I can overhear secrets that you cannot." Zahra flung a hand to her breast. "Still, my heart quivers with apprehension."

"Stop worrying, Zahra. Everything will work out. You will see." Najila tilted her head, listening. "Ah, the cart is here. Let us be off to the baths. I cannot wait to immerse myself in their healing waters. One must make each day one of quality. I refuse to become a prisoner in my own home." Beckoning Zahra to follow her, Najila strode from the room.

Zahra was quite aware that bathing was one of the young woman's fondest pastimes, and once Najila's mind was made up, there was no deterring her.

During the tedious journey from Hawks Hill to the city, Najila mulled over all that had occurred in the past year: the departure from Baghdad; her father's tragic death; her inheritance of the huge estate, and her discovery that her cousin Leopold planned to dispossess her and possibly kill her; the arrival of the mysterious stranger, who turned out to be Leopold's son, Loukios, from whom she was now estranged.

She again remembered and deeply regretted the rash impulse that had caused her to relinquish her father's beautiful, treasured cross. If only she could arrange for its return. Maybe it was time to ask Otrygg to go to Cappadocia, locate the monk Gregori, and find her cross.

Then another thought intruded.

Of course, she exclaimed silently, that is exactly how it shall be accomplished. Otrygg can take Grandmother back to Persia and retrieve the cross on his way home.

Otrygg met Zahra and Najila in front of the building that housed their accommodations. "Did you enjoy your visit to Zeuxippus?"

"Ah! It was a heavenly experience, Otrygg," Najila replied, her eyelids drooping sleepily. "You have not lived until you have basked in the heated waters and received a brisk massage afterward. I do want to speak to you, but right now my mind and body are numb from the pampering they received, and I cannot think straight. I really must take a nap, if you'll excuse me." Najila stumbled off, leaving Otrygg and Zahra alone.

"What is the situation with Najila's cousin, Leopold?" Zahra asked Otrygg. "Is he still here at court?"

"I am afraid so. He managed to retain an apartment on the palace grounds and is therefore too close to the throne to suit me. I am sure Leopold Alexander is plotting something, though I have yet to find any proof."

Zahra clucked her disgust. "Unfortunately, we learned nothing more at the baths. But perhaps during our time at the palace—"

"I would prefer that Najila be at Hawks Hill," Otrygg said, "but as long as I am here, I can watch over her." He gazed at Najila's retreating figure and murmured, "Has she ever forgiven

Loukios for not knowing about Leopold's return? He was not at fault, you realize."

Zahra clucked her tongue. "Lord Loukios assured me that he and his father barely speak to one another. I am sure he was truthful when he said that he did not know Leopold Alexander had returned from Moravia. However, there is no convincing Najila that the relationship between father and son is strained to such a degree."

"Well," Otrygg said, "Loukios will attend the feast tonight. See that Najila is there, Zahra. If I am somehow able to reunite them, young Loukios's shrewdness and strength will be valuable assets as I guard Najila."

Suspecting that Otrygg cared far more for Najila than he let on, Zahra threw him a compassionate glance. "I must attend to her. Until tonight then, Lord Otrygg, the Lord bless ye."

"And thee, Lady Zahra."

Chapter 34

Loukios stood in the great banquet hall, watching for Najila. The minute she walked into the room, their eyes met. Wearing a dress of shimmering Mediterranean blue satin moiré adorned with tiny loops of alternating silver beads and seed pearls, Najila stood out from every other woman present. For this special occasion, Zahra had twisted Najila's thick hair to form a tiered crown on top of her head, securing it with combs and a diamond-and-ruby tiara. At her throat, she wore a matching diamond-and-ruby necklace.

Loukios's sharp intake of breath caused his companions to look in the direction of his gaze. Murmured ahs and appreciative comments—along with several lewd remarks—burned his ears. Loukios half smiled at Najila and performed a stiff, shallow bow.

Otrygg saw Loukios's response and noted the flush that then reddened Najila's cheeks. His heart in shreds, the old Viking knew he had to surrender any fancied claim he might have on her. Though he resented Zahra's expectation that he would mend the chasm between the young people, Otrygg resolutely touched Loukios on the elbow to get his attention.

"We have to talk, Loukios. Alone!"

✝

I knew it! I just knew Loukios would be here!

He stood to the left of the entry with a group of men, including Otrygg Harald. Seeing him, Najila began to tremble. It was as if the drone of more than a hundred voices, the music of a dozen stringed instruments, had suddenly stopped. She had missed him, and she had hoped he would attend the feast.

As Otrygg beckoned Loukios into an alcove and out of her view, Najila spotted another familiar face, her cousin Leopold Alexander Doukas. Dread mixed with anger replaced her joy.

"Zahra, let us be seated ere my cousin comes our way," she said, lifting her chin in Leopold's direction, then walking toward the enormously long, elaborately set table.

Observing Najila steering Zahra toward the table, Otrygg and Loukios moved to a point in the room where their paths would have to cross. "Loukios wishes to speak to you, my lady," Otrygg said pleasantly.

"I have nothing to say to him," Najila snapped and started to go on. Zahra stopped her, firmly grasping her arm. "It is important that you listen. A mistake has been made, and it must be undone for your own welfare."

"Do I have a choice when you two insist I reunite with this oaf?" Najila cried. Though inwardly pleased, she refused to give in or even to look at Loukios. Meanwhile, he waited impatiently for his chance to explain.

Otrygg began first. "Leopold Alexander arrived in Konstantinoupolis two days before the crowning ceremony in the Hippodrome, but even his son did not know it."

Loukios interrupted. "I only recently heard a rumor that my father left Moravia in disgrace after conspiring with the pope to bring Moravia back into the Roman church. That would be blatant treachery, and I doubt that even he would be that thickheaded. I swear by the Virgin that I have had nothing much to do with him in years. He allowed me to stable my horses at Hawks Hill because it enhanced his prestige among his peers, but he also had convinced them that my animals were his. My closer friends and I used to laugh at his transparent ruse."

"That sounds like a made-up tale, Loukios. Why should I believe any of it?" Najila scoffed.

Loukios threw up his hands in despair, but her tirade angered Otrygg, "Then you declare that we all are liars, Lady Najila?" he growled.

On hearing the Viking's tone, Najila realized how childish she must appear to them. Ultimately, what substantial proof did she have that Loukios had wronged her? None whatsoever! She spoke in a low, tremulous voice. "Please forgive me, both of you. Loukios, you sound sincere, and as I have known Otrygg my entire life, I trust his judgment. If he believes you, then what you say must be so."

"What we tell you is the truth. There are those who can vouch for me." Loukios scanned the room, seeking a friend who could support his claim. "Some are here tonight."

Not wanting a stranger to be party to her private affairs, Najila nearly shouted, "No! That is not necessary. Really, I do believe you. I admit it now. I never wanted it to be otherwise." She turned to Otrygg. "Thank you, Otrygg. My pride overcame my better instincts."

Otrygg's grin was wry. "Not an unusual occurrence, my lady."

Najila sighed. "It is true enough, and I have to admire your honesty, Otrygg."

Otrygg knew when it was time to retreat. As Loukios paused to introduce Najila to an admiring nobleman, Otrygg discreetly nudged Zahra. "Loukios can watch over Lady Najila."

Zahra gave him an almost imperceptible nod, and the pair of conspirators exchanged satisfied smiles as they slowly strolled away, arm-in-arm, from the young couple.

When the gushing nobleman finally left them, Loukios swung to face Najila. "My father is here."

"I know; I saw him a while ago. I did not like how his eyes followed my every move."

Loukios groaned. "My father thinks he is sole heir to Hawks Hill, and he will not easily give up the notion."

"Loukas, has no one told you that your father threatened me with death? I overheard a conversation of his during which he stated the threat to another man whose voice I did not recognize."

Loukios's head jerked back. "He would not go that far to capture the estate," he snorted in disbelief. "Even he is not so brash as to employ murder as a solution."

"He at least implied it," Najila insisted, tears glistening in her eyes. "I preferred not to tell you this, but I must. Otrygg and Julian the eunuch, my father's old friend, arranged for your father to be sent to Moravia so neither he nor his cohorts could harm me. I had put him out of my mind." She shuddered. "Then seeing him at the Hippodrome . . ."

She looked up at Loukios, longing for some sign of empathy. "Can you understand my fear, Loukios? I am afraid for my very life."

Torn between the Bible's commandment to honor his father and his blossoming love for the beautiful woman before him, Loukios was not sure how to respond. Though he was not close to Leopold Alexander—and disliked being around him—the man was still his father. Nevertheless, Loukios had long suspected that if Leopold coveted something unobtainable by any other method, he was capable of violence, even as ruthless as to order the extermination of those who stood in his way.

"Loukios?" Najila asked.

Drawing in a protracted breath, and then exhaling slowly, he finally answered her. "I do not doubt it when you say that you may be in danger. I do not, however, think my father bold enough or foolish enough to hurt you, especially now that I have told him how protective I feel toward you."

Her expression softened. "Dearest Loukas, I regret how cruelly I have treated you, but I still do not trust Leopold Alexander."

Later that night, Loukios confronted his father. "It has come to my attention that you have threatened Lady Najila." When Leopold vehemently denied having done so, Loukios countered, "I believe Najila speaks the truth. It has been confirmed by the Viking Otrygg. Let her be, Father. You always knew that Hawks Hill belonged to Michael's heir, be it male or female. Set your sights on something besides Najila's estate."

Leopold's lips thinned. "How is it that my son opposes me when he should be my closest ally? So be it then! I want nothing more to do with you. I no longer claim you as my son." He spun on his heels and stomped off.

Stunned by his father's sudden rejection, Loukios could only stand and watch as Leopold left.

Loukios and Najila lingered in the romantic garden by the stable to enjoy the glowing sunset. A month had passed since the coronation, and the weather had warmed considerably. The two often stopped in the garden on their return from riding on the estate. Those few, precious minutes were the best of Najila's busy day. She marveled that she had ever questioned Loukios's love for her.

All that day, he had been quieter than usual. Tonight, he was even more so, which worried her. "Something chaffs you," she declared.

Loukios remained silent. Then, without warning, he reached forth and pulled her into an embrace. His soulful eyes commanding her gaze, he said, "Will you be my bride, Najila?"

Before Leopold Alexander had reentered the picture and caused so much confusion, she had dreamed, awake and asleep, of marrying Loukios. She certainly was getting older, years beyond the age at which her childhood companions married. But was that enough reason to bind herself to this man? After all, Loukios was a Christian and she was a Muslim. It was a conundrum. Then she remembered that her father, a Christian, and her mother, a Muslim, had come together in a loving and successful marriage, despite their differences.

The adoration in Loukios's eyes overcame all her doubts. "Yes, Loukas. Oh yes!"

It was then that Loukios gave Najila her first, honest-to-goodness, passionate kiss. When they finally drew apart, she pleaded, "Again, Loukas. Kiss me again."

And he did. More than once.

Chapter 35

When Loukios and Najila announced that they would wed the following spring, it surprised few who were close to them. Zahra had no doubt whatever that Loukios and Najila were well suited. Observing Najila's joy, she felt not only pleasure, but also relief at having a great weight lifted from her shoulders. She was confident that Loukios would assume the many responsibilities involved in managing the complex estate, responsibilities that had long been her obligation.

Otrygg was fully aware that he was attached to Najila in a way that he should not be. On the other hand, he knew Loukios was the right man for her. His emotions in turmoil, he looked forward to being away from Hawks Hill for a while. Fulfilling Najila's plans for him to take Shafiqa to Baghdad, and his pledge to return Michael's silver and amber cross to her, kept his mind far too busy to mourn as much as he would have otherwise. Nevertheless, his cheerful whistle no longer echoed in the cavernous halls of Hawks Hill.

Najila missed Otrygg's uproarious joking, especially during meals. A pall settled over the table, and she didn't have any idea of the reason for his somber mood. Her gloom doubled when Loukios told her that he would be going to Iberia within the month to attend the annual Seville horse fair. It would leave her without either of her protectors.

Meanwhile, the prospect of returning to Baghdad had revived Shafiqa's spirits. She hummed a melodious tune as she bustled

sense and he took her then and there, he reluctantly withdrew from the embrace.

"I must go. I have much to accomplish; I leave for Spain on the morrow."

A sudden expression of distress flashed across Najila's face. "I love you, Loukas," she whispered.

"And I love you with my whole body, soul, and spirit, my wonderful, wonderful Najila. An hour will not pass when I shall not long for you."

Chapter 36

It had been five weeks since Loukios had sailed away, his destination the port that lay just south of the mouth of the greatest river in southern Iberia. He had told Najila that from there he would travel by mule or on horseback to Seville and Cordova, where he planned to seek blooded mares suitable for his horse-breeding operation.

Now Otrygg was leaving to take Shafiqa to Persia. Najila was saddened by the thought that her grandmother was going to Baghdad to die. But given her age, it was inevitable. Though Najila could not talk her out of making the arduous trek, she consoled herself with the hope that Otrygg would be able to recover her father's silver and amber cross. Her cousin Leopold's unwelcome presence in Konstantinoupolis, and his long-standing threat, continued to drape an ominous shadow over her life.

Chin in hand, she sat at the writing table in her favorite room at the top of Hawks Hill's east tower. Apart from a stool, a small Persian prayer rug, and a lightweight day bed, the room stood empty. If she walked along the room's curved walls and gazed out each window as she came to it, she had an unobstructed, full-circle view of her estate. Last winter, when chill winds blustered off the Russian steppes and in through the unglazed, narrow openings—turning the room into an uninhabitable, icy mausoleum—she had ordered the furnishings carried downstairs to the main house. Yet, well insulated from the damp cold in wool and furs, she had climbed to the tower every day to pray.

Though she adored the tower room, she much preferred to perch sidesaddle on a pillion behind Loukios, riding his big stallion, one arm snugly wrapped around his waist, her cheek pressed to the warm base of his neck where his silky hair ended in upturned tendrils.

Najila looked up from the documents littering the surface of the table, worry lines furrowing her forehead. Her thoughts drifted south across the Aegean and west over the Mediterranean seas.

What little she knew about the Iberian Peninsula and its inhabitants was only what Loukios had described to her. Iberia was in constant turmoil, immersed in endless wars between the resident Muslim kings and the Christian rulers in the north, who were gradually moving south, conquering as they progressed. It was an unsafe place to be, and she feared for him.

"You are not to fret," Loukios had scolded her when she professed her concern. "I aim to travel as far north as Cordoba and no farther." He had also assured her that he could deal with Muslims and Christians alike; he had obtained much experience on his former trips to Iberia.

Najila knew that she would have to convert to Loukios's Orthodox faith to marry him; Loukios had persistently begged her to do it before he left. Uncertain in her heart, torn between two beliefs, she had postponed her decision. Now, she wondered, did religion really matter? Had she been wise not to give him an answer? Had they been married, they at least could have had a few blissful days—and nights—together. Instead, there were only those brief, stolen moments, lovely to remember and dream about while he was gone.

During the three weeks before he rode off, she had rarely seen him, as he was kept busy in and out of Konstantinoupolis, making arrangements for his three-month journey. And of course, their wedding could not be performed until he returned in late summer or early fall. "Oh, Loukas, how I miss you," she cried softly.

A light tapping on the heavy wood aroused her from her reverie. "Do enter," she called, turning toward the door as Zahra swept through it.

"Otrygg wishes to address you, Lady Najila. He waits below."

"Ah. I want to see him, too," Najila declared. She set a river stone on the batch of parchment sheets on which she had been working. "Will you please straighten things here for me, Zahra? A draft may scatter these documents if they are not held down."

"I will take care of it," Zahra answered, deftly tucking the sheets into orderly piles and weighting them. "Otrygg acts as if he is in a hurry to leave, and your grandmother has been packed and ready for a month." Zahra laughed. "She has so enthusiastically raved about our old home that I actually contemplated going myself."

"Thank you for not doing so, my good friend; it pleases me that you would stay." Najila threw her arms around her lady-in-waiting. "I do need you here, Zahra."

Zahra smiled. "It is the very reason I cannot go, especially with Loukios and Otrygg both absent."

"You are my mother, my dear friend, my confidant. I could not do without you."

Tears formed in Zahra's eyes. "And you are the daughter I never bore; your trials are my trials. I could never abandon you, Najila, particularly when you are to remain here alone."

Najila gave Zahra one more affectionate squeeze, and then started to descend the winding staircase. On the second step, she hesitated, looking over her shoulder at Zahra. "I would be desolate if you left," she said.

✝

Otrygg awaited Najila in the Great Hall. Shafiqa was nowhere in sight, but her fifty or so bundles arranged in stacks and piles surrounded the tall Viking.

"Lady Najila, all is prepared for the journey, but I wish to speak to you first," Otrygg announced. "My thought is that Lady Shafiqa is not well enough for the journey. If you prefer, I could delay our departure again."

Najila shrugged and clicked her tongue. "My grandmother has an iron will; it is impossible to change her mind once she has determined her path."

"Be aware of treachery while I am gone," he warned her. "It worries me to leave Hawks Hill without a man to protect you."

Najila snorted. "I have servants and guards aplenty. They will see to my safety as long as I stay close to home. I have no plans to go elsewhere. And Otrygg, I am unable to tell you how indebted I am to you. You have cared for my grandmother as well as for me all these years. Now you risk significant danger to take her to Persia. When you return, I will see that you are amply rewarded."

Otrygg shook his head. "It is I who should reward you for suggesting this venture, Lady Najila. I have grown weary of trotting to and fro on the dull road between Hawks Hill and Konstantinoupolis. I seek a new experience, and you have provided me with a grand chance to find it." He performed a shallow bow, looking up at Najila, a boyish grin creasing his face. "Yes, it is I who am grateful to you."

He patted a huge, crescent-shaped sheath that hung on gold chains from the belt partially hidden under his broad sash. "I plan to see Grandmother Shafiqa safely home; then while seeking your treasured cross, we shall see what I find to satisfy my restless soul."

Amused, Najila laughed. "I am sure, friend Otrygg Harald, that you will find the excitement you crave, even if you have to create it yourself."

Her cousin Leopold Alexander Doukas might feel permanently secure within the palace walls right now, but his pompous posturing would not survive for very long once his son and
Otrygg were reestablished at Hawks Hill.

Shafiqa entered the great hall, accompanied by the two servants who fulfilled her intimate needs. The appearance of her
grandmother shocked Najila. She seemed unsteady; her skin
was gray, and her inflamed eyes peered out of dark hollows. It
had been several days since she had joined them at mealtime.

Involved in her daily routine, and preoccupied with extra
duties due to Loukios's absence, Najila had presumed that her
grandmother was merely busy preparing for the trip. Now,
ashamed that she had neglected to check on her condition more
frequently, Najila rushed over to her. "Grandmother, you are ill.
I do think it unwise of you to undertake such a journey."

The old woman's rheumy, red-rimmed eyes glared back at
her. "Why do you even say those words? We settled it long ago.
I am going to Baghdad, where I will spend my final hours." She
began to cough in dry, hacking spasms behind her veil. Clear-
ing her throat, she croaked in Persian, "The Viking will see that
I get there, will you not, Viking?"

Throwing Najila a questioning glance, Otrygg nodded. "I
have promised thee, my lady, to see thee safely home to the
country of thy birth," he said, also speaking in Shafiqa's native
tongue.

"Humph!" she sniffed and turned to Najila. "I am saying good-
bye to you now, my only granddaughter." She lifted her face for
Najila to kiss her wrinkled brow. Taking Otrygg's arm and holding on to it tightly, Najila's grandmother urged him toward the
door.

As the small caravan left the courtyard, Najila was positive
that she would never again see her grandmother, her last living

relative. Suddenly grief stricken, Najila ran up the wide staircase to her tower, where she dropped to her knees onto the little prayer rug to pray the rest of the day.

Chapter 37

Despite his tendency to become seasick, Loukios loved the sea. Aboard a sturdy *meizon*—a merchantman version of the larger Byzantine war *dromon*—he was perfectly at ease. Standing erect on the prow, facing a stiff northeast wind, he became a living figurehead. It thrilled him to hear the hissing froth, to see the sleek hull cleaving the Aegean Sea's blue-green waters. Normally, his mind would have been occupied with the voyage's sights and smells. Instead, his thoughts were of Najila and their forthcoming wedding.

He and Najila had never discussed the problems that a marriage between a Christian and a Muslim posed. Byzantines and Muslims were semitolerant regarding other religions. Each frowned on interfaith marriages, though they often happened. Almost without exception, one spouse would convert to the other's religion, although Najila's parents never had. She hadn't told him how they had managed that—or gotten away with it.

Loukios was not exactly sure where Najila stood on matters of faith. Though she accompanied him to specific services and celebrations, she would scarcely talk about them. She was not a baptized Christian, and was therefore forbidden to enter the church sanctuary. When she did go to church with him, he remained at her side in the narthex, or vestibule. He never resented it, yet the necessity of it saddened him. He prayed that Najila would convert and be baptized, because church law required that she do both before they could be married in the church.

When it came to Najila's grandmother, Shafiqa, there was no doubt as to what she believed. The first time Loukios had met her, she had let him know that to her he was an infidel. He smiled as he remembered how fiercely she had protected Najila. Later, when she knew him better, trusted him at least a little bit, and began to see him as a possible mate for Najila, she had earnestly tried to convert him to her Muslim faith.

He had calmly explained his position. "I am Christian and eternally will be. I could never be anything else." But Shafiqa never had given up her proselytizing.

His ruminations were interrupted by the captain's shouted commands to lower the larger of the two lateen sails. Staring ahead over the bow, Loukios saw that the *meizon* was approaching its initial port of call, Crete's Candia harbor.

After the usual exchange of cargo and supplies, the ship left Crete at eventide for Messina, where Loukios was fortunate to catch a Venetian ship bound immediately for Cagliari, the southernmost port of Sardinia. After a brief layover there, the ship would sail on to Palma, in the Balearic Islands, whereupon Loukios planned to change vessels to a small coastal trader going to Valencia, then south along Iberia's east coast.

During the Cagliari-Palma leg, just east of Sardinia, seven writhing waterspouts formed ahead of them. The awesome spouts, though grouped within a kilometer, were of varied circumference and spaced irregularly. The captain prudently changed to a safer course. Otherwise, Loukios found the voyage spanning the Mediterranean to be profoundly dull, particularly for a healthy, energetic man in his prime, who could not get adequate exercise. He was relieved when the largest of the Balearic Islands loomed on the horizon.

Loukios had twice made the voyage down the peninsula's east coast, starting at Valencia. He had decided to take that route again, but this time he intended to see a unique event that he had missed before.

The tiny town of Burriana, just slightly inland, had neither harbor nor wharf. Produce from the surrounding area, mostly oranges and olives, was laded onto barges that had been pulled up on the shore. The merchant ships that would carry the cargo were anchored offshore.

Oxen specially conditioned to salt water swam to the waiting ships, hauling the barges behind them. The animals were guided by men and boys who had learned the technique from their fathers, who had inherited it from their fathers and grandfathers before them.

When the coastal trader arrived at Burriana, Loukios noted that three ships were already anchored, prepared to take goods on board. He watched with interest the loading of the barges, which were then dragged into the water at just the right tide. The sea-toughened individual in charge of an ox team swam alongside his animals, guiding the powerful pair by a firm grip around one massive horn. The only sign of stress the oxen might have felt could be seen in their wildly rolling, white-ringed eyes.

No one knew for certain how many years the custom had flourished. "Who began it?" Loukios asked a grizzled seaman.

"The Romans, it is claimed."

The availability of oranges reminded Loukios that the season of calmer seas was passing and he had yet to find his mares. He would need to complete his business quickly in order to avoid the fall storms. He was beginning to regret his decision to sail the most picturesque route. He knew he should hurry, but he was trapped aboard a slow ship. On the return trip, after he had purchased his Iberian mares, he would take a more direct route.

After three more ports of call, the coastal trader sailed through the Pillars of Hercules, up the Iberian west coast, and finally entered Cádiz harbor. The first thing to grab Loukios's attention as he left the ship was the abundance of flowers festooning every balcony, every park, every street—anywhere a pot could be placed or a plant planted.

Najila, my love, you would so appreciate the color and perfume here, he thought. Despite the commotion along the busy harbor front, he was suddenly lonely beyond telling. How I miss you, my beloved. A sharp pain of longing seared his chest, and he shut his eyes. He opened them at the sound of hoofbeats.

"*Pardoname, Señor,* do you ail?" A young man of medium height, mounted on a splendid gray horse and decked out in Moorish regalia, peered down at him. Concern wrinkled his brow.

Instantly manufacturing an excuse to cover his embarrassment, Loukios stammered, "I am well enough, though my legs still feel as if they are walking the ship's deck."

The man's hearty laugh was sincere. Speaking in cultured Spanish, he said, "Please accept my sympathy, *Señor.* The sea and I rarely agree on our selection of weather. That is why I always travel on horseback." He patted the neck of his fine steed. "I am Don Rodrigo Díaz de Vivar. May I be of assistance to you?"

Loukios understood more Spanish than he could speak, so he responded in Latin, "Perhaps you can. I seek a reliable beast to carry me to Seville." He pointed to a ramshackle building slumped on the opposite side of the road. "When last I was here, a livery stable stood on that very spot. Now the structure seems abandoned."

"Ah, *Señor!* You speak Latin. By your attire I deduce that you are from . . . Konstantinoupolis, no?"

Loukios had not forgotten all his Spanish. "*Es verdad.* Konstantinoupolis is my home." He performed a shallow bow. "I am christened Loukios Alexander Doukas." He shot Don Rodrigo a wry glance and spread his arms. "In truth, my destination is the horse fair near Seville, but it is obvious that I have no mount on which to get myself there."

Don Rodrigo flashed him another broad smile. "The house of Doukas is known to me. An acquaintance has spoken of a Leopold Alexander Doukas. Your brother, perhaps?"

"He is my father," Loukios replied, hopeful that what Don Rodrigo's acquaintance had told him was complimentary to Leopold.

"You are favored by God, Loukios Alexander Doukas. I am also on my way to the Seville fair, to purchase cavalry horses for my lord." He ran his eyes over Loukios from head to toe. "By your appearance, you are a horseman, no? Alas, the *caballeriza* of which you speak no longer exists. The owner cheated a prominent, local Moor once too often, and four years have passed since he lived this side of hell." Uttering a gagging croak, Don Rodrigo sliced his hand edgewise across his neck. "It happened thus."

Taking note of Loukios's evident consternation, the Spaniard continued, "Ah, but do not be concerned. I happen to have an extra steed with me, and he is in need of a rider. Come along with me, and you can take him on."

"That would be most kind," Loukios said, his countenance brightening.

"I should mention, however," Don Rodrigo continued, "that he is a spirited one. No doubt you've heard the saying of the Arabs that a rider always rides with an open grave? I am afraid it is especially true when the rider is seated upon Tornado the Magnificent."

Chapter 38

Don Rodrigo Díaz de Vivar had about him the air of a warrior, and though he appeared no older than his early twenties, he radiated confidence without displaying a dandy's swaggering posture. Loukios instantly liked him.

Politely dismounting to be on equal footing with Loukios, Don Rodrigo commanded, "Come! I will introduce you to Tornado." While leading his gray gelding, he told Loukios, "It is unusual to find me walking. I am far more at ease in the saddle."

Loukios nodded. The Spaniard's bowed legs were shaped like his own. "I, too, prefer to ride. When I am afoot, I feel a part of me is absent."

Coming to a spacious walled villa at the edge of town, Don Rodrigo stopped before a massive door on which some talented Moorish artist had carved an intricate geometric design. The iron knocker was cast in the form of an oversized human fist. Turning to Loukios, the Spaniard said, "Here is my cousin's home. He will hardly notice an additional guest among the many he already has."

He lifted the heavy knocker and thumped it on the door's weathered wood. "Luis, open for us!" he shouted. "We have a visitor from afar." A moment later, a servant heaved wide the door, its hinges loudly protesting, to allow the men and horse through.

That evening, as they were comfortably seated near a refreshing pool within the cloistered courtyard, Don Rodrigo asked

Loukios, "On which ship did you arrive? I shall arrange for your baggage to be carried here from the dock."

Naming the coastal trader, Loukios added, "I travel light; I carry only what you see." He indicated the large satchel resting on the polished tiles at his feet.

"Ah yes, I should have guessed that you are a seasoned traveler. As a soldier, I also travel without luxuries. It is less bothersome." He patted the scabbard at his side. "All I require is a well-honed sword and a fine horse. One does not need much else—a change of clothing, a few essentials perhaps. Ostentation merely attracts thieves."

The Spaniard leaned forward and whispered, "Of course, when traveling among the Moors, it is wise to have a small troop of loyal Christian knights with you. The bandits and mercenaries make it necessary."

Sitting back in his chair, Don Rodrigo took up his wine cup. "The wine is favorable, and though beneath the best, Cádiz has no finer vintage. My cousin imports it from the foothills of La Sierra Morena," he said. "No insult intended, primo," he yelled merrily, waving the mug at his cousin.

"It is excellent," Loukios agreed. "On my estate, I have a modest area where I grow grapes, but the wine they produce lacks such a rich, woody taste."

At that point, two handsome, silver-haired men joined them at the table. Rodrigo introduced one man as his cousin, Don Hidalgo, and then turned with a smile to the second man, cheerfully throwing an arm around his shoulder. "And meet my advisor, Don Minaya Alvar Fáñez. He is also a relative—in his case by marriage. Normally, Iberia's rulers, whether Christian or Muslim, dare not trust their relations. But that has never been my problem. I trust this pair with my life."

Who is this Don Rodrigo Díaz? Loukios asked himself. The man has an advisor? He speaks about a military escort? He noted that the older men acted like subordinates and treated the youthful Rodrigo with respect. Obviously, he was someone important.

✝

After midnight, Loukios was finally ushered to a comfortable, clean pallet in a barracks-type building. The other mats were occupied by slumbering men, apparently the troop Don Rodrigo had mentioned. When he had undressed and flung his weary body prostrate on the sleeping pad, it felt like he was still at sea—the bed seemed to roll and dip under him. He eventually fell asleep just before dawn, but he was awakened soon after by the din of raucous conversation and good-humored teasing. A giant of a man, seeing that Loukios had awakened, approached him, yawning and hitching up his trousers. "Don Rodrigo bade me to tell you, Loukios Alexander Doukas, that the hour is late. It is time to prepare for our journey to Seville."

"I am with you," Loukios muttered. Oh my head, he groaned in silent misery. The wine had been heavier than he was used to, and he had imbibed a bit too much. He sat up carefully, holding his head, then stood slowly to his feet. Dressed only in his breeches, he shuffled outside to the pool and plunged his head into the chilly water to clear his senses.

"Were your dreams pleasant, Don Loukios?"

Rising, Loukios blew his nose and rubbed the water from his eyes. Don Rodrigo stood beside him, tying the thongs of his bull-hide vest.

"The long voyage took its toll, Don Rodrigo, and I overslept. *Por favor*, accept my profound apology."

"¡*Nada!* It is of no importance. Dress thyself, and join my cousin and me for breakfast. We must depart soon after. And," he said, quietly chuckling, "Tornado is eager to be off."

✝

Rodrigo's men ate in the courtyard, while Rodrigo, his host, and Loukios dined at the family table inside the house. Loukios was surprised to be served such a hearty meal so early in the day: polenta, spicy mutton, and fruit, washed down with wine, though Loukios barely sipped his.

"When you are satisfied, Don Loukios, let us be on our way," Rodrigo said, springing from his chair.

The stable yard was a tumult of prancing horses and shouting men. As Don Rodrigo and Loukios neared the low-slung, stucco building that sheltered the horses, one of Rodrigo's men appeared in the doorway, leading a splendid golden stallion with a nearly white mane and tail. The animal jigged and reared as the men approached. At a softly spoken command from Don Rodrigo, the stallion immediately calmed. Dropping his muzzle into Rodrigo's flattened palm, the stallion lipped the grain his master held.

Don Rodrigo reached up to brush aside the horse's ten-inch-long forelock. Rubbing the broad forehead, he nodded toward Loukios, saying, "Tornado, my glorious beauty, meet your *cabalgador nuevo*, your new rider, Don Loukios Alexander Doukas. He has come all the way from Konstantinoupolis to test your spirit." Don Rodrigo grinned at Loukios. "*Un cabalgador temporario.*"

"A temporary rider?" Loukios laughed. "No horse has thrown me yet, Don Rodrigo, but I must admit your Tornado looks to be a challenge."

"He is that, my friend. You have from here to Seville to discover just how much of a challenge he is."

With the stableman holding the bridle, Tornado gave Loukios no trouble as he mounted. As soon as the man released the leather strap, however, the stallion quivered from head to tail, restlessly trying to move forward. The curb bit had extended, curved shanks, and Loukios was able to restrain the powerful animal by using a light, steady hand. Resisting control, Tornado arched his heavily muscled neck until his chin nearly touched his chest. As the rest of the troop began to exit the stable yard, the stallion's front feet danced a different rhythm than his hind feet, while his body remained stationary. The sensation was like nothing Loukios had ever experienced. The ride to Seville promised to be invigorating.

Chapter 39

As Loukios rode at Don Rodrigo's side, leading Rodrigo's troop of knights, he silently thanked God for the circumstances that had brought him into the don's company. Had the ship on which he had sailed continued to Sanlúcar de Barrameda instead of ending its voyage in Cádiz, he would not have met the young Spaniard.

Riding for several days along an ancient Roman road, they angled north until they reached the Guadalquivir River. It amazed Loukios that everyone they encountered along the way seemed to know Don Rodrigo. They were never without lodging; they had been equally welcomed at sugar plantations, beef ranches, and stud farms. The last breeder with whom they had stayed had arranged to send his head groom and a matched pair of handsome, high-stepping bay geldings along with Don Rodrigo's small but well-armed band. The man was confident that his prized horses would come to no harm.

"The Seville horse fair began during Roman times," Don Rodrigo explained to Loukios as they neared Seville, the largest city in Iberia's richest territory. "It was so famous that the Roman generals came to the fair to purchase mounts. As evidenced by your presence, Don Loukios, even today the Seville horse fair is well known to people who live as far away as Konstantinoupolis."

"As far east as Persia, I think."

Don Rodrigo nodded. "I have occasionally seen a Persian at the fair, but never have I seen one bring an animal to sell. They come to buy."

"I can understand the reason. From personal experience, I have been made aware that it is difficult to maintain animals in good condition when taking them such a great distance, especially by sea. For many years, it has been my wish to acquire Iberian horses. I have hesitated, because I have always feared the arduous journey home with them," Loukios admitted, wrinkling his brow. "But now that I have decided to breed an improved chariot horse, I must take that chance."

"Barge them down the Guadalquivir," Don Rodrigo advised him. "It is faster and less tiring to the horses—and to you. One is usually able to catch a ship headed east from Sanlúcar de Barrameda. There is a decreased risk of running into trouble going that way."

"I shall remember what you have said, *amigo mío.* I am not as well acquainted with the ranchers, and I dreaded an overland journey without an escort." Loukios twisted in his saddle to better see Rodrigo. "Unlike the Romans, I seek not a war horse but am after two or three blooded mares of a particular type. That is why I have come to Iberia, Don Rodrigo."

The Spaniard arched an eyebrow. "Of course, and if you describe to me the type you are after, I am sure I can be of assistance."

As they rode into Seville, Loukios took note of the number of mosques he saw. By comparison, the Christian churches were few and scattered. And though he was unable to discern a man's race or religion simply by his clothing, it seemed that most of the people on the streets were Moors.

When Loukios voiced this observation, Don Rodrigo answered grimly, "Unfortunately, *Señor,* the *taifa* state of Seville belongs to the Moors, though Spaniards are allowed to reside here, to do business, and to worship. Ibn Abbad's son, al-Mu'tadid, reigns.

He is ambitious, but an apt ruler. Take note, however, that if he sets his covetous eyes on a certain property, he can also become a ruthless murderer to obtain it.

"For instance," the don continued, "several years ago, he invited the rulers of Morón, Arcos, and Ronda to his palace. They thought they would be attending diplomatic discussions, but the invitation was merely a ruse to dispose of them. Al-Mu'tadid had them suffocated in his private bath house. His bath house! Naturally, he immediately appropriated their domains.

"Al-Mu'tadid's latest acquisition is Carmona," Rodrigo continued. "It fell just last year. We Spaniards wonder what he will seize next. Most of us believe Córdoba is his ultimate goal."

Don Rodrigo waved at an acquaintance who passed them on horseback, then went on with his narration. "The Spanish rulers are no better; the northern territories change hands faster than I can keep track of them. When Ferdinand the Great died in 1065, each of his three sons was proclaimed king of his own realm. The queen mother, Sancha, died last year. Her sons' native greed has already begun to show, and they are presently quarreling over land.

"But make no mistake. All is not peaceful in the south, either. We Spaniards who live here chafe under Moorish rule. Someday, we hope to—" Don Rodrigo stopped speaking while they skirted a crowd that surged around a group of street musicians.

Loukios suspected that Don Rodrigo Díaz de Vivar and his fellow Spaniards planned to change the state of affairs. He prayed a battle would not occur until long after he had departed Iberia.

"En fin! Finally we are here, amigo." Dismounting, Don Rodrigo sighed and, reaching for his kerchief, wiped the sweat off his heat-flushed face.

They entered the courtyard of a prosperous-looking inn, its architecture showing a Moorish influence. A red-tiled roof with wide eaves overhung thick stucco walls decorated with colorful tiles. The many fountains, predominantly of blue tile, emitted cooling mists, offering some small relief from the torrid mid-summer heat.

"This is Seville's best inn," the don declared. "It is well that I reserved rooms before I left for Cádiz. None are to be had without reservation during the horse fair."

Loukios dismounted and turned the stallion over to a stableman. "El Tornado is a fine steed. One of the best I have had the pleasure to ride," he declared with a satisfied grin. "True, he afforded me a stimulating moment or two, but that adds to the enjoyment of the ride. I shall truly miss him."

Rodrigo nodded. "He is my precious one, like my own child. He cannot be bought for his weight in gold."

Just then, a man rushed into the reception hall and shouted, "King Sancho has attacked King Alfonso."

"Hear that, Loukios? Life may be even more hazardous in the north than here. At the fair, I am to buy a dozen horses suitably trained for military use; then my men and I must hurry to Castilla to fight alongside Sancho."

"Why King Sancho?" Loukios asked.

Don Rodrigo shrugged with a crooked half smile. "I command his royal highness's troops."[1]

Chapter 40

Hundreds of brilliant, primary-hued banners, flags, and streamers whipped and crackled in the quickening breeze. The season's first rain shower had fallen during the night, cooling the air and dampening the ground, but as the sun rose, so did the heat. Dust raised by the milling animals and men caused the slanted morning light to lose itself in haze, and the entire scene became enveloped in a mystical aura.

Horses were everywhere of every weight, height, and color. Excited by their new surroundings, jostled by strangers poking and prodding them, the high-strung animals were terribly nervous and gave their handlers a rough go. Loukios skipped sideways to duck a piebald's flailing hooves.

The fancy piebald's muscular lackey, a northerner if one was to judge him by his blond hair and pale skin, smiled an apology, as he gave a hard jerk to the stallion's lead rope, causing the halter strap to rap the animal's Roman nose. The spirited horse obediently dropped to all fours and stood trembling while the man massaged its quivering neck muscles.

After his narrow escape, Loukios was warned by Rodrigo, "You have to keep your wits about you at the horse fair. Some handlers are mere boys—apprentices. Ha! Right there is a typical example." He gestured in the direction of a youngster who was attempting to control a large white stallion. The horse was no less than sixteen-hands tall. The lad, Loukios guessed, was thirteen or fourteen years old. He gripped a stout lead rope in his white-knuckled fists.

The big stallion whirled around the boy, its hind feet slashing out at everyone in sight. The boy was dragged forward helplessly, his heels trailing twin ruts in the dirt. Unexpectedly, the horse lunged backward and the lead zipped through the boy's hands. Screaming an alarm, the stunned child stared at his rope-burned palms as the frightened animal dashed into the crowd, which immediately scattered. Those attracted by the event's noise now joked and shouted bets as if the whole business were a joyous game. Someone finally caught the horse and turned it over to the crestfallen stableboy, but not before the rampaging beast had slammed into an onlooker and knocked the man down.

Amazingly unhurt but shame faced, the upended individual jumped to his feet and sheepishly brushed off his clothes. His companions laughed at his plight and heartily slapped him on the back.

Disgusted, Loukios declared, "That stallion is too powerful and energetic for a boy that size to handle. All that white monster had to do was to lift his head, and the boy came up with it."

Rodrigo chuckled. "*De nada*. It is nothing. Ere this day has ended, you will see far more excitement than that. I guarantee it. But come, my friend! We are here for a predetermined purpose."

Don Rodrigo sent four of his knights to search out promising war animals, which he would personally inspect and test later. Meanwhile, the don stayed close to Loukios to translate when Loukios haggled for mares.

Loukios favored grays. He had heard, however, that they rarely produced permanent color patterns. The two men discussed the problem. "The coat patterns of their foals are known to fade with age," he said.

"The blacks often fade, too," Rodrigo commented, drawing from his own experience. "Perhaps a bay is most reliable to consistently throw true color."

"I am trying to create a swift bloodline endowed with extraordinary stamina—yet one of a different appearance, bearing a leopardlike coat of black or bay spots on white," Loukios explained.

"You ask much," Rodrigo replied. "Even if God wills, it will take years to accomplish what you desire."

"You understand. I must begin by using the best."

"I agree. It is the only way." Rodrigo stopped suddenly and nodded imperceptively in the direction of a fine looking mare. "How does that dark bay over there fit your dream, Loukios, my friend?"

The two men strolled casually toward the mare, not wishing to reveal their interest to the mare's handler. They paused to appraise a young colt that Rodrigo considered a possible addition to his own herd. Gently running his hand down the colt's right leg, he found that the cannon bone was slightly twisted. Standing again, he moved to the front of the colt and stepped back to get a better look. Yes, the hoof turned in. As the seller began his spiel, Rodrigo silenced him with a curt, dismissive word.

Moving on, Loukios and Rodrigo again headed toward their original destination. From a distance, the mare Rodrigo had pointed out looked to be an ideal specimen. The closer they drew, the more interested Loukios became. She had all the qualities of a good brood mare, as well as the three important characteristics of a chariot steed: good muscle, a deep chest, and a long underline. Her progeny could have prodigious speed.

Jabbing Loukios with his elbow, Rodrigo whispered, "Outwardly she looks *más excelente*, most excellent. But first let us thoroughly examine her." Ignoring the eager sales pitch that spewed out of the rat-faced handler's mouth, Loukios began at the mare's head; Rodrigo at the opposite end.

The mare softly lipped Loukios as he rubbed the hollow behind her chin, checking for swollen nodes. Her erect ears were alert, and her prominent eyes, well set in a generous forehead, were keen. Loukios liked her attitude, calm and unafraid, though not aggressive.

The two men's eyes met across the mare's back. Rodrigo dipped his head, signifying his approval. Loukios had come to the same conclusion. As far as he could tell, the mare was perfect. He needed only to be assured of one last thing. Was she fertile? He asked Rodrigo to question the handler.

Encouraged by a prospective sale and windmilling his arms while he talked, the swarthy little man said, "Last year she had a male foal, but she was not bred during this spring's heat. Her yearling is here at the fair. I will take you to him."

They followed the man, he leading the mare over the display grounds, until they came to an area where the younger stock was being shown.

On seeing the yearling, Loukios drew in a quick breath. Though gangly and mildly off-balanced, both normal for the age, the colt was exquisite. Nicely groomed, it had the slender, curving blaze and matched rear fetlock socks of his dam.

How unfortunate. If I were not here only for mares, I would truly like to have this fellow. He could afford to acquire only two horses on this trip, and they had to be brood mares.

After confirming that the colt was out of the bay mare, Rodrigo, Loukios, and the mare's owner commenced with the bargaining process, their fingers a blur as they employed the Arab method of counting by rapidly tapping the palms of their hands. During the next hour, the fee was agreed upon and arrangements were made to have the mare delivered to Loukios at the inn on the morrow.

The two men sauntered on through the fair, Rodrigo keeping an eye open for athletic horses to train for battle, and Loukios looking for a second mare. His gaze landed on a striking liver sorrel that had a mane and tail of a silvery hue. In a certain light, her dappled coat also had a silver cast. He wondered whether the beautiful mare would fit his plan. How would the dappling influence the appearance of her offspring? Would dappling or spots prevail? Suddenly, it didn't matter; he had to have her.

They found the two-year-old to be prime in every respect. Against Rodrigo's advice, Loukios made the purchase without bartering as he should have. Still, Loukios was satisfied that he had paid a decent price for the unproven filly. He would simply have to take the chance that she would produce outstanding foals.

Rodrigo left Loukios to attend to his own arrangements, and set off on his own to purchase his war horses. As Loukios wandered the fairgrounds alone, he came to a rotund, red-cheeked woman selling a litter of very small and fuzzy white terrier puppies. Their black button noses and mischievous black eyes were gleaming contrasts to their clean white fur. "They are newly popular among the nobility," the woman told Loukios.

Remembering his promise, he pictured an adoring Najila holding a puppy on her lap. Loukios picked a male, slipped the woman some coins, and tucked the baby into a large side pocket, where it curled up and fell asleep.

As he walked on, he saw a sweets vendor hawking marzipan, a specialty the Arabs had introduced to Iberia. He bought Najila a large gift packet and departed for the inn, whistling cheerfully.

Chapter 41

The evening before they parted, Don Rodrigo threw a gala celebration in honor of Loukios and other friends who lived in and near Seville. One course after another was served to the diners. Seville was internationally famous for its musical-instrument industry, and with a dozen skilled musicians taking turns playing the industry's finest, the night's singing and dancing was splendid. Wine flowed freely, and by three in the morning, nearly everyone was besotted.

Without exception, the men's eyes were red-rimmed due to the smoky atmosphere and dolorous tears. Loukios tried to still the emotions that threatened to overwhelm him. It especially affected him when he envisioned Najila waiting for him at home.

Suddenly, a celebrant waving a goblet in the air leaped to a table top, sloshing wine on his mates. In a melodious singsong, he began to recite a poem in Arabic. Rodrigo leaned toward Loukios. "Do you speak Arabic?"

"A few words," Loukios replied, blinking away the mist that blurred his vision.

"It is a ninth-century love poem written by the Moor al-Mu'tadid. I will translate for you:

A gazelle's are her eyes, sunlike is her splendor,
Like a sand hill her hips, like a bough her stature:
With tears I told her plaintively of my love for her,
And told her how much my pain made me suffer.

My heart met hers, knowing that love is contagious,
And that one deeply in love can transmit his desire:
She graciously then offered me her cheek—
Oft a clear spring will gush forth from a rock—

I told her, "Let me now kiss your white teeth,
For I prefer white blossoms to red roses.
Lean your body on mine"—and then she bent
Toward me, granted my wish, again, again,

Embracing, kissing, in mutual fire of desire,
Singly and doubly, like sparks flying from a flint.
Oh hour, how short thou was in passing,
But your sweet memory will linger on forever.

Loukios turned his head so Rodrigo could not see just how deeply the verses had affected him. When he had somewhat recovered his dignity, he asked Rodrigo, "Can you obtain a copy of that poem for me? If it is written in Arabic, I will have it translated into Latin or Greek before I present it to my betrothed."

Rodrigo clapped Loukios on the shoulder and rose from the table. "Do you leave at first light?" He yawned, scratching his stomach.

"Not until near noonday. I have many arrangements yet to make," Loukios explained as he pushed back the bench on which he had been seated.

Rodrigo threw his arms around Loukios and exuberantly kissed him on both cheeks. "The poem will be delivered to you

ere you go," the Spaniard promised, his words slurred. Leaving
Loukios standing at the table, he wove a crooked path through
the bedlam, stopping on the way to talk to the man who had
read the beautiful poem.

✟

Though Loukios had imbibed more wine than was his custom, and had slept only three hours, he was abruptly awakened at dawn as a cold, wet nose snuffled his face, and a warm,
wet tongue lapped his chin. The puppy, which had joyously
greeted him when he returned to his room at the inn after his
long absence, had slept most of the night tucked in the curve of
Loukios's neck.

"Hungry, are you?" Turning onto his back, Loukios grabbed
the fat pup and hoisted it aloft. It immediately protested, wriggling and whining, its black eyes peering down at Loukios, its
stubby legs flailing comically.

Loukios laughed and put the puppy down. On swinging his
feet to the floor, his toes splashed into warm liquid. Mumbling
an oath—half at the little dog for doing it, half at himself for
being negligent—he got up. Then he saw the disaster the puppy
had made of the place while he was abed.

"What goes in assuredly comes out," he grumbled as he
swabbed the puddles with a discarded rag. That finished,
he then unwrapped some scraps of cooked mutton—leftovers
from the banquet—and took a bite. He had offered a portion
to the puppy before retiring, but the pieces were too large and
the meat too tough for the pup's milk teeth to handle. Tired as
he was, Loukios had thoroughly chewed each bit, then fed it
to the pup. Now, he repeated the procedure before going to his
own breakfast.

✟

The unmerciful midday sun scalded the deck of the shallow-draft barge that lay at a wharf in the bustling Seville port. Other than several goats and eight crates of squawking chickens, Loukios's horses and the pup were the only animals on board. Rodrigo had lent Loukios his top groom, an Arab named Masoud, who would accompany Loukios all the way home.

Loukios and Masoud encountered no trouble leading the bay mare onto the barge and into her high-walled wooden pen, but the young filly immediately balked at the base of the loading ramp. No matter what the two men tried, she refused to put so much as one foot on the ramp. Finally, they were forced to blindfold her with Masoud's sash.

With Masoud at her near side, Loukios opposite, they at last started the filly up the sloping ramp, though she continued to hesitate and jig. A slight drizzle had begun, causing the ramp to become dangerously slick. The filly's hind hooves skidded from under her. Slipping and sliding, she struggled to regain her balance.

The next thing Loukios knew, he was off the ramp and floundering in the water between the barge and the dock. He did not know how to swim.

Fortunately, a bargeman was near enough to clasp Loukios's hand and pull him out, and fortunately, Loukios was not carrying the puppy in his pocket. He had already stashed it in a makeshift kennel upon the deck.

Loukios merely suffered a bruised ego and a scraped shin. Though the filly was uninjured, by the time she was safely positioned in the second pen, her sleek coat was streaked with dark runnels of sweat. She nervously pounded the scarred planks that made up the pen's floor.

"Calm your beast," the captain shouted at Loukios. "I cannot have her destroying my ship."

"*Si. Si. Al momento.* In a minute." Loukios didn't believe the filly would do more than paw, but instead of removing the blindfold, he left it on. Climbing the wall boards of the pen, he leaned over the top and scratched the filly's neck just above her withers, a maneuver that imitated the nibbling by another horse. The filly gradually calmed until she stood quietly, her lower lip flapping with pleasure. Loukios decided to leave the blindfold in place for the voyage's duration.

The fifty-mile trip down the Guadalquivir River to its mouth at the Gulf of Cádiz was uneventful. Rodrigo had told Loukios the history of the Guadalquivir. Since the eighth century B.C., the Baetis or Betis River had been an important artery on which ancient ships transported merchandise from Iberia's interior to the Atlantic and onward to diverse destinations in the civilized world. The Muslims later renamed it the Guadalquivir, from the Arabic Wadi al-Kabir (Great River). Rain-filled in the winter and fed by melting mountain snow in the summer, the river never lost depth, and good-sized vessels traveled it year round.

Loukios lounged in the meager shade cast by the horse pens, the puppy curled in his lap. It was a rare experience in leisure, following several hectic months that had begun with travel preparations at home. In between spells of dozing, he counted the busy river traffic or watched the peaceful scenery slowly pass.

At the end of the river voyage in Sanlúcar de Barrameda, Loukios tried to find a connecting ship that would sail east within two months. He dared not wait longer than that, but he required a captain able and willing to transport large animals around the tip of the Iberian peninsula and across the Mediterranean Sea. Failing to find such a vessel, Loukios had no alternative but to take the horses by land to the busier and more international port of Cádiz.

After purchasing two donkeys, Loukios and Masoud started out. Loukios rode the mare and led the filly, the pup residing in his pocket, while Masoud rode one donkey and led the second.

They headed south along the rugged coastal road that would take them through swamps and across sand dunes. It was neither the easiest nor the safest route, but there was no other choice.

Chapter 42

The Guadalquivir River delta, the landscape through which Loukios and Masoud rode, was composed of the Atlantic Ocean, dunes, and splendid white beaches that seemed to go on forever. When swollen by feeder rivers in the wet season, the Guadalquivir carried sediment from the higher elevations to what once was a forty-five-mile gulf the Romans called Laces Lagustinus, Lake Lobster. The gulf had gradually silted in until it was little more than a collection of shallow ponds and marshes protected from the sea by a natural barrier of undulating dunes.

In the dry season, according to the tide, the sea forced its way up small channels the streams had cut into the barrier, thus flushing and cleansing the marshes.

Torrid heat rippled the atmosphere as the temperature peaked. It had not rained hard in five months, and the majority of rivers the two men and their animals crossed had been baked arid and were empty of life. The horses constantly shied at the mummified or skeletal remains of a bird or animal. Only near the rare channels yet listlessly flowing were there signs of greenery.

The gulf lay along a major avian migration route, and men had hunted there for centuries. When the channel at the end of the peninsula had finally filled with silt, blocking the formerly unfettered waters of the Atlantic, the gulf metamorphosed into a series of marshes and dunes, but the birds still came. During

the spring and most summers, the area was a paradise inhabited by thousands of land and water fowl, as well as by the pred-
ators that preyed on them.

The great fall migration was in full wing. Never had Loukios
seen such a variety of birds together: species arriving from
Northern Europe and the Arctic to winter in the huge marsh-
land, and those merely pausing to rest and fatten themselves
on the ripening seed before continuing south to Africa and
warmer climes.

Overland travel at this time of year was a mixed bag. On
the plus side, the roads and trails were not crowded with other
travelers, and the tall, seed-plumped grasses were prime horse
fodder. At the same time, drinking water was scarce, and the
stinging insects were intolerable.

Without Masoud to guide them to hidden springs, Loukios
and the animals would certainly have perished. Their periodic
need to slake their thirst made it necessary to meander along
the peninsula rather than track a straight line. They traveled
among rambling dunes that framed seemingly endless stretches
of level shoreline, with the sea always to their right. When it
was essential, they headed inland to look for fresh water.

Loukios rode his new mare, which he had named Damaris,
Greek for "gentle girl." The sweet-natured bay had willingly
taken to the saddle, behaving as if the routine had never been
otherwise. Loukios either led the filly, which he had named
Argyrea, Greek for "silvery," or he let her run free.

The party was following a faint, rock-strewn path through
groves of stunted cork and gall oaks. The thirsty animals, with
their keen sense of smell, knew when they were approaching
water at least an hour before the men saw it. The horses whinnied, snorted, and pranced; the donkeys brayed and stepped up
their otherwise languid pace.

Argyrea, untethered at the time, had been trotting point in
front of Damaris. When she detected the scent of water, the filly

darted forward and eagerly rushed toward the distant spring, her head high, her nostrils distended.

Loukios hesitated only a second, then spurred Damaris after Argyrea, leaving Masoud and his slower donkeys far behind. When Argyrea realized Damaris was closing in on her, she flagged her silver tail above her rump and broke into an all-out run.

Without Loukios having to urge her, Damaris lengthened her canter to overtake the filly. It thrilled him to see the gleeful manner in which Damaris and Argyrea answered the challenge to compete. Both showed the heart required for racing. Now if only their progeny would inherit the trait.

Guiding the speeding Damaris through boulder-strewn terrain required Loukios's complete attention. When he lifted his eyes to search for Argyrea, the filly had already disappeared over the crest of a hill. As Damaris started up the steep incline, a screeching clamor sounded on the other side of the hill, and a big flock of birds—large vultures and smaller kites—flapped into the eastern sky.

Loukios galloped to the hilltop and reined in Damaris. Horror choked him as he took in the scene below. In a verdant glen encompassed by cliffs, a stagnant pool, partly concealed by decaying vegetation, blended into the surrounding weeds. Argyrea had waded in to drink from the murky pool, and was instantly trapped in quicksand.

Plunging and rearing, the filly was trying to disengage her legs from the sticky muck, but the more she fought, the faster she sank. A rotting and flyblown boar's carcass bobbed near the filly. Its stench permeated the air on the rising wind.

Spurring Damaris down the cliff, Loukios leaped off and tied the mare securely to a tree a safe distance from the pool. Neighing and pawing in an effort to reach the water, Damaris pulled back on the rope until she was sitting on her haunches.

Loukios could see that Argyrea was held by something mysterious and threatening, something unfamiliar in his experience. He looked frantically back up the hillside, but Masoud had not yet come into view. Quickly checking his available equipment, his eye fell on Argyrea's four-and-a-half-meter lead rope, which he had fastened to Damaris's saddle. With trembling hands, he loosened the rope and fashioned the end into a loop. Placing his foot at the water's edge, he tentatively tested the underlying mud to see if it would hold his weight. Immediately, he felt an ominous sucking at his boot. Knowing that he had to drop the loop over Argyrea's head, he stretched out as far over the pond as he deemed prudent.

Gathering the length in his hands, he snaked the line toward the filly. But as the rope hissed toward her, Argyrea shied, tossing her head. The noose fell short, failing even to touch her. Fearing that his precious filly was about to meet a horrible end, Loukios pleaded, "Please, most merciful God, I need your help!"

Argyrea's squealing and splashing grew louder as she battled the suction that steadily drew her down to the bottom of the rank pool.

Loukios ran along the bank, seeking some place from which he might get the rope around the filly's neck. Argyrea continued to sink until the water nearly covered her back. She no longer struggled. Her lack of movement was a momentary blessing, because inaction slowed the sinking. Loukios realized that he could do nothing further until Masoud arrived to aid him. More frustrated than he had ever been in his life, he pummeled a fist into his throbbing forehead.

At the sound of hoofbeats, Loukios looked up. Masoud topped the hill.

"Hurry! Argyrea is in trouble!" he shouted to the Arab.

Reading the problem in a single glance, Masoud whipped the donkeys into a reckless, scrambling slide down the rough grade. Jumping off his mount, Masoud swiftly extricated the hemp tether he kept coiled on top of his saddle pack.

Knotted as one, Loukios's lead rope and Masoud's tether were long enough to reach Argyrea. After several vain attempts to set the loop in the correct position, Loukios finally put it over Argyrea's head. But the minute the filly felt the line tighten around her neck, she began to struggle anew.

Getting Argyrea out of the quicksand demanded the combined strength of both men in an ordeal that lasted an hour and a half. By then, all three were coated with stinking slime and thoroughly exhausted.

After securing the filly to a tree near Damaris, the two men went in search of fresh, uncontaminated water. Finding a spring coursing over the rocks uphill and away from the foul and dangerous pond, Loukios and Masoud cleansed themselves and Argyrea, watered the rest of the animals, and filled their water bags. Then they collapsed under a tree.

"Forgive me for neglecting to inform you about the deadly sands," Masoud apologized.

"You are not to blame. I could not have imagined it," Loukios replied. "But," he asked, a wry grin crinkling his sunburned face, "should I expect anything else as extraordinary as that sucking mire?"

"Only the obvious," Masoud said, smiling. "Such things you can see and therefore avoid, but they are few, and our journey is nearly over."

"That is a relief." Loukios nodded. "Then I will soon be aboard a ship sailing home." Yawning, he leaned against the cork bark. "How I long to return to Konstantinoupolis." And how I long for you, my princess Najila.

Chapter 43

When Loukios left Konstantinoupolis to go west to Iberia, Otrygg had traveled east to the Anatolian Plateau. His party now lay encamped by a listless creek that trickled on the outskirts of Iconium, an ancient Roman city.

Having ended his morning meal, Otrygg dropped to his knees in prayer and asked God, with his infinite power and generous mercy, to sustain Shafiqa long enough to get her home. Nonetheless, he was becoming convinced that his prayers were useless. Shafiqa was dying, and Persia was yet a great distance off.

Najila had arranged for her Nubian maid Taraneh to accompany Shafiqa to Persia, assured by the loyal woman that she would dedicate her life to Shafiqa's care. Taraneh had been alone—and lonely—ever since her twin sister, Tala, had died of pneumonia.

From outside Otrygg's tent, Taraneh called to him. "Master Otrygg. My mistress Shafiqa asks that you come to her."

Otrygg rose from his sleeping mat, upon which he had lain to ponder the oppressing situation. "Please enter, Taraneh," he answered.

Taraneh described Shafiqa's worsening condition as Otrygg sat on a stool, glumly listening, his chin cupped in his palm, his elbow resting on a small, ornately carved table. Najila had taught Taraneh to read and write. Not only was the Nubian statuesque and elegant, but she was also an exotic, intelligent beauty. Whenever Otrygg encountered her at Hawks Hill, her calm, dignified presence placated him.

"My mistress grows weaker with each passing hour. She no longer eats, and she drinks barely enough to moisten her throat. I fear she has but a few days to live," Taraneh told the Viking, her expressive, almond-shaped eyes tearing.

The news did not surprise Otrygg. Shafiqa's attempt to reach Baghdad, her birth city and former home, seemed increasingly futile. He should have left for Persia sooner, yet he knew it wasn't his fault that Shafiqa lay dying. From the beginning, he had suspected she could never complete the demanding journey, which would tax a stronger person in the best of health, especially during the year's hottest months. Against his better judgment, he had consented to make the trip because Najila asked it of him.

Sounding a discouraged groan, Otrygg rose abruptly. "It is as I thought; the end is near." He sighed. "Can we do anything to make Lady Shafiqa more comfortable in her remaining time?"

"I believe I have done all I can for her," Taraneh said.

The Nubian followed Otrygg to Shafiqa's tent, which he had ordered placed in a patch of meager shade underneath a scruffy willow, the only mature tree in sight. The tent's heavy, goat-hair sides had been rolled up and secured to give the ailing woman as much air as possible, but the temperature inside the enclosure stayed abominably hot. Despite Taraneh's burning incense and strategically placing perfumed kerchiefs, the foul smell of a grievous illness permeated the tent's dim interior.

Shafiqa lay on a thick bed of carpets and goat-hair throws that cushioned her from the hard ground. Though she wore a night dress and was covered by a silk sheet, Otrygg saw that her emaciated frame had shrunk even more in the past several days.

He asked softly, "You wished to see me, Lady Shafiqa?"

Shafiqa moaned and turned her face away from him. The back of her head reminded Otrygg of a bare skull: yellowed, translucent skin stretched tautly, with scraggly strands of gray hair attached here and there.

Otrygg turned to Taraneh, his raised eyebrows forming a silent question. Taraneh gently shook Shafiqa's shoulder, but there was no response. Her breath came in ragged, shallow bursts, the only indication that she was still alive.

Death and suffering were familiar to Otrygg. After all, was he not a warrior who had fought in major battles? Had he not seen mortally wounded and dead men? And had he not been approached by lepers who haunted the streets of every city from Baghdad to Athens?

At least one could see leprosy's ravaging progress. Never had he been exposed to a terminal disease that savagely destroyed a human being's insides . . . something unseen by others but insidiously active, slowly killing its wretched victim tissue by tissue. It made no sense to him.

The day before, Otrygg had learned that he had another challenge besides fulfilling his obligation to Najila. He had sent Shafiqa's servant, accompanied by two guards, into Iconium to purchase some of the luscious fruits for which the city was known. While there, the men heard shocking news: the Seljuk Turks had attacked and taken Caesarea, Cappadocia's provincial capital.

Rugged, desolate terrain lay between Caesarea and Iconium. Heading directly east toward Baghdad, they would not pass near Caesarea. However, to satisfy Najila's request for the cross, he would have to veer dangerously close to the battle zone. He disliked putting his men at risk, men he had handpicked for their bravery and fighting skill, good soldiers who also were his comrades.

Recalling how an angry and bitter Najila had turned the lovely cross over to the priest after her father had perished in the slide, Otrygg shook his head. "Najila, Najila," he muttered. "You were such a confused, foolish child to give away so precious an object. And now you want to repossess it. Ah, that my mission might succeed."

Early the next morning, Shafiqa died peacefully without regaining consciousness. Her demise presented Otrygg with a fresh problem: he did not know whether to carry her remains on to Baghdad, bury her by the little creek right where they were, or take her body back to Konstantinoupolis.

Najila naturally would want her grandmother buried in Baghdad, but Otrygg preferred not to continue the trek to Persia in the heat with a decomposing body. Even if he gave up going after the cross and immediately returned to Konstantinoupolis, he would face the same difficulty. If he were to bury Shafiqa here, was it necessary to reveal the details to Najila? He thought not.

The next day, Otrygg had Shafiqa interred under the same willow that had shaded her final hours. If Najila confronted him about it, he would have to tell her the truth.

Now he faced yet another difficult choice. Finding the monk and Michael's cross might mean life or death for the remainder of his small band. Either they returned to Konstantinoupolis without finishing his quest, or traveled to Cappadocia in search of the monk, Gregori.

Otrygg had never broken a promise or shirked a duty. And he would not start now. Irrespective of the Turks and the danger they represented, he would locate the monk for Najila, and recover her father's cherished dragonfly cross.

Chapter 44

Otrygg Harald and his men rode swiftly northeast toward the legendary monastery where Najila thought the monk might be cloistered. The party could now move faster because Shafiqa and Taraneh no longer accompanied them.

Certain that Najila would approve, Otrygg had freed Taraneh from further obligation to the Doukas family. When a silk merchants' caravan paused nearby on its way to Persia, Taraneh had chosen to join it. She had never been branded or marked in any way that revealed her status as a slave, and thus could return to her native country and live as she pleased, serving no master but God.

Otrygg sent Taraneh off with a gift of Shafiqa's clothing and jewels. He was certain that Najila would also sanction this generous act. Had Shafiqa reached Baghdad and died there, it was anybody's guess what would have become of her possessions. Taraneh would have little use for the somber, black mourning garb that Shafiqa had worn for decades, but prudently selling the gems might support her nicely in the future.

Before leaving to join the silk merchants' caravan, the grateful Nubian broke into a flood of tears. Falling to her knees, she tried to kiss Otrygg's feet.

Having none of it, the Viking took her hands and raised her. With exaggerated gruffness, he said, "Go, ere I change my mind."

As her strong, erect figure strode by the flank of a huge camel and was about to disappear from Otrygg's view, she turned and gave him one last wave.

The ascent to central Anatolia took Otrygg's party through rugged high desert terrain that could barely support the sparse vegetation that clung to the eroded, rock hills. Along the way, they skirted small, scattered villages, now ruined and deserted and reeking with the smell of scorched homes and violent death. To the men's dismay, the wells in these villages had deliberately been fouled.

Occasionally, a town remained intact and unharmed, proving that its inhabitants had not resisted a Seljuk takeover. Normally, Otrygg avoided contact with the surviving towns, but with water scarce, he was forced to occasionally lead his men into possible danger to obtain it.

Upon entering these villages, they were taken to the recently appointed headman, the Seljuk ghazi, who usually allowed them to draw water after Otrygg paid him a liberal bribe for the privilege.

At last they arrived at the spectacular valley that Otrygg had heard so much about all his life. The amazed Viking reined his big horse to a standstill at the edge of a steep cliff and gawked at the sight spread before him, a broad plain surrounded by towering, ocher-streaked cliffs. Hundreds of peculiar capped columns, riddled with holes and caves, filled the valley beneath and beyond him.

Descending from the valley's rim on a hazardous, narrow trail, Otrygg marveled that anyone could subsist in such an area. But as he dropped closer to the valley floor, he saw evidence of an extensive and productive population: grazing animals, vines heavy with grapes, and ripening grain fields. Since the Seljuk invasion, times were difficult and strangers were suspect. Few outsiders visited the valley now.

Otrygg spotted an aged and sun-withered man who was hoeing an irrigation trench in a field. "Ho, fellow," Otrygg hailed him. "We go to the monastery. Do we ride in the right direction?"

His face displaying his distrust, the man merely nodded, then quickly stooped and continued to hoe his ditch. Otrygg signaled his men to move forward. The people they approached along the way turned their backs or avoided them by scampering into the fields. The expressions they wore alternated between fear and hostility.

Soon Otrygg and his men came to the entrance of a long canyon, an offshoot from the main road, an eroded gash in the tan-colored, porous volcanic hillside. Seeing two monks walking a path that emerged from the canyon, Otrygg guessed that they belonged to the monastery. Riding slowly up the sloping trail to meet the black-clothed figures, Otrygg placed his hand over his heart, his palm flat against his chest as a sign that he pursued a peaceful mission. He pulled up his horse and greeted the two men in Greek. "I am the Varangian Otrygg Harald. I look for a monk who calls himself Gregori."

After the reception he had received from the local peasants, Otrygg expected the monks to respond in similar fashion. Instead, he found their demeanor quite genial. The younger of the two was hardly more than a boy. Grinning at Otrygg, he puffed out his chest and boasted, "Father Gregori is my mentor. He is the finest artist in the entire world."

The older monk grabbed the sleeve of his companion's cloak, silencing him. "Enough! You are forbidden to speak so forthrightly." Turning to Otrygg, he said, "Please accept my apology for Movses's rude behavior." He again shook the lad's arm. "Why do you seek Father Gregori?"

"I have a message from—" Otrygg hesitated. Should he tell these monks who had sent him? What would happen if he mentioned Najila's name? Would her nobility have credence here?

"From Konstantinoupolis," he finished.

"Perhaps you bear a commission for our Gregori?" the elder monk speculated. Extra funds were always welcome at such an isolated outpost.

"I carry a personal message from a lady with whom the priest is acquainted."

Otrygg noticed a sudden interest that flared in both monks' eyes.

Obviously excited by Otrygg's statement, but with a voice now quieter and more respectful than at first, the apprentice asked, "Do you speak of the lady Najila?"

Otrygg nearly toppled off his steed. Did everyone know Najila? Even a lowly novice who lived in so remote a region? Straightening in his saddle, Otrygg flashed the boy a wide smile. It seemed his quest was about to end. "Yes, my lady Najila sent me on this journey."

"Come! We will take you to Father Gregori." The older monk turned away, beckoning over his shoulder for Otrygg and his party to follow.

Chapter 45

G regori descended the scaffold and stepped back to study the portrayal on which he had been working, a benign angel with its wings extended to protect the Madonna and Christ Child. The angel, almost finished, featured a young woman's face. Because he worked from top to bottom when doing a piece, he had merely outlined the child in charcoal.

According to God's Word, neither male nor female existed in heaven, but Gregori had often wondered, Could an angel not look male or female? The Bible in several places spoke of an angel who appeared as a human. He wasn't personally acquainted with anyone who had actually seen such a supernatural being; it was up to him to render what he believed might resemble one. He remounted the scaffold to dab a bit of red ocher on the angel's upper lip.

"Father Gregori, I have brought someone to see you." The magnificent baritone voice that led their daily chants boomed throughout the hollow cave.

"I know of no visitors due today," Gregori said without looking down at Father Marcus. Though visitors to the monastery had become scarce since the Seljuks had advanced on the region, it still irritated him when his work was interrupted.

"And he knows the lady Najila," shouted the impulsive Movses, Gregori's exuberant apprentice. The boy's excited cry echoed loudly in the bare, rock-walled, high-ceilinged chamber: Najila . . . jila . . . la . . .

Shocked at hearing the precious name of the young woman he thought he'd never see again, Gregori staggered. His arm flailed the air, and the brush flew from his hand. He grabbed at it, missed, lost his balance, and nearly toppled off his perch high above Otrygg's head. The brush plopped into the fine, powdered tufa that blanketed the cave's floor at the Viking's feet.

Blushing because the others had witnessed his awkward bumbling, Gregori descended the scaffold to retrieve the brush. As he bent to get it, he stammered, "Na . . . Nah . . . Najila? You have come from the lady Najila?"

"Indeed. I bring her salutations, Father Gregori."

Gregori straightened and squinted, the better to view the giant who loomed over him. Otrygg's indistinct features undulated in the flickering light thrown by the less than adequate oil lamps. During his lifetime, the monk had seen only one other person who fit the big man's appearance—the Viking who had been Michael Doukas Komnenous's companion and bodyguard before the ambassador was killed in a landslide.

"It is pleasant to see you—" Gregori hesitated. It embarrassed him that he couldn't recall the Viking's name, though it was this same man who had summoned him to minister to Najila after her father's tragic death. "What brings you to the Hidden Valley?"

"I have come a long way to present you with a request from Najila," Otrygg declared.

Gregori had mentioned his secret love only to Movses, once when he had slumped into a particularly maudlin mood. Instantly regretting his weak moment and his failure to maintain the dignity expected of a monk, he had severely cautioned the lad never to repeat what he had been told. The name Najila had not been spoken by another in Gregori's presence since the Persian princess had thrust her father's silver and amber cross upon him.

Now, Gregori found it hard to speak, and Otrygg's huge bulk became blurry. Taking control of his emotions with difficulty, the monk finally answered, "You commanded Lord Komne-nous's guards." Gaining courage, he then added, "And, how . . . er, how is the lady Najila?"

"My lady enjoys excellent health and is firmly settled on her estate near Konstantinoupolis."

As he spoke, Otrygg casually scanned the mural on which Gregori had been painting. He suddenly uttered a surprised exclamation. Moving closer, he tilted his chin upward to better examine it. "You have done her portrait. There!" he said with an amazed expression, pointing to the angel.

The Viking spun around to scan the walls and ceiling of the virtually completed chapel, for the excavated cave had become a small church. "And there! And there, too!" he cried.

Every female represented in the paintings was an image of Najila: the slightly upturned eyes and arched brows, the full lips, the aquiline nose, even her smile. The Madonna and the angel bore similar characteristics.

Otrygg turned back to the little monk. "I see you remember the lady well. She will be honored when I describe to her your beautiful creations."

"No! You must not tell her," Gregori protested, horrified. He glanced guiltily at the puzzled senior monk, Father Marcus, who hadn't the slightest inkling as to the reason for Gregori's discomfort.

Then Gregori had an appalling thought. *Have I unconsciously committed a sacrilege by giving the holy ones the face of a living person?* Calming himself, he recalled that artist monks had long used local peasants as models. Having thus convinced himself that his renderings were harmless, he emitted a huge sigh. At last, curiosity replaced apprehension. He asked, "Why did the lady Najila send you to see me?"

"She asks that her father's cross be returned to her."

The monk blanched, thankful that Otrygg could not notice this due to the meager light. "I no longer possess the cross," Gregori mumbled.

"Eh? What did you say? I could not hear." Otrygg drew nearer to Gregori.

"I no longer have the cross," Gregori repeated.

Otrygg stepped back. "Where is it? Can you get it for me?"

"The cross and other monastery treasures, along with artifacts from Noah's ark, were secretly cached when the Seljuk threat first appeared," Gregori explained.

Father Marcus entered the conversation. "The cross lies buried deep underground with our Hidden Valley relics, where the Seljuk heathens will never find them."

Closing his eyes, Otrygg threw back his head and exhaled an explosion of air. He glared down at the two monks. "Tell me where it is!"

"By my oath to God, I cannot reveal its location to a soul. Not even Princess Najila herself would I tell," Gregori said.

Otrygg groaned. He wanted to shake the rotund monk until the answer spewed from his mouth, but he checked the urge. "Well, so be it, Father Gregori. I suppose I have done all that is possible to obtain the cross for her."

On observing Gregori's crestfallen countenance, Otrygg's anger diminished, and his tone softened. "I do believe that our lady Najila will appreciate the fact that her father's cross is in a safe place."

Turning to Father Marcus, Otrygg said, "My men and I are hungry and weary. May we spend the night here? At the monastery?"

"Of course. The Hidden Valley Monastery always offers food and lodging to travelers," answered the senior monk. "Follow me. I will show you to our guest quarters."

Instead of remaining behind and returning to his painting, Gregori followed the others. When Otrygg was free to talk, Gregori discreetly pumped him for information regarding Najila. Otrygg soon realized that Father Gregori adored Najila as much as he himself did. Otrygg felt only sympathy for the lonely monk, who would never again see the one whom he apparently loved. At least, if Otrygg wished to, he could be with Najila every day for the rest of his life. The thought, however, did little to console him. Her heart belonged to another man.

Chapter 46

As she often did after Loukios had sailed for Spain, Najila came alone to the tiny private garden next to the stables at eventide to pray for him. An October cold front had moved down from the north, so she wore a hooded cape over a woolen dress. Still, she shivered a bit as a crisp breeze began to blow in off the Sea of Marmara.

She had been depressed all day. Neither the musical fountain, nor the neatly trimmed foliage did much to improve her disconsolate mood. She stood by a weathered, waist-high sundial that had been carved out of a single, pink-veined marble slab. While the sun's last, half-sphere remnant sank below the horizon, she dreamily fingered the bronze rod that protruded upward from the sundial's concave bowl. The rod's shadow, falling on one of twelve etched lines that radiated around the center point, marked the hour. Her mind in faraway Spain, she paid it little heed.

The motion of something at her feet, reflecting the sun's orange-red glow, caught her attention. Bending to see what it was, she spotted a small turtle. The sun had glanced off its shell as, creeping from plant to plant, it nibbled on the tenderest parts. Enchanted, she watched the reptile steadfastly munch a leaf, its lower jaw laboriously grinding each bite. Time crawls like the turtle. Much too slowly, she mused, her eyes on the fading sunset.

It had been seven weeks and three days since Loukios had left Hawks Hill. He and Otrygg traveled in opposite directions, each intent on his own quest. She missed them both. Terribly. She missed Otrygg for his stalwart presence and faithful protection, and Loukios for . . . well, she missed Loukios for more reasons than she could name.

It was here, in this garden where they had first kissed, that Najila felt closest to him. Her fingers traced a line within the sundial's shallow bowl. "Come home soon, my love," she whispered as the bright evening star appeared in the darkening sky. *Does Loukas watch the same star?* she wondered.

When the sundial's rod no longer cast a shadow, she knew that she must return to the manse while there was still enough twilight for her to see her way. Emitting a great yearning sigh, she turned, preparing to leave through the iron gate. The sound of a displaced rock, possibly stirred by someone's foot, stopped her in her tracks. Though she could see no one nearby, she sensed she was no longer alone.

Thinking it must be Elias, the young groom, who would venture into the garden, Najila called out softly, "Why are you here so late, Elias? Is there a problem with one of the horses?"

A hulking form, silent and indistinct in the dull light, suddenly loomed in front of her, blocking her path. Before she had a chance to react, the form lurched forward and flung a thick cloth over her head. The fabric reeked of mold, decay, and other undecipherable odors. Gagging, Najila clawed at the putrid, smothering rag until she wrenched it out of her attacker's hand and threw it to the ground.

Uttering a rude curse, the man quickly stooped to retrieve the cloth, meanwhile easing his grip on her arm. She jerked her arm loose and started to flee, but another man grabbed both arms and held them tightly at her sides. "If you cease struggling, things will go better for you," the second assailant snarled in her ear.

Najila didn't recognize either voice. Terrified, she fought anew, screaming desperately for help, but no one was near enough to hear her pitiful cries.

For an instant, she was again free of the grasping hands. Run! her mind silently wailed.

Though her feet did her bidding, she tripped over her trailing gown. As she strove to retain her balance, and before she could utter another desperate cry, a hard object struck her on the back of the head.

Brilliantly colored streaks and speckles flashed behind her eyes, followed by intense pain and then utter darkness.

Chapter 47

The first of Najila's senses to reawaken was her sense of smell. Even before she lifted her heavy eyelids, her nostrils shrank from the musty air that stank of decay and things long neglected. She gradually opened her eyes to a blackness so dense that it offered not a clue as to whether the hour was day or night.

She was lying on her back, her arms and legs askew as if someone had carelessly dropped her like a sack of old rags. She cautiously tested each limb; her sore joints and bruises verified that she had been treated less than gently.

Where am I? Sitting upright, she moaned as a sudden wave of pain lanced the spot at the base of her skull where it had been struck. The slightest movement caused dizziness and nausea.

Feeling into the darkness around her, she reached out until her hand struck a hard vertical barrier. Her entire body trembling, she slowly stood and blindly turned in place. Tracing the wall's stony surface with her fingers, she felt damp, chiseled blocks. Cold, slimy rock!

Letting her fingers trace her immediate surroundings, and taking advantage of her dark-enhanced senses, she determined that her bed was a foul-smelling pallet of rancid straw. She could hear water lapping over stone. Again resting a hand on the wall for balance, she moved carefully along until she came to a corner. Shifting her feet, she continued her exploration and soon discovered a massive, ironclad door. Wherever she was, it was solid and secure.

The door had no handle, but by running her hands up the rot-softened planks, Najila used her fingers to outline a tiny aperture near the door's center that was covered by a sliding panel. The panel was loose, and she managed to slide it open.

Tilting her head, Najila looked out the opening with one eye. A bluish glow illuminated what appeared to be a narrow corridor. Though the light seemed to flicker, it wasn't the right color for a lantern or a candle. *It must be daylight,* she thought. But the color didn't seem right for that, either.

Trying not to block the meager light that came through the little gap, she stood with her back to the door and peered around the room. Besides the pallet, she was able to discern the outlines of a battered chamber pot and a pitcher. Water dripped from a corroded pipe into a rank trough of some kind, and then overflowed into a hole in the floor.

A rush of claustrophobic terror overwhelmed her. She began to shiver uncontrollably. "Dear Allah . . . Almighty God," she cried, sinking to her knees, "I am in prison.

"Loukas, help me!"

By coincidence, both Loukios and Otrygg returned to Konstantinoupolis on the same October day.

Loukios, excited and triumphant, proudly led his beautiful pair of horses from the west-side wharves, along the crowded streets, and toward the western walls. Though their velvety winter coats had begun to grow, they were yet glossy and showed their fine breeding.

The mare and filly were full of spirit following a week's confinement aboard the ship after the vessel had left its last port of call. They jigged and pranced, giving Loukios and Masoud an almighty workout with their hijinks. Despite having to keep

Argyrea under control, Masoud had great difficulty keeping his eyes on her; his attention was constantly drawn to the fascinating sights around him. He had been pleased to accompany Loukios to his home, having always dreamed of seeing the fabled city of Konstantinoupolis.

Loukios half expected the crowds along the streets to curse the frisky mare and filly for their skittish, unpredictable behavior, but instead the horses drew admiring stares and comments from everyone. Any person in danger of being trampled obligingly dodged to the road's edge. Loukios shuddered and yanked hard on Argyrea's lead when she kicked out at a boy who ran to pet her, but the child's mother merely tugged her son out of harm's way, saying, "He should not have startled the little horse."

As Loukios approached the western walls, Otrygg's small party of warriors entered the eastern gate. Unlike Loukios, the Viking experienced no joy in his homecoming; he did not know how to tell Najila that her grandmother had not lived to see her family residence in Baghdad, that she had died somewhere on the Anatolian Plain and was buried there. And he didn't know how to give Najila the disappointing news that he had been unable to retrieve her father's cross.

Talking to himself a good part of the way to Hawks Hill, Otrygg practiced his homecoming speech, the excuses he would give Najila. He needn't have worried. Najila was no longer at Hawks Hill to receive him—or Loukios.

Chapter 48

Morning found Zahra cleaning Najila's suite for the fourth time in as many days. The work provided a measure of nervous release. Most of all, keeping busy while surrounded by Najila's possessions made the girl feel near. But fear for Najila had taken its toll on Zahra: new worry lines etched her forehead and large purplish circles underscored her lower lids.

She listlessly fingered Najila's favorite dress, a lovely emerald green ball gown, remembering the last occasion on which Najila had worn it, at a Hawks Hill birthday celebration in her honor. It hung now amidst a dozen others in a mothproof, cedar-lined annex built especially to house them.

After one final check around the windowless wardrobe room, Zahra snuffed the pair of wall sconces and quietly shut the door between the two rooms; then she collapsed into Najila's chair by the bedroom window.

"Where are you, Najila?" Zahra wept. She had simply vanished. Only the clothes she was wearing when she disappeared, twelve days past, were gone. As far as Zahra could tell, not a single item more was missing.

Numb with gloom, Zahra sat staring at nothing. She started when she heard hoofbeats pounding up Hawks Hill's drive. Leaning out across the windowsill, she saw a troop of horsemen approaching at a canter. Certain that they came with tidings of Najila, she ran from the room, dashed downstairs to the mansion's entrance, and flung open the door.

She should have been glad to see Otrygg and his men, delighted to know that they had returned home safely. Instead, her emotions were mixed. It was Najila she wanted to see riding up to the mansion. Then, Zahra had a consoling thought. Now she would have Otrygg's support and no longer have to face everything alone.

Zahra ran to Otrygg as he dismounted, her cheeks wet with tears. "Najila is gone," she cried. "No one knows where she is."

"What?" the Viking exclaimed, not quite understanding Zahra's rapid, jumbled words.

Zahra threw herself at Otrygg, and he automatically dropped the reins to catch her. A bit shocked that the habitually dignified Zahra would approach him with such familiarity, Otrygg stepped back, putting her at arm's length. "Do you say that Najila is not here?"

"She is just gone, Master Otrygg," Zahra repeated, her voice hoarse from crying.

"Gone where? When did you last see her?" the Viking yelled, almost deafening poor Zahra, who reacted to his incredulous bellow by stuttering only incomprehensible syllables.

Impatient for details, wanting to instantly force them out of her, Otrygg grabbed Zahra's trembling shoulders. He managed to say calmly, "I beg you, Lady Zahra, be at ease. Tell me, what happened to Najila while I was absent?" Sensing Zahra's despair, he drew her closer and gently embraced her.

As Otrygg's massive arms encircled and comforted her, Zahra's words finally began to make sense.

"Twelve days ago, Najila was last glimpsed walking toward the stable garden as the sun was descending," she explained. "There has been no trace of her since, though we have searched everywhere."

"Did she go riding? Are any horses missing? Tell me," he demanded. The vision of Najila lying injured somewhere sickened Otrygg.

Zahra shook her head. "I have been told that every animal is here, including Najila's black mare, Jahara. Najila usually has Elias saddle the horses she rides. He claims, however, that he had not prepared a horse for her that day."

Exhausted by stress and lack of sleep, Zahra again slumped against Otrygg. He instinctively tightened his hold on her to prevent her from falling.

"Lady Zahra?"

When there was no response, Otrygg gathered up the woman's slender form and carried her inside. As he entered the great circular rotunda, Hawks Hill's maids fluttered around him like courting butterflies. Otrygg didn't hesitate a moment but quickly carried Zahra to her quarters, which were next to Najila's. They were followed by the whispering and tittering maids.

As Otrygg bent to lay Zahra carefully on her pallet, a commotion sounded in the courtyard. Leaving Zahra in the maids' capable care, he strode in three swift strides to the window. Below, Loukios Alexander was dismounting from an unfamiliar, extremely fine mare. A stranger, an Arab by his raiment, clutched the leads of an equally beautiful filly and a heavily loaded donkey.

Otrygg spun on his heel and rushed to meet Loukios.

"Ho! Otrygg Harald! Alas, you won the race to get home. How goes it with you?" Loukios's huge grin changed to a puzzled frown when he saw the big Viking's ominous expression.

"According to Zahra, Najila disappeared from Hawks Hill twelve days ago," Otrygg shouted as he approached. "Zahra says she has not been seen since."

Loukios paled, a chill crinkling his scalp. "God's crown! Do you think my father would actually . . . kidnap her . . . murder . . . ? Surely not!"

Otrygg nodded vigorously. "What else could have happened? I believe that Leopold carried through his threat when no one was here to stop him. Let us pray that he merely kidnapped Lady Najila and has not killed her."

"We must find her!" Loukios declared, throwing his arms wide. At the motion, his tunic suddenly heaved and bulged. Loukios thrust the mare's reins at Masoud so he could use both hands to unfasten the tunic's top buckle. A very small, shaggy white head with beady eyes popped out of the gapping tunic. Spotting the giant Viking looming above, the puppy bared its milk teeth and uttered a brave if tiny, "Yip!"

"I bought the dog for Najila," Loukios explained.

"You call that a *dog?*" Otrygg scoffed. He gingerly reached out to touch the pup's nose and promptly received a nip on the tip of his thumb. "I have to say, the nasty little beast has spunk," he muttered, sucking his thumb and looking ridiculous. "Dogs dislike me, and I them. What heathen Iberian persuaded you to carry such a miserable, flea-bitten creature across two seas?"

In spite of his concern about Najila, Loukios had to laugh at Otrygg's barefaced disgust. "This 'creature' is from Malta. The breed is quite popular with the Spanish nobility, they say. When I saw it at the Seville horse fair, I realized that the brute I gave Najila ere I departed is not exactly a gentlewoman's pet. This dog is far more suitable."

Mentioning Najila's name jolted Loukios back to reality. He would not let himself think of the most appalling scenario, that his precious Najila could be dead.

Loukios dropped the pup to the ground, where it immediately squatted. After relieving itself, it frantically tore around, its whiskered muzzle pressed to the earth to better absorb Hawks Hill's delicious smells.

✝

Later, Loukios paced while Otrygg sat in front of a fire newly laid in the main dining hall. Normally excluded from the men's private discussions, Zahra, now fully recovered from her swoon, perched on a bench.

"Have you questioned the servants and the stablemen, Zahra?" Loukios asked.

"Yes, of course. I did that very first thing. But if someone knows something, it is likely the person would willingly give the information to you rather than to me, Lord Loukios. Because, well . . . because they consider me a servant, too," she added without malice.

"My primary goal is to examine the staff thoroughly myself," Loukios said. "A piece of the answer may be found there, whether or not any one of them is aware of the fact."

"And I will ride to the palace tonight," Otrygg announced.

"No!" Loukios stated. "Tonight we make additional inquiries here. Tomorrow at dawn, you and I will go to the city together."

Otrygg grunted. "You are absolutely right, Loukios. We should find out what is known here at Hawks Hill."

"Yes. Then we must go to the palace as you suggest and tell Julian what has happened. Anything occurring within the empire, no matter how trivial, is known to almost everyone connected to the palace. Nothing gets by the court." Loukios smiled ruefully. "For once, rumor may be a good thing."

Chapter 49

Unusually quiet, Loukios, Otrygg, and Julian sat in the eunuch's comfortable palace suite, each man contemplating his own disturbing thoughts. The investigation at Hawks Hill had turned up empty, and Julian's discreet inquiries among the courtiers had not revealed so much as a hint of Najila's whereabouts.

The trio waited until a servant finished pouring wine for Loukios and Julian, and for Otrygg the honey-flavored mead favored by his ancestors. Julian spoke first, breaking the silence. "Do you deny that Leopold Alexander is capable of murder, Loukios? I think he is.

"There was quite a scandal when your mother died; the cause of her death is still a mystery. He lived with her for many years, yet he never married her. You were too young to remember, of course. Poison was suspected, but never proven. Though you, Loukios, are considered Leopold Alexander's ba—" Julian abruptly stopped when he realized what he was about to say.

Loukios was long past taking offense at comments about his birth, especially by one as unassuming as Julian, a longtime family advisor who always had been forthright and reliable. "Be not afraid to speak the truth, Julian. I am, after all, his illegitimate son. I have no doubt that my father has planted his seed widely throughout Byzantium. Nevertheless, I am his only acknowledged heir; he has personally assured me of it."

"Exactly!" Julian exclaimed.

Loukios's eyes suddenly widened. "Are you saying that I am also in jeopardy? I know my father cares for me. In his own way, he loves me. I cannot accept that he would destroy me or the woman I love, because if he did destroy her, it would destroy me."

"What of his close companions?" Otrygg barked. "Do they not cater to his demands?"

Loukios flashed Julian and Otrygg a crooked half smile. "I think I am acquainted with every simpering member of his alliance. I would never trust a one of them when it comes to political matters, but I cannot imagine any of them willingly killing a girl who is personally of no threat. Word of such a deed would speedily get back to court. Those who surround my father are like sheep. They are followers, not killers. I doubt they would commit murder, even for their lord, my father. No one wants to be shunned by the throne."

Otrygg shrugged, shaking his head. "Rarely is a female done in, but it does happen, Loukios. Do recall Byzantium's brutal history. Its nobles are noted for eliminating their rivals."

"My blood lacks official nobility," Loukios reminded them.

Julian waved a dismissive hand. "Humph! Small difference. The emperor is God's representative, and God supposedly speaks to him, yet emperor after emperor is assassinated. What chance has a less-esteemed man or woman? I feel that our Najila is in mortal danger."

"I am fully aware that greed's hard shell encloses my father's heart, but I will again attempt to clarify why I do not think he would slay either of us. Leopold Alexander Doukas is too vain, too clever a man to hazard the unwelcome notoriety that such an assassination would bring him. Besides, what would he gain? I mean, by slaughtering me? I have nothing he values."

"Ah! You are wrong, Loukios. Najila has the title and fortune he obviously craves. If you marry her, you will be at risk, too. Believe it!" Otrygg bellowed.

"That may be true. Still, I refuse to accuse my father of so grievous an act until definite proof is given me."

"Loukios, we know that Leopold has already threatened Najila with death," Julian interceded.

"Lady Zahra knows this, too," Otrygg added.

"Yes. Lady Zahra also knows. But none of us has mentioned it to anyone else," Julian said. "Is it not time we let it be publicly advertised that Leopold is a menace to Najila, Loukios? Perhaps to you as well? Those most loyal to you should be told. Explain this miserable situation to them before he does do something serious. I pray to God that he has not done it already."

Jabbing an index finger at his chest Loukios declared, "Najila is alive. I sense it. Here. Inside."

Julian's voice softened. Leaning across the table, he patted Loukios's wrist. "She will be found, my dear friend."

Najila had seen no one since her internment. Few sounds penetrated the thick stone walls. All she heard was the constant lapping of water, a rhythmic background to her own breathing. Thankfully, her captors had left her hooded cloak, which offered a barely effective barrier to the cell's damp chill. Her only relief during the endless, lonely hours came when, twice a day, a faceless phantom shoved a bowl of watery gruel through the cell door's small portal.

As bad as the food was, she began looking forward to those brief breaks when she thrust her bowl out the opening for a ration. The portions were tasteless, insufficient in nourishment, and scarcely enough to keep her alive. Quality did not matter; she had little appetite.

She despised herself: hated her tangled hair; her lice-infected, itching scalp; the stench of her unwashed body. The awful smell of the overflowing chamber pot nauseated her. Why did somebody not come to empty it? Was anyone searching for her? If she were not soon rescued, she would go mad.

Suddenly, she heard a different sound. Someone was coming. It was the first time since her incarceration that she had heard a human voice. Now there were two voices, and she recognized one of them. Leopold Alexander Doukas!

As the men neared her cell, their words became clearer. Apparently, they were unaware of the place's acoustics, or they did it deliberately, because Najila could understand every terrifying syllable. They were planning to hold her prisoner indefinitely—to hold her prisoner forever.

Najila scuttled along the cell's slimy floor to her filthy pallet. Trembling like a cornered rabbit, she crouched against the dank wall and sobbed.

Chapter 50

"The Varangian Guard has been alerted to keep their eyes and ears open for any hint of Najila or her whereabouts," Otrygg reported when he met with Loukios and Julian that evening.

"I scouted the grounds again, but found no sign of her," Loukios added. "Those I questioned knew nothing, or did not admit it if they did."

Julian stood near the huge fireplace, warming his pudgy hands. He had attended an important court function during the day. The gilt and jewels that adorned his official robes glittered in the fire's flickering light. "I may have learned something of value," he said. "There is a rumor going round that a crazy woman is imprisoned in the cistern under the palace. Slaves who clean the walkways hear her cries."

As one, Otrygg and Loukios sprang to their feet. Loukios reached the fireplace in a single stride, grabbed Julian none too gently, and spun him around. "Can you find out which slaves heard her?"

Otrygg stood with clenched fists. "It has to be Najila!"

Julian shrugged. "I do not know. I am merely repeating what I heard from others, not from the slaves themselves. Loukios, I pray that it is Najila down there, but we have no way of knowing if the rumor is even based on truth."

"Tonight, Julian!" Loukios began to pace the room, his footfalls muffled by the thick oriental carpets. "We have to search the cistern tonight. If it truly is Najila, she has been there almost a fortnight. We cannot leave her another minute." He clawed through his hair in frustration.

Otrygg draped his arm across Loukios's tense shoulders. "I agree. We must at least take a look."

Julian nodded. "The underground reservoir is large, and it is absolutely dark in places. It can be dangerous, especially at night when no illumination comes in through the ventilation slots. But allow me to change out of this finery, and I will gather torches for our foray into that forbidding place."

Long after Leopold Alexander Doukas and his coconspirator left, Najila huddled in the corner. One part of her floated above her body, the rest remained on the pallet. She was aware of her surroundings but drifted in and out of a nightmarish, semi-stuporous state.

When she recovered her wits, she rose laboriously from her cramped position. Her joints were stiff, and she moved awkwardly, like an old arthritic. *I will not allow him to do this to me.* She stretched her arms and stamped her feet to increase circulation. "I simply cannot," she moaned. "Allah, please keep me sane."

Fighting the miasmic condition her mind sought to reenter, she continued to pray and exercise. When her limbs stopped tingling, she once again began to trace the cell's perimeter by cautiously brushing a guiding hand along the wall. Her single focus: find a way to escape.

Groping blindly in the absolute darkness, Najila came to an area she had not thoroughly explored. She almost fell when she stumbled over something lying on the floor. Stooping, her fingers gingerly probing, she touched a long curved object. As she lifted it, she heard a brittle rattling. Where the floor met the wall, she found more of the same pieces. They felt like wood or pottery. Searching further, her hand closed around a large sphere. When her fingers slid over protuberances, slipped into a hole, then into other holes, the thing's overall shape became clear. Recognizing what it was, she flung it down. Whimpering, she scurried toward her pallet on all fours like a crab scuttling to safety amid the pilings of a wharf. Her cellmate was an ancient, moldy skeleton.

Several hours later, or so it seemed to her sensory-deprived mind, as she was finishing a measure of cold, runny gruel, she heard a dry scratching on the cell door. As she listened with heightened awareness, the scratching progressed upward to the aperture and stopped.

Standing slowly, Najila set the half-empty bowl onto the straw pallet and quietly made her way to the door. Digging with her broken nails at the panel that covered the small window, she was able to slide it slightly open. In the dim light, a grotesque silhouette outside suddenly appeared. Uttering a piercing scream, Najila reeled backward.

A rat, the size of a small cat, hovered in the opening. The rodent had not managed to penetrate the cell's closely fitted stones, but the faint odor of food had filtered through the cracks in the door jamb and drifted into its den. Whiskers twitching eagerly, the rodent had followed the scent. Scrambling up the door, it now perched on the sill of the open aperture, its body filling the space and blocking the corridor's bluish light.

When Najila realized that what she saw was merely an animal—though a detestable one—her fear was replaced by a determination to prevent it from invading her territory. She lunged forward, fists clenched. As the rat put its front paws at the aperture's edge, preparing to clamber down the inside of the door, Najila knocked it, screeching and clawing, off the frame.

✝

Glancing neither to the right nor the left, the old deaf mute shuffled along the tunnel that led away from Najila's cell, located in an isolated niche of the vast underground cistern. He carried a sputtering torch and an empty pail. The man who paid him a pittance to take meals to the remote cell twice a day had explained to him, through gestures, that the occupant was mad. In his endeavor to communicate, the man performed a weird dance, circling an index finger at his temple to imply that the cell's inhabitant was a demented being. The deaf mute wisely, but with much difficulty, hid his amusement at the fat man's contortions.

The old man remembered the first day he had fed the woman. Her pale, delicate hand protruded through the door's window to clutch the chipped ceramic bowl he offered. He noted the soft white skin, the well-cared-for nails. He had also spotted a magnificent ring with a large cabochon emerald enhanced by faceted rubies on the woman's middle finger.

All that night, the slave had pondered the incongruity of an incarcerated madwoman wearing such a valuable bauble. The next morning while ladling gruel, he had none too gently grabbed her wrist before she could take the bowl. Brutally pulling her hand farther through the opening, he had yanked off the ring and palmed it. He experienced no guilt. The ring was there. Its wearer didn't need it. He did.

As the days passed, the woman's hands had become black with grime, the nails ragged and clogged with dirt. Trapped in his silent world, the deaf mute could not hear Najila's pleas for help.

✝

The deaf mute politely lowered his eyes as three men holding torches approached. *How strange,* he thought. *They are too richly clothed to be water inspectors. And why are they here at night?*

A giant of a man, his face contorted with anger, seized the slave's arm and shouted something.

The deaf mute grinned and shook his head to show he didn't understand. Again, the big man shouted something, this time thrusting his face toward him.

Loukios tapped Otrygg's arm. "He cannot hear you. Let me try something." With questioning brows, Loukios touched his ear, then his lips, and pointed to the deaf mute's toothless mouth. The man nodded vigorously and started to leave. When Otrygg moved to stop him, Loukios said, "Let him go, Otrygg. We will find her without him."

"Did you notice the bucket?" Julian asked. "It contained food scraps. He must have delivered a meal to someone."

A shrill scream pierced the corridor ahead. For the briefest moment, the three men stared at one another. Najila! Thrusting their torches high, they raced toward the sound. As they rounded a corner and entered the connecting hallway, they saw a gigantic rat fly through the air, thud against the opposite wall, and fall to the floor.

A muffled, unladylike curse followed the rat's flight. "Stay away from me, you filthy creature!"

"Our precious Lord, that is Najila!" Loukios bellowed. He and Otrygg leaped to the door from whence the rat had flown.

Trembling in anticipation, Loukios unlatched the heavy, ancient, warped door. It squealed and squeaked as they tugged it open.

As soon as the gap widened, Najila flung herself into Loukios's arms. Unmindful of her strong odor and the vermin in her hair, Loukios hugged and kissed her until she begged for the chance to catch her breath.

Book Two

Chapter 51

Loukios drew Najila closer. A week had passed since her rescue, and she looked much better, having regained a bit of the weight she had lost. Her repeatedly washed hair again shone with copper highlights in the setting sun.

Hand in hand, they stood together in the Hawks Hill stable garden where her abductors had attacked her. Loukios held her tightly, his face buried in her hair as if he could never bear to release her. "I love you, Najila," he murmured. "When I imagined that you might have been murdered, I also wanted to die."

"I knew you would come for me, Loukas," Najila said, trying not to relive her capture. With Loukios she was safe. She thought she'd never have the courage to return alone to the garden. Besides, Loukios would worry should she ever dare to do so.

"My love for you and the faith that you would eventually rescue me are what kept me from going insane," she told him.

"We have Otrygg and Julian to thank. If it were not for their aid, you might never have been found."

"There is yet another we have to thank, Loukas."

"Who? Zahra could not have helped much."

"Not Zahra, Loukas. While I was down in that terrible place, during my lowest moment, there came to me a spirit."

Loukios treated her comment lightly. "Perhaps you were dreaming. Anybody might do so under the same circumstances."

It embarrassed her to tell him what had happened; he would think her truly mad. She bravely continued. "But Loukas, he was as real as you are standing there before me. He even spoke to me."

"Spoke to you? A supernatural being?" Loukios raised a dubious eyebrow. "What did it say?"

"He said, 'Believe in me!' Oh dearest Loukas, he was surrounded by a golden light, and I felt the most glorious sensation of peace and goodness in his presence." Feeling the skin of her arms tingling at the memory, she began to rub them.

Loukios simply stared at her. "It must have been Jesus Christ," he whispered, awestruck by the thought. "Else why would he have said, 'Believe in me'?"

"I do not know why, Loukas." She remembered that his robe was such a shining white, that he was so beautiful and brilliant she could hardly keep her eyes on him. She lowered her chin and mumbled, "I am finally beginning to believe what I have been told all along. I mean, what you and the monk Gregori told me about Jesus the Son of God and about the Holy Spirit." She gazed up at Loukios, biting her lip. "I want to learn more about them all."

"All?"

"Yes, all! Your three Gods. I am so confused. The Jews, Christians, and Muslims alike are called the people of the Book, are they not? But what is the difference between my one God, Allah, the Jews' one God, Jehovah, and the Christians' three Gods? Do you understand what I mean, Loukas?"

"Not three Gods, Najila." Sighing, Loukios shut his eyes, pondering how he could explain it to her. At last, he said, "They are all one. We call them the Trinity."

"I will try to understand that concept, Loukas, but I do believe in the prophet Jesus." Her face was radiant.

"Yes, when Jesus was born as a mortal man, he did become a prophet. But more importantly, he is the Son of God. Saint John wrote, 'For God so loved the world that he gave his one and only Son, that whoever believes in him shall not perish but have eternal life.'"[1]

"I have seen him. He told me to believe in him, and I do.

"You cannot guess how happy it makes me to hear you say those exact words, darling Najila. By that statement, you solve a problem I have fretted over since we became betrothed. In fact, I once considered withdrawing my proposal due to the futility of trying to convince you."

Stepping away from him, Najila paled, tears glistening in her eyes. "Not marry me? Why?"

"Until you accepted Jesus, understood that he died for us, and you were baptized in the Orthodox faith," Loukios said, counting the three points on his fingers, "we could not wed within the church. It is the law."

Loukios gently held Najila's shoulders and peered deeply into her eyes, as if looking into her very soul. "I want to hear it. Say it again. From your heart. For me." He then shook his head. "No! Not for me, for yourself. Do you accept Jesus as the Son of God, the Savior who died for your sins?"

Najila did not hesitate. "I do, Loukas. I truly do!"

Loukios threw back his head. "Praise be to God!" he shouted, declaring his joy to heaven.

Chapter 52

In no time, Najila fully recovered from her ordeal in the underground cistern. As her condition improved, so did her vigor and ambition. She had always been healthy. Now, because of her participation in outside activities, she was more robust than most women of her class. Regaining the weight she had lost took longer; she didn't have a large appetite, and her activities used up the food she ate as quickly as she consumed it.

After Loukios rescued Najila and returned her safely to Hawks Hill, he deliberately avoided contact with his father. He still sought proof, however, that Leopold Alexander was behind Najila's abduction. Despite his efforts, and those of Otrygg and Julian, no incriminating information could be unearthed. If his father had been involved, he had thoroughly covered his tracks.

Desperately cautious when it came to Najila's welfare, Loukios turned possessive, urging her with sharp words to stay inside the manse, and above all, never again to venture out by herself.

Though her dreadful experience had not made her timid nor intensified her fear of Leopold Alexander Doukas, she wanted to please Loukios. Therefore, she gave up riding solo and took Zahra along as her chaperone whenever she left the estate. Her life became like that of every Byzantine female of her station: cloistered, mundane, and to Najila, emphatically boring.

"I hate sewing, but I suppose it is necessary," Najila complained to Zahra one day. "I prefer to be at the stables or riding Jahara." They sat in Najila's quarters, concentrating on executing exquisite needlework pieces for Najila's wedding chest. She and Loukios were without parents who would normally exchange traditional gifts. Nevertheless, Najila was determined to bring a proper dowry to her upcoming marriage.

The wintry afternoon sun slanted its rays through the window glass, and the two women enjoyed its meager warmth. Not lifting her eyes off her stitching, Zahra lectured Najila on Byzantine customs and traditions. "You are expected to attend church with Loukios once you have been baptized. It is also understood that you will play a prominent role in various celebrations, especially religious ones. When you are officially betrothed, you should not be seen in public alone."

Najila's lips tightened, and she mumbled, "As if I did not already know that!"

"And"—a corner of Zahra's mouth twitched—"lately I have been hearing harsher comments concerning you two. Regardless of words Loukios speaks to the contrary, you and he are constantly together without a chaperone."

"I do not care what others say, Zahra. You sound like my grandmother, Allah bless her soul."

Zahra ignored Najila's protestations. "A person of your position must pay heed to what is said," she calmly continued as if there had been no interruption. "Since we arrived here, I have tried to learn all rules regarding your title. For example, a Byzantine lady should only be seen in church, at the baths, attending specific festivals, and visiting the home of a relative," Zahra said. "In many ways, the Byzantines restrict women more than we Persians do," she added, to Najila's growing irritation.

Najila threw down her needlework and stalked to the window. Hands on hips, she spun to face Zahra. "I cannot tolerate being housebound."

"You never have had much patience. When you and Loukios are married, it will be different. Yes, you still must live within restrictions. But think about it, Najila. Loukios can then escort you to places to which you were previously forbidden to go, and incidentally, you will be gaining certain privileges. Meanwhile, you have to obey the law and perform actions that are socially acceptable."

"At least I am choosing my own husband," Najila snapped. "Having no parents to arrange a match suits me well." But a bitter note underlined Najila's statement. Though she remembered little of her mother, she wished both her parents were alive to witness her vows with Loukios.

Zahra emitted a soft cackle. "I could find you a matchmaker," she suggested.

Najila's skin crawled at the idea. "Zahra, how dare you even say such a thing. I love Loukas. I look at no other man."

Catching Najila's indignant tone, Zahra laughed. "I am merely teasing you. Loukios is the perfect mate for you. I am sure there is nobody in Byzantium more suitable."

Zahra recalled just how relieved she had been when Loukios had assumed the entire responsibility of controlling Najila. Since he had, her own life had grown increasingly peaceful.

"Truly," Zahra said, pausing a beat, "you are quite fortunate to have had as fine a gentleman as Lord Loukios court you. Listen to the sad story I recently heard at the baths."

That caught Najila's attention. Zahra's gossip was always interesting, unless, of course, the talk involved Loukios and her. Anticipating a spicy tale, she swished back to her chair, flopped into it, and picked up the frustrating needlework.

"A few years ago," Zahra began, "a woman, actually a girl of fourteen, disliked the man her father found for her. She refused to marry him, so they sent her to a convent in Macedonia. She is there yet today. A nun!"

Najila shuddered. "I do not intend for that to happen to me." Deep in thought, she remained quiet for a few moments.

"Everyone who is my age is promised or already married. I will not wait any longer. I feel that I am an outcast at court; I fit into no age group. I am getting old!" At twenty, she was considered well into spinsterhood.

"You need not worry," Zahra chuckled. "Use your good sense and God-gifted beauty to win our royal court's acceptance, Najila. When you are wed, you will have as much or more influence there as do other noblewomen. You will fit in everywhere."

Pacified a little, Najila murmured, "Keep reminding me of that fact, Zahra. Chatting with palace aristocracy is not a pastime I relish, but neither do I wish to become a nun."

Chapter 53

Konstantinoupolis, 1071

Holding her two-year-old son, Andreus, Najila peered out the palace apartment window to better observe the turmoil in the street below. Awful news had reached Konstantinoupolis only that morning. Campaigning since spring in an attempt to recapture Seljuk-held Armenian fortresses, Emperor Romanus IV's forces had suffered abject defeat by the ambitious sultan and war leader Muhammed ben Da'ud, renowned as Arp Arslan, the Valiant Lion. Though the Byzantine army was heavily armed and had fought valiantly at Manzikert, the emperor's sixty thousand troops, mostly mercenaries, were overwhelmed by one hundred thousand enemy forces.

All Byzantium feared that Arp Arslan's victory at Manzikert might open Asia Minor to the Turks and further decimate the empire.[1] Where would this dreadful day lead? Shifting Andreus to one arm, Najila rubbed her stomach, fighting to overcome early morning nausea, now compounded by her worry over recent occurrences.

At that moment, tall and handsome Loukios hurried into the room. He kissed the tip of Andreus's pug nose and tenderly brushed a hand over the boy's silky hair. "Rumor has it Romanus IV is alive but has been taken prisoner by Arp Arslan."

Najila shook her head, a touch of sadness souring her welcoming smile. "That information is little more gratifying than we initially heard. I cannot understand Eudokia. First, she summons Romanus IV, a famous general and respected warrior but also a man awaiting execution because of his treason against her former husband's sons. Then, she unexpectedly pardons him and marries him. What was she thinking?"

Loukios playfully nudged Najila. "It is said that he is quite a charmer. Our passionate Eudokia probably needed another man, particularly one of his mettle."

Najila rolled her eyes. "I think she is demented, Loukas. Ever since they wed, Eudokia and Romanus, in a sense, have coruled with Eudokia and Konstantine's three sons, the very same men that Romanus had plotted against. The two sons that Eudokia and Romanus whelped seem to be of no significance."

Loukios shrugged.

"And then Eudokia sends her husband off to war? To get killed? Indeed! What good is that? And how must she feel now that he has been captured?"

Loukios frowned. "I am not so sure it was Eudokia who sent Romanus to the front. I doubt that she was at the bottom of it, anyway. The Doukases, including my father, would like to see Romanus stripped of power and out of the picture."

As a man who strove to live his life as Jesus Christ would have him live it, Loukios struggled to obey God's fifth commandment, "honor thy father and mother." After Najila's kidnapping, he wanted nothing further to do with Leopold Alexander. It had never been proven that his father had participated in the plot, but Loukios believed Najila that she had twice overheard Leopold planning her destruction. He could not help it; he had come to despise his own father.

"Down, Mama! Anda want down!" Little Andreus squirmed to free himself from Najila's restraint. When Najila let the toddler slide to the floor, he instantly ran to straddle Behrooz, the big bloodhound. Unable to pronounce the dog's name properly, Andreus yelled, "Go! Go, Boof!" at the top of his lungs.

As the youngster landed on the dog's back, Behrooz flinched and raised a droopy eyelid. Realizing it was only Andreus tormenting him, he resignedly groaned, closed his eye, and rolled to his side, dislodging his attacker.

"Our son grows heavier every day. I can barely carry him," Najila said, arching her spine, then stooping to plant an affectionate, noisy kiss on Andreus's rosy cheek. "Behrooz mothers him to death; or should I say he 'fathers' him?" They both laughed.

Najila had greatly enjoyed naming the pair of dogs that Loukios had brought home to her. "Their individual names are a bit shy of the bull's-eye" is how Loukios was fond of putting it. She named the hound Behrooz, which in Persian means "lucky" or "hopeful." Loukios thought the name perfectly suited the big dog, "because he's lucky he has us, and he is forever hopeful for food." But Najila insisted the dog was lucky that anyone loved him, "because he looks so forlorn and is so atrociously homely."

The little white Maltese terrier she had named Galen, even though his demeanor was anything but tranquil, which the Greek word implied. He followed Najila everywhere she went, constantly yapping until she picked him up. Tranquil indeed.

Loukios bent to stroke Behrooz, whom he considered his personal pet, though the massive dog seemed to favor Andreus, no matter that the child outrageously mauled him.

Loukios hoisted his delighted son to his shoulder. "Getting back to our discussion, Najila, perhaps Romanus IV was simply bored with court affairs and left of his own volition. He has always been a man of action. Should the Seljuk sultan release him, the Doukas nobles will never allow him to return to Konstantinoupolis or regain any semblance of power."

Najila turned again to survey the ruckus going on below the window. She murmured, "I have been so isolated since we have resided in our palace apartments. Even though Andreus is weaned, I am afraid to leave him. The sparse news I get is what

I receive from you and Zahra, or if Otrygg deigns to bring me tidbits of this and that. I miss the freedom I had at Hawks Hill to wander the pastures and work with the horses. I am eager to put on some comfortable clothing, to ride through my beautiful woods again. Oh, Loukas, here I am surrounded by the foolish chatter of vain, idle women. I neither belong nor want to. I feel trapped! I wish your court duties were over and we could go home."

Andreus began wriggling, and Loukios set him on the tiled floor. The youngster started to whimper, lifting his arms to be held again.

"He wants down; then he wants up. Does nothing please him?" Loukios complained.

"He is unusually cranky when he cuts a tooth," Najila answered, her mouth pinching with strain. Taking Andreus by the hand, she led him to a toy horse. Galloping the wooden toy across the tiles, Najila caught the child's interest. "There! That may keep him busy for a scant lepta," she sighed.[2]

Loukas merely grinned. "I have waited to tell you the best news, news that should elate you, my beloved. The political meetings are over for me. We travel to Hawks Hill in three days. Can you be ready?" he asked.

Uttering a joyous squeal, Najila ran to Loukios and threw her arms around his neck. "I have so longed to return," she cried. "The sooner, the better."

"It is overdue," Loukios breathed, his lips brushing her cheek. "The big equinox race is next month; I must check the progress of my horses. Hawks Hill has entered two chariots. One is to be drawn by Argyrea's first colt, Odysseus, in whom I have great faith. His harness mate has already won several races. They are a promising team."

Najila spun, confronting him. "And how is Elias doing? Has he fully recovered from his accident in the last race?" Elias's chariot had locked wheels with another, and both had overturned. Though the other driver died as a result of his injuries,

Elias escaped with a broken finger, several large bruises, and a few scrapes.

"Age only improves the lad; he is prepared and fit," Loukios affirmed. "At eighteen, his strength is nearly at its maximum. He successfully maintains his light weight and has an ever-increasing ability to handle horses, already having won half-a-dozen races. I expect him to win the equinox without difficulty."

"Elias is a sweet young man." Najila smiled. "I pray that he completes every lap safely."

Loukios curled an arm around her waist. "I pray every day for us all, especially for Elias when he drives," Loukios reassured her. "If Elias were badly injured—or worse, killed—I would mourn him as I would mourn a son."

Chapter 54

When Loukios and Najila arrived at Hawks Hill, Otrygg and Zahra descended the gleaming marble staircase to greet them.

Otrygg grinned his pleasure at their return. "Salutations, friend Loukios and wife. What gossip do you bring me from Konstantinoupolis? Any news about Romanus IV?"

"Ere we left the city, we heard that Andronicus Doukas and his followers had deserted Romanus. It was their fault he was captured," Loukios barked as he helped Najila and Andreus step down from the cart. "Bearing the Doukas name shames me."

Freeing Andreus to run to Zahra, Najila snuggled against her husband's chest. "You had no part in the duplicity, my love. Suffer no guilt."

"I am sure my esteemed father was somehow involved," Loukios snarled. "He causes the empire nothing but grief. Well, when Romanus IV returns—if he returns—he will take his revenge. And I, for one, will remain loyal to him. It is difficult to honor one's father when that father dishonors everything with which he associates. I have trouble even being around a man who is so evil that he would kidnap his son's wife." Loukios stomped up the steps, as angry as Najila had ever seen him.

Najila lifted a shoulder. "At times, no matter what I say, I cannot ease his mind," she confided to Otrygg. "I am no longer as concerned for myself, but I detest Leopold Alexander for what he is doing to Loukas."

"I know," Otrygg replied. Then, seeing Najila's face suddenly blanch, he said, "You seem ill. Let us take you to your rooms." He beckoned for Zahra to assist her.

"Zahra, I think I am again with child," Najila whispered as they mounted the staircase. "It is unfortunate timing."

"No time is a bad time to have a baby," Zahra replied, highly pleased at the prospect. "Your children are the children I never had. While I live, I will care for them as if they were my own."

That is the problem, Zahra, Najila thought. *You must be almost eighty and you are growing frail. How much longer will you be with me?*

A few weeks later, Loukios was at the palace's impressive reception hall when Romanus IV and his priestly escort entered. While the emperor was a prisoner of the Seljuks, his captors had treated him as their guest. And then they had released him. It was a common practice among the Muslim leaders. Romanus showed no sign of his ordeal. Coming home, he had been well received by the throngs that had lined the streets of Konstantinoupolis to welcome him.

Now at the formal reception, however, Loukios noticed a group of men, including his father, huddled in a remote corner. They gave no indication they were glad to see the old warrior come home, and there was something sinister about their demeanor. Their words were too quietly spoken for Loukios to understand, but by their furtive glances at Romanus, he suspected they were plotting against him. What discouraged Loukios was that he was powerless against their strong coalition.

Events soon proved that Loukios's misgivings had been well founded. Old Romanus IV was blinded and poisoned, eventually dying after enduring days of agony. The plotters placed Michael VII Doukas Parapinakes, the late Konstantine X's son, on the throne in Romanus's place. Michael Psellus, a scholar, became his chief adviser. The grieving Eudokia fled into a monastery.

That same terrible year, Byzantium experienced one more devastating setback. The Normans, under Count Robert Guiscard, took the Adriatic port of Bari, releasing Italy's last parcel from Byzantine domination.

The Byzantine empire had shrunk to a vestige of its previous size, but within the great city of Konstantinoupolis, life continued, especially carefree court merriment, as if there had been no change in the empire's might and prestige.

Chapter 55

"Z ahra!" Najila called. "Loukios is at the track. Let us join him so Andreus can see the morning exercise sessions." Loukios planned to work his two best teams on the oval that he had ordered graded the previous year, and she was dying to watch. Loukios might not protest as much if she used Andreus as an excuse to go there.

"It is a good idea. The child needs to get out into the fresh air," Zahra agreed. She carried Andreus from the adjoining nursery, his legs circling her waist, his plump little arms around her neck. Walking any distance was becoming increasingly difficult for her arthritic bones, but she had made up her mind to remain active in spite of her limitations. "The day promises warmth. We will not have to wear heavy clothing."

"We should take cloaks anyway," Najila suggested. "One never knows if an early morning, even in August, will stay mellow and calm, or if perhaps a chill wind will come roaring upon us from the northern steppes."

Najila took Andreus from Zahra and gathered him into her arms. His breath smelled like sweet milk. He pawed at Najila's vest, trying to unfasten the buckle. "Stop, Andreus! You are too old to nurse."

"A month of drinking goat's milk and one might believe he would have forgotten his mother's," Zahra commented.

"Do they ever forget how to suckle?" Najila laughed.

The spinster ignored Najila's remark and began to straighten the room. She bent to retrieve a stray toy and involuntarily moaned when her lower back twinged. "Is it absolutely necessary that I accompany you?" she asked Najila.

Noting Zahra's pained expression, Najila said softly, "I see that it is harder each day for you to move about. Worry not. The dogs can come, but I cannot imagine either one coming to my rescue if I encountered trouble, though Galen is a proficient ankle biter."

Zahra had to smile at that. "Galen would bark anyone away, I think." Her smile abruptly changed to a frown. "Is not Andreus too much for you, knowing you may carry his brother or sister?" Not completely sure she was pregnant, Najila had yet to inform Loukios of her suspicion.

"If I am with child, it is by just a few weeks. I can handle Andreus. Besides, the track is not far. Andreus needs to watch his father and Elias train." Loukios had told her he hoped someday to give their son a chariot of his own and teach him to drive. Aware that a charioteer's life span was unusually short, Najila dreaded that time.

Elias had begun to drive under Loukios's colors before Loukios and Najila married. Possessing strong, sensitive hands and powerful arms, shoulders, and legs, he was born to hold the multiple reins. He also exhibited the innate ability to judge his horses and to foresee the tactics of his competitors.

Even so, after several years of racing in the Hippodrome, it was a miracle Elias was not only alive but that his body remained whole, as well. Few charioteers survived beyond their midtwenties. Grave injuries and the grave itself removed most of them before they reached twenty. Nevertheless, the chance to gain enormous wealth or freedom from bondage attracted young men, predominately slaves, from everywhere in the known world.

Chariot racing had been popular with the Etruscans, who practiced it as early as the sixth century before Jesus Christ's

birth.[1] The list of famous drivers and horses that had com-
peted since Rome's beginning was long, though still familiar
to Byzantine racing fans. Najila did not want her son's name
added to it.

Following the worn path to the track, Najila allowed Andreus
to explore wherever his curiosity led, as long as he stayed within
her sight. The sun barely shone through the haze blanketing
the landscape, but its glare caused her to squint.

The dogs—one a mere ball of fluff with protruding legs, the
other a lumbering, flop-eared giant—coursed back and forth
across the trail. They chased a rabbit, then returned to check on
Andreus. When the boy ignored them, they ran circles around
Najila, barking with excitement.

"They cover three times the distance we do," Najila said to
Andreus. She suddenly grabbed his hand and pried from his
grubby fingers a semipoisonous, orange-red berry that he had
plucked from a shrub. He was ready to pop it into his mouth.

"Not to eat, Andreus!" she scolded, glowering at him in exaggerated disgust. Tossing the berry aside, she immediately re-
directed his attention elsewhere.

Soon they crested the last rise. Below them lay the dirt race
track. Loukios and four grooms stood at one end, attending to
a chariot. Elias exercised the second team counterclockwise on
the oval, holding the horses to a beautiful, collected trot.

Loukios had decided the infertile field lying to the stable's lee
side and formerly planted in wheat was not worth the meager
modioi it produced.[2] He had concluded that the grounds were
a good place for a practice track. His foresight proved sound; it
was the perfect setting.

Chariots were commonly drawn by two horses—*biga*—or
four—*quadrigae.* In previous decades, larger teams had been
the fashion, but now they were rarely used. The more animals
that were harnessed, the more danger the charioteer faced. A
man who preferred to see his horses fit and his drivers survive,

Loukios chose only the less-risky, two-horse hitch, though it limited the races he was able to enter.

"No, Andreus!" Najila cried in vain when the boy squealed and ran ahead of her, his arms outstretched.

Loukios looked up at Najila's agitated cry. Seeing Andreus heading toward him as fast as his little legs could toddle, Loukios squatted to receive him. Grinning, he slapped his knees to urge the child and the dogs onward.

So much for my discipline, Najila thought. But she enjoyed seeing father and son interact in such a loving manner.

The dogs, swifter than Andreus, got to Loukios first and knocked him down. He tried to defend himself against their playful lunges, but eventually had to submit to a thorough face washing.

Then, just as Loukios righted himself, Andreus arrived at full speed and knocked him flat again. "I concede! I give up!" Loukios shouted above the giggling boy's head.

"It serves you right!" Najila snickered. Gripping Andreus by his tunic, she hoisted him off her husband so he could sit up. A mischievous gleam in her eye, Najila leaned forward as if to lend Loukios a hand, but before he could guess her intent, she pushed him over for the third time. In a quick move, he seized her wrist and pulled her down on top of himself with Andreus squished between them. "I, too, can play the game," Loukios chortled.

Choking with laughter, Najila couldn't devise a clever retort. When Andreus loudly complained, "Me off! Me off!" Najila released the boy, who was none the worse for his minor squashing. Loukios held her wrists, preventing her from rising.

"Let me up, Loukas!" Najila's demanded in an amused whisper. "What will the grooms think?"

Loukios suddenly remembered they were not alone and that they had acted with extreme impropriety in front of the stablemen. He looked toward them, and to his relief noted that their sole attention was on Elias and the horses galloping along the track.

Embarrassed for Najila, Loukios rose and helped her to her feet. A layer of fine dust soiled their clothing. They were brushing themselves clean when they both saw Andreus run onto the chariot track. Najila gasped and then screamed.

Andreus was on a collision course with the speeding chariot.

Chapter 56

Aghast at seeing tiny Andreus toddling across the track, Elias heaved back on the reins, his biceps bulging from the strain. Fortunately, he had begun to slow the thundering team as they rounded the near pylon.

The powerful horses, trained for one unwavering goal, continued to pull for the finish line.

Unafraid, yet in awe of the thundering hooves and iron wheels, Andreus froze and stood stock-still.

Elias unleashed strength he did not know he had. Leaning back, his body nearly parallel to the floor of the chariot cab, he managed to bring the belligerent stallions to a reluctant, sliding halt a mere three lengths from where Andreus stood.

Tossing their heads, fighting their bits, their mouths frothing, the horses pranced in place as Elias restrained them, his knuckles and face as starkly white as the oval's chalked perimeter.

Loukios, with Najila close behind him, sprinted onto the track. Lifting the unfazed child to his shoulder, Loukios noticed how Elias's hands trembled. "Well done, Elias! It was not your fault. Andreus should not have been allowed to wander."

Turning to Najila, his lips thinning, Loukios growled, "Nor will it happen again, will it?" Najila saw something in his eyes she had never seen before—a fierce, protective rage.

"No," she replied, her voice meek and shaky. "From now on, I shall bring someone to look after him when we come."

257

"A sensible decision," Loukios hissed between clenched teeth. Giving Andreus a quick hug, he handed the boy to her.

Striding past the still snorting and blowing animals to the chariot, Loukios again assured Elias, "You are not at fault." He climbed into the cab and took the reins from the youth. "I wish to test the team myself." Driving the spirited horses would be a tonic for his taut nerves in the aftermath of Andreus's narrow escape.

Grateful that no one blamed him, Elias attempted to steer everyone's mind from the near tragedy by tactfully offering information about the two horses. "My lord, Odysseus continually improves but should be kept on the outside for the present. He is almost as durable as Skorpus, and he may be faster. However he lacks the wisdom that Skorpus has gained through experience."

Skorpus had belonged to the heir of an unfortunate nobleman killed at Manzikert. Knowing the heir's disinterest in racing, Loukios had tendered an acceptable offer and had become the horse's new owner.

Poised like a statue within the chariot, ready to wield the whip, Loukios nodded. Referring to the turn posts, he said, "Skorpus skims the *metae* as smoothly and skillfully as a falcon stoops to snatch the lure."

"Skorpus is your stable's finest beast," Elias agreed, "but Odysseus is a close second. He just needs a year or two to develop his muscles. He already matches Skorpus in heart."

"You should do well in the equinox, Elias. Another win for Skorpus, and he will have achieved his one hundredth victory and thus earn the title of centurion."

Confident he would wear the laurel wreath, Elias replied, "I expect to take the lead from the first."

"If I were not sure of it, I would hire an alternate driver." Loukios good-naturedly thumped Elias's shoulder.

Elias grinned with pleasure. Though Loukios was a stern taskmaster, he cared about his men and animals. "I shall do my very best for you and Lady Najila," Elias promised.

Chapter 57

All eastern Byzantium focused on the equinox chariot races. At Hawks Hill, tensions increased in the stables as race day neared.

Eager to see how the training was progressing, Najila walked with a brisk step toward the stables. A young maid followed with Andreus. Since Andreus's close call the month before, she had assigned a trusted servant to watch the toddler when she took him to the practice track.

An early morning frost sparkled on the shriveled grass alongside the well-trodden trail that led to the training oval. With someone else looking after Andreus, Najila wallowed in sensory indulgence. She breathed in the pungent smell of needles crunching underfoot; the musky perfume coming from brightly colored foliage; the gentle, salt-laden breeze that streamed inland from the Sea of Marmara.

Even so, as she walked, Najila couldn't stop from wondering which of the *demes*—politically powerful parties that zealously supported their personal favorites—would eventually sponsor Loukios's team. The demes factions dated back to the Roman games and had once been numerous. Over the last centuries, they had merged into just two groups: the militarily inclined Greens and the civic-minded Blues.

In previous decades, the demes came closest to expressing the people's will. Governed by officials called demarchs, they energized fifth- and sixth-century uprisings, the most famous being the Nika riots, during which the population protested Justinian's high taxes. Those riots resulted in the torching of the Hagia Sofia and approximately thirty thousand deaths. Loukios had told Najila that the factions now functioned as ceremonial dressing—as greeters at coronations, as well as at Christmas and Easter services. Their roles were played largely, and ironically, in the rebuilt Hagia Sofia, the edifice they once destroyed.

The Hawks Hill chariots presently raced for the Greens, but before Loukios and Najila were married, his vehicles had carried the Blue. It all depended on whose ethics or politics an owner favored. Because the Blues now supported Leopold Alexander, Najila was sure that Loukios would choose the rival faction as his backer.

When it came to politics, Najila paid little heed. Playing with Andreus and overseeing her household's complex daily routine demanded her full attention. Nevertheless, she loved to see the horses run, and she took advantage of every opportunity to go to the Hawks Hill exercise track. She had expected to see Elias compete in the Hippodrome, but Loukios had dashed that idea emphatically, declaring, "A gentlewoman's presence at the chariot races is frowned upon. It has always been thus in Byzantium."

When Najila suggested that she could go dressed in her male riding outfit, Loukios snorted, then marched off, mumbling and shaking his head. His stubborn attitude hurt, but Najila was even more determined to go to the great Hippodrome.

The equinox would be run in two weeks. It was the race to which the Byzantine world most looked forward. Try as she might, Najila couldn't envision how to circumvent the traditional ban against the attendance of women other than by going disguised as a man. It was the only way, she finally decided. And she would go without Loukios's knowledge.

As she devised her plan, she realized she would have to enlist a fellow conspirator, a trusted companion, someone willing to obtain her admission ticket and perhaps sit with her.

In whom could she confide? Otrygg would naturally side with Loukios. And apart from being a woman and thus forbidden to go, Zahra was too frail to partake in such an adventure. Najila resolved that she would not even tell Zahra; it would be unfair to needlessly upset her. Whom, then, should she ask? Najila was unable to come up with a solution right away.

Every chariot team that entered a race had to be fully guarded against an opposing faction's sabotage. In the past, spokes had been sawed half through and filled with clay or wax to mask the cuts. Contending horses were either drugged or lamed, and drivers too often endured the same fate. At Loukios's instruction, Otrygg assigned four stalwart bodyguards to the Hawks Hill teams, to the chariots, the horses, Elias, and the second chariot's driver. The closer to race day, the tighter the security.

At Hawks Hill, Loukios examined the two pairs of handsome horses that had been hitched to light racing chariots in preparation for a sort of dress rehearsal. When they trained seriously, they pulled heavier, unadorned rigs.

The harnessed horses were held in place side by side for Loukios's inspection. It was a challenge and a matter of pride to field perfectly matching teams. He had been fortunate to assemble two such pairs. His principal team included two golden sorrels, Skorpus and Odysseus. What a pleasant surprise it had been to discover how efficiently they worked as a unit when harnessed together. Of course, Elias drove them.

The second driver, and Elias's substitute should one be necessary, held the other team, which consisted of two almost black, liver-bay stallions, with striking, full blazes.

"Tomorrow we take them to Alioth, Loukios declared. "There, they will rest until the day before the equinox, when they are to make their test runs at the Hippodrome."

After their wedding, Loukios and Najila had decided to keep his estate, not only because it embraced profitable agricultural land, but because it was also conveniently situated on the city's perimeter. The teams would be going from Alioth on to the Hippodrome, leaving Najila behind at Hawks Hill.

Loukios strode back and forth in front of his two teams, scratching beneath a forelock or fondly stroking a velvety muzzle. The animals' pelts glowed with health and regular grooming. The well-rubbed harness leathers gleamed, and the sun's rays reflecting from the chariots' elaborate and polished brass, silver, and gold ornamentation hurt the eyes.

Loukios nodded at Elias in appreciation. "They are fit and ready to do their best, thanks to you and your grooms, young Elias."

Elias nearly burst with pleasure.

The nearer to the date of the big event, the more Najila fumed. To her frustration, Loukios and Otrygg increasingly retreated into their own male world, with nothing on their minds except the great race. She had to find a way to enter the Hippodrome unnoticed, without embarrassing herself or Loukios. Then she had an inspiration.

She rushed to the desk in her private quarters. Snatching up a parchment, she hurriedly penned a note. After holding a sealing wax stick over a candle flame, she dropped melted wax on the rolled document and pressed her signet ring's hawk impression into the soft wax. Finished, she summoned a servant she knew to be discreet. Handing him the note, she gave him oral directions, stating to whom it was to be delivered and telling him to wait for an answer.

On reading Najila's message, Julian smacked a palm on his brow. This was asking too much. Though Julian's true loyalty was to Najila, the daughter of his boyhood mentor, Michael, Loukios was like a younger brother or beloved nephew. Najila's plot, which required his participation in order to succeed, was completely preposterous.

The eunuch paced his palace suite, spending hours weighing the danger to Najila. Late that evening, he arrived at a decision. Yes, he'd do it for her, meanwhile making certain she suffered no harm. Julian sent back his written reply with the same messenger: *At dawn on race day, meet me inside the wall's western gate.*

It was doubtful that anyone, especially during such a special celebration as the equinox race, would question the appearance of a beautiful boy in the company of a high-ranking court eunuch.

Tearing open Julian's note, Najila quickly read his response and triumphantly whirled around the room.

Chapter 58

Earlier in the week, Loukios and his teams had gone to Alioth, leaving Najila at Hawks Hill. A day later, he went on to the city to participate in the equinox trials.

When Najila knew for sure that Loukios was in Konstantinoupolis, she quietly made her own arrangements to go to Alioth. She took two people along, her cart driver and fourteen-year-old Amara, a new maid she had acquired to help Zahra.

Andreus stayed behind in Zahra's care, and the pair stood at the top of the staircase waving good-bye. Holding little Andreus's hand, Zahra asked herself why Najila would leave without her son. She also wondered why Najila's black steppe mare, Jahara, was tethered to the back of the cart. But Zahra's memory wasn't what it once was, and by day's end, she had forgotten any misgivings she might have had.

After arriving at Alioth that evening, Najila beckoned Amara to her private suite. "Sit by my side, Amara." She patted the bed. "I have a secret I want to share with you."

"A secret?"

"You and I are going to change my appearance," Najila told the girl. "No one is to know. I expect—no, I demand—your loyalty. Do you understand?"

Amara glanced nervously at Najila, then away, her eyelids rapidly blinking. "Yes, my lady, but—"

"There is more. You are not to tell another person what I am about to divulge. It is a secret between you and me. Can I trust you?"

Amara placed her hand on her breast. Meeting Najila's steady gaze, she answered, "No one shall ever steal a word from me."

Amara listened while Najila detailed her plan. Timid and inexperienced, never having ventured more than a mile or two from where she had been born on a neighboring estate, Amara was excited and exceedingly flattered that the beautiful and noble lady Najila trusted her enough to confide in her. To take part in such intrigue was an honor.

Najila had carefully picked the cart's driver, an amiable, middle-aged man who had been simpleminded since his birth. He had been Najila's personal driver the past three years, and he adored her, doing only what she asked of him, and unquestioningly following her gently spoken instructions.

As she prepared for her epic undertaking, Najila's exhilaration increased each minute. Making such decisions gave her an immense sense of power and freedom. She danced instead of walked, sang instead of talked.

Amara had sewn a male outfit for Najila, styled in the fashion worn by urban youths who were apprenticing a trade. Najila's early pregnancy did not show; her form was still slender and firm. But her hair was much too feminine, too long and thick to easily disguise. It delighted Loukios to entwine his fingers in its silken curls when he made love to her. Yet if her plan were to be successful, the hair would have to go.

Najila sat stiffly in a straight-backed chair. Closing her eyes and taking a deep breath, she commanded Amara to start cutting. Amara had never touched anyone's hair other than her own, which she wore braided and wound around her head. The girl's entire body trembled as she picked up the sharp kitchen knife that Najila had ordered her to use.

Gathering a strand of Najila's hair, Amara set the blade's keen edge on it, then stopped, afraid the knife would slip and slice her mistress's soft, pale skin.

Najila opened an eye, raised a brow, and peered at Amara. "Well? Why do you not begin?"

"I should not want to injure you, my lady."

"That is something we must chance, Amara. No one will blame you if you are unskilled at barbering. You will learn by . . . by working on me." Now that the deed was about to commence, she was more than a bit concerned, though she sought to hide the fact with bravado.

Amara wavered, her right hand poised in the air.

"Please, just do it, Amara. Do it before I change my mind."

At the operation's conclusion, Amara stepped away. Holding a tiny bronze mirror, Najila checked the result and nearly fainted. She looked so different! Released from the pull of a waist-long length, her cropped hair had tightened into ringlets. The ends, fairly even with her earlobes, were ragged, and her bangs crooked. Loukios would be horrified at what she had done, but it was too late to undo. Unbidden tears of regret suddenly clouded her vision.

Amara paced a circle around Najila to examine her handiwork. "My mistress is very attractive," she said.

Tilting and turning her head, Najila stared at her reflection. She was rather pretty in a boyish manner, quite comely in fact. Maybe Loukios would like it after all.

"Shall I remove more?" Amara asked.

"No," Najila replied quickly. "This is sufficient."

As dawn's first blush illumined the city's eastern skyline, a light breeze blew off the Bosporus, swirling the dust and debris stirred by thousands of feet that tramped the road to

Konstantinoupolis. Though it had been too dark to see much and only bobbing torches carried by others lit the way, Najila had enjoyed feeling the wind ruffle her new coiffure. Nevertheless, she was aware that it was now prudent to cover her head as well as her features.

Mounted on Jahara, she drew near the gate in Konstantinoupolis's massive western wall. Due to Jahara's extensive schooling and willing temperament, Najila had no trouble handling the mare, though it was physically uncomfortable to ride on a sheepskin pad instead of her broken-in saddle with its sturdy, ornate stirrups.

She wore a loose, belted tunic that reached to the top of her cotton-stockinged knees. For the tunic, she had chosen material dyed a faded blue. The tunic's style and color were indistinguishable amid the clothes of those around her. Flexible hide boots covered her legs to mid calf.

Najila reined Jahara to a secluded patch within a roadside glade. Remembering the tricky procedure her father had taught her years ago when they had traveled from Baghdad, she wrapped her head in a scarf, turban-like, securing the end to conceal her lower face. She hoped no one could identify her.

People of every nationality had come on foot, on horseback, seated in swaying sedan chairs, and driving a medley of horse-drawn vehicles. The unruly mob jostled Jahara as it closed ranks to funnel through the gate; horse and rider were swept on the tide into Konstantinoupolis.

Fearing she had missed Julian in the surging throng, Najila anxiously searched her surroundings for his portly figure and cherubic countenance. As she was about to panic, she saw the eunuch astride a fat pony that stood placidly in the shadow cast by a large church. Wearing neither his habitual costly fabrics nor brilliant jewels, he had garbed himself as a common, middle-class citizen.

Traversing the milling crowd, Najila managed to maneuver Jahara diagonally across the wide thoroughfare to approach Julian.

"Greetings, Julian. I thought I would never find thee midst this lot."

On hearing Najila's voice, Julian searched the surrounding sea of faces. Recognizing the "boy" who was nearing his side, his tension eased. "Lady Najila, you strain my old heart." But his relief segued to despair when he saw she had come alone. "No guard accompanies you? What you do is lunacy. My folly is that I agreed to collaborate in your foolish plot." He groaned, rolling his eyes heavenward. "By the holy God and all his saints, why did I encourage you?"

Najila grinned. "I am safely here. Is that not proof that I am capable of taking care of myself?" Her attention shifted to observe a duo of harlequins who artfully juggled a half-dozen squawking chickens, their feathers flying everywhere. To make the hapless birds easier to toss, their legs had been bound to their bodies with many-colored streamers. After the harlequins, a flute-playing clown danced past.

Throwing Julian a merry smile, Najila jerked her head in the direction of the traffic. "It vexes me to delay. Come, let us go to the Hippodrome," she said, her heels giving Jahara's ribs a hefty kick.

In order to be heard over the clamor, Julian shouted at Najila's retreating back. "Wait! Follow me! I know the best route." He kneed his mount into the dense crowd to head Najila off. "Madness!" he muttered. "The woman is insane!"

Najila had never been this way before. The alleys that Julian led her through were narrow and less traveled than the broad, commercial boulevards that she and Loukios normally used. Despite her disguise, Najila received curious stares. She rode too fine a horse for an ordinary boy, and she had neglected to substitute plainer tack for Jahara's decorative, red-dyed leather.

They soon reached a great square near the Hippodrome and the Hagia Sophia. For the first time, Najila saw the ancient *milion*, a gold-plated milestone on which distances to the empire's most important cities were displayed. An arched, four-pillared, domed edifice enclosed it. Another day, she would have insisted they stop to ponder the strange, far-flung places the *milion* listed, but already the spectators in the Hippodrome were emitting provocative roars.

"Hurry, Julian! Something is happening."

Julian sighed. "Be at ease Lady Najila. We have time ere the ceremonies start. Patience! You know we cannot take our beasts into the Hippodrome." He led Najila to his favorite stable to leave their horses.

"Lady Najila," Julian began.

"Shh! Do not call me Lady Najila," she cautioned him. "Someone may hear you. I am a simple peasant boy named Jon," she smugly declared. Her eyes above the concealing cloth were bright with anticipation.

Chapter 59

Najila's and Julian's seats were uncomfortable, bare stone and remote from the plush boxes designated for nobles and influential persons. Despite his respected office, Julian knew he would be knee-deep in goat manure should anyone recognize Najila, though it was unlikely that Loukios or any other close acquaintance would see them amidst such a throng.

This was only the second time that Najila had been inside the Hippodrome. It was more crowded than it had been when Loukios took her to Romanus IV's impressive coronation, and this audience was noisier. Rowdier.

Soon, every seat filled, and those who had not obtained a seat vied for standing room. "It certainly shows the people's preference for horses over a royal spectacle," Najila observed to Julian. She was staring at the kathisma, the royal box in which no one was yet seated. Purple banners and purple and gold streamers fluttered in the quickening breeze. Loukios had told her that the emperor or empress does not always attend the races but usually comes long enough to start the first one by personally dropping the *mappa*.

The new emperor, Michael VII, Eudokia's son, was a mild-mannered, unassuming aesthetic who preferred his books and studies to large public gatherings. *Surely though,* Najila thought, *he will attend the prestigious equinox.*

Julian pointed out Loukios's recently acquired box, up front and close to the arena. Loukios was not in it. She panicked, then relaxed. Of course her husband was not there; he was behind the starting gates, overseeing preparations for the race.

As in Rome's glory days, chariot race ceremonies began with a procession. Individual officials who sponsored the various teams led the parade. The factions touted their colors and hoisted statues of celebrities, past and present. Troubadours and dancers performed their arts. Priests carried ornate crosses and effigies of saints, instead of gods and goddesses as was customary in the old Circus Maximus. Military notables dressed for battle rode their prized *destriers*, war horses that reared and twirled in response to their riders' invisible prompts.

Behind the gates, bedlam reigned. Reacting to the tension and noise, the high-strung horses pawed the ground and worried their jingling bits. Bred to run and eager to get started, the powerful animals had to be continually restrained by their handlers.

The pit teams made their final harness checks. A scream, then guttural cursing echoed in the long corridor as a groom's sandaled foot was crushed beneath a fretful hoof. Hurried, last-minute instructions to the drivers occupied their trainers and owners, as everyone awaited the first heat. Loukios adjusted Odysseus's cheek straps, slightly lifting the bit for a tighter fit. Annoyed by the increased pressure, Odysseus arched his neck and tongued the metal.

"Be on your guard; beware of the Blues," Loukios warned Elias for the umpteenth time. "We know my father's teams are excellent, but Leopold Alexander's top pair has entered the twelfth and final race. His second team will compete in this race against our first team. There is no serious challenge, and you should win without stressing the horses. If you do as I say, Skorpus will definitely earn his centurion. Try to save Skorpus and Odysseus for the critical twelfth race. That should give them sufficient rest. Above all, Elias, you must avoid harm—a disabling injury to you or the horses. My foremost concern is that you finish the day safely."

When drawing lots for the third race, Loukios had picked the fourth position from the spina, the low wall running down the length of the Hippodrome's center. Not bad. Not ideal.

Elias gripped the reins firmly in one hand. Like other charioteers, he wound the ends around his waist. He wore a leather helmet and minimal body protection. If he were involved in an accident and entangled, he carried a hefty knife with which to cut himself free. Few charioteers, however, survived a serious crash, which usually happened at the turns.

The huge Hippodrome became breathlessly silent as a bank of trumpeters stationed under the four bronze horses above the gates heralded Byzantium's emperor. Along with everyone else, Najila focused her attention on the royal box, where Michael VII Doukas held the *mappa* over his head. His slender form stiffly erect, he slowly turned so all could see. Then as the onlookers shouted their approval, he nonchalantly straightened his fingers and released the white silk cloth. The wind carried the piece of silk higher and higher until it disappeared against the gray sky.

At the same instant, the wondrously constructed, automatic gates clanged open. The crowd's appreciative roar echoed throughout the city.

From the race's start, Elias trailed two teams, including his Blue rival. As the chariots gained momentum, racing counterclockwise around the spina, they came together. Elias held third place for nine laps. During the tenth lap while rounding the nyssa, the pylon at the dolphin end of the Hippodrome, he managed to work his way inside and past the second chariot, leaving him just one to pass. When Elias let Skorpus and Odysseus have their heads, they flew to the lead, winning by a full length.

Cooling the horses, Elias had them trot the winner's lap.

"Hail, Skorpus! Centurion!" Najila shouted, joining the rest. She couldn't help jumping up and down. "Loukios will be so pleased. I wish I could see his face," she cried to Julian.

"It was a fair race. But remember, it is not as important to Loukios as the twelfth race will be," Julian answered. "Meanwhile, there is still much to happen." Despite his unease at the situation into which Najila had lured him, he was delighted by her enthusiasm.

The track was cleared and the trumpets again sounded. In lieu of gilded chariots drawn by dazzling steeds, wooden carts hitched to mules raced round the oval. The crowd alternately chanted and hooted. Mules were neither fast nor beautiful. Nevertheless, the gaily painted carts and raucous braying of animals provided colorful, albeit comic, relief.

"There is always entertainment between races," Julian explained when things quieted. "I think you will especially enjoy the race of the foals."

Najila's scandalized expression showed her dismay. "You mean they hitch *babies* to chariots?"

Julian chuckled. "Be patient. You will see soon enough. It is a popular event, so it is held at day's end between races eleven and twelve." He turned away, hiding a grin. "I should not have told you. Ah well . . ."

Najila needn't have been anxious. Each weanling pulled a miniature, foal-size chariot. Driven by prepubescent boys, the small vehicles were to attempt just one lap. Harnessed with soft leathers and ropes—no bits in the long-legged foals' tender mouths—the toy-like chariots zigged and zagged back and forth across the track, from spina to stands. Most never made it completely around, and a sponsor, groom, or parent ran onto the oval to lead a vanquished, often weeping child and foal out. Rarely did someone get hurt, and it was great fun.

"That was not so bad," Najila admitted afterward.

By late afternoon, the wind increased and the weather deteri-
orated. Strong, intermittent gusts snapped the flags and banners
until they sounded like cracks of the long whips the charioteers
snaked along their horses' backs. Ominous pewter clouds hid
the sun, and the heavy, humid air smelled of impending rain.

The day had been bloody, the first eleven races taking their
toll on man and beast alike. Two lesser-known drivers were
killed, and six were hurt badly enough to require a trip to the
hospital—among them a famous Persian charioteer. Five good
horses, critically lamed or fatally injured, mercifully had their
throats cut.

Thanks to the skills of Elias and his fellow driver, the chariots that belonged to Loukios had so far finished every race
unscathed.

Trumpets heralded the twelfth race. When running fresh,
the fastest horses could accelerate to forty miles per hour, but
by late afternoon, the weather had become hot and humid and
would retard their speed. The spina contained a water channel.
Boys stood by it, prepared to dodge the rocketing chariots in
order to throw cool water on their particular team. More boys
and men lined the arena edge, ready to briefly run alongside
their favorites and encourage them onward to the laurels.

Najila and Julian had been in the Hippodrome all day. Earlier, Julian had bought food from vendors who plied their trade
to those in the stands, selling goat cheese, olives, pomegran-
ates, bread, and wine. The plain food satisfied their hunger.

Julian had left their seats only one other time, when Najila
had to relieve herself. This simple act proved a major problem.
She was a female dressed in male's clothing. A public toilet
would not do.

"We have no choice, Naj . . . er . . . Jon," Julian muttered, his
normally pale skin crimson. "I must take you to my quarters in
the palace, which is a short walk through the private royal passage. Everyone knows me and will pay you scant heed under
the circumstances. It is your lone option."

Julian's suggestion worked. They didn't encounter a single interested soul.

A little giddy from the heat and too much wine, Najila sat with her hands flattened beside her, bracing her unsteady body. Trumpets again blared, and the crowd jumped to its feet. Shakily, Najila rose, too. Holding on to Julian's arm, she stood on tiptoe in order to see over the heads in front of her.

As one entity, six chariots shot out of the gates. As they rounded the first turn, they thundered directly toward the area from which Najila and Julian watched.

Najila suddenly cried out, her nails digging into Julian's arm. "Loukas is driving the Green!"

Chapter 60

Seeing Loukios on the oval amid iron-rimmed wheels and slashing, iron-shod hoofs, Najila experienced overwhelming alarm. Never mind his radiant expression, his obvious joy in what he was doing. It was her *husband* down there driving his best team, the pride of his stable.

Julian draped an arm across Najila's tense shoulders. "Not to worry," he said, in a useless attempt to console her. "Loukios is a fine horseman, a superb driver, better than most professionals."

"But Julian, Loukas is too old for this. What if he is hurt or killed? I could not live without him." Najila's fingers dug deeper into Julian's arm, her nails clawing through the sleeve's thick cloth and into his flesh. "It is terribly dangerous! I cannot bear to see it." Squeezing her eyes shut, she turned away.

"Have faith in God," Julian replied gently. "He will protect Loukios. I know it to be so. Pray to him for your husband's safety."

Najila quickly bowed her head, and her lips moved in a silent prayer. Calmer, she whirled to once again watch the speeding chariots. "I am praying, Julian, continually, as hard as I am able."

Tension built in the Hippodrome. Counting the laps one by one, the bronze dolphins dipped at the far end of the oval. Silver eggs dropped at the near end by the starting gates. From the race's beginning, heeding his own advice, Loukios kept Skorpus and Odysseus contending, but not leading. He knew the team that led, the number-one White, to be slower. He would easily catch it when the opportunity arose. His real competition, the primary Blue driver, played an identical game, holding his dappled-gray team even with Skorpus and Odysseus.

The four magnificent animals ran hip to hip: silvery grays and golden sorrels, sweat darkening their shining coats. Entering the sixth lap's first turn, a fourth competitor, the number-one Red, managed to squeeze between Loukios and the Blue and on up to second place. This left Loukios and his father's team vying for third place.

Loukios accepted the situation. He sensed that the Red and the leading White teams' horses were tiring. Their low-hung tails showed that they had been pushed too hard, too soon.

While completing another lap, Loukios, the Blue, and the Red rapidly closed the gap between themselves and the front-runner, the weakening leader hugging the spina.

Biding his time, waiting a chance to overtake the two chariots in front of him, Loukios maintained his position at his rival's outside. During the seventh lap, the next-to-last circuit, every driver except Loukios and Elias began lashing their horses with impunity. The leading White at last fell back, dropping behind the Red. The other White moved to the outside, passing Loukios. Both Whites now ran together in second place.

"Skorpus on! Odysseus on!" Loukios shouted, snapping the whip over their ears. The eager pair strained against their traces, stretching their strides, rushing onward ever faster.

What a race! Berserk, the crowd leapt to its feet. As the chariots approached the first turn of the eighth lap, the leading Red chariot's right wheel loosened, wobbled on its axle for five meters, and then broke free.

Loukios saw the wheel separate from the Red chariot. To his horror, it spun into the path of the two White vehicles that followed. He had mere seconds to make a decision. Either he had to swing wide of the Whites, pass them, and then immediately bear sharply inward to avoid the wheel, or he could whip Skorpus and Odysseus cruelly to an even swifter gait and hope they would speed past the wheel before it shattered their legs.

The whole thing was happening right in front of Najila and Julian. They glimpsed only a mixed blur of spokes, legs, and hooves.

Najila uttered scream after scream.

Chapter 61

It had begun to rain, and the slick, sand-covered track had become increasingly treacherous. As if in a trance, his ears numb to all but Najila's cries, Julian was unable to tear his eyes from the appalling drama that was taking place before them.

After losing his wheel, the Red driver shifted his weight to his lurching chariot's left side, managing to temporarily balance it.

Loukios also tilted his body to the left at a sharp angle, forcing his chariot in that direction. At the same time, he hauled on Skorpus's inside rein, pulling the animal's head hard toward the Blue team's outside horse. The chariot's sudden drag and the twisting of his neck in one step forced Skorpus to bear inward, slowing his pace almost imperceptively. Harnessed to Skorpus, Odysseus had no choice but to do the same.

Controlling the strong horses as they fought to hold their momentum took every ounce of Loukios's considerable strength.

The second-string White, attempting to avoid the damaged Red, swung outward and rapidly overran the speeding wheel. In a great leap, the White's inside horse jumped the wheel. That action yanked its teammate off balance, and the outside horse was broadsided by the loose wheel, the impact smashing the hapless animal's left rear leg below the gaskin. The badly injured horse bounded once before its sagging hindquarters collapsed.

As the White chariot struck the bodies of its two floundering horses, it flipped, sending the driver head over heels across the track. Desperately trying to escape the horrendous mess, Loukios instinctively lashed his two horses. Skorpus and Odysseus, the whip stinging them to renewed energy, spurted forward, barely missing the overturned chariot's luckless driver.

The second Blue, trailing the pack, crashed into the pileup. The consequence was a colossal mass of screeching metal and writhing, screaming men and horses.

Najila couldn't take her eyes from the terrifying scene. It had all happened so fast—in a scant half breath, it seemed. When accidents had occurred during previous races, she had not been personally involved. This was different. Her Loukios was in the middle of it. But thanks to God, he was safe—this time! Never, she promised herself, would he drive in another race.

Crews immediately dashed onto the oval, untangling and removing the wreckage before the last chariot rounded the next pylon. Even the blood disappeared, soaked up by the sand, which was then raked.

During his wrenching maneuvers, Loukios felt his thigh slam against the rim of the chariot. The resulting pain was so intense that, for a moment, he thought he couldn't continue, but his superb physical condition and competitive nature drove him on.

Meanwhile, the rival Blue chariot and undamaged White moved ahead. Loukios stung Skorpus and Odysseus's rumps once with the lash, and they flashed by the open-mouthed White and Blue drivers. Loukios won by less than a chariot length.

When Loukios, wearing the victor's laurel wreath on his brow, took his victory lap, he dropped his grip on the reins. Skorpus and Odysseus, their necks gracefully arched, circled the spina at a beautiful, synchronized trot.

Totally exhausted, Najila mutely watched Loukios pass the area where she and Julian stood. Her husband's arms were raised high, his hands waving to the cheering crowd. For an instant, their eyes met. She thought he recognized her, but no, his broad grin did not shrink.

Najila underwent three powerful, conflicting emotions: pride, anger, and relief: pride in his achievement; anger because Loukios had done such a foolish thing; and relief, profound relief, that he was uninjured.

As the victor triumphantly sped out through the gates, Julian said to Najila, "Let us go below to congratulate our man."

"What a grand suggestion! We will surprise him," Najila agreed, forgetting her disguise. Then, recalling what she had done, she mumbled, "Oh, Julian, how can I face him? What will he think of me?"

Renowned for his clever tact, Julian had a ready reply. "Loukios will be so exultant that he will forgive you for anything. Right now is the best time to reveal your ruse to him."

"What about those who surely surround him?"

"Allow your eyes to meet only your husband's. He will know they are yours. I believe that, under the circumstances, he will say nothing. It is when you both return to Hawks Hill that you must defend your actions." Here Julian lowered his voice to a whisper. "Even should another man recognize you as the Lady Najila, he would not dare mention the fact in front of Loukios. I myself plan to silence court gossip if it occurs."

Behind the starting gates, jabbering, jostling admirers surrounded Loukios, Elias, and the Hawks Hill grooms. The noisy group suddenly split as Leopold Alexander Doukas rudely elbowed everyone aside. He confronted his taller son. "Loukios, you caused that collision! You should not have been driving."

His eyes narrowing, Loukios calmly answered, "It was nobody's fault. The wheel detached itself."

"From where I sat, it appeared to be your fault!"

Loukios turned away. Arguing with his father would only worsen the schism between them. Reasoning with his father was pointless.

Leopold Alexander thrust his face at Loukios. "You refuse me an explanation?"

Loukios just shook his head.

Leopold Alexander grabbed Loukios's arm, swinging him around. The twisting movement caused a painful cramp in Loukios's bruised thigh.

Massaging his leg, Loukios roared, "I am no longer the cowering child you abused. Leave me and mine be."

"Or . . . ?" Leopold Alexander snarled.

"Or you will feel my wrath, Father. You should have felt it years ago," Loukios said, again turning his back.

Balling his fists, Leopold Alexander sputtered a vile curse. Without another glance at his son and heir, he stalked off.

Approaching at the corridor's opposite end, weaving through a throng of babbling men and boys, clanking chariots, and whinnying horses, Julian and Najila missed the clash between father and son. When they finally joined Loukios, Julian declared, "A magnificent win, my friend."

On hearing Julian's voice, Loukios, still angry due to his encounter with Leopold Alexander, looked up from examining Skorpus's left hind leg. A piece of metal or a flailing hoof had lightly scraped the cannon bone. Fortunately, the wound wasn't serious. Loukios let the hoof drop. "Never have I experienced so intoxicating a pleasure," he laughed, his anger vanishing. "I cannot wait for next year's equinox."

The very idea! Najila bristled. She marched up to Loukios, hands on hips, dark brown eyes flashing above the scarf across her nose and mouth. "Never again, as long as I live, are you to undertake such a blockheaded, dangerous stunt," she scolded. "I nearly died watching you risk your life."

Loukios instantly identified the impertinent boy's voice as his wife's. He reacted with an expression of shock and then ire. He was about to give her a good tongue-lashing, when, just in time, he remembered the hangers-on with big ears who lingered nearby, basking in their hero's shadow.

"What are you doing here?" Loukios whispered through gritted teeth.

His obvious rage caused Najila to step backward. "I . . . I . . . I had to come."

Loukios caught her arm. "You had to come to an event forbidden to decent women? What demon possesses you?"

"Dressed as I am, no one knows me except you, my husband," Najila meekly protested. She reached to straighten a side of the laurel wreath that had slipped down to one of Loukios's ears when he bent to check his stallion's cannon bone.

Loukios jerked from her touch. "And you, Julian? I cannot believe you played a part in this deception."

Julian was not as easily intimidated as Najila. "I truly had no choice. Your wife insisted on attending the equinox. I came along to protect her. Is that not as you would have preferred?"

Loukios threw up his hands. "Julian, she has duped us both. I suppose neither of us could have prevented this Persian woman's flaunting of Byzantine tradition."

That night, lying in bed when Najila came to him, Loukios saw her shorn hair for the first time. The lovely long, wavy tresses, once flowing to her waist, were gone. Instead tight, burnished curls framed her delicate features.

Thunderstruck, Loukios shouted, "Is that all you have done, or is there yet more to dismay me?"

"There is nothing more, but . . ." Najila lazily unfastened her nightdress. She was so proud of him. Demurely fluttering her eyelashes, she slowly slid the gown off her shoulders, murmuring a sleepy, "No, there is nothing more, Loukas, except . . ."

Loukios sighed. What was a man to do?

Chapter 62

Seven months after Loukios's triumph in the Hippodrome, Najila gave birth to a second child, a girl they named Shadea after Najila's Persian mother, Shahdi. Julian doted on Andreus and Shadea, children he never could himself have. Over the next ten years, he often came to Hawks Hill just to see them and to update Loukios and Najila on court gossip.

On a visit in the spring of 1081, Julian wryly described yet another new emperor, Nikephoros III, over a late supper. "I have come to know him quite well. He is not only naive, he also is awkward at diplomacy, lacks court etiquette, and is unfit to defend Byzantium against the Normans who invade our western borders."

"So I deduced," Loukios said, shooting Najila a quick glance that told her to keep quiet. Though protocol didn't allow her to eat with the men, Najila usually sat at the same table when Julian was at Hawks Hill.

Shaking his head, Julian smiled scornfully. "The single wise move he has made thus far was to promote General Alexios Komnenous as commander-in-chief of the western armies."

Loukios was astounded. "I did not know that. It is good news. Even if Alexios has lost more battles than he has won, I believe he is worthy of the honor."

Najila refused to be left out of such a stimulating conversation. "Are you aware that Alexios Komnenous is a cousin to both Loukas and me?" she asked Julian.

"I knew something of it, though not exactly how you were related," Julian replied.

"The late general Manuel Eroticus Komnenous is Alexios's and my grandfather. And he is Loukas's great-grandfather," she explained.

Julian grinned and winked at Loukios. "It amazes me how the Komnenouses and Doukases can always track their eligibility to the throne. At court, I must be surrounded by dozens of your relatives." He laughed.

Loukios chuckled. "It is fact, not speculation, old friend. When Alexios married Irene Doukas, it melded the two families once and for all." His expression turned serious. "But let us continue our discourse on Alexios and how he might improve our empire's unfortunate state of affairs. We know that Michael VII was chiefly concerned with academia. He had limited vision and so neglected the military—thereby weakening it—that our borders are drastically reduced."

"Which ultimately led to Michael VII's abdication and our present ruler's appointment to the throne," Julian interceded.

"And is it not true the abdication was instigated by the very generals Michael denied his endorsement?" Najila asked.

"Absolutely. Still, there are those of us who believe Nikephoros III will further ruin Byzantium," Loukios said, clicking his tongue.

"I agree." Julian delicately sipped his wine before continuing. "Alexios supports Michael VII, yet Nikephoros rewards Alexios by assigning him to a highly responsible position. Is that not peculiar?"

"Yes, it is peculiar." Loukios lay back in his chair. "Julian, I would like to meet with General Alexios the next time he is in Konstantinoupolis. Extend to him my invitation to a boar hunt at Hawks Hill."

"I am sure it can easily be arranged." Julian smiled, smelling fresh intrigue.

Three weeks later, Julian notified Loukios that the general had returned from the eastern front. From Hawks Hill, Loukios sent word back to Julian, confirming his invitation to the general and inviting Julian to come, as well. Loukios possessed a certain agenda that he wished to propose to Alexios for him to consider. Though Loukios knew that Julian abhorred hunting, he wanted to take advantage of the eunuch's abundant wisdom and incomparable tact.

Najila had ordered her staff to stoke a roaring fire in the huge fireplace of Hawks Hill's library, where the men would meet. She rightly sensed that Loukios had confidential matters to discuss with Alexios, so she did not resent his request that she leave him and the general alone to talk. Anyway, it was not the first time Loukios had actually told her to stay out of sight while he entertained important male guests. After completing preparations, Najila retired to her tower.

Tall and lean, his ebony hair and beard slightly wavy, General Alexios sat at ease in a comfortable chair facing Loukios. His tanned face gleamed in the flickering light. Though Alexios was barely thirty-three years old, three years older than Najila, he had made a name for himself during his initial campaign in 1073.

General Alexios's family relationships were political as well as complex. He was not only the grandson of a Byzantine emperor and closely related to other rulers, but also his older brother, Isaac, had governed Antioch until the Turks captured him in 1077.

Though Loukios was not intimidated when in the presence of powerful men, Alexios, by his very reputation, was not a man with whom one trifled. The proposal Loukios had in mind required thoughtful presentation.

"Because I am nonmilitary," Loukios began, "I deem Hawks Hill neutral territory. Tomorrow's hunt will pause for its midday meal in a remote glen where men may freely express their ideas."

Alexios raised an eyebrow, knowing there had to be more. "And . . . ?"

Loukios hesitated, then plunged ahead with the question that might cause his downfall. "Ere I go on, I need to know how you stand, my cousin. You once swore your allegiance to Michael VII. Do you now favor our new emperor?"

General Alexios cocked his head and peered sideways at Loukios. "What do you mean? I have earned the respect of both."

"If forced to choose, whom would you follow?"

"That is a choice I hope I never have to make."

"Why?" Loukios dared to ask.

Alexios emitted a heavy sigh. "Given what has happened, and what continues to happen, I have come to one conclusion: the two are equally ineffectual leaders. As Nikephoros III gave me my command, however, I am naturally loyal to him. That is probably the reason he favored me. But I realize that it was a clever move to win the military to his side."

"Precisely!" Loukios exclaimed, slapping his knee. His gaze intense, he leaned forward. "Many others favor you above Nikephoros; I among them. Tomorrow we will offer you a proposition."

The next morning, the hounds quickly cornered a large boar. By noon, when the hunters dismounted to partake in the repast set out in a treed glade, servants had already gutted and hung the carcass to bleed out. A tender young sow, flayed and spitted, roasted over glowing coals to a tantalizing golden brown.

Every attendee except Loukios was a top-ranking army officer, so mealtime conversation was decidedly war oriented. All
ate ravenously.

Soundlessly rehearsing the speech he was about to make,
Loukios had no appetite and merely poked at his food.

Too soon, the rest finished, some sitting relaxed, some
lying on furs spread on the ground. Most had imbibed the fine
wine Loukios had generously provided, but no one was yet
intoxicated.

By previous arrangement, Julian arrived in a cart, ready to
act as mediator should there be the need. When the rattling cart
stopped at the fringe of the glade and Julian climbed down,
Loukios stood and strode to a spot near the fire pit. Only when
he held everyone's attention did he begin to speak.

"Most of you may have correctly assumed that we gather here
for something other than hunting boar and feasting. Lucius
Annaeus—commonly remembered as Seneca—once said, 'Fire
tries gold; misery tries brave men.' Seneca also observed, 'Life,
if you know how to use it, is long enough.'" Loukios paused for
effect.

His audience silently awaited his next words.

Loukios nervously cleared his throat before proceeding. "The
latter comment in mind, my intent is to reveal to you a plan
thus far kept secret from all but a few."

To a man, his overfed and listless guests became alert.

Ignoring an undercurrent of muttering, Loukios went on.
"We have among us a particular noble who has been tried by
misery, as well as by fire." Loukios felt their anticipation build.
He inhaled a deep breath before he announced, "Alexios Komnenous, there are those present who wish you to take the
throne."

The hum of voices ceased. Dead silence filled the glade.
Then, united as one body, the assembly jumped to its feet.
Clenched fists jabbed the air. Loud shouts echoed throughout
the forest. "Aye, Alexios! Aye, Alexios!"

Weary beyond belief, Loukios collapsed on a log, his lips silently whispering, "Thank you, oh mighty and holy God. I pray your guidance has caused me to choose our man wisely."

Chapter 63

The year had been one of turmoil. The empire was threatened by rebellion within and attacks from without the realm. When the military's plan to put Alexios on the throne was discovered by the emperor's henchmen, Alexios fled to Thrace.

While in Thrace, Alexios lived on the estate of Caesar John Doukas. Later, Caesar John bribed a mercenary officer to unbar the gates of Konstantinoupolis so the military units under Alexios could enter. But once inside the walls, instead of maintaining order, Alexios's soldiers plundered the city. Meanwhile, Caesar John convinced Nikephorus III to abdicate.

As all this was going on, Loukios stormed about Hawks Hill, in a bad temper and hard to approach. Fortunately, the emperor had not discovered that Loukios had instigated the coup.

Najila managed to stay out of her husband's way during the worst of his moods. Everyone was greatly relieved when Alexios was finally secure on the throne in 1081 and peace returned to Hawks Hill.

Najila had things other than politics on her mind. It still distressed her that she had not successfully carried another child to term after Shadea was born, but the doctors forbade additional children when she suffered three miscarriages in rapid succession. Until recently, caring for her two lively children and helping Loukios oversee the two estates and a compartment within the royal palace compound had left Najila little time for her own pursuits. But twelve-year-old Andreus now spent his hours being academically tutored, and with Shadea old enough, at nine, to entertain herself, Najila experienced renewed freedom.

Her fiery nature having mellowed with age, she used the time to meditate or read in her isolated tower room. Loukios and the children usually found her there whenever they sought her.

Najila heard Shadea's light footsteps echoing on the spiral staircase, and her daughter gracefully danced into the circular room. She had inherited Najila's tawny skin, raven hair, and exotic, slightly slanted eyes. She had her father's wonderful smile and lean build, but her hazel-green irises ringed in deep blue and framed by dark, sweeping lashes were her own.

Shadea threw her arms around Najila's neck. "Mama, can I go to the kitchen to watch the preparation of our evening meal?"

Najila struggled to keep a serious countenance. Asking permission was a needless, daily ritual between them that Shadea had started several months ago. Najila guessed that Shadea's preoccupation with cooking was secondary. She suspected that the true attraction in the kitchen were the generous samples offered by the cooks who, like the rest of the family's servants, dearly loved Shadea. Despite these frequent handouts, Shadea was not the least bit plump; like her mother, her boundless energy burned off any excess fat.

Najila, a pampered princess raised in a noble household where her every wish was fulfilled, had never so much as boiled water. Shadea's interest in what seemed to Najila an onerous, messy process both puzzled and amused her. She decided not to protest her daughter's excursions to the kitchen as long as it kept the girl's inquiring intellect and busy hands occupied.

"That is fine, Shadea. Why not make something special?"

Shadea thought a moment and then performed a little hop of anticipation. "I will bake a surprise treat for you," she bubbled, her face glowing. "You shall have it tonight at supper." She smacked a wet kiss on Najila's cheek and skipped out the door. Najila heard her daughter's sweet voice humming all the way down the staircase.

Najila let her gaze wander over the brilliant silk and wool tapestries she had hung to warm the cold stone wall. Her eyes settled on a cross-shaped icon mounted on the opposite wall. Suddenly nostalgic, she remembered the silver and amber cross. *How sad,* she mused, *that Otrygg failed to recover it. The loss was my fault, not his, though he has never forgiven himself for not bringing it back to me.*

"Well," she said aloud, "if I cannot have the original, I must design a duplicate. I should have thought of it years ago." Newly motivated, she jumped out of her chair and, moving very much like Shadea, fairly skipped from the room.

The tower became Najila's studio. For the best light, she sat at a writing table that she had placed under a narrow window. She had been taught to read and write as a child in Persia, but drawing an accurate image of an object, especially something strictly from memory, posed a new challenge.

During the passing years, it had become increasingly difficult to recall details of her father's cross, and drafting a copy proved even harder. Biting her lip in frustration, Najila bent over her last sheet of rare, fine-textured rice paper. She had already attempted half-a-dozen vignettes, which now lay in wadded balls beneath the table.

The basic cross itself wasn't difficult to draw; she easily sketched a typical Byzantine form with triple flared ends— models were available everywhere. Her most complicated task was to imitate the amber with its fossilized dragonfly. Michael's cross had been one of a kind. She would never be able to duplicate the amber chunk, let alone the insect it contained. For several days, she sought an answer to the problem.

One night, just as she was falling asleep and her mind lingered in that twilight previous to oblivion, the solution came to her. If the hour were not so late, and decent illumination were available by which to see detail, she would have dashed up to her tower and carried out her vision.

Awakening at dawn the next morning, and leaving Loukios still sound asleep, Najila raced up to her studio. She had to apply her idea to paper before the rest of the household stirred and disturbed her concentration.

When she at last completed it, her design portrayed the replica of a dragonfly enclosed in painted amber, outlined in what would be gold wire. "Yes!" she cried, holding up the drawing to study it. "That is how to add color. Why did I not think of it before? I shall use enamels!"

With the design finished, she had to contact the various guilds whose members would translate her crude sketch into reality. When she knelt to perform her daily prayers, she asked God to find for her the most talented artisans.

Chapter 64

Najila, with Amara along as her escort and lady-in-waiting, searched the guild-controlled, precious metal and gem shops that lined Konstantinoupolis's Mesê. The powerful guilds were a law unto themselves and tightly controlled. A silversmith was not permitted to work with gold. Nor was a goldsmith allowed to style silver. And neither of those crafts-men could facet a gem, which must be cut by a member of yet another guild.

Najila had chosen a good time to give the Byzantine crafts-men some work. The government was in serious trouble; the economy's depressed state made it difficult for artisans to earn a living.

When Najila was ready to proceed, she summoned a renowned Armenian silversmith to Hawks Hill. As Amara led the way up the staircase to the tower studio, the corpulent, gray-haired guildsman puffed and wheezed. On reaching the top landing, his chest heaving, he mopped his florid, moist brow.

"Lady Doukas," he panted as Amara ushered him through the doorway, "may we meet elsewhere? I fear I cannot again bear the climb."

Sitting at her work table, Najila looked with pity on the red-faced Armenian. "I thought it better to meet here because my drawings are here. I did not account for how tiring the journey from Konstantinoupolis would be, and then the ascent to my tower." The guildsmen she had chosen were all advanced in age, but they were also the most experienced. "I selected you to do the work because you are the very best," she said, flattering the man, "but I suppose that's small consolation if you were to expire on the tower steps. Come," she said, rising.

"On this day, let us confer in the dining hall, where there is ample space to display my drawings." She briefly touched the guildsman's elbow to guide him toward the door. "In the future, we will meet in the more convenient Komnenous quarters at the old palace."

Rolling her papers into a compact bundle, she followed the relieved silversmith to the mansion's ground level. The artisan collapsed onto a comfortable chair. "I am deeply thankful to you, my lady."

Najila waved away his gratitude. "Let us wait for the other guildsmen. I expect them at any moment." She laid the rolled papers with her drawings on the surface of the huge dining table.

Soon, the Jewish goldsmith and the Greek enameler arrived, and Amara ushered them into the great hall. After introductions, the three men contemplated one of Najila's preliminary sketches.

"An unadorned cross?" questioned the Armenian. "Is it truly as you wish, so modest, Lady Doukas?" he asked, jabbing a pudgy finger at the drawing.

"Not quite. But you must see this version first to truly understand what I want." Najila flattened a second sheet and held it down to keep it from curling. "This is the final view. My ability to illustrate what I feel inside me is at best weak, but do you recognize the winged creature?" she asked, eyeing the goldsmith.

"An insect?" the man murmured tentatively, not wanting to offend her by uttering the wrong reply.

She nodded. "It is a dragonfly, a golden dragonfly."

"What part am I to play in the manufacture of such an artistic and unique piece?" probed the Greek enameler, immensely interested.

Najila pointed to the amber nugget, the dragonfly's body, and the gems pictured on the four arm tips of the cross. "The insect's coloring, the amber, and the simulated cabochon jewels are to be framed in gold and then enameled."

Still not understanding it all, the Armenian planted his thumb on the cross's center. "And what purpose has this asymmetrical line that surrounds the insect?" he asked, frowning.

"It is supposed to be an amber nugget," Najila explained. "Of course, it is impossible to obtain genuine amber of that shape, so I have created its representation."

"How so? In silver?"

"No, just the cross itself is silver. I wish the rest to be of gold and enamel."

Peering more closely at the faux amber, the Armenian craftsman exclaimed, "Ah, I see it now, an amazing idea, my lady. Your finished cross will be lovely."

"Thank you," Najila purred proudly.

"Why do we not make the dragonfly wings of filigreed gold?" interposed the goldsmith.

Najila's enthusiasm grew. "That is a splendid idea. It should lend a certain delicacy to the overall design, as well as lighten the weight hanging from the neck chain."

"You mention a chain. What do you have in mind?" said the goldsmith, perceiving the possibility of additional profit.

Pondering, Najila nibbled her lip. "The cross is silver. A silver chain would look better, I think," she answered.

The silversmith grinned and rubbed his hands together. The goldsmith, however, hated giving up a chance for a larger commission. He glanced at his rival, then shrewdly observed,

"But your design, my lady, shows the cross crafted in both metals, their amounts are nearly equal. I have to say, the greatest
advantage of gold over silver is that gold does not tarnish but
forever remains gloriously brilliant. The entire presentation
would be handsomer with a *gold* chain, would it not?"

When Najila's eyes lit up, the goldsmith knew he had scored
his point. He would not only have the pleasure of rendering
the most intriguing part of the piece, but he would also earn
the greater fee. Satisfied that the silversmith was left with only
the basic form to manufacture, the goldsmith threw the other
man a triumphant smirk.

Their rivalry was lost on Najila, who was concentrating on
her drawings, trying to visualize the proposed amendments to
her original ideas.

Three months later, Najila wore the cross in public for the
first time, at a royal ball. Set against an elegant gown sewn from
ecru watered silk, the beautiful object glittered on her breast.
She had decided to add a pair of matching earrings to the original commission she had given the guildsmen, but she wore no
other ornamentation besides a filigreed gold band to discipline
her unruly ringlets. The unusual cross, with its dragonfly design
repeated in the dangling earrings, was the evening's chief topic
of conversation among the women. When the noblewomen discovered that Najila had created her own jewelry, they mobbed
her, imploring her to design jewelry for them.

Thus, with Loukios's encouragement, jewelry design became
Najila's new avocation. God had made her life exceptionally
fulfilling. She could ask no more of him.

Chapter 65

The day he turned seventeen, with a bit of help from both Julian and Otrygg, Andreus was accepted into an elite guard unit. It wasn't Otrygg's famed Varangians, who had to prove that Viking blood ran in their veins, but another, almost as significant unit assigned to royal protection.

During the short, midwinter days, Najila rarely had time to take her usual morning rides; she was too busy fashioning baubles for her wealthy patrons. The Byzantines considered it crass for a gentlewoman to practice a trade, so Najila claimed jewelry design as her hobby. She loved it.

Unlike Najila, Elias had more idle moments during the winter months, especially because Najila didn't come as often to the stables. Besides accomplishing his regular duties, he took it upon himself to exercise the neglected Jahara. At nearly twenty years old, the small, tough steppe mare was in fine condition, her coat shining. She had gentled with age, but her attitude was still sassy on occasion. After handling the highly strung chariot stock, Elias enjoyed quietly riding Jahara over Hawks Hill's expansive rolling fields and through its dense woods. This he did almost every day at the same time, usually around dusk. But this day, he decided to take an early morning ride.

To break the monotony, Elias sometimes urged Jahara into an easy trot. He hummed a lively tune as they traversed the tree-lined trail. Giving the mare her head, he let her slow to a lazy walk. His cloak's wool cowl, extending as much as three inches beyond his face, protected him from the freezing air and sharp branches. A wide scarf that wrapped his nose and mouth further concealed his features.

Jahara took every opportunity to scavenge tidbits from one side or the other as she passed something suiting her taste. Elias paid no mind, though she had been previously disciplined whenever she did it.

"You have earned leniency, little mare," he murmured.

Jahara swiveled her ears, listening to his softly spoken words. She was craning her neck to snatch a particularly attractive morsel when her head shot up, and she stopped dead in her tracks, throwing Elias forward, across her neck. He grabbed a fistful of mane to stay aboard.

A deer, thought Elias, straightening. He tightened his hold on the reins, preparing to curb Jahara if she tried to bolt. But instead of deer, two riders emerged from the forest, barring his way. The rough-looking men were well equipped with weapons: swords and daggers. Each of them clutched a nocked bow held in readiness.

"Ho!" Elias challenged them. "This is Hawks Hill property, belonging to Lord and Lady Doukas."

The strangers didn't answer.

Elias warned them again. "Hunting is not allowed here."

The pair just sneered.

The sound of smashing foliage came from the thicket behind Elias. He whirled Jahara to face it. Two more men on horseback materialized among the trees. In his peripheral vision, Elias saw the first pair moving closer. He spun Jahara to face them again.

Elias realized that he was surrounded, but surrounded by whom? Poachers? One man carried a mace—a chain with a short wooden handle at one end and a heavy iron ball at the other. Poachers were common these days in depressed Byzantium, but poachers typically bore spears and bows and arrows, not maces.

"Though it is not the woman, he rides her horse," growled one of the men.

"He has seen us. We cannot permit him to return to the manse," said another, menacing Elias with his drawn sword, its point circling ominously.

With no help within shouting distance, Elias knew he was in dire jeopardy.

Disliking her rider's nervous pressure on the bit, Jahara jigged in place, catching Elias off guard. As his attention shifted to controlling the mare, the men tightened their circle around him.

An excruciating blow struck the back of Elias's head. Fire erupted behind his eyes . . . and then nothing.

"Come ride with me. It is a beautiful morning. Let us take advantage of it," Loukios begged Najila.

"I have to finish a pin design. Lady Deena is coming for it on the morrow."

Loukios carefully turned Najila's sketch face down on the tabletop. Gently drawing her to her feet, he said, "You have been at it for days. Neither of us can sleep when your legs twitch all night because you have sat all day."

"You are right, of course." Najila sighed. "I truly do crave some physical activity. The design is nearly finished; I have only to add color to the jewels. Let us go then."

When they arrived at the stable, they found Elias and Jahara already gone, so a different horse was prepared for Najila. Relishing the crisp air, simply appreciating their togetherness, the couple rode the same trail that Elias had taken earlier.

The animals' hooves crushed and crackled the leaves and needles that formed the trail's thick, fragrant surface. Deciduous trees, their leafless limbs entwined with conifer branches, created a lacy canopy through which the ascending sun lanced, seeming to seek elusive shaded spots on which a light snow had fallen the previous night. The rays hitting ice crystals reflected in rainbow-hued, diamond-bright sparkles.

Najila was dreamily trailing along when, without warning, Loukios abruptly halted in the middle of the track, forcing Najila's horse onto the heels of his mount. As her gelding bumped his mare, Loukios's mount lashed out a hoof, which narrowly missed the gelding's vulnerable knees.

"Why did you stop like that?" Najila yelled peevishly. "My horse was nearly kicked."

"Something lies in the trail ahead." Loukios prodded his jittery mare up to the motionless form, swung from his saddle, and stooped over it. "It is Elias!" he cried.

"Oh no!" Najila exclaimed, sliding off her mount. She looked about them. "I do not see Jahara. Do you think she threw him?"

Loukios checked Elias. "He is breathing, but he is badly injured." When he lifted Elias's head, blood covered Loukios's arm and hand. "Najila, go back home! Get help! Hurry!"

Najila remounted and savagely kneed the gelding's ribs. The horse lunged forward then broke into a rapid canter, heading to Hawks Hill.

Even in winter, one normally heard birds, but the woods were eerily silent as Loukios knelt by Elias. He doubted that Jahara would have dislodged Elias, an excellent horseman, from his saddle. So what had happened?

As Loukios brushed a speck of dirt from Elias's pale cheek, four heavily armed horsemen trotted up. Noting their menacing demeanor, Loukios rose to his feet. He started to ask, "Who—?" but one of the men rammed him with his horse.

Loukios staggered backward, trying to recover his balance and at the same time drawing his saber from its scabbard. From the corner of his eye, he saw the wickedly spiked ball of a mace coming at him, but he was unable to dodge it or deflect its path. The heavy iron weapon struck him on the forehead, knocking him to the ground. His arms flailing wildly, he bounced obscenely on the icy earth, twitched, and then lay still.

Returning with a contingent of men to aid Elias, Najila encountered Leopold Alexander Doukas and a second man heading in the same direction. Meeting him, her longtime adversary, on her own property outraged her. She hadn't seen her father-in-law in years, except from afar at court functions. Never an accomplished equestrian, his flabby frame slumped awkwardly in the saddle. Observing his sagging jowls and mottled skin, she noted that his life at court had been less than beneficial for his health.

That he possessed the nerve to trespass at Hawks Hill astonished her. But with so many of her own men to protect her, Najila did not fear him. When Loukios learned of his father's presence, he would be furious.

"Loukios forbade you to be anywhere near me or Hawks Hill, Leopold Alexander. Why have you come?"

On seeing his son's wife, Leopold Alexander's florid cheeks blanched. Just then, her attention was drawn to four horsemen who cantered out of the woods. Before Leopold Alexander could stop him, one of the men gleefully shouted, "We missed the woman, but got her two men. Both are dead." He rode up to Leopold, triumphantly twirling a bloody mace around his head.

Two!

"No! Please not Loukas!" Najila cried. She spurred the gelding to a full run and dashed recklessly into the tangled woods.

When she reached the spot where Elias lay, she saw her husband also prone, his head in a red pool. She jumped from her mount and flung herself across his unmoving shape, kissing his face, rubbing his frigid hands.

Feeling no response, Najila screamed, "God, why have you killed my beloved?" Then, mercifully, she fainted.

Arriving at the tragic scene, Leopold Alexander entered a nightmare of his own creation. Immediately identifying his son's crumpled body on the icy turf, he swayed in the saddle, his right hand clutching at his chest. From his mouth came a guttural, gasping cry. As he arched backward, his left hand jerked the reins so hard that his horse reacted by rearing and squealing.

Leopold Alexander Doukas was catapulted from the saddle into the trunk of a large pine tree, but he was already dead. His body slumped in an awkward heap at the side of the trail.

Chapter 66

Najila recovered from her swoon as someone gently lifted her off her husband's body. She stood to the side, propped against a tree, helplessly wringing her hands while the men worked rapidly to staunch the flow of blood from Loukios's head. He didn't stir during their ministrations.

"Though weak, your lord's heart still beats, Lady Najila," said one of the men. "But Elias is dead."

Having brought no means by which to transport the gravely injured Loukios, the men draped his limp body crosswise on the saddle of one of the horses. Though his head and neck were stabilized by a man who walked alongside the horse, holding a makeshift bandage in place, the wound continued to ooze blood. Loukios remained unconscious during the entire trip home. Lashed to the saddle of another horse, Elias's corpse made its sad, final journey.

✟

"Time will tell us if he will fully waken," said the doctor whom Najila summoned to Hawks Hill. "Meanwhile, it is best to let him rest." The physician bled Loukios before he left, but when Najila noticed that Loukios was weaker afterward, she refused to allow any more medicinal bleeding.

In the days that followed, she left her husband's side only when absolutely necessary. Though she usually curled next to him in their big canopied bed, she had servants bring a pallet for her to use when Loukios was exceptionally restless.

More than a week passed before Loukios became aware of his surroundings: hushed whispers, women's skirts rustling, glass clinking on glass. Then came pain, pain so intense he almost screamed, but the effort proved too great. He opened his eyelids, but he saw only blackness riddled with brilliant sparks that gradually faded.

Something enveloped his skull tightly, and he reached up to touch it. His shaking fingers discovered a thick cloth binding his head, but his eyes were not covered. Why couldn't he see anything except darkness shot with flashes of color? *It must be the middle of night,* he thought as he again slipped into uncomplicated sleep.

A few days later, he awakened again. The voices were louder now, some of them unfamiliar. People seemed to move around in the night without the benefit of candles or lanterns. But whose were those mysterious voices that came and went? It was all too much to comprehend.

Hardly resting, and barely eating enough to sustain herself, Najila hovered over Loukios twenty-four hours a day. When she spoke to him, he often opened his eyes, but she couldn't tell if he actually heard her.

Faithful Zahra had died peacefully in her sleep the same week that Elias and Loukios had been attacked. It was an additional burden with which Najila was forced to cope. She pleaded with the aging Otrygg to oversee the running of Hawks Hill, which he did willingly, despite his own infirmities and grief.

Two souls dear to her were dead, and Loukios was incapacitated. Najila longed for Zahra, longed to cry on her shoulder. In a way, she felt, like a newborn infant—helpless and yearning to snuggle against its mother's comforting breast.

Najila had immediately sent a message to Andreus, notifying him of the attack on his father, but so far, he had not responded. His guard unit had been reassigned and sent to fight a war in a remote region. The conflict and location rendered him unreachable.

Najila's message to Shadea told of the attack, but encouraged the newlywed to stay with her husband. Shadea complied with her mother's request and did not travel to her side, but her return message asked Najila to summon her if she was needed.

Najila bitterly wished that it had been Leopold Alexander who had suffered the painful injuries he had caused to be inflicted on his own son. Not only had his henchmen so heinously injured her beloved husband, but they had also killed poor, innocent Elias. Now, her precious Loukas lay abed, a different person, his body withering, unresponsive to her love. Leopold Alexander Doukas should have had to suffer, too. Sudden death was much too easy for one so evil.

Najila managed to feed Loukios a variety of thin soups and watered-down wine. Three times a day, she would raise his head and shoulders on pillows and then prod his lips with a spoon until he responded. Careful not to choke him, she coaxed the liquids down his throat sip by sip. He always gazed at her when she fed him, but his eyes held a vague, unfocused appearance, and he appeared to dwell within a world of his own.

Eventually, Loukios began to reconnect with the world around him, but it was a tenuous connection at best. All he really knew was that he was a man. He wondered why he could not recall the simplest matters, such as his name and the name of the woman nursing him, who seemed to know him intimately. Three questions constantly plagued his mind: *Who am I? Where am I? Who is she?* She was the soft-voiced woman who slept beside him, draping her slender arm across his chest, soothing his fierce headaches with gentle fingers, and who called him "Loukas."

His sightless eyes struggled in vain to visualize what his other senses perceived: things that smelled faintly familiar, pungent herbs, perfume, and candle wax. He heard a woman hum as a straw broom rasped the floor, and he listened to the chatting of the two women who changed the bed linens every day.

When his bandages had been removed and the headaches had apparently decreased, Najila saw her husband's normally blank expression brighten when he recognized her footsteps as she entered the room one day. It so astonished her, she dropped the tray she was carrying to him, splattering dishes and food everywhere.

"Najila? Is that you?" he croaked, his throat dry, his voice hoarse. "Why is there not a lamp in this dark room?"

Running to him, she threw her arms around his neck. When Loukios unexpectedly returned her embrace, her joyous laughter rang throughout the manse. "You are back at last," she cried.

"Back? Where have I been?" He recalled having ridden with her into the woods that morning. Throwing off his covers he pushed her away. "Why are you up and about and stumbling around in the dark?" Fighting to move his legs to the edge of the bed, he found his muscles weak and trembling. Something was not right. Nauseous, he collapsed backward, his lungs pumping in huge gasps.

"My legs won't work," he cried. "What is wrong with me, Najila?" He rubbed his eyes. "And why can I not see anything?"

Tears streamed down Najila's cheeks. How could she explain to him that he had been blinded in an attack meant to kill her? Never, never could she bear to tell him that his own father had been behind it all. She'd leave that onerous chore to someone less vulnerable to her husband's inevitable rage, perhaps Otrygg or Julian.

As she studied Loukios's familiar features, she saw an expression of shock suddenly change his face. Moaning, he rolled to his side and into a fetal position, arms covering his head.

"Why am I blind?" he cried.

Najila stroked his hair, not knowing what else to do, but he resisted her touch, hunching his body into an even tighter ball.

At that moment, Najila realized how much their lives would be forever changed.

Chapter 67

"With Alexios on the throne, I am sure to go to war again soon," Andreus declared to his parents one day in 1096 while dining with them in their Konstantinoupolis suite.

Loukios stopped eating, a bite halfway to his mouth. "All things have not gone well during the fourteen years Alexios has ruled, but Andreus, our emperor is not entirely to blame," he declared. Fully healed except for his blindness, Loukios had become a valued counselor to the emperor.

Loukios added, "The emperor has always proclaimed his wish to rebuild Byzantium to its previous glory, which is an unending struggle and requires force. I have done all I can to help him in his effort, I might add."

"I am afraid I have to agree with your father," Najila interjected. "Our empire's decline began long before Alexios took the throne."

At Loukios's right, Najila sat across the table from her tall, handsome son and his beautiful, eighteen-year-old wife, Laliyne. Ponderous with her first child, Laliyne, a blonde, fair-skinned Circassian, was also taller than any other woman Najila knew. She and Andreus made a stunning contrast. Laliyne seldom participated in family discussions, as she spoke neither Greek nor Latin fluently. Najila was unsure how the couple could even communicate, but anyone could tell that they obviously cherished each other.

Now twenty-seven, Andreus commanded a full battalion. He had grown a bit taller than his father, but both had strongly formed features, heavy manes of dark auburn hair, and wonderful gray eyes that darkened to nearly black when they were angry.

They are so much alike, Najila said to herself on more than one occasion.

Discounting his unpredictable outbursts of temper, Loukios seemed to have adapted to his blindness. But each time his vacant stare sought Najila's face only to sweep over and beyond her, she ached to make eye contact, to see recognition in his blank gaze.

"Ten years of fighting to regain and keep the land," Andreus growled. "Since I have been a part of the military and for as long as I can remember, Robert Guiscard has constantly invaded our western border." He pounded the table with his fist. The tankards jumped like fleas, sloshing wine over the rims. "When he died, thank our Lord God, we thought we were done with the Normans, but then—"

"Then Guiscard's son, Bohemonde, steps into his deceased papa's shoes, and the conflict goes on," Loukios finished for him. "That is precisely why Alexios successfully promoted an alliance with the Venetians, and later the Kumans. Using that alliance five years ago, we were able to defeat the Pechenegs, who had the gall to attack the very walls of Konstantinoupolis itself."

Andreus huffed derisively. "It is said the Kumans are true-hearted to none other than their own people, though I recall that they and the Pechenegs once united to conquer Thrace."

Loukios nodded. "I told Alexios that both are inconsequential nomadic tribes, with whom we never should have had a relationship." Thoughtfully, he chewed a morsel of savory, baked white fish caught that morning in the Bosporus. Swallowing hard, he continued, "Our traveling merchants recount stories of how the tribal members—men, women, and children—cheat, bribe, and steal to get what they covet. Alexios should refuse to trust any of them."

Andreus broke in, "What I cannot understand is why Alexios used cavalry from the Seljuks, formerly our most bitter enemy, to stop Bohemonde."

Loukios smiled. "That was a clever ploy. And it worked, did it not?"

"I suppose so."

"Yet I have to believe we are well rid of such pagan coalitions," Loukios said. He relished these heated discussions with his son.

Andreus would not be pacified. "Humph! Maybe we are rid of the pagans, but now, thanks to Alexios having sought aid from the West, Rome's crusaders run wild through our fine city. As a result of their rampaging, I even question their claims that they are genuine Christians."

"As sometimes do I," Loukios agreed. "Nevertheless, Scripture says that we are not to judge them. God will perform that act on Judgment Day."

"Still, we ought to throw them out," Andreus insisted. "Let them fend for themselves. Instead, we empty our storage houses in order to supply them."

A ruckus sounded in the street below. Andreus ran to the window to see what was happening. "Look at that! Six of those so-called crusaders are arguing with a poor cart vendor," Andreus snarled. "Now they strip his cart of everything. I am going down to stand with him." Andreus reached for his sword.

Loukios shook a finger in the direction of his son's voice. "Hold on! You are outnumbered by five, Andreus," he cautioned. "Have they physically harmed the vendor?"

"No. They have left him shaken but unhurt."

"Then let him be. It is over." Loukios clicked his tongue and shook his head. "That is just a sample of what would happen if

the crusaders were left to fend for themselves, as you suggest,"
Loukios snorted. "Well, my son, left to their own devices, they
would surely ravage every field and slaughter every meat animal from here to their ultimate destination."

"Our friend Alexios hopes to hurry them along by donating
goods and services," Loukios continued. "I already sense signs
they are leaving. And do not forget that Alexios urged Pope
Urban II to send us help to begin with. Besides, not all crusaders are riffraff. Last week during a ceremony at court, I met
many noble knights who seem honestly dedicated to Christ and
who are eager to free Jerusalem. I particularly recall one young
man, named Tancred, who promised allegiance to Alexios. He
claims he is Robert Guiscard's grandnephew. Unlike his uncle,
Tancred feels that crusading is far more crucial than laying
siege to Byzantium."

"That may be, Father," Andreus interrupted. "But Urban, a
Roman pope?" he snickered. "Since when are we Greeks col-
laborators with the Romans? It irks me to death."

Groping for his walking stick, Loukios pushed back his chair.
He used the stick to rise. "Though Romans and Byzantines
disagree on doctrine, we do mutually maintain one critical
objective: we must retake the lands and holy places that once
belonged to us Christians."

Najila had been aware for some time that the blow to his
head had subtly altered Loukios's personality. He remained
intellectually alert, but he often retreated within himself and
easily grew irritated when annoyed by someone or something.
True, he exhibited the same devotion to her that he had always
shown, but other than politics, he had no outside interests and
rarely visited the stables. She had tried but had never been
able to get him to go to another chariot race. He did attend
one presentation at court, where he met the crusaders he had
mentioned to Andreus, but only after she had coaxed him into
going with Otrygg.

"Do you think the emperor will have your guard join the crusade?" Najila asked Andreus.

Her son rose from the table. "I and my men have already been given orders to join," he said wryly. "My obligation is to do that which is required. Tomorrow, I shall return to Hawks Hill to prepare." He hesitated, then said, "Naturally, Mother, you and Laliyne do not wish me to go, but go I must. Am I not a duty-bound military officer?"

Understanding the gist of what had just been said, Laliyne arose clumsily and then collapsed in her husband's arms.

Najila averted her face so the others would not notice her distress. "We will go to Hawks Hill, too," she told Andreus. What more could she say? Like his father, loyal to a fault, Andreus would do what he deemed proper, despite how his wife and mother felt about it.

A few days later, Najila, Loukios, and Laliyne stood at the top of the portico staircase at Hawks Hill. The two women wept as a squire helped Andreus mount his great black war horse. Loukios could not see his son ride off and fade from sight, yet his eyes were also wet.

Having returned to their city apartments, Loukios and Najila sat on the third-story balcony as crusader caravans passed beyond the royal compound on their way east. Najila described the parade to Loukios. "First are foreign leaders, armored Norman-French barons riding resplendent horses and proudly carrying their province or country flag. Over their armor, they and the soldiers of Christ who follow wear sleeveless white tunics marked with red crosses."

Najila and Loukios shouted encouragement and shed proud tears as the Konstantinoupolis contingent, including their son, rode by. After those units came the war machines: massive catapults, rams, and miscellaneous instruments of siege, pulled by long teams of bullocks.

Common peasants, and unsavory individuals who expected to obtain land, wealth, or both during the venture plodded at a considerable distance behind the Byzantines. Next, the supply wagons, sagging beneath their bales of food and ammunition, lumbered into view.

Trailing everything else, hauling their personal possessions, trod a motley band of camp followers. Some of these were legitimate families of fighting men, but others were street women who would practice their profession along the way.

Children prodded livestock and yelled at sorry-looking curs that ran alongside the procession with their tails between their legs. Many of the travelers rode skinny nags or donkeys. Most of the stragglers trudged by on foot, coughing in the dust stirred up by those ahead.

When Najila finished describing the latter group, Loukios tightened his arm about her shoulders and muttered, "It is not a promising lot, is it, my love."

"And it worries me," Najila exclaimed, rubbing her taut forehead. "Our son depends on that very rabble for support when he is on the battlefield."

"Then we must continually pray and have faith that God will protect him," Loukios added quietly.

"Praying is what I do best," Najila answered.

Chapter 68

Loukios and Najila continued to divide their time between Hawks Hill and the city.

News from the eastern front, where Andreus fought with Alexios and the crusaders, arrived infrequently, usually in the form of rumor, distorted or sparse in content. Andreus's wife, Laliyne, and their daughter, Chloe, lived at Hawks Hill during his absence. They had heard nothing from him in months.

With Andreus gone, Loukios aged noticeably, and his moodiness affected Najila. Keeping up her spirits was difficult, and she battled an ever-encroaching depression.

For her husband's sake, she had taken over his quest to breed the perfect chariot horse. She continued to hope that Loukios would revive his interest and participation in the project. After several generations, she had reached her goal of an ideal conformation. But it was merely part of the goal Loukios had set long ago. She had never found the acceptable, brightly colored stallion that was needed to sire the spotted foals Loukios had wanted.

After Elias was killed in the attack meant for her, Najila had hired a young man named Thadeus to oversee the stables. He was truly a gift of God, which was what his name meant in both Greek and Hebrew. Like Elias, Thadeus supervised the breeding and race training, and he was scrupulously attentive to all of his duties. He was also as clever with the horses as Elias had been, but Najila knew she would never feel quite as close to Thadeus as she had to Elias.

"I suppose I should be content that we win consistently," she remarked to Loukios as they strolled with her hand in the crook of his arm gently guiding him. "Yet, I would have enjoyed entering a spectacular team that sported those distinctive spots you always desired, to fulfill your original plan." She paused for a moment and then added wistfully, "I so wished I could have done it for you, my love."

She stood on tiptoe, reaching up to finger-comb his wind-blown hair. Though he had recently turned sixty-eight, his snowy white hair had not thinned with age. Najila, at fifty-one, was showing gray streaks that gleamed silver-rose in the late afternoon sun.

It was such a lovely evening. She had coaxed Loukios into walking her to the stable garden, her favorite place. If only he would take an interest in her efforts; they used to work so well together.

Loukios fumbled until he found her hand. Squeezing it, he murmured, "I was sure you would discover the fine steppe stallion we sought, but I guess the spotted beasts are rarer than we believed."

Najila shivered with hope. He hadn't mentioned it in years. "None I see are adequate in all aspects," she answered, sighing. "You would not have approved of them either."

"That may be, but I really do not care anymore." He shrugged and turned away, seeming to lose interest, once again barring her from his sightless world.

Hurt, Najila suppressed a sharp retort.

Fortunately, Thadeus hastened into the garden. "Lord and Lady Doukas," he shouted, "there is a new foal. Just dropped. It is a beauty, as black as the blackest onyx stone."

Najila had been biased toward black horses ever since her father had given her Jahara, now long deceased. She grabbed

Loukios, tugging his arm. "Hurry, let us go see. Another black! How wonderful!"

"Is it a colt or filly, Thadeus?" Loukios asked.

Thadeus stammered, "I . . . er . . . ah . . . I did not check."

"It makes no difference to me," Najila chortled. No matter what it was, she loved every baby. She adored stroking their fuzzy coats, watching them cavort in the pasture, flagging their perky tails. She especially liked to hold their delicate heads near her face, to inhale the sweet, milk-fragrant breath expelled from their velvety nostrils.

Najila knew that Loukios thought her exuberance endearing, but she was also aware that her reluctance to sell off extraneous stock undermined her efficiency as a breeder.

Impatient, she strode ahead of the two men and on to the brood barn. Approaching the long, low shed, she heard the high-pitched whinny of a newborn foal. Again it whinnied. She followed the shrill sound to an expansive box stall that held a stunning, dark, liver-bay mare with golden mane and tail. The mare was Najila's special darling.

The light within the stall was dim, but Najila made out a small, shadowy shape nuzzling its dam. Cooing to the nervous mother, Najila opened the stall door. Responding to Najila's quietly spoken words and familiar voice, the mare nickered deep in her throat.

Loukios and Thadeus joined Najila in the roomy stall. Mortified because he had not had the presence of mind to check earlier, Thadeus captured the foal and hoisted its short tail. "It is a colt," he pronounced sheepishly, embarrassed to his toes.

Loukios emitted a rare chuckle. He once had made the same mistake in the early days of the Hawks Hill horse-breeding operation. "Describe him to me, please."

"He is the image of Ebony, your two-year-old with the same sire and dam; they are full brothers. He looks exactly like Ebony even to the star and thin snip on his nose. The pair will be a perfectly matched team should they prove to have ability."

Pointing his ears toward Najila, the foal wobbled on awkward legs over to her. She cupped her palms around his muzzle and softly breathed into his nostrils, presenting her personal scent. She knew that foals bonded best to their handlers while less than a week old.

Glancing over at Loukios, Najila noted he wore a cheerful expression—a nice change from his usual scowl.

"Thadeus, when he can take care of himself, put this one out with Ebony," Loukios ordered.

Thadeus nodded. "I agree. As soon as our boy here is strong enough, I shall see if the mare still tolerates her rambunctious two-year-old. If so, I can put the three in the same field."

Alarmed, Najila spoke up. "Is that not too soon, Loukas? Might the bigger colt harm his little brother? A two-year-old is too frisky to be fenced in with a mere baby."

Loukios smiled at her concern. "Thadeus will not leave them alone until he is assured everything will go well."

Thadeus vigorously bobbed his head. "Lady Doukas, I myself will make sure they get along, make certain that the younger is not in danger of being bitten or trampled."

More good news arrived at Hawks Hill later that night. Najila and Loukios were awakened by the clatter of hooves sounding in the courtyard below their bedroom window. Najila peered from the window and saw a man jump from his sweating horse. Without tethering his animal, he leaped up the marble stairs two steps at a time. His pounding on the great, iron-studded door rang throughout the mansion halls.

Najila hurriedly donned a dressing gown over her nightdress and was starting toward the main floor when a manservant who had served the family for many years called out, "Lady Doukas, Lord Andreus is coming home."

Najila immediately rushed back to their suite to give Loukios the happy tidings. "Andreus is safe! He is on his way back from Jerusalem," she cried.

Loukios broke into a brilliant smile. "It has been so long since we have heard from him that I feared he would not return to us at all." Despite his disability, Loukios unerringly closed the gap between himself and Najila. His hands clasped her still tiny waist. Lifting her, he spun in mad, careening circles.

"Put me down, Loukas," Najila shrieked, choking with laughter. "We will fall." But they didn't.

Unexpectedly, it had turned into one of the best days of her life.

Chapter 69

Too restless to settle in one spot, Andreus stalked the dining hall at Hawks Hill where the family, including his wife and daughter, gathered to hear his story. His once husky physique was rail thin. Silver-gray wings painted his temples. He had aged ten years in the five years he'd been gone.

Some major changes had occurred while he was away: Otrygg had suddenly dropped dead one day while walking back from the stables. Julian had retired from court and had joined a monastic order; Loukios and Najila had sold off one third of the Hawks Hill land to clear debts against the manse's upkeep.

"Conquering Jerusalem was a month-long ordeal," Andreus told his rapt listeners. "True, our crusade was victorious in the end, but it cost an appalling loss of life, not only during the siege of the Holy City itself, but also before then at Antioch. In nine months fighting at Antioch, Bohemonde's troops lost five thousand horses due to starvation or disease. The human toll was nearly as bad—and perhaps far worse, if you count the injured who died later."

Andreus paused to stare out one of the floor-to-ceiling windows at the lush, peaceful landscape. A soft rain was falling, and in the distance a brilliant rainbow shone, its arc stretching fully from edge to edge on the horizon. He had yearned to see this very scene when he marched amid the bleached and sere cliffs of the arid Holy Land. He heaved an enormous sigh. "I am extremely glad to be home at last." He remained silent for a long while. Sensing his pain, his parents waited patiently.

After a minute, Loukios leaned forward in his chair, intent on Andreus's tale. "Please continue, Son. Tell me. Exactly how was Jerusalem taken? We received confused and fragmented reports here at home."

Andreus whirled from the window and returned to his pacing. "It is difficult for me to talk about it, not so much about the siege in particular, but regarding events after we entered the Holy City. I tried but could not prevent what happened. A lone man could do nothing.

"Thousands upon thousands—not just soldiers, but civilians—were killed by our troops until flowing blood stained the streets red. Elegant mosques and ancient synagogues were torched, burned to mere coals and scorched rubble. One was hardly able to breathe for the smoke and ash. It was such a deplorable waste." His voice broke.

"But you have returned to us safely, praise be to Allah," Najila stammered in Persian. "Er . . . er . . . God," she amended when Loukios scowled and opened his mouth to correct her. Though he knew that Najila had long been a devout Christian, it annoyed him when she slipped up and said something having to do with her previous Muslim faith.

Shaking his head, Andreus stopped in back of Laliyne's chair and barked, "I should not be here; there is still fighting to do, but I can tolerate no more. I am fearfully weary."

"Is it not enough that you are now with your wife and daughter?" Laliyne cried, turning around, her eyes pleading. "Your daughter, Chloe, does not even know you. She will not go to you despite my coaxing, and your mother's."

"I am not the same man who left Hawks Hill five years ago," Andreus growled, his hands trembling as he gestured. "The sights . . ." Remembering some incident, he bowed his head and covered his eyes. "The sounds of battle, wounded men crying for help, screams of mangled animals, the stench, all haunt my dreams."

Laliyne extended her arms to console him. Unwittingly ignoring her, Andreus was off again to wander the room. Apparently, he had no further information to impart, at least not voluntarily.

The family sat ill at ease. Loukios spat toward the great fireplace—and missed. Then he broke the silence, saying, "After what you and your men went through, we learn Godfrey has somehow become king of Jerusalem. It sorely vexes me," he blurted, slamming his fist into his palm. "By a camel's reeking cud! Jerusalem is ruled by a Norman! Whoever let that happen?"

Andreus ceased his pacing. "Well, Father, the Normans did organize and lead the crusade. I am not in favor of Godfrey's assuming the title; but neither can I condemn those who chose him. It seemed a natural progression, leading to his enthronement. I believe that he truly earned it."

"Humph!" snorted Loukios. "But a Norman?"

By the year 1104, Najila had joyfully attended many Hippodrome chariot races—seven years of them since Andreus had returned. When Andreus came home unharmed, Loukios became a new man. He willingly went to the races with Najila. Because he needed and wanted her guiding hand, and because the local nobility respected both of them highly, the rules had been relaxed to allow her into the great arena. Najila refused to be intimidated by the few men who openly resented her.

As many races as she had seen, Najila never felt her excitement diminish, nor her anticipation in seeing the Hawks Hill teams run. Soon after that first time long ago when she had sneaked into her first race disguised as a boy, the ban against women had somewhat eased, though not entirely.

Najila described the races lap by lap to Loukios. His legs would no longer let him leap up to cheer his favorites on. Unable to do more, he enthusiastically rocked back and forth in his seat, waving his walking pole dangerously close to neighboring spectators' ears.

This day, they would introduce their brace of black stallions, which had turned out as promising as Thadeus had predicted at the younger colt's birth. Thadeus handled behind-the-scenes preparations completely, relieving the aging couple from enduring the hardships one encountered in the dark, dusty corridor behind the starting gates.

The fine black team easily won its initial race; it wasn't even a contest. Najila, who had stood up to better see the finish, smiled down at Loukios. On hearing the crowd roar its approval at their win, he flushed with pleasure. His happy shouts blended with the rest.

Najila felt her heart swell as she witnessed her husband's delight. Taking hold of her arm, Loukios attempted to rise to his feet but faltered. Najila tried in vain to catch him as he slid down between the rows of seats, clutching his chest.

Chapter 70

They had brought Loukios home to Hawks Hill. It made no difference that the room, lit by a few candles, was so dark that one could barely make out the bed on which he lay. Even had he been conscious, he would not have needed a well-lit room. He had been comatose for nearly two weeks, ever since his collapse at the Hippodrome. Najila kept the room dim because it soothed her.

"How long will this condition continue?" she asked the doctor, fatigue straining her voice. The doctor stood slightly behind her by the bed, both of them looking down at Loukios.

She heard a rustle as the doctor shrugged his shoulders. Retrieving a candelabrum from a corner table, he held it close to Loukios and leaned over him to lift his eyelid. Straightening, he told her, "Once, soon after he was blinded, your husband told me that he was ready to die at any time. I have learned, however, during many years of practicing medicine, that it is God who determines the exact instant he collects a soul." The physician smiled sympathetically. "Lord Doukas could journey to heaven in the next hour, or he might linger for days. There is no way that I can tell his future."

Najila stifled a sob. Her throat ached, and her eyes were red and irritated from crying. It was so difficult to accept the fact that her Loukas was dying. It was fortunate that she had already sent for Shadea. Their daughter would arrive from Baghdad any day.

✝

Emerging from his coma ten days later, Loukios gradually became aware of muted voices. He heard Najila and Shadea at his left, while the doctor, pressing his fingers on the side of Loukios's neck, mumbled unintelligible comments under his breath.

Loukios struggled to turn his head toward Najila. He knew he was dying. If only he were able to see her once more. Enfeebled as he was in body, his mind was surprisingly sharp. He cursed the blindness that prevented him from seeing his loved ones, and prayed for the miracle of restored sight.

The doctor, again stooping over the bed, lifted his patient's eyelid. He felt a wet tear. "My lady," murmured the doctor, rising. "Though Lord Doukas does not move, I believe he has the ability to hear you. Do speak to him." The doctor then discreetly left the room.

Shadea drew nearer as Najila knelt at Loukios's side. "If thou hearest me, dear one, know that neither Shadea nor I will leave you." She bent to kiss the frail hand that lay limp on the coverlet. As her lips touched Loukios's palm, his fingers slowly flexed to brush her cheek.

The servants tiptoed in and out of the room as the waiting family spoke in whispers. At times, they were forced to raise their voices to be heard above the fierce storm that blew outside the manse. Lightening gashed the sky, its flashing penetrating the heavy drapery as hail rattled the windows.

Four days passed as Loukios hung on, now fully conscious but growing weaker by the hour. His shrunken form was lost in the massive, canopied bed. Using much effort, the dying man lifted a skeletal arm from the thick furs.

Taking his icy hand into her warm one, Najila lay down beside him. "I will not leave you, my beloved," she whispered.

His translucent eyelids quivered, the only sign that he may have understood.

Later that evening after Najila had sent the servants off, she and Shadea dozed by Loukios's bed. Rising, Shadea came to stand before Najila. "You have constantly been at Father's side, Mother. Why not take a moment to freshen yourself?" Shadea suggested. "I am here to tend him while you do." Shadea had temporarily left her own family in the care of servants in order to help Najila nurse Loukios. Mother and daughter knew that Loukios's remaining days were few.

Najila fingered her skirt. "I do feel the need for a clean frock. This garment I am wearing is soiled and beginning to smell." She hugged her daughter. "Thank you, Shadea. I am grateful that you are here to wait with me—more than you can ever guess."

After they had taken turns washing themselves and donning clean clothes, the two women at last fell into a restless half slumber.

In the very early hours of the next morning, Najila and Shadea were abruptly awakened by Loukios.

"I can see you!" he shouted.

His grey eyes were wide open, reflecting the candle flames, a strange new light glittering deep within the pupils. He focused on Najila as he had not done in the years since Leopold Alexander's ruffians had injured him. An expression of awe illuminated his face.

"There is a wonderful glow surrounding us. Turn around, Najila. Is it our blessed Lord who stands behind you?"

Apprehensive, Najila peered at where he seemed to be looking, but she saw nothing unusual. She stooped to raise her husband's head and shoulders by propping pillows under him. As

she did, he suddenly sat up, stretching out welcoming arms,
reaching beyond her. His features were radiant.

"The Lord Jesus greets me. He has come for me, Najila."
Emitting a joyous laugh, his voice young and strong, Loukios
slumped back on the bed and drew his last breath.

Chapter 71

Najila arranged for Loukios to be temporarily entombed in the small forest chapel where they had first met. She and Loukios had long ago discussed the design of a larger, more secure burial location, but they had never quite gotten around to actually starting it. Now it was up to Najila alone.

She found decisions hard to make. Should she have the tiny existing chapel expanded to make room not only for Loukios, but also for herself? Or should she find another place separate from the lovely chapel in the woods that had meant so much to both of them? Grave robbing was a common problem. Otrygg's unprotected, aboveground tomb in Konstantinoupolis's easily accessible Varangian cemetery had been desecrated by unknown thieves less than a month after his body was interred. Najila hated to think the same thing might happen to Loukios. She finally decided to create a vault close to the chapel, but well hidden from unwelcome eyes.

The tomb was to be seven meters north of the chapel itself, with a secret underground tunnel leading to it from the chapel. The church-end opening of the tunnel was set into the floor and squarely centered at the front of the chapel altar. The tunnel entrance was covered by a tiled slab that incorporated a design so cleverly matching the surrounding floor that the trap door was virtually undetectable.

Najila made sure the tomb's site was known to few others: Andreus and Shadea; Andreus's wife, Laliyne; Najila's personal maid, Amara; and the half-dozen trusted men who worked on it—the same men who, when construction ended, carried Loukios's inner coffin from the chapel to his final rest. Enough space had been left in the tomb for Najila to lie next to Loukios when the time came.

Lastly, Najila commissioned a noted sculptor to render her husband's outer sarcophagus and lid of fine, pure white, imported marble. The lid would show a bas-relief statue of Loukios. The image reclined upon its back, hands clasping a long sword, an idea Andreus came up with. Though his father had been neither a knight nor a soldier, Andreus believed the sword represented his father's strength and determination, as well as his struggle to compensate for his blindness. Najila thought it a splendid addition, though she wept as Andreus described it to her.

The sculptor carved the sarcophagus lid in a shed adjacent to the manse, but he wasn't told where the body would lie. When the cover was finished, Andreus paid for the work and dismissed the craftsman. He then personally supervised the same men who had carried the sarcophagus to the tomb as they toted the heavy marble lid to the chapel and through the tunnel and then placed it on its matching base. The entire project took three months to complete.

"I am weary," Najila told Andreus the day she turned sixty-nine, in the year 1117.

"You should again visit the stables," Andreus suggested. "You used to enjoy the horses, but now you do not go to see them at all. Thadeus is doing a fine job with our teams." He smiled, and his expression so resembled his father's that it made her throat ache. "Why not come with me to the next races? You have not attended a single chariot race during these past thirteen years. Not since Father died. I worry about you, Mother."

Najila shrugged. "Do not fret about me; worry is needless. I am perfectly fit," she declared.

"Join me at the stables today then," he pleaded. "We have five nice foals you can pet and spoil: two colts and three fillies."

"I cannot walk that distance, Andreus. It is a chore to rise from my bed in the morning; I hurt in every joint," she grumbled, suddenly feeling very sorry for herself and contradicting her previous claim to being perfectly fit. She poked at a smoldering log in the fireplace, causing acrid smoke to pour into the room and set them both to coughing. "It is just that I am so alone. I have outlived everyone: Loukas, Zahra, Otrygg, Julian, Elias. When you are away, there is no one," she softly moaned.

Andreus put his arms around her. "I never think of you as old, Mother. Surely there is some way to make an outing easier for you. Why is that so hard?" he asked. "It seems to me that you no longer even try to enjoy living."

His remark angered her. "Andreus," she snapped, "just living life is the most difficult part of life." She turned to avoid having to look at him. "But what would you know of that?" She instantly regretted her words. While crusading, Andreus had known far more trouble than he deserved. "I should not have said that; I did not mean it."

"Ah! But what you said is true," Andreus agreed. "I only know that if the Lord Jesus is by my side, he holds me up in toilsome times. I certainly learned as much on the way to Jerusalem."

Najila offered a half smile. "Oh, my dearest son, I wish I had your strong conviction and faith. Our Orthodox religion is so complex, and I have so much yet to learn." Picking at her fingernails, she murmured, "I have been wondering. What would you think if I joined a monastery . . . to seek further instruction?"

At first, Andreus was dismayed at what his mother was contemplating, but when he realized that she still grieved for his father and that the busy routine of a monastery might replace the emptiness in her heart, he knelt beside her chair. Taking her hands in his, he said, "I would miss you. We all would."

"I am not going to my demise, Andreus," she laughed. "And you will often come to see me, will you not?" She coyly tilted her head as she sought his approval.

"Naturally I shall. Why would you think I would abandon you?"

"Please, Andreus, you know I did not mean exactly that. I merely fear that you and Shadea might forget your mother, the nun," she said a bit petulantly.

"Never!" Andreus vowed. "But what monastery do you prefer? Among the many in and around Konstantinoupolis are several that admit women. Do you have a particular one in mind? You have not said."

"The Pantepoptes. Anna Dalassene, the mother of Emperor Alexios I, founded it more than thirty years ago."

Andreus nodded. "I know the Pantepoptes well. It is a beautiful monument. Those who ship in or out of Konstantinoupolis cannot miss seeing it perched on the hill overlooking the Golden Horn." He had sailed the harbor on several occasions in the line of duty. "If you must become a monastic, I believe you would be happy there." He gave her fingers a light squeeze.

"I am glad you concur, Andreus, as I have already applied and have been accepted."

He grinned slyly. "I heard about it last week."

Najila glared at him. "Do you know everything that happens around here?"

Andreus emitted a satisfied chuckle. "Especially when it has to do with the ones I love."

She could never stay angry at him. "How would I survive without you, my beloved son?"

"As you always have."

She sighed deeply. "I shall immediately arrange to enter Pantepoptes, and you may take me there."

Chapter 72

Before entering the Pantepoptes Monastery, Najila signed over Hawks Hill and Alioth to Andreus, though she first donated a large parcel of Alioth land with a productive vineyard to Pantepoptes. "You would have inherited the estates anyway," she told Andreus. "You might as well take on the entire responsibility of running them now."

She had sold the Konstantinoupolis apartment long ago, but retained enough assets to ensure her continued comfort and to regularly—and generously—donate to the institution's various charities and many in-house needs.

Shadea had her own household to look after. Her husband had been appointed the Byzantine consul to Persia. The couple and their two children lived in Baghdad. Najila had taught Shadea to speak fluent Persian from babyhood; it had helped ease her son-in-law's appointment. His placement, however, was a two-edged sword. It was an honor to have Shadea married to an important diplomat. But Najila was deeply saddened to think she might never again see her daughter or her grandchildren.

Because she was from a noble family, Najila was given a modest suite furnished with her own belongings. Though she was also permitted to bring a limited staff with her into the monastery compound, she brought only one person: her maid, friend, and confidant, Amara.

Despite her vow of humility, Najila proudly related to anyone who listened, "Thanks to my son's clever and capable management, Hawks Hill is flourishing beyond my expectations."

A single tiny window of her suite afforded Najila a view of the Golden Horn with its busy harbor. From the window she could watch the ships come and go: French, Roman, Scandinavian, and numerous others. On special occasions, the majestic royal galley sailed by, flaunting an eagle figurehead and gold-emblazoned banners that fluttered from its yards.

The walls of her room were bare except for two items. On one wall hung the duplicated silver dragonfly cross that she had designed. On another was a wooden plaque carved with the beautiful Nicene Creed which she read daily:

I believe in one God the Father Almighty,
Maker of heaven and earth,
and of all things visible and invisible.
And in one Lord Jesus Christ,
the only-begotten Son of God,
begotten of His Father before all worlds,
God of God, Light of Light,
very God of very God,
begotten, not made,
being of one substance with the Father,
by whom all things were made;
who for us and for our salvation came down from heaven,
and was incarnate by the Holy Spirit of the Virgin Mary,
and was made man,
and crucified also for us under Pontius Pilate;
He suffered and was buried,
and the third day He rose again according to the Scriptures,
and ascended into heaven,

and sitteth on the right hand of the Father;
and He shall come again with glory to judge both the living
and the dead;
whose kingdom shall have no end.
And I believe in the Holy Spirit,
the Lord and Giver of life,
who proceedeth from the Father and the Son,
who with the Father and the Son together is worshipped and
glorified;
who spoke by the prophets.
And I believe in one holy universal and apostolic church;
I acknowledge one baptism for the remission of sins;
and I look for the resurrection of the dead,
and the life of the world to come.
Amen.

✝

To Najila, the creed summed up what she had heard from
Loukios and the priests over the years. She now believed it with
all her heart.

More often than she wanted to, Najila recalled that the monastery's hilltop site was directly above the dank underground
cisterns where her father-in-law had confined her. Visibly shuddering at the grim memory, Najila told Amara, "My bed here
could be directly over the filthy, rat-infested cell in which I was
imprisoned."

However, after only a few weeks in residence at the monastery, Najila knew she had made the right decision in choosing Pantepoptes from among the seventy or so monasteries in
Konstantinoupolis.

"For the first time in a decade, I am experiencing utter,
uninterrupted peace," she wrote in a letter to Shadea. "The
Pantepoptes Monastery is surrounded by lovely flower beds

and bountiful vegetable gardens that support the kitchen. The population within Pantepoptes is small, the greater percentage being monks."

At first, Najila had planned to maintain her status as a guest of the monastery. But as she became increasingly involved in its activities and truly mature in her Christian faith, she decided to become a full-fledged nun, a part of the great, all-embracing brotherhood of Orthodox servants of the Lord.

In 1118, while Najila was yet a novice, Alexios I Komnenous died at the age of seventy. He had ruled Byzantium well for thirty-seven years. His son, John II Komnenous, succeeded him. John would carry on the Komnenous dynasty for another twenty-five years.

When news of Alexios I's passing reached Pantepoptes, it was a day of mourning for those within, as the emperor was much loved and respected.

After serving a three-year novitiate, Najila achieved her goal of becoming a nun. She hadn't eaten meat in that time, nor would she ever again. In the beginning, she missed sinking her teeth into a thick slice of venison, but she eventually grew used to a meatless diet.

During the day, she spent six hours attending church services. If not at church, eating, or sleeping, she served the monastery in a way that few others were able. She became an esteemed member of the Literati because she could read and write. When the others learned that she could also draw and paint, she was given the task of copying and illuminating manuscripts. She especially enjoyed the latter occupation, as it allowed her a measure of creativity within the bounds of religious convention.

Though her eyesight wasn't as sharp as it had been when she was younger, it was still good. She praised God for a reliable drawing hand, which had remained fairly steady.

Occasionally, if a particularly critical situation arose at the monastery stables, the monks sought her horse-breeding expertise. If she was unable to personally see to the problem, she nearly always had a solution to be relayed by someone else to those in charge of animal husbandry.

Once a nun, Najila wore the plain habit, or schema, and took a new name, Naomi. She had given half her jewels to Shadea, and half to the monastery. She kept just one special piece, the first design she had ever created, the silver cross that resembled the one she had given away to the monk Gregori. She asked that it be buried with her when she joined Loukios in death.

Najila! It is time!

The voice came to her early in the morning hours, long before dawn when the monastery was at its most silent. "Eh? Who?" she grunted. She had nearly forgotten her former name.

Amara instantly became alert. Had her mistress called her? Not hearing anything further, the maid frowned and rose from her cot. Going to Naomi's side, she found her breathing irregular.

"How may I help you, my lady?" Amara softly whispered.

Naomi suddenly opened her eyes and focused on something above Amara's head. An ethereal radiance illuminated her alabaster-pale features.

"Look! They have all come to meet me," she said, sounding surprised.

Amara quickly glanced around the room. Seeing nothing unusual in the flickering candlelight, she shivered, and her nape hairs stiffened. "I see no one else."

"My Lord!" Naomi cried, thrusting her hands upward. She uttered a great sigh, and her body went limp.

She was ascending swiftly, rising up a shaft of nacreous, blue-white light. Ahead, she saw figures robed in shimmering, snow-hued garments, their arms spread to welcome her. Among them was a tall horseman. She immediately recognized both the man and the horse. Loukas! It was her own darling Loukas riding Damaris, his Iberian mare. Then she saw her father, Michael, mounted on Sabiya. What a marvelous dream, *she thought.* I wish never to awaken.

Bounding toward her were two dogs, a huge wrinkled hound and a tiny bundle of fluff. Laughing, she knelt to greet them.

Epilogue

News of Najila's death spread quickly through Konstantinoupolis. Andreus wrote Shadea the sad news and sent it by courier to Baghdad:

✝

My dearest sister,

This letter bears the sad news of our precious mother's passing. May God bless her soul. I know you regret that you were unable to come home in time to bid her farewell, but please do not bear guilt for it. The distance is far, and your husband and children must come first.

As agreed by the family many years ago, I have arranged to have Mother's remains entombed next to Father's in the mausoleum prepared for them both.

You will be pleased to learn that I have also seen to it that she holds her favorite object, her own enameled cross and chain. It lies upon her breast.

All Konstantinoupolis shall miss our darling mother, the lady Najila, Sister Naomi.

I pray that everything is well with you and your family.

Your loving brother,
Andreus Komnenous Doukas

✝

For Andreus, no one could ever replace his mother, but every time he remembered the pages of Scripture she had carefully copied and illuminated, or saw the elegance and speed of the horses in his stables, or watched the growing faith of his children, he knew that the influence of his mother, Najila, would live on for generations.

Afterword

Someone has suggested that six million Westerners are descendants of Byzantine royalty.

The Western world has never lost its fascination for Constantinople (Konstantine's City). Founded in A.D. 432, it was the first city created as a true Christian metropolis. It wasn't until early 1930 that its name was officially changed to Istanbul.

The original community may have been built on the rudiments of a settlement begun as early as seventy-five hundred years ago when a great flood drove shore dwellers inland. Dr. Robert Ballard, president of the Institute for Exploration and senior scientist emeritus at Woods Hole Oceanographic Institution, recently detected signs of human habitation lying 328 feet below the Black Sea's surface, eight to ten miles off Sinope in Turkey. Though his find is not approximate to Istanbul, it does not preclude the discovery of similar underwater archaeological sites elsewhere along the Black Sea's ancient submerged shoreline.

Current belief is that the present site of Istanbul began as an early Greek town called Byzantium, but the first Roman inhabitants called it Romaioi (Romans). When the Roman emperor Constantine selected it as his new capital, he named it Constantinople.

Emperor Constantine gave freedom of worship to all who dwelled there, no matter what their faith. Constantinople's inhabitants were a blend of many races, speaking a multitude of languages and dialects. Greek, then Latin, and later Greek again were the languages of trade. The influx of such diverse peoples influenced the city's rise as a major crossroads and trade center.

At forty-one degrees latitude and surrounded on three sides by water, Istanbul's climate is similar to that of San Francisco, but more humid without the Pacific Ocean breezes to cool it. Divided by the Bosporus Strait, Istanbul is the only city in the world that lies on two continents—Europe and Asia.

Except for fifty-seven consecutive years when Western powers ruled it, Constantinople stood as Byzantium's capital. Byzantium's borders continually changed during the varied emperors' reigns, and its lands and power gradually waned until only Konstantinoupolis remained in Byzantine hands. In 1453, the great city, the last bastion of Byzantium, surrendered to the Ottoman Turks, thus ending Byzantine or East Roman rule.

Like Rome, Istanbul is built on seven hills. Istanbul University (established in 1453, the same year the Ottomans defeated the city) claims to be the oldest institution of higher learning in the world. Modern Istanbul still has almost two hundred Christian churches and holds the headquarters of the Eastern Orthodox Ecumenical Patriarch and the archdiocese of the Armenian Patriarch of Turkey.

Appendix A

**Byzantine Rulers Who Reigned
During the Years the Book Spans**

NAME	BIRTH–DEATH	YEARS RULED
Macedonian Dynasty		
Romanos III, Argyros*	968–1034	1028–34
Michael IV, The Paphlagonian*	1010–41	1034–41
Michael V, Kalaphates (The Caulker)*	1015–42	1041–42
Zoe Porphyrogenita*	978–1050	1028–50
Theodora Porphyrogenita* (1st reign with Zoe)	980–1056	1042
Konstantine IX, Monomachus*	1000–55	1042–55
Theodora Porphyrogenita (2nd reign)	980–1056	1055–56
Nondynastic		
Michael VI Stratioticus		1056–57
Komnenous and Doukas Dynasty		
Isaac I Komnenous	1007–60	1057–59
Konstantine X Doukas	1006–67	1059–67
Audokia (Eudokia) Macrembolitissa*	1021–96	1067–68

Romanus IV, Diogenes*	1032–72	1068–71
Michael VII Doukas Parapinakes*	1050–90	1067–78
Nikephoros III Botaniates	1001–81	1078–81

Komnenous Dynasty

| Alexios I Komnenous | 1057–1118 | 1081–1118 |
| John II Komnenous | 1087–1143 | 1118–43 |

*ruled jointly

Appendix B

The Byzantines were tough on their rulers. From 1183 on, the following emperors were tortured and/or assassinated:

1185	Andronicus I—mutilated and tortured
1193	Isaac II—blinded
1204	Alexius IV—strangled
	Alexius V—blinded and maimed
1261	John IV—blinded
1374	Andronicus IV—blinded
	John VII—blinded

Author's Note

In researching *Najila*, I discovered that the old Byzantine names and places varied widely in their spelling. Two of many examples are Alexius/Alexios/Alexus/Alexas and Doukas/Doucas/Doukus. Though not a Greek scholar, I've tried to use Byzantine Greek to the best of my knowledge and to be consistent throughout the book.

There are differing opinions regarding the exact dates an emperor, empress, or regent reigned. Any errors are my fault alone.

The "vision" of Jesus that occurred as Loukios lay dying actually happened to a personal friend, a retired pastor who died after a long battle with prostate cancer. The event was related to me by his wife.

Notes

Chapter 8

1. Paraphrased. Millard J. Erickson, *Christian Theology* (Grand Rapids: Baker, 1983), 1:342.

Chapter 15

1. Halley's comet appeared in October 1066 and was seen October 14 at the Battle of Hastings, in southwest England at 51 degrees latitude. Istanbul lies at 41 degrees latitude.

Chapter 25

1. Loukios's tetrapylon structure is pure fiction. The one in Constantinople is known to have existed. Built in the fourth century and later called the Anemodoulion, it was destroyed on April 13, 1204, when the armies of the Fourth Crusade ransacked the city.

Chapter 28

1. The lions are believed to have been gilded bronze or wood.

Chapter 31

1. The gold byzant was first minted in the fifth century. It became the longest-lived, most consistently used coin in history.

2. 1 Timothy 5:23.

3. Ephesians 5:18.

Chapter 39

1. Don Rodrigo Díaz de Vivar would later achieve notoriety as the famous soldier *El Cid* or *El Campeador.*

Chapter 51

1. John 3:16.

Chapter 53

1. Manzikert. Also called Malaz Kard. Once an important trading post of ancient Armenia, it is modern Malazgirt in eastern Turkey.

2. A *lepta* is approximately twenty minutes.

Chapter 55

1. Archaeologists have found spoked wheels at the sites of the ancient Greek cities Knossos, Mycene, Tiryos, and Phylos, hinting that chariots predated the Etruscans. The Hittites fielded 3,500 war chariots in the battle of Kadesh (1275 B.C.). Chariot racing is mentioned in Homer's *Iliad*. It is believed the Greeks raced chariots as early as 1300 B.C.

2. A *modio* (*modioi* pl.) is equal to about eight modern bushels.

An Epic Adventure
Across Continents and Through Time

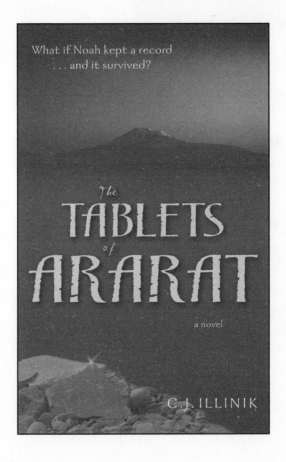

What if Noah kept a record
. . . and it survived?

The
TABLETS
of
ARARAT

a novel

C. J. ILLINIK

It is rumored that the biblical Noah carefully noted each animal that he took into his ark on twelve gold-plated tablets. But when the floodwaters receded, many of these tablets were destroyed and lost. Now only three survive. This riveting precursor to *Najila* traces the remnants of these legendary tablets across centuries and continents into modern times, where an American archaeologist, Arianna, is about to make a life-changing and world-shaking discovery.

"Readers of all ages will be captivated by this extraordinary first novel by C. J. Illinik."
—Dr. Gloria Randle
Professor of English, Michigan State University

978-0-8254-2908-8 | 352 pages